# THE TOWER

VALERIO MASSIMO MANFREDI is professor of classical archaeology at the Luigi Bocconi University in Milan. He has carried out a number of expeditions to and excavations in many sites throughout the Mediterranean, and has taught in Italian and international universities. He has published numerous articles and academic books, mainly on military and trade routes and exploration in the ancient world.

He has published ten works of fiction, including the 'Alexander' trilogy, which has been translated into twenty-four languages in thirty-eight countries, and *The Last Legion*, made into a major motion picture starring Colin Firth and Sir Ben Kingsley. He has written and hosted documentaries on the ancient world, which have been transmitted by the main television networks, and has written fiction for cinema and television as well.

He lives with his family in the countryside near Bologna.

VALERIO MASSIMO MANFREDI

# THE TOWER

*Translated from the Italian by Christine Feddersen-Manfredi*

PAN BOOKS

First published 2006 by Macmillan

First published in paperback 2007 by Pan Books
an imprint of Pan Macmillan Ltd
Pan Macmillan, 20 New Wharf Road, London N1 9RR
Basingstoke and Oxford
Associated companies throughout the world
www.panmacmillan.com

ISBN 978-0-330-43827-8

First published in Italian 1996 as *La Torre Della Solitudine* by
Arnoldo Mondadori Editore S.p.A., Milano

3 5 7 9 8 6 4 2

A CIP catalogue record for this book is available from
the British Library.

Typeset by SetSystems Ltd, Saffron Walden, Essex
Printed and bound in Great Britain by
Mackays of Chatham plc, Chatham, Kent

Visit www.panmacmillan.com to read more about all our books
and to buy them. You will also find features, author interviews and
news of any author events, and you can sign up for e-newsletters
so that you're always first to hear about our new releases.

TO BONVI

Gilgamesh said, 'I have come to see Utapishtim, my elder, who was allowed to go beyond. I wish to know life and death.'

The scorpion man laughed and said, 'Never has a mortal done that, Gilgamesh. No one has ever gone beyond these mountains, travelled the remote path.'

*The Epic of Gilgamesh*, Tablet IX

# PROLOGUE

THE COLUMN ADVANCED SLOWLY in the glare of the sky and the sand. The oasis of Cydamus, with its clear waters and fresh dates, was no more than a memory. It had been many days since they'd departed, wary about their mission from the very start, and the southern horizon continued to recede – empty, false, slipping away like the mirages that danced among the dunes.

Centurion Fulvius Longus rode at their head, back and shoulders straight, never removing his sun-scorched helmet, setting an example of discipline for his men.

Longus was from Ferentino in central Italy, from a family of small landowners. Before this mission, he and his men had been rotting away for months at a redoubt on the Syrtes coast near Tripolis, prey to malarial hallucinations, drinking spoiled wine and longing for the delights of Alexandria. Then the governor of the province had suddenly summoned him to Cyrene and given him new orders, orders that came from Caesar himself: Longus was to cross the desert with thirty legionaries, a Greek geographer, an Etruscan haruspex and two Mauritanian guides.

The emperor had learned, from an explorer who had been down the Nile years earlier with Cornelius Gallus, that – according to certain ivory traders – a fabulous kingdom existed at the southernmost confines of the great sea of sand, and that this kingdom was ruled by black queens, the descendants of those who had built the pyramids of Meroe, which had lain empty and hollow as an old man's teeth for all these centuries.

The centurion's instructions were to reach those remote lands, establish trade relations with the reigning queen and perhaps even discuss a possible alliance. Longus was pleased at first that the governor had chosen him for the assignment, but his satisfaction was short-lived. As soon as he considered the itinerary on a map, he realized that the hellish trail crossed the most arid and desolate stretch of the desert, right through the middle. But that was the only route; there was no alternative.

The Mauritanian guides rode at the centurion's sides; they were untiring horsemen, with skin as dark and dry as leather. Close behind came Avile Vipinas, the haruspex, an Etruscan soothsayer from Tarquinia. It was said that he had lived for years at Caesar's palace in Rome, but had been sent away when the emperor grew weary of his dire prophecies. In banishing him, Caesar had called upon Homer's words from *The Iliad*:

> 'You visionary of hell!
> Never have I had fair play in your forecasts.
> Calamity is all you care about, or see.'

Maybe the whole mission had been devised so that the troublesome prophet would drown for ever under a sea of sand. That's what the soldiers muttered among themselves as they trudged behind him, heads lolling in the heat.

Vipinas had even foreseen this unseasonable heat: although they had left at the beginning of winter, he had predicted that the sun would grow as bold as during the dog days.

They were crossing an ever more desolate expanse of pebbles as black as coals, and wherever their gaze roamed they saw nothing but endless fields of stones and teasing, quivering mirages flitting here and there.

The Mauritanian guides had promised a well to break up their march that day, but something else stopped them before the time had come to pitch camp.

All at once, the haruspex jerked his horse's reins and urged him towards a spot alongside the trail. Vipinas jumped to the ground to examine a rock on which he had seen the carving of a scorpion. His fingers hovered over the image, the only thing not made by nature in all that boundless solitude, and then, just then, he heard a lament. He turned towards the men, who were watching him. They were perfectly still and he could see nothing but silence. He turned then to the four corners of the horizon and the emptiness cut his breath short and made a shiver run down his spine.

The diviner stretched out his hand towards the carving again and the lament was deeper this time, sorrowful, dying off into a kind of rattling sigh. It was distinct, unmistakable. He turned again to find the centurion observing him with puzzlement in his eyes.

'Did you hear it as well?'

'What?'

'A sound, a moaning . . . the sound of infinite, cruel suffering.'

The centurion turned towards the men waiting on the trail; they were talking tranquilly among themselves now, drinking from their flasks. Only the Mauritanian guides seemed uneasy, eyes darting around as if danger threatened.

The centurion shook his head. 'I didn't hear anything.'

'But the animals did,' said the haruspex. 'Look at them.'

The horses were strangely restless: they pawed at the ground, snorted and shook their bits, jingling the metal bosses. The camels were agitated as well, spilling greenish drool onto the ground and raising their grating cries to the sky.

Vipinas's eye twitched: 'We must turn back. This place is inhabited by a demon.'

The centurion shrugged. 'My orders come from Caesar, Vipinas, and I cannot disobey them. I'm sure we're almost there. In five or six days, we'll have reached the kingdom of the black queens, where we'll find immense treasures. Unimaginable wealth! I must deliver my message and establish the terms of a treaty. We'll have honours heaped upon us.' He paused. 'We can't turn back now. We're exhausted and tormented by this heat, that's all, and the animals have been pushed to the limit as well. Come now, we must resume our march.'

The haruspex shook the dust from his white robes and returned to his horse, but there was a deep shadow in his eyes, like a dark premonition.

They continued their journey for several hours. Every now and then the Greek geographer dismounted from his camel, drove a stake into the ground, squinted at the sun on the horizon through his dioptre and noted their position on a sheet of papyrus and on a map.

The sun set that evening on a dim horizon and the sky darkened quickly. The soldiers were preparing to pitch camp and make dinner when a sudden gust of wind revealed a light glimmering in the distance, at the limits of that dark expanse. Just a single point of light, for as far as the eye could see.

The soldier who was first to notice it pointed it out to the commander. Longus scrutinized the beacon, throbbing like a star in the depths of the universe, then motioned to the guides. He called over the haruspex as well. 'Come along with us, Vipinas. It must be a campfire. There will be someone there who can give us some information. You'll be persuaded that we don't have much further to go and that your fears are unfounded.'

Vipinas did not answer, but dug his heels into his horse's belly and galloped off alongside the others.

Perhaps they had been deceived by the false light that follows the sunset, but the fire seemed to get further and further away as they rode towards it, despite the fast clip of the four horsemen and the compact terrain, covered by a mere veil of dust that the gusty wind blew around the horses' hooves.

They finally reached the solitary campfire. The centurion breathed a sigh of relief to see that there truly was a fire blazing there; not just a figment of his imagination, then. But as he drew nearer and was able to size up the situation, an expression of amazement and dismay came over his face. There was a man sitting alone in front of the fire and nothing else: not a horse, not a water bottle, no supplies or gear of any kind. It was as though he had been disgorged by the dry earth. He wore a long robe and his face was covered by a cowl. He was tracing signs into the sand with his index finger, while his other hand clutched a stick.

At the very instant the centurion put his foot on the ground, the lone man stopped drawing and raised his skeletal arm, pointing in the direction from which the strangers had just come. Vipinas's gaze fell to the sand and the haruspex shuddered at what he saw, distinctly: a roughly sketched scorpion.

The man got to his feet and, gripping his curved stick, silently set off in the other direction. What remained was the scorpion, brought to life by the glow of the dying flames.

Panic turned the faces of the two guides ashen as they exchanged tense, whispered words in their native dialect. The wind picked up sharply and raised a dense cloud of dust in front of them, although the rest of the territory all around was clear and undisturbed at that tranquil hour of the evening.

The haruspex turned dread-filled eyes towards the centurion. 'Do you believe me now?'

The officer's response was to take off on foot after the old man, who amazingly managed to elude him at first, appearing and disappearing from sight in the cloud of sand that whirled about him. But Longus finally spotted him in the distance, a dark figure in the vortex, and had soon caught up with him.

Longus reached out to grab his shoulder. He meant to look him in the eye and force him to speak like a man, whatever language might come out of his mouth, but his fingers clutched at an empty cloak hanging from a stick driven into the ground. The remains of an unreal creature, cast off into the dust. Longus dropped the rag in horror, as though he had touched something repugnant, while the hiss of the wind began to sound more and more like a sigh of pain.

The centurion turned back, daunted, to where his companions awaited him. They rode west towards their camp, which gradually came into sight. There they found the men lined up at the top of a dune, one alongside the other, silhouetted against a halo of reddish light. They were looking at something intently.

Longus dismounted and made his way to the top of the hill, pushing his men aside to discover the object of their attention. Before them stood a solitary monument: a cylindrical tower topped by a dome. The walls of the mysterious construction were as smooth as bronze: not an inscription, not an ornament, only that inexplicable reddish halo all around that cast its light onto the sand like a bloodstain. At the base of the tower was an archway, completely shrouded in darkness, that led inside.

The centurion observed it for some time, his confusion mounting, then said, 'It's too late to move now. We'll stay here. No one is to stray from camp without my permission. None of you, for any reason, is to go any closer to that . . . thing.'

The strange reddish glow died slowly away and the mystifying tower was nothing more than a shadowy black mass. The camp was plunged into darkness. The only light came from the fire that the two sentries had lit to ward off the chill of the desert night.

The Etruscan haruspex alone was wakeful, and staring at the point where he had seen the opening at the base of the monument. He had veiled his head and brow like a dying man and he was chanting a dirge under his breath and jingling his sistrum. Once everyone else had fallen asleep, the two Mauritanian guides waited until the sentries' backs were turned, then crept silently towards their horses and slipped off into the darkness.

The sentries were talking, looking at the dark bulk of the tower. 'Maybe we've already reached the land of the black queens,' said one.

'Maybe,' replied the other.

'You ever seen anything like that?'

'No, never. And I've seen plenty, believe me, marching behind the eagle of my legion.'

'What could it be?'

'I don't know.'

'I think it must be a tomb. What else could it be? A tomb full of treasures, like the ones the barbarians build. I'm sure of it. That's why the centurion doesn't want anyone going near it.'

The legionary fell silent, reluctant to go along with what his comrade was suggesting. The idea of profaning a tomb offended him, and he feared that it might be protected by a curse that would haunt them for the rest of their days.

But the other insisted. 'What are you afraid of? The centurion is sleeping, he won't find out. We'll just take a few precious stones, a golden jewel or two, stuff that's easy to hide in the folds of our cloaks. We can sell them as soon as we get back at the market of Lepcis or Ptolemais. Come on, don't tell me you're scared! That's it. You're afraid of some sort of magic spell, aren't you? What crap! What have we got an Etruscan wizard with us for? He knows all the antidotes, trust me. Hear him? That's him, with his rattle. He's keeping all the evil spirits away from the camp.'

'You've convinced me,' said the other sentry, 'but if we're found out and the centurion has us whipped, I'll say it was all your idea.'

'Say what you like, but let's get moving now. We'll be in and out in no time. No one will even notice.'

Both of them took a brand from the fire to use as a torch and cautiously approached the entrance to the tower. But just as they were about to cross the threshold, each holding out an arm to light up the interior, a low groan sounded in the hollow of the tower, rumbling hoarse and deep under the immense vault and then exploding into a thunderous roar.

Avile Vipinas trembled in the darkness so suddenly rent by the agonized screams of the two legionaries. Panic kept him rooted, cold and stiff, to the ground.

The soldiers sprang from their camp beds, grabbed their weapons and shot off in every direction, shadows running wild. Longus burst from his tent, sword in hand, shouting loudly to rally the men, but what he saw nailed him to the spot.

'By all the gods . . . what is it?' he barely had time to murmur as the screams of his soldiers rang in his ears, before the tremendous roar, which ripped the air all the way to the horizon and made the earth shake, exploded in his brain and destroyed him. His body was blown to pieces as if the jaws of a vicious beast had torn him to shreds and his blood was sprayed over a vast stretch of sand.

Avile Vipinas, frozen in horror, raised his spirit in the night against that monstrous voice. He rallied all the strength of his soul against the slaughterer, against the blind ferocity of the unknown aggressor, but he knew he had no chance. Unmoving, his eyes staring, he watched as his white tunic became spattered with blood, besmirched by scraps of flesh. The howl was getting stronger, drawing closer. He could feel the beast's boiling breath on his face. He knew that in a moment it would suck up his life's blood, but somehow he found the strength to start chanting his song, to shake the sacred sistrum in his numb fingers.

And the silvery jingling suddenly shattered the fury. The savage onslaught ended abruptly. Vipinas continued to shake the sistrum, his eyes wide and glassy from exertion, his ashen face dripping sweat, and the beast's roar faded into a hoarse rasp.

The camp all around him was plunged into the silence of death.

He got to his feet then and staggered across the ground, through the mangled limbs of the soldiers of Rome. No one had escaped death. The lifeless human bodies were mixed with the cadavers of animals – the horses and camels of the unfortunate expedition.

Vipinas approached the tower's yawning black arch. He stood at its threshold and peered in at the live, threatening presence he felt there. He continued to shake his sistrum steadily. 'Who are you?' he cried out. 'Who are you?'

The only sound to be heard from the opening was the weary, aching breathing of what seemed to be the tower's prisoner. The haruspex turned his back then to the mysterious mausoleum and began walking north. He walked all night long. At the first glimmer of dawn, he made out a motionless shape at the top of one of the dunes: one of the expedition's camels, still laden with a skin of water and a bag of dates. Vipinas caught up with him, grasped his halter and hoisted himself onto the packsaddle. The jingling of his sistrum echoed at length in the dazed silence of the desert, fading finally into the pale light of dawn, into that endless expanse.

# 1

PHILIP GARRETT HURRIED TOWARDS the Café Junot on Rue Tronchet, weaving his way through the late afternoon rush, when all the clerks in the city seemed to be swarming out of their offices to head for the tram stops and metro stations. He'd had a phone call the evening before in his office at the Musée de l'Homme asking him to meet with a certain Colonel Jobert, whom he'd never seen before or even heard of.

He took a look around the café, trying to work out which of the people here was the officer who wanted to talk to him. He was struck by a man of about forty-five sitting at a table all alone, with a well-trimmed moustache and an unmistakably military haircut. The man gave him a polite nod.

He approached and placed his briefcase on a chair. 'Colonel Jobert, I presume?'

'Yes, and you must be Dr Garrett of the Musée de l'Homme. It's a great pleasure,' he said, shaking his hand.

'Well, Colonel,' said Philip, 'to what do I owe the pleasure of this meeting? I must confess that I'm rather curious. I've never had dealings with the Armée before.'

The colonel opened a leather bag and extracted a book, which he placed on the table. 'First of all, allow me to give you a little gift.'

Philip reached out his hand to take the book. 'Good heavens, it's—'

'*Explorations in the South-eastern Quadrant of the Sahara* by Desmond Garrett, published by Bernard Grasset, first edition, practically unobtainable. It is, I believe, the most important work your father ever wrote.'

Philip nodded. 'That's true, but . . . I don't know how to thank you. How can I repay such kindness?'

Jobert smiled and ordered two coffees from the waiter, while Philip continued to leaf through the book that his father had written when Philip was little more than a boy. Jobert passed over one of the cups and took a sip of his own.

'Dr Garrett,' he began, 'we have learned from our sources in the Foreign Legion that your father . . .' Philip suddenly looked up, an intent, anxious expression on his face. 'It may be nothing more than a rumour, you understand, but . . . well, it seems that your father is still alive and has been seen at the oasis of El Khuf, near the border with Chad.'

Philip dropped his gaze and pretended to look at the book again, then he spoke. 'Colonel, I am truly grateful to you for this gift, but, you see, it's not the first time that someone has claimed to have seen my father alive. I've left my work at least three times to go off searching for him in the most unlikely places, but I've always returned home empty-handed. You will forgive me, then, if I do not jump for joy at your news.'

'I can understand your disappointment,' replied Jobert, 'but, believe me, this time is different. It is highly probable that, this time, the rumour is true. The high command of the Legion is convinced of it, and it is precisely for this reason that I have asked to meet you and that I myself am about to depart for the Sahara.'

'To look for my father?'

Jobert ordered another coffee and lit up a cigar. 'Not only that. You see, Garrett, there are details that you are certainly . . . unfamiliar with, events regarding your father that you are unaware of. I can tell you about what happened ten years ago, when your father suddenly disappeared in such a remote and solitary corner of the desert. But I've also come to tell you that I need your help.'

'I don't see what I can do. It seems that you know so much more than I do.'

Jobert took a sip of coffee and inhaled a mouthful of smoke. 'One month ago you published a very interesting study in which you demonstrated that a number of expeditions attempting to enter the south-eastern quadrant of the Sahara vanished abruptly, without leaving any trace. Entire armies of tens of thousands of men even—'

'I've done nothing more than develop a thesis outlined by my father many years ago but never published.'

'Yes, so you say in the preface to your work, which I haven't had the pleasure of finishing unfortunately.'

'Well, five centuries before the birth of Christ, a huge army led by the Persian emperor Cambyses that was heading for Ethiopia disappeared. The emperor survived, along with very few others, but what had happened to the rest was never revealed. It was said that the survivors devoured one another, that many went insane and that the sovereign himself died some time later in the throes of madness. Another army, led by the pharaoh Soshenk, had been wiped out in the same area five hundred years earlier. Not a single survivor. But, as I'm sure you realize, Colonel, we are dealing with a very hostile environment. The area is completely devoid of water, swept by scorching winds, sandstorms. It's not entirely surprising that—'

Jobert interrupted. 'Dr Garrett, the same phenomenon has repeated itself quite recently, in the absence of adverse weather conditions. The units were modern, well organized and equipped. One of them was a British contingent which had received French authorization to cross the area. The entire unit vanished without trace, swallowed up into the desert. A caravan of slave traders travelling from Sudan with expert Ashanti guides suffered the same fate. And no sandstorms were reported at the time. What we are asking you to do is to incorporate certain facts that we will provide you with into your research and, even more importantly, to pick up your father's trail from when he was last known to be in Europe. Specifically, Italy.'

'Why Italy? My father travelled everywhere: Aleppo, Tangiers, Istanbul.'

'True. But there is a reason. Ten years ago, your father had been carrying out research at the oasis of Siwa when he left suddenly for Italy. He apparently spent some time there before returning to Africa. He was in Rome for two weeks and then went to Naples, from where he left Europe, heading for Oran. From this point on, we actually know a great deal about what happened to him before his disappearance and are willing to share these details with you. What we don't know is what he was doing in Rome and Naples: what he was looking for, whom he contacted. We believe that his time in Italy holds the key to what happened to him later.'

Philip shook his head doubtfully. 'I find it very hard to believe, Colonel, that my father has been alive all this time and has never tried to contact me.'

'Perhaps he hasn't been able to do so. Perhaps he's been prevented from contacting anyone. You know that anything can happen in such desolate places, Dr Garrett. You see, I'm firmly convinced that, after this little talk of ours, you will wind up any unfinished business you have here and leave as soon as you can for Italy, but before you do, there are some things you still need to know about your father's last journey.'

Philip frowned. 'Colonel, I imagine you must know how many times I've tried to obtain reliable information regarding my father's last days in Africa, from the Foreign Legion, from the War Office and from the Colonial Office. You must also know that all my efforts have come to nothing. My own search for him failed, thanks to a total lack of cooperation from the military authorities, and now all of a sudden here you are, asking to meet me, telling me you have all sorts of information to give me and expecting me to set to work as if nothing had ever happened, as if we'd always enjoyed the most cordial of relations—'

'Please allow me to interrupt,' said Jobert, 'and to be frank with you. I completely understand how you feel, but, my dear Dr Garrett, you are anything but naïve. If we were unable to give you information in the past, there was most certainly a good reason. And if you had got the information you wanted, what might your reaction have been? What would you have done next? We were in no position to control that.'

'I understand,' Philip said, nodding. 'And now you're in trouble because you just can't explain what's going on in that cursed south-eastern quadrant. That must mean that the government, or one of her foreign allies, has plans for that area and needs to clear the field of any sort of obstacle. At this point you feel I might be useful and you want to exchange information for collaboration. I'm sorry, Jobert. It's too late. If my father is truly alive – and I'm sincerely grateful to you for this information – I'm certain he'll contact me sooner or later. If he does not, it means that he has very serious reasons for not doing so and I have no choice but to respect his wishes.'

Philip picked up his bag and turned to go. Jobert's features twitched in frustration and he raised a hand.

'Please, Dr Garrett, sit down and listen to what I have to tell you. Afterwards, you can make your decision, and I promise to respect it, whatever it might be. But first listen to me, for God's sake. It is your father we're talking about, isn't it?'

Philip sat down again. 'All right,' he said, 'I'll listen, but I'm not promising anything.'

Jobert began his story. 'I was a captain in the Foreign Legion, stationed at the fort of Suk el Gharb, when I first met your father. My commander had spoken to me about this American anthropologist who was carrying out research in the south-eastern quadrant and had asked for our help. He also told me that Garrett had neglected to inform him of the true purpose of his expedition, or rather that the explanations he had provided were not very convincing.

'I was asked to organize things so that we could keep an eye on Garrett, unobtrusively but attentively. The Legion has always been responsible for the Saharan territories, and, given his renown, your father's explorations were certainly of interest to us. I was in charge of the entire Suk el Gharb fort then and could not see to the matter personally, so I assigned one of my men, a Lieutenant Selznick, to discreetly learn what your father was doing and to keep me informed. He volunteered for the job himself, saying that he'd already worked with Garrett in the past and was familiar with his research.

'Now, as you know, the Legion has a tradition of accepting anyone among its ranks, without asking questions about their past. Many of our men have chosen this way to escape the rule of law in their countries of origin. They see the harsh, dangerous life of the Legion as a good alternative to rotting away in a prison cell somewhere. They find new dignity under our banner, they rediscover endurance and discipline, solidarity with their comrades . . .'

Jobert immediately picked up on Philip's impatience. 'What I mean to say is that we don't ask about the past when we're hiring soldiers, but that's not the case with officers. All of our officers are French and their lives, their backgrounds, hold no secrets for the Legion. Unfortunately, that wasn't the case with Selznick. We had been led to believe that he was a naturalized Frenchman, born in eastern Europe, but he succeeded in hiding his true identity from us. We have learned since then that a man named Selznick was stabbed and killed many years before in a bar-room brawl in Tangiers, and that someone stole his documents and assumed his identity. A marked physical resemblance to the deceased man helped him to carry it off. We have still not managed to learn the true identity of the man we knew as Selznick, but we have well-founded suspicions that he is, in reality, a highly intelligent and frighteningly ferocious criminal . . . a ruthless man who, during the Great War, carried out a number of missions for various governments, missions that required enormous courage, an absolute lack of scruples and the capacity to strike out at anyone in any way, by any means.'

Jobert paused and swallowed hard as he noticed the pallor of Philip's face.

'For ours as well?' asked Philip.

'Pardon me?'

'You understand me perfectly well, Jobert. You're saying that that man did our government's dirty work during the war, aren't you?' Jobert's embarrassed silence seemed an eloquent answer. 'So, in other words, you put a bloodthirsty monster on my father's tail as his guardian angel—'

Jobert interrupted again. 'Let me finish before you judge me, Dr Garrett, please. You have to understand the context we're working in, the forces to be reckoned with, the pawns to be moved. This is a very big game. We have to play the game, but most of all we have to win.

'At first Selznick was diligent in reporting your father's movements. I learned that Dr Garrett was following a very ancient trail, marked by recurring rock carvings which portrayed . . . a scorpion, I believe. It seems that he had succeeded in discovering something – what, I can't tell you, I'm afraid. That was when he disappeared. And so did Selznick, along with several men from his unit. The others were found murdered. One survived to tell us what I've just told you. He reported that some of the men refused to follow Selznick. A gunfight broke out, and apparently there was a duel, a sword duel between him and your father, in which Selznick was wounded. We have been searching for him ever since. He is wanted for desertion and homicide. When we find him, he will suffer the fate of all traitors. He will be shot in the back.

'So, what I'm offering you is the chance to find your father. In exchange we need your help in order to achieve two enormously important objectives. The first is to lay our hands on Selznick, as there's much he still has to tell us. The second is to establish exactly what is happening in the south-eastern quadrant of the Sahara and to find out if these events are connected with your father's studies. Do you accept?'

Philip took a deep breath. 'You see, Jobert, there's something that doesn't make sense in all this. The gap between what you expect from me and what I can effectively give you. As far as finding my father is concerned, you have much more information, greater means and a far better knowledge of the territory than I could ever hope to have. And thus a much greater chance of success.'

Jobert pointed his well-manicured hand at Desmond Garrett's book, which was still on the table. 'Dr Garrett, there's one more thing you must know. We believe that this book contains a coded message for you. We discovered it quite by chance. It was in a post office in North Africa that had been destroyed by a sand-storm some seven years ago. It was addressed to you, although you obviously never received it. We have been going through it for months in vain. There are several phrases written in pen at the start of some of the chapters. We imagine that they must have a precise meaning, meant for you, and that only you can decipher them. That's why your role in this matter is absolutely essential. I will be leaving for Africa in two days, going straight to the place this book was posted from. I need your answer now.'

Philip leafed through the book with much greater attention than he had a few moments before, pausing to read the added phrases. It was, without doubt, his father's handwriting, although what was written didn't seem to make much sense, at least not at first glance. He looked up and stared firmly into Colonel Jobert's eyes. 'I accept,' he said. 'I will leave for Italy as soon as possible and I will carry out my own investigation, but that doesn't mean that our paths will ever cross again.'

PHILIP GARRETT caught a train to Rome one hot, hazy day in late September. He found a seat, took out his notebook and began for the hundredth time to copy out the handwritten phrases. The first was at the beginning of the opening chapter and was in Latin: *'Romae sacerdos tibi petendus contubernalis meus ad templum Dianae.'*

After having considered the various possible translations, he thought the most likely was: 'Look in Rome for the priest who lived with me at the Temple of Diana.' He knew that whenever his father visited Rome, he used to stay in a *pensione* on the Via Aventino, near the ancient Temple of Diana. The message was clear to him, although it would be incomprehensible to anyone else.

As soon as Philip arrived at the station he took a cab to the *pensione* on Via Aventino where his father had most likely stayed when he'd come to Rome ten years earlier. Luckily, the little hotel was still run by the same person, Rina Castelli, a robust, jovial woman who loved to chatter. As she bustled around, preparing the room, Philip asked her a few questions about his father. Oh, she remembered him well: such a good-looking man, no more than fifty, refined and elegant, but he kept mostly to himself, she recalled, always immersed in those books of his.

'Do you remember if there was anyone who came to see him regularly, someone you knew?'

The woman placed the fresh towels and lavender soap she was carrying on an oak chest. 'Would you like coffee?' she asked, and at Philip's nod she called out to the maid from the doorway, then sat down next to a little table, her hands in her lap.

'Did he see anyone here? Well . . .' she continued, slightly embarrassed, 'your father was a good-looking man, as I was saying, very elegant, quite a hit with the ladies . . . And, you know, back then most people were quite badly off. Not that things are much better now but, believe me, life was tough then. The Great War had just finished. There was no work to be had, no bread. A man like your father . . . he was a good catch. And a widower to boot.'

Philip raised his hand to interrupt her. 'No, that's not the kind of encounter I'm wondering about, signora. I was thinking of someone who may have struck you as peculiar, caught your attention. Someone who may have had something to do with his work.'

The maid entered with the coffee and Signora Castelli poured a cup for her guest, who sat down beside her.

'Someone a little out of the ordinary, you're saying. Well, now that I think about it, I do remember him meeting several times with a priest, a Jesuit. I think his name was Antonini or Antonelli . . . Yes, that's right. His name was Father Antonelli.'

Philip was startled. 'Do you know if he's still alive? If he lives here in Rome?'

The woman took a sip of coffee and gave a voluptuous little lick of her lips. 'Still alive? Goodness, I would imagine so – he wasn't very old – but I have no idea where he might be now. You know how it is with men of the cloth. When their superiors give an order, they have to jump. As soon as they get settled in, they are transferred somewhere else. Who knows? He may even have gone abroad as a missionary . . .'

'Are you sure he was a Jesuit? That could be a very important starting point.'

The woman nodded. 'Yes, sir, he was a Jesuit all right.'

'How can you be sure?'

'Only a Jesuit could let his trousers show under his robes in Rome in the 1920s. Any other priest would have worn knicker-bockers, so only his stockings showed, like a woman's. Believe me, there's nothing I don't know about trousers.'

Philip couldn't hold back a smile. He finished his coffee and then said, 'Signora, you don't remember this Father Antonelli's first name, do you? If I knew his first and last names, perhaps the order could locate him and I could arrange a meeting.'

'His first name . . . no, I don't remember it. Wait, wait, I know. Maybe I can help you. I'm a person who likes to keep my things in order. I never throw anything away. I remember that he stayed here at the hotel one night, because he was working or studying, I'm not sure which, with your father. I'm sure I must have had him sign the register, for the police. I certainly don't have the time to go through them all myself, but the old registers are still in my office. If you have the patience to look through them, I'm sure you'll find him. It must have been 1920 or 1921, if I'm not mistaken, in September or October. It was the early autumn, like now. All you need is a bit of patience.'

Philip thanked her and followed her down to her office on the ground floor, a small room with curtains at the windows and a bunch of daisies in a vase on top of a wooden column.

'Here,' she said, opening a cupboard. 'They're all here. Take your time.'

Philip sat at a little table and began to take out the guest books, big registers with stiff marbled covers tied with a black ribbon. He began to leaf through them one by one, until he saw, his heart quickening, his father's signature.

That brief, forceful scribble instantly brought the man to mind. Philip could see him in his mind's eye, sitting at his work table, in a study crowded with an unimaginable quantity of papers. His books were kept in strict order on the shelves: texts in Latin, Greek, Sanskrit, Arabic and Hebrew. Philip had expunged the tragic circumstances of his mother's death from his mind, and what he most remembered of her was the photograph that his father had kept on his table; she was at the height of her beauty, wearing her long opera-singer's gown.

Philip had always considered his father the man who had an answer for everything. Desmond Garrett would apply the most rigorous logic to his investigations of the past, but his mind remained open to any hypothesis, no matter how foolhardy it might seem. He had handed his passion for research and his boundless curiosity down to his son, along with his sense of just how immense the mystery of the past could be.

Desmond had even been affectionate with Philip, as affection-ate as a man alone could be, giving him the insecure, distracted attention of someone who had never got over the loss of his one love.

When he disappeared into the desert, the event was not wholly unexpected. Philip was at university when it happened and had already taken his first steps on the road to what would become a brilliant career. He knew that he could navigate the world on his own and he was aware that his father would probably just leave one day, without saying goodbye, without saying where he was going and whether he would ever be back.

Philip brushed the faded ink with his fingers. That name identified the only person who had meant anything to him after the death of his mother and he swore that he would find him. He had a question to ask and his father was the only one who could answer it.

He focused on finding Antonelli's signature as well. There it was, Giuseppe Antonelli, SJ. The signora hadn't been wrong; Antonelli was a Jesuit. It all fitted perfectly: Antonelli was a *sacerdos*, a priest, and had stayed under the same roof as his father and was thus his *contubernalis* or 'tent companion'. Easy. Even too easy. But if he knew his father, the tough part wouldn't be long in coming.

THE NEXT DAY Philip left the *pensione* early in the morning, walked over to the Circus Maximus and started down Vico Jugario. To his right, he could see archaeologists at work up on the Palatine Hill and a little later on there were more down below in the Roman Forum, digging in the area of the ancient Temple of Vesta. The new regime had given quite a boost to the excavation of ancient Rome and the whole city was crawling with demolition and reconstruction crews. He'd heard they were undertaking a major overhaul of the Mausoleum of Augustus and were opening a road that would connect the Castel Sant' Angelo district to St Peter's Square, razing all the houses of the ancient Spina del Borgo that stood in the way. Another road would connect Piazza Venezia to the Colosseum, demolishing the medieval and Renaissance quarter built among the ruins of Nerva's Forum. Philip did not understand how the Italians could tolerate a political administration that boasted of reviving the glories of a millenary past, as they proceeded to tear down a sizeable portion of that very past in such highly questionable projects.

He hailed a cab in Piazza Venezia and made his way to the Curia Generalizia, the headquarters of the Society of Jesus, where he was greeted with polite interest.

'Father Antonelli? Yes, he lived with us for several years, but he is no longer in Rome.'

'I must speak to him about a very urgent matter.'

'May I know the reason for your request, Mr . . .'

'Garrett. Philip Garrett. I'm American, naturalized French. I live in Paris and have been working for several years as a researcher at the Musée de l'Homme.'

'Garrett, you said? No relation, I suppose, to—'

'That's right, Father, I'm the son of Desmond Garrett, the American anthropologist who was working with Father Antonelli on some research here in Rome ten years ago. Father Antonelli was the director of the Vatican Library back then, I believe.'

The Jesuit fell silent for a few moments, as if trying to collect his thoughts, then said, 'That's true, Dr Garrett. But unfortunately it's not possible for you to meet Father Antonelli. You see, our brother is quite ill and cannot receive anyone.'

Philip could not hide his disappointment. 'Father, I must speak with him. It concerns a matter of the utmost importance. You see, my father vanished without trace ten years ago in the Sahara, and I'm trying to find him by piecing together the last journey he made, here, before he disappeared. Father Antonelli may have precious information. Please excuse my insisting, but I'm sure I won't need more than a few minutes of his time . . .'

The Jesuit shook his head. 'I am sorry, Dr Garrett, but Father Antonelli's state of health will not allow him to receive visitors.'

'Can't you even tell me where he is?'

'No, unfortunately not.' The priest rose from his chair, walked around the solid walnut desk that separated them and led Philip to the door. 'Please believe me when I say that I truly regret being unable to help you,' he said again with a polite smile. 'I wish you good luck, nonetheless.' He closed the door behind his guest and went back to his desk.

# 2

PHILIP WALKED DOWN the long waxed corridor that led to the exit with quick, nervous steps. He was soon back out on the street.

The sunlight blinded him and brought home the reality of his failure. His first attempt had led him straight down a dead end. All he could do was go back to his father's book and try to decipher the remaining messages.

He reached Piazza del Popolo and hailed a cab, but just as he was about to get in he stopped suddenly and waved the vehicle off. On the other side of the square, near the start of Via del Corso, he'd spotted a man in a light-grey suit holding a briefcase under his arm. It was an old friend with whom he'd studied for a couple of years in Paris. He hurried to catch up with him, laid a hand on his shoulder and called his name: 'Giorgio!'

'What the devil . . .' the man answered. 'Philip Garrett! Where have you crawled out from?'

'Do you have half an hour for a cup of coffee with an old friend?'

'I swore to my wife that I'd go with her to pick out a dress for her sister's wedding, but she'll have to wait. Good grief, Garrett, I can't believe it's you!'

They sat at Rosati's café and Philip ordered two coffees. In ten minutes they had gone over the last ten years of their lives. Giorgio Liverani had married and had two children, a boy and a girl, whose photographs he carried in his wallet. What's more, he had become the curator of the classical art collection in the Vatican Museums.

'I knew you'd been working there for years. Congratulations! When were you promoted?'

'Last year. What about you?'

'I've taken a year's sabbatical from the Musée. I'm trying to track down my father.'

Giorgio Liverani dropped his gaze. 'I'd heard he was . . .'

'Dead? That may very well be,' replied Philip. 'Or perhaps not. I've received a . . . sign that he may be alive.'

'I hope you're successful. Your father was a great man.'

Philip looked him straight in the eye. 'Giorgio, maybe you can help me.'

'Me? Well . . . of course, but how?'

'Ten years ago my father worked for a while here in Rome with a man who was then the director of the Vatican Library, a Jesuit named Antonelli. Have you ever heard of him?'

'Giuseppe Antonelli. I remember him well. He's from Alatri, the town I was born in. Father Antonelli retired some time ago. Health problems, I believe.'

'I know. I've been to the Society's headquarters, but they won't tell me where he is.'

'I'm sorry, but I have no idea where he is myself.'

'Do you know who has taken his job?'

'I don't think a successor has been nominated. The acting director is the prefect of the Vatican Observatory. Father Ernesto Boni.'

'The famous mathematician? Do you know him personally? Can you get me an appointment with him?'

'I've met him a few times, at the meetings of the Pontifical Academy. I can try.'

'I can't tell you how much I appreciate this, Giorgio. It's a matter of life and death.'

'I believe you. I know how close you were to your father. His disappearing like that . . . so suddenly . . .'

Philip lowered his head.

'I'm sorry, I didn't mean to bring back sad memories.'

'You mustn't be. I believe that my father deliberately chose to drop out of sight ten years ago. His hypotheses interpreting Genesis in an anthropological way had stirred up a hornets' nest and greatly challenged his scientific credibility. He felt besieged by the whole academic community. He went into the desert, I think, to find definitive evidence for his theories. And maybe even to face up to himself. The desert is like a crucible: it melts away everything that is not in perfect equilibrium, so all that's left is the true stuff that a man is made of.'

'You said that your father has sent you a sign . . .'

'I think so.'

'Maybe he wants to tell you what he's found.'

'Maybe. Or maybe he wants to pass on what he's learned, so he'll be free to continue whatever it is he's up to, delving deeper into the unknown. If I know him, that's more likely.'

'Where are you staying?'

'On Via Aventino, at Pensione Diana.'

'Nice place. I'll call you there as soon as I've arranged a meeting with Father Boni.'

'I'm very grateful.'

'Well,' said Liverani, 'I'm afraid I've got to go. I'll be getting an earful from my wife.'

'Giorgio?'

'Yes?'

'Do you have any idea why they don't want me to meet Father Antonelli?'

'No. There may not be any particular reason. I'd heard that he had been behaving strangely before he left his post . . . but maybe it was because of his illness.' He glanced at his watch. 'I have to run. I'm really sorry. I would have liked to spend more time with you. If you're staying in Rome for a few days, maybe we could get together again. We could go out, go somewhere for dinner. You know, seeing you has made me feel good . . . and bad, actually. It's taken me back to our boyhood dreams, our plans for adventure. Now look at me. Eight hours a day behind a desk. Every blessed day. Christmas in the mountains and August at the sea. Every year. Every blessed year.'

'You have a beautiful family.'

'Right,' said Giorgio. 'I've got a beautiful family.' He stood and walked with a brisk step to the tram stop.

TATTERED CLOUDS galloped across the leaden sky that hung low over Bernini's grandiose square, over the pallor of the deserted colonnade, over the solitary spire, as straight and unyielding as the finger of God. Angry gusts of wind mixed showers of rain with the spray from the fountains and sent ripples through the veil of water that covered the basalt pavement as if it were the surface of a narrow inland sea. At every flash of lightning, the black mirror reflected the fleeting light towards the dome and its white bulk was illuminated against the night sky, witnessed only by the mute throng of statues crowning the top of the Vatican portico.

A black car passed the Leonine Walls and stopped in front of the San Damaso Gate. A Swiss guardsman wearing an oilcloth cloak left his sentry box in the driving rain to peer through the windscreen. He recognized the driver despite the incessant motion of the squeaky wipers, then backed up to examine the occupant of the rear seat: a man of about fifty with a hat pulled low over his eyes. The guard waved them on and the car entered the courtyard, where a man in a long raincoat awaited them with an umbrella.

He leaned over as soon as the driver had opened the back door so the newcomer would not get wet. 'Thank you for coming,' he said. 'I'm Father Hogan. This way, please.'

The man gave a short nod, turned up his coat collar and followed the priest towards the big bronze pinecone which sparkled like a diamond in the downpour. They turned left to enter the Papal Palace and then walked outdoors again through the gardens, heading towards the Vatican Observatory, whose lit dome rose above the wind-tossed trees.

They climbed the stairs to the very top of the observatory. The large telescope at the centre of the vault was pointed at the sky although not a single star was visible through the thick blanket of cloud. An elderly priest was sitting on a stool, taking notes on a pad.

Father Hogan turned to his guest. 'Allow me to introduce Father Boni, my direct superior.'

They shook hands and then the three men walked towards a complex instrument that was emitting an insistent signal: a distinct, modulated sound.

The man removed his coat and hat and turned his ear towards the sound. 'This is it, isn't it?'

Father Boni nodded. 'This is it, Mr Marconi.'

Guglielmo Marconi approached the empty stool in front of the instrument and sat down. He put on a set of headphones and leaned in close, eyes shut in absorption. The fingers of both his hands were pointed at his temples, as if to focus all his powers of concentration there. He sat for a long time without moving, listening, then took off the headphones.

Father Boni drew close with an anxious, questioning expression. 'What is it? Or . . . who?'

The scientist put a hand to his brow as if searching for a plausible explanation, then shook his head. 'It cannot come from any source known to man.'

'What do you mean?'

'That there is no transmitter on earth capable of launching this signal.'

Father Hogan's bewilderment was clear as the scientist turned back towards the telescope. 'You're not saying that it comes . . . from out there?' he asked hesitantly.

'That's exactly what he's saying,' observed Father Boni wryly. 'Isn't it?'

Marconi continued to listen for hours, occasionally consulting the chronometer he had placed on the table. 'There's something I just can't understand,' he kept repeating. He suddenly sprang up from his stool as if an idea had flashed through his mind and turned to the elderly priest. 'Father Boni, you are one of the world's most brilliant mathematicians. I need you to construct a system of equations for me, right now, in which the two trajectories of a parabola and an ellipse interact. The unknown is the point at which the speed of translation along the parabola meets with the speed of rotation along the ellipse . . .'

'That can be done,' replied Father Boni, 'as long as we have some information on the parabola. But I don't really understand . . .'

'Well, you see, the signal is intermittent but the interval between one emission and the next is shrinking, albeit by a very small amount. I'm wondering if this depends on the "free will" of the transmitter or if it is externally conditioned.'

'Conditioned?'

'Exactly. It may be that the source of the signal we're hearing is not, in reality, a simple transmitter that is awaiting a return signal from another fixed source at an extreme distance. This second source may actually be approaching along a parabola, which would explain the reduction in transmission intervals. You see, each time our hypothetical repeater sends us the signal, it's from a different position along an ellipse upon which it is travelling at a speed infinitely slower than the signal, which arrives at the speed of light. The solution of the system would allow me to establish if another source really does exist, how far away it is and at what rate it is approaching.'

'I can try,' replied Father Boni.

'Good,' said Marconi. 'Very good.' And he went back to his listening.

At every pulse of the signal, the scientist jotted down a sequence of data, scribbled in a nervous hand, which Father Boni reinterpreted, making his own calculations on a large white sheet of paper spread out on the table next to the apparatus. Every once in a while the two men would raise their heads from the sheet and their eyes would meet in a kind of direct, intense transmission of thought. They went on for hours as the storm began to abate and wide rents opened between the ravaged clouds.

The basilica bells had tolled five times when Father Boni got up and went over to the telescope. He looked through the eyepiece. The point of light he saw twinkling in space did not appear on any map of the cosmos. 'Oh, my God,' he gasped. 'Good God . . . what is that?'

Marconi came close and looked through the eyepiece himself. 'That's where it's coming from,' he said. 'There's no doubt. That could be the repeater.' Then, with a start, 'It's gone out! Look for yourself. The light has gone out but it's still transmitting.'

He turned back to the apparatus and began to write again, feverishly.

By dawn, the two men had filled the sheet of paper with a sequence of complicated calculations and a pencilled drawing. They both raised their eyes from the table in the same instant as they acknowledged the truth.

Marconi spoke. 'It's an object suspended at approximately half a million kilometres above the northern hemisphere which is revolving at the same speed as the earth, but it may be merely a repeater.'

'Yes,' agreed Father Boni, 'the true source seems to coincide with a point in the constellation Scorpio which is approaching along the parabola at an amazing and constantly increasing speed.'

Father Hogan finally drew close. 'Are you saying that there's some sort of machine or something up there that's sending us a message . . . an intelligent message?'

Marconi nodded. 'I believe so.'

'But what's the message? And who's sending it?'

The scientist shook his head. A bead of sweat on his temple and a tousled lock of hair on his forehead were the only signs of the sleepless night. 'It's expressed in a binary system, but I can't manage to decipher it . . . It's in code. See this symbol that recurs every three sequences of signals? See? This has got to be the key . . . a key I don't have.' He glanced at Father Boni with an enigmatic expression. 'Perhaps you . . . you can find the key.'

Father Boni dropped his eyes in silence.

THE DOOR of the Vatican Observatory opened and two men crossed the garden with a brisk step, passing among the age-old cedars dripping rain. The night sky was paling.

'Will you inform the Holy Father?' asked Marconi when they were back at the deserted square.

'Yes, of course,' said Father Hogan, 'but we'll have to finish our calculations first. It will take time. And there's no saying that we'll come to a definite conclusion. Thank you, Mr Marconi. Your help has been of enormous value, but we must ask you to maintain the most rigorous silence about what you have seen and heard here tonight.'

The scientist nodded and then lifted his eyes to the sky, where the last storm clouds were moving swiftly away. The stars were fading out one by one. His car materialized from the dark, silent as a ghost, and stopped alongside him.

The driver opened the rear door, but Father Hogan's hand touched his shoulder. 'What did you mean when you said before, "Perhaps you can find the key"? Why didn't Father Boni answer you?'

The scientist looked at him with an expression of ill-concealed surprise. 'You were the ones who asked me to build that apparatus. The first ultra-short-wave radio ever built with those characteristics. The only one that can receive signals from cosmic space. An instrument that no one else has access to, nor will for years.' Seeing Father Hogan's bewildered expression, he continued, 'Don't tell me you didn't know. No. You didn't know, did you? Well, then, let me tell you something else.' He drew closer and whispered in the priest's ear. 'Be careful!' he added, and slipped into the car.

Father Hogan crossed the square, which was still immersed in darkness, and vanished between the huge travertine columns. At that moment, a light came on suddenly in the window of the Pope's apartments.

FATHER HOGAN put his glasses back on after nervously wiping them clean with his handkerchief. He replaced the big register that he had just finished consulting and took down the next from the large cupboard. He started to leaf through the book with great patience, running his finger down the list of the works consulted in the Vatican Museums during September 1921. The dusky light streaming through the window was reflected on the frescoed faces lining the empty, silent room. His finger abruptly stopped on a date, a signature: 'Desmond Garrett, PhD.' He pressed an interphone button.

'Have you found something?' replied a voice at the other end.

'Yes, Father Boni. Ten years ago, someone probably saw the Stone of the Constellations and may have read the text you've enquired about. His name was Desmond Garrett. Does that name mean anything to you?'

There was a moment of silence at the other end of the line and then the voice again. 'Come here, Hogan, immediately.'

Father Hogan replaced the register on its shelf and left the consulting room. He descended two flights of stairs to the ground floor and then took a lift down another couple of levels. He walked along corridors lit by dim bulbs until he found himself in a room dominated by a large painting which hung on the wall, picturing a cardinal in his purple robes and rochet. He touched a golden curl on the frame and a sharp click was heard. The painting rotated on itself and Father Hogan disappeared behind it. Another brief, blind corridor lit by a single bulb led to an anonymous door.

He knocked and heard the lock turn twice on the other side. The door opened and Father Boni appeared. 'Come with me,' he said.

On a large wooden table was a model of part of the earth's surface in three-dimensional relief. The wall behind it had been papered over and was completely covered with mathematical calculations. A three-faced glass pyramid had been carefully positioned over the plaster cast. Father Hogan examined it carefully and then raised his eyes to Father Boni's. 'So this is the model.'

'Yes, I believe so,' replied the elderly priest. 'The symbol which recurs every three sequences of signals contains topographical data corresponding to each of the vertices of the base. The vertex of the pyramid coincides with the source of the signal – that is, with the repeater.'

'What about the receiver?'

'I don't know. The signals are retracting from our listening position. They seem to be concentrating on a different point . . . perhaps the final receiver . . .'

'And where is the final receiver?'

Boni shook his head. 'I don't know. Not yet. I'm considering two hypotheses: either the receiver is at the centre of the base, at the point of vertex projection, or it is in one of the three vertices of the base triangle.'

Father Hogan observed the luminescent pyramid. The vertices of the base triangle were widely spaced: one in the Azores, a second in Palestine, the third in the heart of the Sahara desert. He slowly moved his finger towards one of the vertices of the pyramid, where a little light pulsated.

'It's connected to the radio,' said Father Boni. 'It pulsates with the same frequency as the signal.'

'The signal,' repeated Father Hogan. 'A message in a bottle cast ashore at our beach . . . a message from the infinity of the cosmic ocean . . . Oh, God.'

Father Boni looked at him over the top of his glasses. The close light of the table lamp carved out his features. 'Are you so sure? And what if it comes from here on earth instead?'

Father Hogan shook his head. 'That's not possible. Even

Marconi said so. Neither America nor Germany, Japan nor Italy possesses such advanced technology ... not even all of them together. I am sure of this, and you know it as well. An object that could transmit such a signal is conceivable only in the distant future.'

Father Boni let out a deep sigh and shot an intense look at Father Hogan. 'Marconi is nothing but a technician, Hogan, albeit a very ingenious one. This ... object is described in a text that comes from a civilization older than any we know. A document handed down to us by the dying empire of Byzantium, which had got it from the Great Library of King Ptolemy in Alexandria, where in turn it had been copied from the Temple of Amon at the oasis of Siwa. The transmitter comes from the past, my friend, from such a remote past that it may, perhaps, coincide with our possible future. Time is a circle, Hogan ... and the universe has a curved shape as well.' His eyes went back to staring, as if hypnotized, at the pulsating light at the top of the pyramid.

'You're making fun of me. All this is pure fantasy. A man of your scientific rigour, of your intellectual stature, cannot seriously believe such—'

'Don't contradict me, Hogan,' burst out the old priest, cutting the other man short. 'I know exactly what I'm talking about. And you are here to assist me with the most important endeavour that has ever been attempted on the face of this earth since the time of Creation.'

Father Hogan held his tongue, startled and confused. The atmosphere in the locked room had become unbearable.

'Who is Desmond Garrett?' he asked abruptly.

Father Boni shook his head. 'I don't know much about him yet. What we do know for certain is that he managed to get access to the Stone of the Constellations and "The Book of Amon", both of which had been barred from public viewing for centuries. His signature on that register proves it.'

Father Hogan thought about this for a moment. 'That's

not necessarily true,' he protested. 'His signature means that he requested a consultation.'

'Oh, no, I'm sure he actually saw them. When I discovered the existence of the cryptographic section of the Vatican Library, where such texts are held, I found a safe there. Inside was a note from my predecessor, Father Antonelli, which mentions Garrett and speaks of a bilingual text that they seem to have been working on together. Antonelli was later rushed to hospital after a sudden deterioration in his health, not leaving him the time, apparently, to find a better hiding place for his notes.'

'But how could a foreigner have been given access to such a document?'

'I don't know and I can't explain it. Nothing of this sort should ever have happened.'

'Father, who was your predecessor?'

'As I told you, a certain Giuseppe Antonelli. A Jesuit from Alatri.'

'Where is he now?'

'I don't know. Not yet. The Jesuits have raised a wall of silence. There's something very strange about all this. Confound it, Hogan, you're a Jesuit. It's your order! Find out what they have to hide! And find out where Antonelli is. We absolutely must speak to him before it's too late.'

'I'll do what I can,' said Father Hogan, 'but I can't promise anything.'

He left the room and retraced his steps to the library's reading room and then back to his office. He went in and closed the door swiftly behind him as if he were afraid of being followed. He felt as though he had just returned from hell.

PHILIP GARRETT met Giorgio Liverani in a café on Vicolo Divino Amore, where the Italian scholar was renting a small house. Philip was so pleased to hear that his friend had managed to arrange a meeting with the director that he gratefully accepted an invitation to dinner at Giorgio's place that evening.

'Let me tell you,' began Liverani, after having ordered *gelato* for both of them, 'Boni, who's usually such a cantankerous old character, didn't object in the least. As soon as I told him who you were, he seemed very keen to meet you. He'll see you this afternoon at five in his study on Via Mura Leonine.'

'Giorgio, I don't know how . . .'

'Oh, come on now, I've done nothing at all. And good heavens, I'm really pleased to have met up with you again! I wish you could stay a while. You have no idea how I miss the old days in Paris. You will let me know how things go with Father Boni?'

'You bet,' said Philip. 'Tonight, dinner at your house. I'll tell you everything.'

FATHER BONI'S STUDY was very simple and austere, lined from floor to ceiling with bookcases full of bound manuscripts and extracts from scientific journals. Behind the priest's desk, in the only space free of bookshelves, hung portraits of Galileo Galilei and Bonaventura Cavalieri.

His desk was oddly uncluttered and tidy. A few volumes to his right were ordered by decreasing size. A folder of Moroccan leather lay before him with a finely wrought seventeenth-century stiletto on top – ostensibly a paper cutter, it was shiny and sharp, as though it could well be put to another use. A calculating machine, jewel of the most modern technology, sat on his left, along with a slide-rule.

'If I believed in telepathy,' the priest began after asking Philip to sit down, 'I would say that I had been expecting your visit, although we've never had the pleasure of meeting.'

'Is that so?' said Philip. 'I'm happy, then, because you're the only person in the world who can help me right now.'

'I'll be glad to do so if I can,' said Father Boni. 'Tell me, please, what is it you need?'

'As you may know, my father, the anthropologist Desmond Garrett, disappeared in the south-eastern quadrant of the Sahara desert ten years ago without leaving any trace. An officer of the Foreign Legion recently contacted me and passed on what may be a sign from my father in the form of a coded message. In ten years, I've been up any number of blind alleys trying to search for him, but this time I'm convinced I'm on the right track.

'I've learned that shortly before he vanished, he spent some time here in Rome and met with a man who may have been very important for his research: the director of the Vatican Library, a Jesuit named Giuseppe Antonelli. I contacted the Curia Generalizia to learn what I could about him, but the answers I received were rather evasive. Since you are his successor at the library, I was wondering if you could give me any information about this man and perhaps tell me how I can find him. It's vitally important to me, as I'm sure you will understand.'

Father Boni widened his arms. 'Father Antonelli left his job a year ago due to ill health. I'm afraid I never met him.' Philip lowered his head in disappointment but the priest quickly began speaking again, as if afraid of losing the young man's interest. 'However,' he said, lifting his index finger, 'that's not to say I can't help you. You see, I need to see Father Antonelli myself, regarding a matter of certain library funds that I am responsible for. I was meaning to call the Father General of the order this very evening to request a meeting. If I can arrange this, I may be able to ask Father Antonelli to see you as well.'

'You'd be doing me an immense favour,' said Philip, without managing to hide a touch of scepticism.

Father Boni nodded, then said, 'Father Antonelli was always a very private person, even when he was in good health. I imagine that he would want to know the reason for such a request on my part, especially now that he is suffering from such a grave illness. I'm sure you understand . . .'

'Naturally,' replied Philip. He admired the man's ability to move his words as carefully as pawns on a chessboard. 'You can tell him the truth. That Desmond Garrett's son asked to see him to learn what was said ten years ago, when he and my father saw each other here in Rome, and what the true object of my father's research was.'

'Do forgive me,' said Father Boni, 'but it's hard to believe that your father told you nothing at all about his research. I wouldn't want to arouse Father Antonelli's suspicion. As I told you, he's quite a reserved man.'

Philip betrayed a barely perceptible twinge of impatience. 'Father Boni,' he said, 'you'll have to excuse me, but I'm not used to this subtle verbal sparring. If there's something you want to know, ask me straight out and I'll answer. If I can't, I'll be glad to explain the reason why.'

Accustomed to the tortuous, diplomatic tones of curial discourse, Father Boni was embarrassed at first and then irritated at this brash young man, but he restrained himself. 'You see, Garrett, we're speaking of a man who is very ill, weak, racked by pain, a man who is facing the mystery of death and eternity with the fragile forces he has left to him. Vague . . . curiosities may well seem distant and practically meaningless to him.

'I seem to remember hearing that your father had discovered the key to reading a very ancient language, older than Luvian hieroglyphics, than Egyptian or Sumerian. I imagine that this was the interest he had in common with Father Antonelli, who, as you will know, was an expert epigraphist. You realize, of course, that we too are extremely interested in the key for interpreting this language . . . We do not want all Father Antonelli's efforts to go to waste with his death, which unfortunately seems near. Especially since, as you tell me, your father, the only person on earth who may have been privy to this knowledge, has disappeared. There, I've said what I know. It might be helpful if you would let me know what "sign" your father has sent. Perhaps, if we combined forces . . .' He paused, without concluding his thought.

'I hope to see Father Antonelli quite soon,' he continued, 'and you have my word that I will attempt to arrange an appointment for you as well, but if your father has revealed something more to you, something that might help us and convince Father Antonelli to receive you, I'd ask you to let me know about it. That's all. As you can see, I'm only trying to assist you.'

'Please forgive me, I didn't mean to be rude,' replied Philip. 'Allow me to be frank: I had the impression that you were trying to see my cards without revealing your own. What you've told me, instead, is very interesting and explains a number of things. It's possible that knowledge of this language you speak of may have been essential to the research my father was conducting on the Book of Genesis.

'As far as the sign, the clue that I've spoken of, I'm afraid there's not much to tell. On my honour, Father. All I have is a book, a scientific study that my father wrote many years ago, *Explorations in the South-eastern Quadrant of the Sahara*, in which he has added phrases at the beginning of several chapters, the meaning of which I'm still attempting to decipher. Actually, I have no idea why he saw Father Antonelli and what they had to say to each other.

'If I could find a way to meet him now, he might be able to give me some information, some useful lead to help me locate my father in the middle of that endless sea of sand. I hope this is enough to convince Father Antonelli to see me. I hope so with all my heart . . .'

'The Book of Genesis . . .' repeated Father Boni, as if he'd heard nothing after that. 'The Book of Genesis is no small topic. How could your father have attempted research in such a difficult field without any training as a Bible scholar?'

'I have no idea. I only know that he'd come to the conclusion that the characters in Genesis were actual historical personages.'

Father Boni could barely contain his surprise. 'Did you use the word "historical"?'

'I did.'

'I'm sorry, but I don't understand what you mean by this term. You realize, of course, that not even the most conservative

40

scholars believe that all humanity was born from a single couple, from a man and a woman named Adam and Eve . . .'

'Not in that sense,' said Philip. 'No, not in that sense. If I remember correctly from my father's writings and notes, he came to the conclusion that it was not the actual origin of man that was narrated in Genesis, but rather the passage from the Palaeolithic era to the Neolithic era. He postulated that the Garden of Eden was nothing more than a symbol for or a parable of the era in which man was part of nature and lived on the fruits of the earth and was nourished by the animals around him – that is, a symbol of the early Palaeolithic. Then man chose to eat from the tree of knowledge, of good and evil – that is, he evolved into a perfectly conscious being, a being who was equipped with a complex system of knowledge. This made him aware of the possibilities of evil and resulted in the loss of his primeval innocence.'

Philip became more and more excited as he spoke, as if his father's convictions were the fruit of his own research.

' "Ye shall earn your bread by the sweat of your brow," ' he continued, quoting from the Bible. 'That was their punishment. "Ye shall work the land." It was in Neolithic times that man became a sheep-herder and a farmer, developed a sense of property, forged metal to craft agricultural tools . . . But not only tools; weapons, as well. Especially weapons.'

Father Boni raised his eyebrows. 'Quite a simplistic hypothesis, and very banal all told. Hinted at long ago by the ancient poets of the pagan world in the myths of the age of gold and the age of iron.'

'You say so? Then tell me, did man ever have the choice of not evolving, of not becoming conscious of good and evil? Wasn't evolution an unavoidable process, provoked by a series of uncontrollable events like climatic and environmental changes and, in the final analysis, by man's genetic predisposition as well? And if this is the case, Father, if man had no choice, what is original sin?

What was the human race so guilty of? Why was man forced to bear the horror of violence, the awareness of decay and death?'

'The author of Genesis was simply trying to explain the mystery of why evil is present in the world. It's an allegory that can't be interpreted literally.'

Philip smiled ironically. 'A similar affirmation would have sent you to the stake just a couple of centuries ago. You surprise me, Father Boni. But furthermore,' he continued, 'if evolution is not the fruit of chance but rather of the will of a divine providence who dictated the rules of the universe and the development of every form of life, well, then the problem gets even thornier, wouldn't you say?'

Father Boni broke in. 'You're running away with yourself, Garrett. In the first place, the Darwinian theory of evolution has not yet been definitively accepted, or demonstrated, in particular as far as the human race is concerned. And nor have theories about the expansion of the universe. The mind of God is a labyrinthine mystery, Garrett, and our presumption to fathom it is ridiculous,' the priest concluded. 'But tell me, what did your father hope to find in the desert to support theories that, do pardon me, are debatable at the very least?'

'I don't know. I swear to you I do not know. But perhaps . . . there was a document . . . something that my father had discovered. Perhaps it led him first here to Rome and then into the heart of the desert. Can't you see that only Father Antonelli has the answer?'

Father Boni did not let on how excited he felt. Could this 'document' be the bilingual text mentioned in Father Antonelli's notes, so hurriedly stashed in the safe? What Desmond Garrett had found in the desert had provided him with the key to reading 'The Book of Amon'!

He merely nodded. 'I'll try to help you, Garrett. I'll ask to have Father Antonelli meet you, but on one condition. If you find out something about this text that your father discovered, you'll tell me about it.'

'I will,' said Philip. 'But I'm curious to know why this text interests you so much. You're not an epigraphist, you're a mathematician.'

'That's right,' replied Father Boni. 'You see, I suspect that that text may contain a mathematical formula of revolutionary importance, given that we're dealing with such a remote era, in which it is supposed that mathematical knowledge was quite elementary.'

Philip was puzzled and felt tempted to push matters further, but he was certain that no more answers would be forthcoming. Boni was the type of man who gave nothing without getting something in return.

Philip said goodbye and went towards the door, but as he gripped the handle he turned around. 'There is more,' he said. 'It seems that something inexplicable has been happening in the south-eastern quadrant of the Sahara. That's where my father disappeared ten years ago.' He left.

As he walked down the long, dim corridor, he crossed paths with a young priest heading in the opposite direction with a hurried step. He instinctively turned around and saw that the other man had turned as well. They exchanged glances for a moment, but neither spoke and each continued in his own direction.

The young priest paused a moment in front of Father Boni's door, knocked lightly and entered.

'Come in, Hogan,' said Father Boni. 'Any news?'

'Yes,' replied Father Hogan. 'He's in a rest home, outside a small town between Lazio and Abruzzo.'

'Very good!' exclaimed Father Boni. 'And how is he?'

Father Hogan darkened. 'He's dying,' he said.

Father Boni sprang to his feet. 'Then we must leave immediately. I absolutely have to speak with him, before it is too late.'

Shortly afterwards a black car with Vatican number plates left through the San Damaso Gate, entered Spina del Borgo and disappeared down Lungotevere.

PHILIP DINED THAT EVENING at Giorgio Liverani's house but his conversation was less than brilliant. He couldn't get the meeting with Father Boni out of his mind. The priest's explanations were strange and ambiguous and the story of the mathematical formula was not really credible. What was he truly looking for?

Philip went back to his room rather early and, although he felt quite tired, he picked up the book of his father's that Colonel Jobert had given him.

The first step had not been difficult, but unless he managed to meet Father Antonelli, it led nowhere. He wondered whether the other clues followed on from the first. If that were the case, he had found himself on another road leading nowhere. He leafed idly through the pages. It seemed that the dedication to him on the title page was written with the same pen and ink as the subsequent messages, but he saw no meaning in it. Perhaps his father had prepared the book years before as a gift for him and then had never given it to him.

Fatigue won out as he struggled to give meaning to those words and he fell asleep, still fully dressed, on the sofa on which he had stretched out to read.

# 3

THE CAR WAS JUST beginning to wend its way up the curving Apennine road when the first drops of rain fell. The tarmac instantly turned shiny and black and the trees lining the road were soon bending over in the gusting wind. Father Hogan switched on the windscreen wipers and slowed down, but Father Boni, who had remained silent at his side until then, protested. 'No, don't. We can't afford to lose any time at all.'

Hogan stepped on the accelerator again and the big black car raced through the night, illuminated now and then by flashes of lightning from the storm.

The tarmac ended a few kilometres later and the road became a kind of mule track, furrowed by streams of muddy water descending from the scarp above.

Father Boni turned on the reading light and consulted a topographical map. 'Turn left at the next crossing,' he said. 'We're almost there.'

Father Hogan did as he was told and, a few minutes later, started down a narrow path paved with rough cobblestones which ended in a courtyard. There they found a building dimly lit by a couple of street lamps. They got out under the driving rain, pulling their coats close, crossed the small, illuminated square and entered the building through a glass door.

A very elderly man sat behind a desk reading the sports pages. He lifted his head and pushed his glasses up to his brow, considering the newcomers with considerable surprise. 'Who are you?' he asked, looking them over from head to toe.

Father Boni showed his Vatican identification. 'We're from the Secretary of State,' he said. 'Our visit is strictly confidential. We must see Father Antonelli with the utmost urgency.'

'Father Antonelli?' repeated the man. 'But . . . he's very ill. I don't know whether . . .'

Father Boni stared him down with a look that brooked no objection. 'We have to see him now. Understand? Immediately.'

'Just a moment,' said the man. 'I must notify the doctor on duty.'

He picked up the telephone and a very sleepy-looking doctor soon appeared, quite elderly himself.

'Father Antonelli is in a critical condition,' he said. 'I don't know if he'll be capable of understanding or answering you. Is this really necessary?'

'It's a matter of life and death,' replied Father Boni. 'Life and death, understand? We've been sent by the Secretary of State and I've been authorized to assume all responsibility.'

The doctor shrugged. Such a commanding, self-assured individual must certainly have had a very good reason for coming all that way in such awful weather.

'As you wish,' he said resignedly, and led them down a flight of stairs and along a long corridor that was badly lit by a couple of lamps. He stopped in front of a glass door.

'He's in here,' said the doctor. 'Please, be as quick as you can. He's on the brink of death. He has suffered atrocious pain all day.'

'Of course,' agreed Father Boni opening the door, beyond which the faint glow of a night light could be seen. They entered.

Father Antonelli lay on his deathbed, pale and sweat-drenched, his eyes closed. The room was in semi-darkness but, as soon as he became accustomed to that dim light, Father Hogan could make out the austere furnishings, the crucifix at the head of the bed, a breviary lying on the bedside table, along with a rosary, a glass of water and several medicine bottles.

Father Boni approached and sat on the bed without even taking off his raincoat. He leaned down and spoke into the sick man's ear. 'I'm Father Boni, Father Ernesto Boni. I must talk to you . . . I need your help.'

Father Hogan leaned back against the wall and watched.

The man slowly opened his eyes and Father Boni continued in a low voice. 'Father Antonelli, we know how much you are suffering and I would never have dared to disturb you at such a time were it not out of desperate necessity. Father Antonelli . . . can you understand what I'm saying?'

The man nodded with great difficulty.

'Listen to me, please. Ten years ago you were in charge of the cryptographic holdings of the Vatican Library, and you received a man named Desmond Garrett.'

The old man gave a violent start, his chest heaving with a painful intake of breath. He nodded his head again with a moan.

'I read . . . your diary, in the safe.'

The old man clenched his teeth and turned his head towards Father Boni, astonishment in his eyes.

'I found it . . . by chance, you must believe me,' continued Father Boni. 'I was looking for some documents and I found it by chance. Why? Why did you show Desmond Garrett the Stone of the Constellations and "The Book of Amon"?'

The old priest seemed on the verge of drifting into unconsciousness but Father Boni gripped his shoulder and shook him. 'Why, Father Antonelli? Why? I must know!'

Father Hogan felt paralysed, stunned at that brutal violation of the old man's pain. Father Boni seemed not even to notice him and continued to torment the dying man with pitiless insistence. Father Antonelli finally turned towards his interrogator with an immense effort and Father Boni lowered his ear to the old man's mouth so as not to miss a word.

'Garrett could read "The Book of Amon".'

Father Boni shook his head in disbelief. 'That's impossible!'

'You're wrong,' rasped the old man. 'Garrett had found a bilingual fragment . . .'

'But viewing of that text has always been absolutely banned! How could you lift such a prohibition and let an outsider see that text? Why did you do it?'

Two tears fell from Father Antonelli's nearly lifeless eyes and his voice sounded like a wail. 'The desire . . . desire for knowledge . . . ungodly presumption . . . I too wanted to read that forbidden book, to penetrate the meaning buried within it. I agreed to show him the Stone of the Constellations and "The Book of Amon" if he would teach me the key for deciphering them. Absolve me, Father, I beg you . . . Absolve me!'

'What did you learn? Did Garrett manage to read all of the text or just a part of it?'

The old man's fleshless cheeks were lined with tears. His eyes were staring and haunted by pain. His voice became hollow, hoarse, full of uncontrolled terror. 'A Bible . . . a different Bible, the story of a fierce, alienated race, maddened by their own arrogance and intelligence . . . They had reached the oasis of Amon from an ancient ceremonial site buried in the southern desert . . . from the city . . . the city of . . .'

'What city?' demanded Father Boni relentlessly.

'The city of . . . Tubalcain. In the name of God, absolve me.'

His hand reached out towards the man who was questioning him, who might have lifted his own in the sign of the cross, but they never met. His last strength abandoned him and the old man collapsed onto his pillow.

Father Boni got even closer. 'The city of Tubalcain . . . what does that mean? What is it? The translation, where is the translation? Answer me. Where is it, in the name of God!'

Father Hogan moved away from the wall then and confronted him. 'Can't you see he's dead?' he said in a steady voice. 'Leave him. There's nothing more he can tell you.'

He drew close to the bed and closed the dead man's eyes with a light gesture, nearly a caress. He raised his hand in the sign of the cross. *'Ego te absolvo,'* he murmured with shining eyes and a trembling voice, *'a peccatis tuis, in nomine Patris et Filii et Spiritus Sancti et ab omni vinculo excommunicationis et interdicti . . .'*

THEY RETURNED to the car amid gusts of wind and squalls of rain. Father Hogan started it up and the vehicle shot off, cutting a path through the deep green of the dripping forests at every turn. The silence weighed heavily on both men.

Father Boni was the first to speak. 'I don't want . . . I wouldn't have you judge me too harshly, Hogan. That text is just too important . . . We have to know. I only . . .'

'You haven't told me everything about that book. What else do you know? I must be told, if you want me to keep working with you.'

Father Boni raised his hand to his brow. 'It all started with Father Antonelli's diary. I found it in that safe when I took over his office. As I told you, he was suddenly taken ill and didn't have the time to find a good hiding place for his private papers. The diary refers to a text called "The Book of Amon", which foretells of a message that was to due to arrive from the heavens on a precise day, month and year. Had he gone mad, I asked myself, or could there be a germ of truth in what he asserted? I thought his words over long and hard before I decided to act on them, even though at the time the probability of getting anywhere seemed very small indeed.

'That's why I first asked to meet Marconi. What I asked him to do was a true challenge to his intelligence. I wanted him to build a radio for the Vatican Observatory, a radio with very specific characteristics. An ultra-short-wave radio. Something that no one had ever heard of or was capable of building.'

An old lorry laden with timber was making its way up the road, groaning and creaking, and Father Hogan slowed down to let it pass. As he turned his head towards his companion, the lorry's headlights carved out the older priest's sunken features and put a disturbing gleam in his light-coloured eyes.

'The patent for such an invention would earn a fortune for its creator,' Father Hogan mused. 'Marconi has been working with you for three years. What have you promised him to persuade him to keep this a secret? You don't have access to that much money . . . or do you?'

'We're not talking about money here. If we succeed in our intent, I'll explain, in good time . . .'

Hogan dropped the subject. 'Tell me more about the text,' he said.

Father Boni shook his head. 'There's not much to tell, I'm afraid. A Greek monk brought "The Book of Amon" to Italy five hundred years ago, shortly before the fall of Constantinople. He was the only person on the face of this earth who could understand the language it was written in. He read the text directly into the ear of the reigning Pope, who did not dare destroy it, but insisted it be buried for all time in the vaults of the library. The monk was exiled to a desert island, his whereabouts kept a secret from everyone. There's a well-founded suspicion that he was poisoned . . .'

Father Hogan didn't speak for quite some time: his eyes seemed to be staring at the alternating movement of the wind-screen wipers.

'Where is the city of Tubalcain?' asked Father Boni abruptly.

The car was back on the tarmac stretch of the road now and was travelling at a faster and more steady pace under the still-driving rain.

'A city of that name never existed. You know what the Book of Genesis says: Tubalcain descended directly from Cain, and was the first man to forge iron and to build a walled city. I'd say he personifies the non-migratory peoples whose technology permitted them to settle in one place, as opposed to the nomadic shepherds that the Jews tend to identify with in the most archaic phase of their civilization. But, as you are well aware, current opinion holds that Tubalcain, as well as all the other figures in Genesis, are merely symbolic.'

Father Boni fell silent as the car started down Via Tiburtina in the direction of Rome.

'Have you ever heard of a theory, a hypothesis set forth by Desmond Garrett, that the people of the Bible can be traced to a very precise period of prehistory, between the end of the Palaeolithic era and the beginning of the Neolithic?' asked Boni again.

'Well, yes, I've heard of such hypotheses, but they really don't change much. We use the word "technology" in talking about a Neolithic or even a late Bronze Age city, but the means they had at their disposal were no more than what an Amazon – or Central African or South-East Asian – tribe has access to today.'

'Of course. But you can't deny that we have a radio source – suspended at 500,000 kilometres above the earth in a geostationary orbit – emitting signals that seem to match up with the message from the heavens described in Father Antonelli's diary, taken from a translation of those ancient documents. Coincidence, you say? I'm afraid I can't believe that. And if we want to get at the real meaning of that message, we absolutely have to find the way to read the entire text. What we have learned up to now is extremely alarming, I would say. We certainly can't afford to sit back and ignore the rest.'

'But Father Antonelli is dead. And who knows how long it took him to translate those few lines?'

The car was now crossing the practically deserted city. The rain had stopped and the streets were swept by a cold, damp wind. Father Hogan started down Lungotevere and was soon on the other side of the Vatican walls. He parked in the San Damaso courtyard.

'Father Antonelli had the key for deciphering "The Book of Amon". He must have translated much more than just those few lines. Why else would he have been ranting on about a "different" Bible? Antonelli just didn't want to reveal what he'd learned, not even on his deathbed.'

'Perhaps he destroyed his translation.'

Father Boni shook his head. 'A scholar never destroys the fruit of his life's work, especially when we're talking about the discovery of a lifetime. A poet maybe, a writer even, but not a scholar. It's not in his nature. All we have to do is look and we'll find it.'

He left the car without saying another word and walked across the abandoned square, disappearing into the darkness of an archway.


PHILIP GARRETT WOKE EARLY, after a restless night. He had a bath and went down for breakfast. Along with his caffè latte, he was brought an envelope from the Vatican. A few lines from Father Boni, informing him of Father Antonelli's death. Boni apologized for not having been able to do anything for Garrett, and hoped to have the pleasure of meeting him again.

Disconsolate, Philip dropped his head into his hands. His search had aborted before he'd begun. Played for a fool again by the irony of fate. He thought of returning to Paris at once and forgetting about this crazy idea of finding his father. But he knew that would be impossible.

He walked out in the direction of the Circus Maximus. It was a splendid sight under the early autumn sun after the night's rain. The sloping sides of what was once a gigantic racecourse, echoing with the screams of rapturous crowds, were empty and smelled like earth and grass, reminding him of the walks he used to take with his mother as a child. A fleeting memory.

Strange, whenever he thought of his mother it was a sound he remembered more than words, the sound of a little wooden music box playing an odd, indefinable tune. It had been a present from his father, on his fourteenth birthday. A little black-bereted soldier on the top, his uniform shining with gold braid, sprang up and down as if mounting guard.

A sad birthday. His father had been absent that day, far away doing research, and his mother had been taken ill for the first time.

He would play the music again and again, even after she until one day the box disappeared from his bedside table. It had died, been no use asking where it had gone, or who had it; he never got an answer.

One day his father had called him into his study and said, 'I will not be able to see to your education for some time to come. You'll be going to boarding school.'

Shortly after that Desmond left for the war, and he began to write to his son from the front, from a number of battle positions. He would always enquire as to how his studies were progressing. He would even send mathematical problems for Philip to solve, conundrums to puzzle out. He would write in Latin at times, or in Greek, and it was only when he used those languages that he would let himself go with an affectionate form of expression, as if only those dead, sterile words allowed him to let out emotion or feeling. Philip had hated his father for that.

And yet he realized that it was his father's way of staying close, of taking an interest in his personal development and the growth of his mind.

Philip suddenly remembered that his birthday was only three days away, and the dedication that his father had written in the book flashed into his mind. The date: 'Naples, 19 September 1915'. It was clear now! That was the clue, how could he not have realized it? In 1915, Philip had only been fourteen: how could he have read and understood that book? His father's gift that year had been the music box.

Could his father's message be in those notes, that music? Philip tried hard to remember it, but he just couldn't pin it down. Although it seemed impossible, that brief tune that he had listened to hundreds of times had been snatched from his mind and he couldn't call it back.

He returned to his *pensione* and sketched out a stave on a sheet of white paper so he could try to jot down the notes of the music-box tune, but it was no use. In the sitting room there was an old piano pushed up against the wall. He sat down and put his hands on the keys, hoping that a stray note might bring the lost melody back into his head. The notes rose incoherently up the stairwell and rained back down inert and meaningless onto the keys. All he could see in his mind's eye was the little soldier with the black beret, blue jacket and gold frogging, with his jerky movements, mounting guard on his lost memories.

Philip picked up the book again and read the phrase that preceded the second chapter: 'The brown friars can hear the sound by the volcano.'

He moved on to the third, imagining that the chapter numbers provided the sequence with which the notes were to be read: 'The sound is beyond the gate of the dead.'

The last phrase was written in before the fourth chapter: 'Find the entrance under the eye.'

Perhaps the 'sound' mentioned in the second phrase referred to the music box whose tune he had tried so hard to remember, but still there was no sense to be made out of the sequence.

Philip felt frustrated and irritated at being dragged into a stupid, infantile game, a ridiculous treasure hunt. A seasoned researcher like himself, trapped by such a childish puzzle! But then he thought of Colonel Jobert's words when he gave him the volume ... there must be a reason why his father had chosen such an apparently nonsensical approach to guiding him through this enigma, an approach that would take him back to his childhood ... and he must surely have taken into account the possibility that Philip would be unable to decipher his messages, or meet with Father Antonelli.

That same afternoon Philip went to the Angelicum Library to look for a directory of the religious orders in Italy. It didn't take him long to find a Franciscan monastery near the Church of the Madonna of Pompeii. 'The brown friars can hear the sound by the volcano.' All right, so he had Mount Vesuvius and the friars: what sound could they hear? Philip decided that he would leave for Naples the next day.

FATHER BONI OPENED THE SAFE and took out Father Antonelli's diary. At the end, between the last page and the back cover, was an envelope with a single line, written in ink: 'To be delivered into the hands of the Holy Father'. Boni had never dared either to deliver it to the addressee or to open it himself. He decided to open and read it.

I beg the forgiveness of God and of Your Holiness for what I have done, for the presumption that enticed me into seeking knowledge of evil, and swayed me from the true path of Infinite Good.

I have dedicated my life to deciphering 'The Book of Amon', only to discover a temptation within it which I have not been capable of resisting! A temptation that, were it known to man, would overwhelm the resistance of most human beings on this earth.

It has taken a relentless disease to save me from damnation. Or so I hope, at least, in these last days that remain of my life. I am resigned to the illness that is destroying my body. I accept it as a sign from the Almighty and hope that it may serve for the remission of my sins and atone for at least a small part of the punishment I deserve. The only other person who knows the secret of reading this text has disappeared into the desert and will never return.

As for me, I shall take the secret which I was driven to learn with such arrogance into the tomb. I implore Your Holiness to absolve my sins and to intercede on my behalf with the Most High, before whose presence I shall soon appear.

Father Hogan was awakened not long after that, in the middle of the night, by a soft but insistent knocking at the door of his room. He felt his way to the light and put on the robe lying on a chair. When he opened the door he found Father Boni standing there. He was wearing a dark overcoat and a homburg hat.

'I think I know where the translation of "The Book of Amon" is hidden. Hurry and get dressed.'

PHILIP GARRETT FOUND a room at the Ausonia hotel, not far from the Franciscan monastery. The next morning, he introduced himself as a specialist in art history and asked to visit the monastery. He was received by a quite elderly and very loquacious friar who apparently had not had much occasion to entertain guests. He showed Philip his own studies regarding the monastery, which had risen on the foundations of an ancient Benedictine cenoby built, in turn, over the remains of an ancient Roman domus. This extraordinary stratification of events and cultures found only in Italy never ceased to amaze Philip, who did his best to gratify his host, complimenting him on the insight and diligence of his studies.

The visit then began. They saw the church with its frescoes and paintings by Pontormo and Baciccia in the side chapels, they visited the small *antiquarium* with its early Christian tombstones and fragments of Roman floor mosaics and then, finally, the crypt. It was situated at a depth of five or six metres below ground level and it contained the remains of all the monks who had lived and died between those walls over the previous four centuries. It was quite a disturbing sight, and as his host chattered on at length about the history of the monastery and its occupants, Philip couldn't help but stare at those stacks of time-yellowed skulls and shin bones, those empty eye sockets, those grotesque, dusty smiles.

'What's the purpose of all this, Father? To remind ourselves that all men must die?' he asked suddenly.

The friar's tongue stopped suddenly, as if someone had shattered the entire scholarly exposition that he had so painstakingly constructed under those ancient vaults.

'A monk lives for the hereafter,' he replied. 'You who live in the outside world cannot understand, because too many things distract you, but we monks know very well that life is but an instant, and that what awaits us will guide us to the eternal light. I realize,' he continued, inclining his head towards the skull-cluttered shelves, 'that all of this appears grotesque, macabre even, but only for one who refuses to consider the truth. Even a fruit, when it has lost its fresh juicy pulp, is reduced to a stone, to a dry, hard stone, but we know that it is from that stone that new life is born.'

'Inside the stone is a seed,' agreed Philip, 'but here,' he added then, taking a skull from the pile and turning it upside down to reveal the internal cavity, 'here I see nothing . . . no trace of the veins and nerves that once throbbed under this dried-up face and conveyed the thoughts and emotions, the knowledge and the hopes of a human being . . . The truth is, Father, that we are enveloped by mystery, and we've not been given a light to explore it, apart from this mind of ours. A mind perpetually aware of the relentless passage of time and terrified by it.'

'We believe that we have been given a light,' replied the friar. ' "Light from light, true God from true God". We firmly believe that God entered history to speak with us. Once and for always.'

'I know that's what a true believer will tell you. But you tell me, my friend, how you can see the hand of God in this world of ours, in this obsessive, monotonous alternation of births and deaths. In this throng of bodies in heat who, in seeking a few moments of pleasure, perpetuate the curse of pain, of illness and old age, the raging of war, hunger and epidemics . . . You monks, you who refuse to couple with females, aren't you saying that the way to reach perfection in life is to refuse to perpetuate it, to rebel against the mechanism that drives us to reproduce ourselves before we die?

'Do you know what the world is, Father, for those of us who have not renounced it, as you have? A desolate land beaten by the hooves of the four horsemen of the Apocalypse . . . Our world is pain, above all, and we who live in it are completely responsible for that.'

'We are no different from other men,' replied the friar, 'as strange as that may seem to you. If you could share our experience, you would realize the truth of my words. You could say that we have gambled our entire existence on a single number in the roulette of life. We have accepted the word of the Son of Man. Although, as you remember, He himself trembled and cried and shouted, sweating blood, at the thought of losing His life.' The friar lowered his bald head and his beard touched the worn cowl. 'But this is not the reason you've come, and nor have you come to see the art treasures this monastery holds. I feel as though I've met you before. A long, long time ago.'

Philip started. 'Why? Why do you say that?'

'I have the feeling that I've seen you before . . . but if it had been you, you'd be much older by now.'

Philip could not hide his agitation. 'Perhaps you saw my father, Desmond Garrett, ten years ago. Could that be?'

The friar's face lit up. 'Yes, of course! But his eyes were black, weren't they?'

Philip nodded. 'What was my father looking for? I must know. He disappeared in the Sahara desert ten years ago, shortly after he left here. I'm trying to find him, but my search is going nowhere.'

The friar pondered his words for a while before answering. 'The first time he came to the monastery was much longer than ten years ago. I think it was chance that brought him here, if I remember well. Just as he was about to leave for Africa. Back then, you see, there were rumours that the usual tomb robbers had found a certain something here, in the area. Your father did everything he could to find out more about the discovery; I don't know why. He went down time and time again, underground. There are countless galleries under the city, dug into the tuff that was deposited by the eruptions of Vesuvius in ancient times. There were some things he told me, but others, I'm sure, that he kept to himself. He ended up here at the monastery and convinced me to help him. I suggested a route that he could follow. He stayed for a while. Then, one day, he had to leave quite suddenly. His wife – that is, your mother – had been taken ill . . . or perhaps her already precarious condition had taken a turn for the worse.'

Philip lowered his head in silence and in his mind's eye saw his mother lying among hundreds of white flowers, his father kneeling next to her with his face hidden in his hands.

'Years went by before we heard from him again,' continued the friar. 'But he did come back and he stayed with us for a brief time. That was about ten years ago. I don't know if he ever found what he was looking for.'

'Thank you, Father,' Philip said, 'for your kindness. I regret what I said before. In reality, I admire your faith. Actually, I envy it, in a certain sense. Let me ask you this: in looking for my father, I've found a . . . a clue, I suppose you could say, a phrase that he wrote, which seems to be devoid of meaning, but perhaps it might mean something to you. This place just brought it to mind.'

'Speak freely, son,' said the friar.

'The phrase is: "The sound is beyond the gate of the dead." Does that mean anything to you? Could there be a door beyond all these shelves full of bones?'

The friar smiled, nodding. 'Do you know the legend of the earthquake bells?'

'No. I've never heard of it.'

'Well, it seems that every time an earthquake is about to take place, a bell can be heard ringing in the underground passages of this monastery. A soft, silvery sound of just a few notes. They say that the sound has always protected these walls, which, in truth, have never given way. But that may be because they stand on the formidable structure of a Roman villa.'

'Have you ever heard the sound?'

'No. But your father told me that he had heard it. There was a tremor here in the area just when he was visiting. But it might have been the power of suggestion. Your father was a very emotional man, was he not?'

Philip did not answer. 'Please, could you tell me exactly what my father said about the sound he had heard?'

'I don't remember well, I'm afraid. What I do remember is that he was dead set on finding out where it came from.'

'Before . . . you said you suggested a route my father could follow . . .'

'Come with me,' said the friar, walking towards the end of the crypt. 'You surely don't believe that a monastery as ancient as ours has no secret passageways?'

'I'd be surprised if there weren't any,' admitted Philip.

'To tell you the truth, it's no great secret. Look. Behind here,' he said, pointing at a shelf full of bones that covered most of the wall, 'is the passage to the lower levels, a true labyrinth of tunnels. Mostly catacombs; their location corresponds to what may have been the south-eastern quarter of ancient Pompeii. You know how little of the old city has been explored.'

The friar stretched out his hand and unhooked a bracket that held up a shelf, which rotated on a hinge fixed to the floor. He swung it out, revealing the little iron door behind it, which was bolted shut.

'As you can see,' continued the friar, 'no mysterious mechanisms. An unsophisticated secret, worthy of the poor friars of St Francis.'

' "The sound is beyond the gate of the dead . . ." Fantastic! Can I get official permission to go down?' asked Philip with a certain apprehension, indicating the door.

The friar shook his bald head. 'No. Your father wasn't able to either. My superiors don't want anyone venturing down there. Not because there's anything particularly exciting apart from our mysterious bell, but someone could easily get hurt down below and we don't want trouble if anything should happen. As far as I'm concerned, you can start as soon as you like, but you'll need an acetylene lamp, a miner's hat and a haversack for your gear. Keep me informed, if you will. Your father always did. Somewhere I think I still have the map he drew up, with a partial layout of the tunnels, at the end of his first week of exploration. I'll find it for you. Officially, you'll have permission to study the structure of the Roman *domus*. Mind you, be careful and don't do anything foolish: it really is dangerous down there.'

'I won't,' promised Philip. 'Thank you, Father.'

'Fine. You'll find,' he said, sweeping a hand towards the stacked bones, 'that after a while these brothers of mine will seem less disturbing. You'll feel their spirits hovering under these vaults. Do you know what I think? I think that the ancient Egyptians were on to something when they said that the *ka* remained close to the buried body. There must be some trace of our thoughts and feelings that remains behind after we're gone . . . And before you leave, perhaps you'll tell me the real reason you are so cynical.'

He walked back up the stairs that led to the church's main altar.

EVENING WAS FALLING on the city of Alatri and the mighty cyclopean walls glowed with crystalline reflections. Great black and pink cumulus clouds rose from the hills like colossi and flocks of crows glided on the northern wind, contending dominion of the sky that stretched over the bell towers and domes of the churches with the swallows.

Father Hogan looked out of the window of his hotel room and let his eyes roam over the rooftops of the old city, towards the setting sun.

Father Boni's voice rang out behind him. 'We have an appointment with the pastor in half an hour, outside the city. We've quite a way to go, so it's best we get started.'

They went down to the street, both in civilian dress, and walked down the roads that flanked the cyclopean walls.

'Legend has it that these walls were built by giants at the time of the god Saturn,' Father Boni mentioned to his companion. 'But no one really knows who could have built them, or how . . . What mysteries still exist on this earth!'

They set out towards the open countryside and a small cemetery soon came into sight.

'I'd like to know what you have in mind,' said Father Hogan at a certain point, as he realized where they were heading.

'We'll exhume Father Antonelli's body,' said Father Boni. 'I thought you'd understood.'

Father Hogan was completely taken aback. 'I don't believe we have the right . . .'

'We have the duty, Hogan, the duty to do so! Don't you see?' He stood motionless for a few moments, as the valley was flooded with golden light. 'It seems that you still do not fully appreciate what we're trying to discover. Or – if you do understand – you're trying unconsciously to back away. Why?'

'Because this thing that we're looking for has already had perverse effects on us, while we still have no idea of what, exactly, we are pursuing. I don't recognize you any more, Father Boni. I watched you react with complete indifference to a dying man, a fellow priest, imploring you to absolve his sins, and now I see that you are ready to profane his grave. What is happening to us, damn it?'

They were now less than a hundred steps from the cemetery. Father Boni glared at his companion with icy eyes: 'If you don't feel up to it, leave. Now.'

Hogan nodded. 'That's exactly what I'm going to do,' he said, turning back in the direction they'd come from.

'But remember,' said Father Boni, 'if that signal is coming from a civilization as fierce as it is intelligent, it is our duty to decipher the message it bears and even to attempt to extinguish it, no matter what the cost.'

Father Hogan stopped.

'Well?' asked Father Boni.

'What you're saying is absurd. But I'll come with you,' said Father Hogan.

'Fine. And from now on, try giving me a hand instead of hindering me. I consider your decision definitive.'

They started back down the path, reaching the churchyard entrance in a few minutes. The pastor was waiting for them.

'We're ready,' said Father Boni.

'I'm sorry. There's a problem,' said the pastor.

'A problem?' asked Father Boni, visibly unnerved. 'What kind of problem?'

'The late Father Antonelli is not in this cemetery.'

'I don't understand.'

'Well, you see, three hours ago I was expecting his coffin, for the funeral.'

'And?'

'A Jesuit came instead of the coffin. Not just any Jesuit but the secretary of the Father General. He came to tell me that Father Antonelli's last wish was that his body be cremated.'

Father Boni blanched. 'You can't be serious. A priest cannot be cremated.'

'And yet his request was authorized. The coroner was here with me and the papers we were shown were the original, signed documents. The Jesuit's credentials were in order as well. I wanted to contact you, but I didn't know where to look for you. You would have already left Rome by that time. So I decided to wait for you here.'

'Were you told where the body was taken?'

'To Rome, I think. But if you want my opinion, I say there's not a bit of truth in that story about his last wishes. I say that Father Antonelli had some disease. He was a man who travelled a lot, all over Africa and the East . . . That's why they had to burn his body. They'll have asked for some special dispensation from the Pope.'

'I thank you,' said Father Boni. 'We must leave now. Please do not say anything to anyone regarding our visit.'

They quickly made their way back to Alatri.

'Your fellow Jesuits have trumped us, Hogan.'

'No, I don't think so. It was probably Father Antonelli himself who arranged to have his body cremated.'

'Well, I haven't lost hope yet. Let's hurry back to the car. I know a way to get to Rome in less than two hours, if you don't mind driving fast.'

THEY LEFT SOON AFTERWARDS and in half an hour found themselves on the unsurfaced bed of a road still under construction. The car sped off, leaving a black cloud of dust in its wake.

Just before nine p.m. Father Hogan stopped in front of the Verano cemetery in Rome. Father Boni had not opened his mouth once during the entire journey, except to spit out terse directions.

He rang the bell repeatedly, nervously, until the custodian showed up.

'Who are you? The cemetery is closed.'

'We know,' said Father Boni, 'but, you see, we just happened to be passing through Rome when we heard that one of our brothers had passed away suddenly, and that his body had been brought here, to the funeral chapel, awaiting cremation. We have to leave Rome tonight, but we wanted to pay our last respects. We were good friends in our youth . . .'

The custodian shook his head. 'I'm very sorry, but I can't let you in at this hour. I've been given strict orders.'

Father Boni opened his wallet and took out a banknote. 'Please,' he insisted, 'you can't imagine how important it is for us.'

The man eyed the money and then took a quick look to make sure no one was around. He opened the gate to let the two men in.

'It's against the rules,' he said, swiftly pocketing the cash. 'I'm risking my job. But I'm not a man to deny someone in their time of grief . . . Hurry, this way. What was the good father's name?'

'Antonelli. Giuseppe Antonelli.'

'Excuse me a moment,' said the man, stopping in front of his living quarters, 'I have to get the register.' He was soon back. 'Follow me,' he said, 'this way.'

They walked down a gravel path between two rows of cypress trees, past a long series of vaults, until they found themselves before a low, grey building. The custodian turned the key in the lock.

'But this is not the funeral chapel,' protested Father Boni.

'No, it's not,' replied the custodian, opening the door and switching on the light inside. 'This is the incinerator. Your brother has already been cremated.'

Father Boni turned to Father Hogan. He had paled and his eyes were wide in disbelief.

'You can pay your respects to his ashes,' continued the custodian, 'if you so desire.'

Father Boni seemed about to turn on his heels but Father Hogan gripped his arm and practically forced him to follow the man into the large empty room.

'There,' said the custodian, pointing to a little chest on a metal shelf, 'that's the urn with his ashes.' He read the label to make sure he wasn't mistaken. 'Yes, it's him all right. Giuseppe Antonelli SJ. What does SJ mean?'

'It means Societatis Jesu, the Society of Jesus. He was a Jesuit,' replied Father Hogan.

He lowered his head and said a prayer. He recited the Requiem under his breath, then raised his hand to bless the urn.

'Thank you,' he said to the custodian, 'it's been a great consolation for us. Our heartfelt thanks.'

'Don't mention it,' replied the man.

'Well, we'll be going then.'

Father Boni strode off without waiting for the custodian to lead them out and Father Hogan followed. They'd covered perhaps ten metres when the custodian called them back. 'Wait!'

'What is it?' asked Father Hogan.

'No, nothing. I just remembered that . . . Well, the personal effects of the people we incinerate are kept for their relatives. But this man had no one at all – at least, not according to the register. If you were friends, perhaps you'd like to have something as a keepsake.'

Father Boni spun around and practically ran back.

'Yes, yes, of course!' he said. 'We'd appreciate it greatly. As I said, we were very close, very close indeed.'

'Well, he didn't have much actually.' The custodian opened a side door and led them into a little office. He used a key to open the top drawer of a filing cabinet.

'This is it, I'm afraid,' he said. 'His breviary.'

'Are you sure there was nothing else?' Father Boni asked anxiously.

'No. Look yourself. There's nothing else here.'

The custodian looked on dumbfounded as an expression of deep dismay transformed Father Boni's features. Father Hogan fingered the little book with its cover of shiny black leather, worn by years of use, and pictured it in the bare room of the dying priest, in the dim lamplight of his bedside table. In his mind's eye he saw the old man's ashen forehead, beaded with sweat.

'Thank you,' he said. 'Please give it to me. We'll take good care of it.' He took the breviary and they left the room.

HOGAN SAT AT THE WHEEL of the car and drove in silence through the practically deserted streets of the city. Father Boni never said a word the whole time. He calmly placed his hands on his knees and stared into the distance without blinking an eye. When they reached their destination, he opened the car door and walked off across the courtyard in silence. Father Hogan's voice stopped him before he could disappear under the portico. Father Boni turned and saw him in the centre of the courtyard with the breviary in his hand.

'What is it?' he asked.

Hogan raised the open breviary, gripping it between his thumb, index and middle fingers, and turned it so the print faced him.

'It's here,' he said. 'The translation of "The Book of Amon".'

'I imagined as much,' replied Father Boni. 'But I didn't have the courage to look. Don't lose it now. Goodnight.'

# 4

PHILIP GARRETT FOUND HIMSELF three levels down, in a tunnel that he estimated was about ten metres below the ground. The map that his father had drawn years before ended here, more or less; beyond this point there was nothing other than a very cursory sketch that indicated a fork in the tunnel that then broke off into a labyrinth of sorts. Philip realized he was in a fix. Whichever direction he chose, he'd no doubt end up lost in this maze of underground passageways. It would take months to survey the network and explore it centimetre by centimetre. His only option was to skip ahead to the last instruction: 'Find the entrance under the eye.'

'Under the eye' – what could that possibly mean? Another one of his father's brain-teasers. But was there really something worthwhile behind all this, something that would justify all this effort? Philip was feeling increasingly frustrated, and the situation brought up all those feelings of hostility and even resentment he'd felt for his father as a boy. He'd realized for some time now that he had always unconsciously held his father to blame for the death of his mother, no matter how implausible and unreasonable that was.

His father was living in Italy when he'd written those messages; perhaps he meant them to be read as a literal translation of the Italian? He remembered how his father had been fond of word games and of setting puzzles using different languages. 'Under the eye' would be *sott'occhio* in Italian, which also meant 'close at hand'. Could the solution be close at hand? Right there, where he least expected it?

Philip set down the acetylene lamp and sat on a row of flat stone blocks. The atmosphere was stifling and stank of mould, but every once in a while a slight breeze would waft by, a kind of dusty puff of air drifting through those dark galleries. Philip strained his ears. What was that sound he'd just heard? He looked at his watch. It was late, nearly midnight, and the slice of bread and cheese that he'd forced down an hour before with a little water had certainly not been much of a dinner.

He got to his feet and realized that the stone blocks he had been sitting on were not part of the pavement; they belonged to the outer wall of an ancient Roman house and had been reused to support the wall of the tunnel dug out long years later in the volcanic tuff.

Philip heard the sound again, and in that absolute silence it made a chill run down his spine. It sounded as if it was coming from the other side of the wall. He lifted the lantern and saw, on the wall directly in front of him, faded and dust-covered, but still identifiable, an eye. An eye run through by an arrow, between an open-clawed crab and a scorpion. The ancient apotropaic sign displayed on the houses of Pompeii to ward off the evil eye. He'd seen one just like it a few days before, a mosaic, on the wall of a recently excavated house of the ancient city.

'Under the eye'. He started to explore the wall with his hands, little by little, but all he found was a compact surface. He didn't want to use his pickaxe, because he had no idea how thick the wall was, and because it was against his principles to blindly attack an ancient structure that might even be covered with precious paintings on its other side.

He dropped down to the pavement again and tried budging the blocks of stone. It didn't take long to discover that a couple of them were loose, because dust had replaced the mortar that had once held them together. The mortar had been scraped away (by his father, perhaps?); small lumps of it were still mixed in with the dust.

Philip took a mason's pick from his haversack and used the

tip to work at the sides and then the bottom of one of the blocks until he managed to loosen and then remove it. A puff of air blew out at him from inside, proof that he had opened a passage with a room of some sort that had been closed off by the tunnel. And then he thought he heard a weak jingling that died out almost immediately. Was it possible? Could the legend of the bell that announced earthquakes have some basis in fact? Could it be announcing an earthquake now? The idea of being buried for ever in that catacomb made him shudder. Philip listened intently, but he could only hear the sound of his own breathing. He forced such worries out of his mind and started to cautiously remove the second block. He slowly scraped away enough of the earth underneath to make a crawlspace big enough to allow him to get to the other side of the wall.

He found himself in a smallish square room, surely a *cubiculum*. As he raised his lantern, he could in fact see a wooden bed frame which had fallen to pieces, as well as a chest with bronze latches, pushed up against a wall. The metal had a greenish patina while the wood, almost completely mineralized after centuries, had taken on a greyish colour.

He found himself in the home of an ancient Roman, almost surely sealed shut by the eruption of Vesuvius in AD 79. He explored the walls of the room by lamplight and saw that it had been separated from the rest of the house by an earthslide, and it was plainly evident that the collapse must have happened more recently. His father may even have set it off himself as he was trying to get to the inner rooms of the ancient house. And then perhaps he'd never had the time or the opportunity to come back and continue his exploration.

It was getting quite late and Philip thought it would be better to return the next day, after he'd rested and made a plan, but the thought of crossing that last threshold and roaming those silent rooms – he'd be the first person to enter them in almost two thousand years! – gave him the energy to go on. He ate a last chunk of bread and gulped down some water and then began to remove the tuff blocks and clear away the rubble, taking care not to start another cave-in. Two hours later, he had succeeded in opening a passageway. Dripping with sweat, his hair all white from the dust, Philip wormed his way through the opening, mindful not to bump against a beam that seemed to be miraculously keeping the whole structure from collapsing. His fingers grazed the beam, and he realized that long years of calcareous water infiltrations from above had once again mineralized the wood, preserving a certain solidity, although it was certainly fragile.

What he saw defied imagining. A fortuitous equilibrium of load and pressure had left most of the rooms standing. The house was largely intact, and mostly accessible. Only the large central peristyle had been inundated by ash, which had, however, settled and compacted behind the balustrade which encircled the garden on the ground level. In fact the ash had consolidated to such an extent that it formed a sort of barrier, allowing him to walk along the boundary walls at the sides.

Philip was amazed at the incredible state of preservation of the frescoes that adorned the walls. A flowered garden appeared in the halo of his lamp as he advanced, replete with splendid trompe-l'oeil effects: palm trees and fruit-laden pomegranate trees, apple trees with shiny red orbs, lentisks and myrtles, brambles full of blackberries. Through the boughs of that magnificent garden peeked blackbirds and magpies, goldfinches and chaffinches, turtle-doves and jays, multiplied infinitely by an artist's hand at the behest of the master of the villa. It seemed to Philip for a moment, in the wavering light of his hand-held lantern, that those branches and leaves were moving, as if swayed by a sudden breeze. The birds seemed poised to burst into song and take flight under those dusty vaults.

He wandered on to the *atrium*, which was almost completely filled by the ashes which had fallen from the *impluvium*, although he managed to make his way through. On his left a little shrine was filled with images of divinities and demons, each bearing an

Etruscan name. The most impressive was Charu, the ferryman who transported souls to the otherworld. It seemed strange to find such symbols and statues in a first-century Pompeian home. As he lingered to examine the images in the flickering lamplight, he had the clear sensation of hearing a weak sound and then, immediately afterwards, feeling a puff of wind. Could anything still be moving in that dead air, in that timeless space?

Philip stood stock still and listened for a long minute, but he heard only the beating of his heart. He walked to the threshold of the *tablinum* and drew up short. The master of the house had appeared before him.

The upper part of the skeleton – the head, the arms, part of the ribs and the backbone – lay on a table. The pelvic bones rested on a chair, while the legs and feet were scattered over a lovely black and white mosaic floor. His white robe was intact and still showed faded red embroidery at the hem.

Philip approached on tiptoe and, as he crossed the threshold, saw an odd object out of the corner of his eye, hanging from an arm of the standing candelabrum: it was a perfectly preserved sistrum in black metal, the colour of tarnished silver. The friar's mention of the earthquake bells echoed in his mind and, as he looked at the instrument, he could almost imagine its silvery sound, as if he himself had heard it once, long, long ago. He reached out a trembling hand and gave it a little swing. The beads slipped along the rods and touched the frame. Just a few notes rang out, on the little instrument that no human hand had touched for twenty centuries, sounding like a sweet, short elegy in that world of ash.

This must be the sound that had made the monks startle out of sleep whenever the earth was about to shake! It was obviously amplified by whatever strange play of echoes was at work down here. A quiet voice, buried through the millennia.

What other marvels did this place hold?

He turned back towards the skeleton sitting at the table and watched as the last bones of his hand disarticulated under his eyes, as the sound waves disturbed the miraculous equilibrium that had held them together until that moment. It was the man's right hand, crumbling to pieces over a sheet of parchment. He had died in the act of writing.

The inkwell still sat on the table and the reed stylus still rested between the bones of his index finger and thumb. Philip quickly took his Leica from the haversack and captured that stupefying scene in the cold light of his magnesium flashbulb. He walked around the table, then gently moved the bones one by one from the parchment and took another shot. Just as Philip was about to lift the parchment to have a closer look, the noise he thought he'd heard a few minutes before became louder and more distinct. It was the sound of footsteps, and voices. He turned to where the sounds were coming from and saw what he had missed when he had first entered and his attention had been captured by the incredible scene. There were traces of human activity in the dust covering the floor, traces obviously much more recent than that ancient tragedy. He backed up towards the threshold and instinctively grabbed the sistrum, dropping it into his haversack. He had just enough time to extinguish the light in his lantern and retreat behind one of the columns in the *atrium* when he heard a creak, like that of a door opening. The light of another lamp, and the acrid smell of carbide, flooded the room.

Three men came in. Two of them, miserably dressed, looked like typical Neapolitan lowlifes, while the other had his back turned to Philip. All he could see was that the man was tall and heavy-set, dressed simply but with great elegance.

'See?' said one of the first two. 'It's like we said. Just take a look at this! And it's all perfectly intact. Never been touched.'

The man briefly examined the scene. 'Never been touched?' he repeated. 'Look at the bones of his hand. They've been moved by at least thirty centimetres. You assured me that no one had ever set foot in here.'

'Hey, buddy, I don't know what you're talking about. What

we told you was the truth! You're not looking for an excuse to back out of our deal, are you? If it's trouble you want . . .'

'I won't give you a cent unless you tell me who else you've told about this place . . . You buggers thought you could dip into the same nest twice, didn't you?' The Italian the man spoke was quite correct, but he clearly had a foreign accent, vaguely Central European.

The first man stepped forward, by no means intimidated. 'We brought you here, now you pay.'

'No,' said the foreigner. 'Our agreement was clear. Either you tell me who has been in here or I won't give you a cent.'

'No one, as far as we know,' said the second man, who hadn't opened his mouth until then. He turned to his companion and said in dialect: 'There's that American in the monastery who's always wandering around underground. Could it have been him?'

The foreigner immediately understood the word 'American', even though they had been speaking dialect. 'American? What American?'

'I do odd jobs sometimes for the Franciscans,' said the second, 'and there's been an American hanging around the monastery the last couple of days. They say he's studying the stuff that's here underground. He must get in through the catacombs under the crypt.'

Philip jumped at those words and flattened himself as best he could behind the column, holding his breath. The dust clinging to the stone was so fine that any tiny movement released it into the air and he was afraid he would sneeze and alert the intruders to his presence.

The foreigner seemed calmer now. His attention was attracted to the papyrus open on the table. He went closer and took a long look in silence. The expression of his face changed dramatically. His brow became beaded with sweat and his eyelids blinked faster and faster. His hands neared the sheet.

'What about our money?' demanded one of the two men.

The foreigner turned and Philip could finally see his face. He was a good-looking man with handsome features, perfectly clean-shaven, but the gelid look in his blue eyes hinted at a capacity for great cruelty. Philip shuddered.

'I'll give you your money,' he said, 'but first I want to make sure that you haven't brought any one else down here.' He picked up the papyrus with the intention of slipping it into the bag he was carrying, but one of the men tried to snatch it away. The fragile sheet ripped in two.

'Idiot!' hissed the foreigner. 'You imbecile! Look what you've done!'

'We've never brought anyone down here until now,' insisted the other.

'Then we have to look for other passages,' said the foreigner. 'If you've never brought anyone down here, it means that he got in some other way. He might even still be around. Find him.'

Philip felt his heart sink and he tried to creep back to the collapsed wall, in the dark. But after a few steps he bumped a doorjamb and the sistrum he had with him tinkled. He muttered a curse and continued to feel his way towards the opening that let on to the peristyle.

'That way!' shouted the foreigner. 'There's someone over there! Quick! Don't let him get away!'

Philip, realizing that he'd been discovered, set off at a run, stumbling and knocking against all sorts of obstacles in the dark, but he managed to reach the entrance to the *cubiculum*. He heard the foreigner's voice shouting, 'I'll give you twice as much if you catch him!' and the sound of hurried footsteps. All at once, he heard a scream of pain, and couldn't help but look back. The foreigner had run into the balustrade and was holding his right side. His face was twisted into a grimace.

The halo of the carbide lamp was getting dangerously close now, as the other two men continued the chase. Philip crawled up the pile of stone blocks and debris towards the opening he'd made under the beam. As he was trying to get through to the other side, lamplight flooded the room and the dark shadows of his pursuers loomed up behind it.

'Stop or I'll shoot!' shouted the foreigner, but Philip frantically dropped to the ground and rolled through the hole to the other side of the collapsed wall. He stumbled to his feet and saw the light nearing the opening from the passage on the other side. There was no time left and Philip realized he had no choice. He crawled back up to the top of the heap of debris and, as he spotted one of the two men already peering into the room, he repeatedly struck the wooden beam with his pickaxe. As soon as he saw that the beam was about to give, he scrambled down towards the wall and found the opening to the external pavement. He could hear the entire structure collapsing behind him. A cloud of dust filled his lungs and nearly suffocated him and a hail of stones threatened to crush his legs, but with a final effort he pulled himself through to the tunnel outside and took a long gulp of fresh air. He hacked and coughed at length before he could catch his breath, then rubbed his aching, bloody legs. Thank God, it didn't look like he had any broken bones. When he had recovered, he put his ear to the wall. There was nothing but silence on the other side. He must have killed them. All three? A sensation of distress engulfed him and his limbs felt numb.

His lantern had broken and was useless to him, but he managed to find his way back out by sparingly using a cigar lighter and then the matches from his haversack.

He emerged into the monastery crypt harrowed by the fatigue, pain and upset he had suffered. The skulls piled up in their niches greeted him with grotesque grins. Right then they looked to Philip like the smiling faces of old friends.

PHILIP MANAGED TO GET to the service exit that led to the laundry and then out to the garden. He tidied himself up as best he could and limped towards the hotel. It was the middle of the night and the streets were completely deserted. He tried to pick up his pace, gritting his teeth against the pain; he couldn't wait to get back to his room, take a bath and collapse onto his bed.

However, he was soon forced to acknowledge that this endless day was not yet over. The sound of footsteps accompanied his own, stopping whenever he did. A few steps later, at the end of an alleyway dimly lit by gaslight, Philip found his path barred, both in front and behind, by shadows which had materialized out of nowhere.

A voice said, 'Drop your haversack and get out of here. You won't be harmed.'

That voice! Philip flattened himself against a wall, shouting, 'Help! Help me!' But none of the windows in the nearby houses opened. No one came to his defence. There was no way out. Not only had the man escaped, he'd managed to get out before Philip! And now he wanted to take away everything Philip had struggled so hard to get, cutting him off for ever from all trace of his lost father. Could he mean to take his life as well? Who could he be?

Philip grabbed his pickaxe and backed up against the wall. He'd go out fighting. Shadows began to emerge into the halo of light projected onto the ground by the lamp. There were four of them, thugs, armed with knives, but the man who had spoken remained hidden in the gloom at the head of the alleyway.

The attackers were very close now and one came forward brandishing his knife, while another made a move to snatch the haversack hanging at Philip's side. Philip landed a kick, screaming out at the pain in his own leg, and escaped the blade slashing towards his right arm by a hair's breadth. He swung his pickaxe, forcing the cutthroats to back off, but he knew he had no chance. He cursed his foolishness; had he removed the film from the camera he could have dropped the haversack and tried to break away, but it was too late for regrets now.

The four thugs were just steps away from him and their

knives were teasingly close when a man appeared from a dark passageway behind him: a figure cloaked in black, his face covered. A deep voice rang out with a syncopated accent – '*Salam alekhum, sidi el Garrett!*' – as two dark hands shot from under the cloak: the right held a scimitar and the left a *jatagan*.

One of his assailants, the first to spin around to meet the newcomer, took two deep cuts to his face and fell to the ground howling, hands clutching at his cheeks, which had been slashed from temple to jaw. Another was hamstrung before he could even turn and he collapsed in a twisting, screaming heap. The two remaining took to their heels.

The warrior regained his stance instantly and sheathed his weapons. He turned to Philip and bowed his head, briefly touching his chest, mouth and forehead with his right hand.

Philip was still backed up against the wall with his pickaxe in hand, stunned and unable to move.

'Pure folly, *el sidi*. They would have gutted you like a goat and your father would never have forgiven me,' said the man, baring his face. 'Luckily I thought of following you on these night-time jaunts of yours, when peril is at its height.'

Philip looked at the square jaw, the straight nose, the big, black, shining eyes. 'El Kassem! Oh, my God, I can't believe it's you!'

'It's best we leave,' said the Arab warrior. 'This city is more dangerous than the medina in Tangiers.'

'Did you say "your father"? Is it true, then, that he's still alive?'

'If Allah has kept him from harm, yes, he is.'

'Where is he?' asked Philip as they walked off in great haste. He couldn't help but glance around for more attackers.

'This I do not know. He has surely walked a long path since I left him and we will have to find him again. Come now, follow me. You can no longer stay in your serai. Your things have already been moved to a safe house.'

THE SKY WAS beginning to pale to the east when they reached an old house with chipped walls. They went in and found themselves in a large courtyard crossed by long lines of fluttering laundry.

'This way,' said El Kassem, slipping around the obstacles with familiar ease. They reached a staircase and started up.

'Strange folk, these Naples . . .' observed El Kassem, the steep rise of the stairs not taking away his breath in the least.

'Neapolitans,' corrected Philip, gasping.

'Yes. How can they think to win a fight with such short *jatagans*? At our oasis, only the children play with those.'

'We're not in the desert here, El Kassem. I can't understand how you've managed to get around dressed like you are in a place like this, where everyone sticks his nose into everyone else's business.'

'Oh, it is not difficult,' said El Kassem. 'If you remove the rope from your keffiyeh, wrap it around your shoulders and walk with your head down, you look like one of their widows.'

They stopped at a landing on the third floor and Philip leaned against the wall to catch his breath.

'If we are to find your father you must strengthen your muscles and your limbs,' said El Kassem. 'If three flights of stairs take such a toll . . .'

Philip knew it was no use answering. He had known El Kassem since, as a boy, he had accompanied his father as far as Oran, before one of Desmond's many departures into the desert. El Kassem was his father's guide and bodyguard, bound to him by the loyalty that only the men of the desert are capable of. Stalwart and untiring, he could ride for days without a sign of weariness, catching a bit of sleep now and then without leaving his horse's saddle. He was extraordinarily skilful in the use of any weapon and could bear up under any hardship, heat or cold, hunger or thirst.

El Kassem knocked at the door and the shuffle of slippers

could be heard on the other side. An old man's voice called out, 'Who is it?'

'It's us,' answered El Kassem in passable French.

The door opened and an old man greeted them. He was wrapped in a creased dressing gown, but his hair was neatly combed.

Philip recognized him and opened his arms. 'Lino!'

The old man looked puzzled for a moment, then said, 'Is that you, master Philip? Oh, Holy Virgin, it is you! Come in, come in. But look at you! Look at what a state you're in!'

'My dear old friend,' said Philip, embracing him.

The old man dried his eyes with his sleeve and had them sit down so he could make them coffee. El Kassem sat on a carpet with his legs crossed, while Philip settled in an old armchair with worn upholstery. Everything in the little apartment seemed frayed and shabby, and Philip couldn't help but think of how things had changed for the old man. When he'd met Lino, Philip was an adolescent, living in Naples in an elegant residence on Via Caracciolo with a stupendous view of Mount Vesuvius and the bay. Natalino Santini had worked for them back then as his father's valet and driver. He would accompany Desmond to the Piazza Dante bookshops that specialized in rare and antique books and manuscripts, and introduced him to all the city's hidden secrets. There was not an alleyway in the Spanish quarter that Lino was not perfectly familiar with. When Philip and his father left Naples, Lino was living respectably and had found another job.

The *caffettiera* began to perk, so Lino took it off the flame and turned it upside down, in true Neapolitan fashion.

'I'm sorry, *signuri*,' he said, 'to receive you in such humble surroundings but, you see, when my poor wife fell ill with consumption, I spent my last penny trying to help her.' He shook his head. 'I've lost her, along with everything I had, and no one will hire me any more at my age. But I scrape by with a few odd jobs now and then ... Ah, the good times are long gone, *signuri* ...'

He served their coffee in elegant porcelain cups, a reminder of better times, and sat down himself to sip at the steaming black brew, closing his eyes. It was one of the few luxuries he could still afford.

'What brings you back to Naples?' the old man asked Philip.

'I've been investigating the passageways beneath the old Franciscan monastery,' he replied.

The old man regarded him with an expression of surprise. 'Just like your father,' he murmured.

'My father, did you say? Lino, what was my father looking for in the catacombs?' Philip asked.

The old man took another sip of his coffee, then set the little cup on its saucer and breathed a deep sigh.

'You'll think it strange, but he was looking for a sound.'

'A sound?'

'Yes. A soft metallic sound, like the notes of a music box. The Franciscans claimed they could hear it when an earthquake was coming. The people believed them and would seek shelter between the monastery walls, because they said that the sound would protect them from any cataclysm. And in fact the walls have never been damaged. Didn't the guardian tell you?'

Philip passed a hand over his forehead. Everything fitted together perfectly, even though, for the time being, nothing made sense. 'Yes, but ...'

'Your father asked for permission to explore the catacombs. He heard that sound and was deeply affected by it. I don't know, maybe he only thought he'd heard it, but afterwards he had no peace. He would hum that little tune continually, obsessively. He asked me to find a craftsman who could make a music box that would reproduce those notes. I had it made and he gave it to you as a gift, remember?

'Then one day he gave it back to me, telling me to take good care of it. Look, I'm not making this up,' he added, getting up

from his chair and opening the door of a little cupboard. 'See?'
And he took out a little wooden box topped by a lead soldier.
'Remember it? He gave it to you the day of your fourteenth
birthday, but when he had to leave for the war, he brought it to
me and made me promise not to say a word to anyone about it.'
He opened the cover and turned the key and a brief, plaintive
melody filled the little room.

Philip blanched. 'My God . . .'

'What's wrong?'

'I know . . . where this music comes from. Look.' He got up,
went over to his haversack and took out the sistrum under the
mystified gaze of the old manservant and the Arab warrior. He
hung it on the doorjamb and gave it a little push with the tip of
his index finger. It swung and the bronze beads slid on their rods,
tapping the metal frame one after another and producing a silvery
sequence of notes.

The old man reached out a hand with tears in his eyes.
'You're right! This is the true source of the music, my son.'

'Yes,' said Philip. 'This has sounded for centuries in the
underground labyrinth every time the earth shook. This is what
my father was looking for. But why?'

The old man shook his head. 'I don't know, and neither did
your father. It was something he couldn't explain. There are
forces that guide us at times without our realizing why. Don't
you believe that?'

'What about you, El Kassem? Don't you know either?'

'No. But it must be very important. There was someone else
looking for it tonight. Remember?'

'Yes. I saw his face.'

El Kassem jumped. 'You saw his face? Why didn't you tell me
right away? It was so dark that I thought . . .'

'No, not there on the street. When he was underground. He's
tall, blond, with a square jaw and icy blue eyes.'

El Kassem paled. 'O merciful Allah! It was Selznick.'

# 5

COLONEL JOBERT HAD REMAINED at the El Aziri fort for a month in the hope of receiving news from Philip Garrett which could help him in his search. Seeing that no message was forthcoming, he decided to leave the fort at the end of October with two companies of legionnaires. Although the heat should have been tolerable so late in the season, the summer was unusually prolonged that year and their advance to the south-eastern quadrant became more strenuous and punishing with each passing day.

He managed to get information from the bedouins at the oases. They spoke of two foreigners: one – a tall infidel with light eyes, suffering from a pain in his right side – sounded like Selznick; he had been seen in April heading north towards Fezzan. The other had left the well at Bir Akkar, directed east, at the beginning of September. This second *nabil* had dark eyes and silver hair at his temples; he was certainly Desmond Garrett. Although he felt sure of their identities, Jobert could not understand why Selznick was going north. Where could he be headed, and for what reason? Perhaps Garrett had confided in Selznick years earlier, when he still thought he could trust him, and the trail he was following might be based on the very information he'd received from Garrett.

Aware of the fact that dividing one's forces in the desert was invariably a mistake, Jobert sent a telegraph from the last outpost to the garrisons along the coast, ordering them to watch the caravan routes and the ports and to stop Selznick should he try to take ship, although he didn't have too many illusions about the success of such an operation. If Selznick had managed to get to Libya and gone to Gadames and Tripoli, he would be able to reach Italy or Greece or Turkey without problems. Jobert was nonetheless sure that their paths would one day cross again.

He had saved the most difficult task for himself: the exploration of the south-eastern quadrant, a desolate and practically inaccessible area, cursed by extremely high temperatures and very few wells. A report dating back to the early 1800s, cited in Desmond Garrett's study, spoke of an oasis beyond the inferno: a little Eden, with luxuriant palms, fig and pomegranate trees, where clear water flowed abundantly. The oasis was completely hidden in a gully of Wadi Addir and was protected by its banks from incessant sandstorms. This small but completely independent realm was ruled over by an ancient family who claimed to be descended from an Egyptian son of Joseph the Hebrew. They reigned over their land from an impregnable fortress: the castle of Kalaat Hallaki.

No one knew what there was beyond this oasis. The bedouins claimed the territory was haunted by spirits and called it the sands of the djinn. The Sand of Ghosts. It was there that Colonel Jobert hoped to find Desmond Garrett, sooner or later, and it was there that he was convinced he would discover the reason behind the disturbing phenomena that he had been sent to investigate.

For days and days they advanced over a land scorched by a merciless sun, losing horses and camels along the way, without ever meeting a single human being.

They camped one night near a well half-buried in the sand. After they had laboured long and hard to clear away the sand, just a little bitter water gurgled out, barely enough to slake the thirst of the men and animals. As the soldiers were setting up camp, Jobert sent one of the captains to reconnoitre the surrounding area with a patrol before darkness fell. The officer returned some time later, alone, at a gallop.

'Colonel!' he cried out, without dismounting. 'You must come and see this!'

Jobert jumped onto his horse and followed the man. They rode for a couple of kilometres until they reached the spot where the patrol had stopped, in front of a low, jagged ridge that rose from the sand like the crest of a dragon.

'You'll never believe what we've found!'

Jobert dismounted and followed him to a point at which the rocky ridge was interrupted by a smooth surface a couple of metres long. It was completely covered with carvings depicting strange creatures: headless men wearing grotesque masks on what appeared to be their chests.

'The Blemmyae, Commander! Look! The race of headless men with their faces on their chests spoken of by the ancients!'

Jobert immediately noticed the agitation that his words were producing in the soldiers nearby and he shot his subordinate a withering look. 'They're just pictures on a stone, Captain Bonnier,' he said. 'Control yourself. We've seen much worse over the years!'

They returned to their camp to eat some biscuits and dates. Before retiring for the night, Colonel Jobert summoned the captain to his tent.

'Bonnier, you must be mad! How could you spout such foolishness in front of the men? They are soldiers, but they're vulnerable under these conditions. Good God, man, you should know them by now! Make them face a pack of marauders on horseback in the middle of the desert and they won't bat an eye. But if you fill their heads with strange imaginings you'll have them trembling with fear in this cursed land. Do I really need to explain it to you?'

Bonnier lowered his head in confusion.

'I apologize, Commander. But you see, in those rock carvings, I saw the truth behind an ancient legend reported by Pliny the Elder. He speaks of a fierce race of beings who live on the edges of the southern desert. The Blemmyae: men with no heads, who wear their faces on their chests.'

'I am astounded at you, Bonnier! Do you think you're the only one to have read the classics? I'm sure you'll have noticed, in your reading, that any area, any area at all, that is out of reach, inaccessible or unexplored, on land or at sea, is populated by monsters of every description by the ancients! Your Pliny describes a race of men in India who have but one foot, which they lift above their supine bodies to shade themselves in the heat of noon!'

'You're right, Commander. But this is proof! While we have no evidence of those other stories.'

'Well, then, I can tell you that whoever carved those figures had heard of Pliny! Do you know how many fakes have been cunningly fabricated by well-read travellers over the last couple of centuries?'

'I beg to differ with you, sir. The chances that a traveller arrived at this very point during the last century or two with the intention of creating an archaeological forgery are close to nil. What's more, allow me to remind you that I am something of an expert on primitive art, and I can assure you that those carvings are very ancient indeed. I cannot hazard a precise date, but I would say they go back to the early Bronze Age, at the very least. We're speaking of over five thousand years ago. I hope you understand, sir. It's obvious that no one believes in the existence of such a being, but it would be interesting to decipher the symbolism hidden behind this type of representation.'

His subordinate's insistence irritated Jobert, who was already tense because of the difficulties inherent in their advance. He cut him off sharply. 'The subject is closed, Captain Bonnier. In the future you are to keep any such considerations to yourself. That is an order. Goodnight.'

Bonnier clicked his heels and withdrew.

KALAAT HALLAKI STOOD OUT at the top of the hill that dominated the oasis of Wadi Addir, the sky behind it darkening as the sun sank into the expanse of sand. Sparrows took to the air from the trees dotting the orchards and gardens, soaring to the castle bastions that were bleached white by the sun of infinite summers, while on high a hawk spread its wings in solemn flight. All at once, in the silence that precedes the deep peace of the evening, a woman's song rang out from the tallest tower, soft at first and then more intense, high and warbling, a hymn sweet and agonizing, which rose like a silver stream towards the evening star. The swallows' chirping stopped and the bleating of the sheep died down as if nature were intent on listening to the elegy flowing from the veiled figure that had appeared on the ramparts of the immense fortress. Then, in an instant, the melody was distorted into a shrill, delirious scream that dissolved into heartbroken weeping.

The oasis below was immersed in the light of dusk. The tops of the palms swayed in the evening breeze and the walls of the castle all around were enveloped in twilight as in the glow of a fire. The dying sun was mirrored in the canals that divided the terrain into verdant squares of emerald green nestled between the silvery waters and the golden sands.

Against the disc of the sun sinking at the horizon there appeared a swarm of warriors wrapped in a cloud of golden dust. They were returning from battle, bearing their wounded and the memory, perhaps, of their dead left unburied on the Sand of Ghosts.

The woman had disappeared. In her place stood the black-cloaked figure of her husband, the lord of that place, Rasaf el Kebir. He trained his eyes on the throng of warriors, trying to count them as a shepherd does his sheep as they return to the fold in the evening. He could make out at their head a man wrapped in a light blue *barrakan*, gripping a purple standard: their commander, Amir. He recognized the silvery shields of the mailed lancers on horseback and the riflemen on their fast *mehari*. Their losses did not seem to be too great; but as the army approached and he could distinguish between one man and another and even make out their spears, he was overwhelmed with astonishment as his gaze fell upon something that no one had ever seen under the walls of Kalaat Hallaki. A prisoner! Bound to a saddle, his hands in chains behind his back. For the first time in living memory, a prisoner had been taken!

He hurried down the stairs and ran into the courtyard as the gate was swinging open to allow the warriors to enter. Amir was the first to dismount, handing the standard to a footman as Rasaf rushed forward to embrace him. As the wounded were being seen to, the woman's sobbing could suddenly be heard again from above.

'Where is she?' Amir asked.

Rasaf raised his head towards a stair that led up to the women's quarters.

'They caught us by surprise again, damn them. They spring out of the sand, all at once, hundreds of them, from every direction. Their energy seems to have no limits. Even after they're down, and you think they're dead, that's when they suddenly pounce. Many of our men were wounded that way.'

Rasaf's expression was full of anguish. 'We must find a passage! The time is coming. I can no longer sleep at night, nor find peace by day.'

Amir gestured behind him. 'We have a prisoner!'

'I saw him,' replied Rasaf, 'although I couldn't believe my eyes.'

As he spoke he looked beyond Amir's shoulders to behold the Enemy: the scorpion of the desert, the denizen of the Sand of Ghosts. The prisoner's head was wrapped in a turban, knotted at the neck, which completely covered his face. The fabric had small holes slashed at the eyes and mouth. His bare chest was tattooed with a horrifying mask. Two curved blades hung from his belt, like the claws of a scorpion. The lower part of his body was covered by long, black camel-hair trousers. His skin was dry and very thick, as wrinkled as an old man's, but his physical vigour was incredible. Every yank he made at his chains threatened to topple the four gigantic lancers who held him down on all sides.

'How did you do it?' Rasaf asked. 'None of us has ever managed to capture one of them.'

'They are not invulnerable,' said Amir. 'Your ancestor Prince Abu Sarg once wrote that they were terrified of fire. When we saw that this one had separated from the rest to finish off one of our men who was trying to drag himself off the battlefield, my mounted guards encircled him with a ring of naphtha and set fire to it with a gunshot. His terror was so great that he lost consciousness. And so we captured him. He's yours, my lord. Do with him as you wish.'

'Fire,' murmured Rasaf. 'Fire will get us through! But how can we light enough flames to open a passage? It's just not possible. Even if we felled all the trees in the oasis, even if we took down all the cedar beams in the castle, it wouldn't be enough.'

A flash lit Amir's eyes. 'Perhaps there is a way. If you allow me to draw upon the treasure of the ancestors in the Horse's Crypt.'

Rasaf's head dropped as the suffocated wailing of his woman continued to rain down from above. As if she sensed the presence of the enemy.

'The treasure of the ancestors,' repeated Rasaf. 'Even if I gave you permission, you know that it's almost impossible to open the crypt . . .'

He turned towards the prisoner, who had finally been bound, in the centre of the courtyard. Rasaf approached him, overcoming the disgust the creature aroused in him, and stretched out his hand towards the edge of the turban that covered his face.

'No!' shouted Amir. 'Don't do it! No one can see a Blemmyae in the face! Your bride, Rasaf! Think of your bride . . . how her mind has been ravaged, destroyed for ever!'

Rasaf retracted his hand. 'Not for ever, Amir. We shall

succeed in opening a passage to the Place of Knowledge and we shall take her there on the appointed day. But now this scorpion must be destroyed. Take him out of the oasis and burn him. Then grind his bones in a mortar and sprinkle the dust in the desert.'

Amir gestured to a group of warriors, who approached the prisoner. He writhed and struggled, letting out strange sounds like a terror-stricken animal as they dragged him away from the castle.

Rasaf turned and went up the stair slowly, his head low. He walked down a long corridor punctuated by wide Moorish windows that looked out on the western desert until he found himself before a door. He opened it and entered with a quiet step. Lying on the bed was an incredibly beautiful dark-skinned woman whose gaze wandered absently to the arabesqued beams on the ceiling. He caressed her forehead lightly, then brought a bench near the bed and sat watching her silently. When she closed her eyes as if she were dozing off, he rose and went up to the castle bastions. The moon appeared in the east while the flames that were devouring the prisoner's limbs rose to the west.

WHEN HE SAW AMIR turn from the blaze and mount his horse to ride back to the castle, Rasaf went down to his apartments. He awaited him there by lamplight, sitting near the great window that gave onto the desert.

'Do you truly believe that we can open a passage to the Tower of Solitude?' he asked as soon as he heard Amir enter.

'I do,' replied Amir. 'And today I had the proof that we will succeed. The Blemmyae are terrified of fire.'

'How can you be certain?'

'The reason they fear it is because they've never seen it. No one knows what they live on in that inferno of sand and wind, but there is nothing in their territory that can catch fire. Give me the chance to draw from the treasure in the Horse's Crypt. I will go to Hit in Mesopotamia, where a spring of naphtha flows, and

I will bargain with the tribes that live there. I will buy an enormous quantity of it and bring it all the way back here by camel, inside thousands of skins. And when the day arrives, our warriors will advance all the way to the Tower of Solitude protected by two walls of fire. I have heard that there are rifles which are immensely more powerful and precise than those we have: I will buy them as well, if you allow me to take from the treasure.'

'I would do anything for my bride to regain her lost reason . . . anything. You cannot understand my torment, Amir. To see her body at the height of its splendour and then to look upon those empty eyes, staring into the void . . . to hear the agony in her song whenever the nightmare takes over . . .'

'Then allow me to leave as soon as possible. There's no more time. And let Arad leave as well. I will meet her in the Horse's Crypt on the third day of the new moon of Nisan.'

'Arad!'

'Yes,' replied Amir. 'Your daughter and I have tested ourselves thousands of times. We cannot fail.'

'You've thought of everything then. You've been planning this for a long time . . .'

'Yes, my lord. Your daughter cannot bear her mother's folly.'

'But it's a terrible risk, Amir. How can I risk the life of my daughter to save her mother?'

'Life itself is a terrible risk, Rasaf, from the moment we first see the light. Let us leave now, I beg you. The time is right. We cannot abandon the task that lies before us. It is not by chance that our people have managed to survive for so many centuries in this marvellous and forgotten place. We must win. Please, allow us to take the keys and to go.'

Rasaf lowered his head. 'Does Arad know you want to leave so soon?'

'Arad wants it as well and is ready to leave at any moment to reach the appointed place. I shall speak to her this very night.'

'Go, then,' said Rasaf. He opened a coffer of cedar wood,

rimmed in iron, and took out a small rosewood case. He opened it and showed Amir two arrowheads lying on red leather. One had a square tip, while the other was shaped like a star.

'Choose your arrowhead, Amir. Arad will take the other.'

Amir gazed at the two shining steel tips, then chose the star.

'The most difficult and the most deadly,' said Rasaf. 'The wound it provokes is devastating. Incurable. Do not fail, Amir. I could not bear it.'

'I will not fail,' he said. 'Farewell, Rasaf. Tomorrow I shall leave as soon as possible.'

'Farewell, Amir. May God protect you.'

AMIR LEFT THE ROOM, walked down to the courtyard and headed towards the spring, sure that he would find Arad there at this hour. There she was, her sheer white gown fluttering in the moonlight on the evening breeze that had descended upon the oasis. Her gracious figure and long gazelle's legs showed through the light fabric. She was a ravishing sight in the glow of the full moon reflected in the crystalline spring: she seemed to be bathing in the diaphanous light which flooded the air as if it were a lake without shores or a bottom. She could remain in silence for hours, listening to the voices that came from the gardens and the desert, breathing in the wind-borne scents of blossoms hidden in distant, arid valleys.

Amir loved her profoundly, with a proud, moody love, and even if Arad had never spoken to him openly about her own feelings, he was sure that no woman could prefer another to him in all of Kalaat Hallaki. No one could rival him in courage, generosity or devotion. He was certain that one day he would sway her, that passion would consume her like the fire that devoured the endless plains of grass beyond the sea of sand at the end of every summer.

'Arad.'

The woman turned towards him and smiled.

'Arad, your father has agreed. We will open the Horse's Crypt and take what we need from the treasure accumulated by our ancestors. And when the time comes, I will open the way to the Tower of Solitude so that your mother may regain the reason that was stripped from her the day she was kidnapped and held prisoner by the Blemmyae. I will leave tomorrow. And you too must leave as soon as you can, if you want to be at the appointed place on the third day of the new moon of Nisan.' He stretched out his hand and showed her the tip of the arrow. 'It's a game we've played since we were children, but this time the tips will be of tempered steel. Neither of us can fail.'

'I am not afraid,' said Arad, taking the arrowhead into her own hands.

'Will you love me if I lead the warriors through the Sand of Ghosts and your mother's reason is restored?'

'Yes. I will love you then.'

Amir lowered his gaze and seemed to be watching her reflection in the water of the spring. 'Why not now?' he asked, without daring to look her in the eyes.

'Because . . . it's what my father wants, it's what our people want, but . . . my soul is oppressed by sadness whenever my mother's madness flies from the highest tower of Kalaat Hallaki.'

'Arad, every time I have risked my life in battle, I've wondered if I might die without having tasted your lips, your breasts, the rose between your thighs, if I might die without ever having slept in your hyacinth-scented bed and, every time, the thought filled me with despair. I would die without ever having lived. Can you understand me, Arad?'

The woman took his face between her long fingers and kissed him. 'Lead the warriors through the Sand of Ghosts, Amir, and you will sleep in my bed.' She slipped off her light muslin gown and offered her naked body to his gaze for an instant before she dived into the spring and disappeared in a trail of silvery bubbles.

ARAD LEFT TWO DAYS LATER, accompanied by a small group of warriors. She was dressed and armed as a man herself, but with her she brought many gowns and jewels because her journey would be long and because only she had the authority to pass the many barriers that protected the Horse's Crypt.

It took Amir six days instead to prepare stocks of water and food, to load the packs on the camels and to choose the best warriors and horses of Kalaat Hallaki. The journey that awaited him was different from Arad's and even more arduous. He would have to cross the driest parts of the desert until he reached the banks of the great Nile. From there he would have to push on through arid and inhospitable lands until he reached the sea, where he would find the fishing boats he needed in the villages that lay in the shadow of the mysterious ruins of troglodytic Berenike.

From there he would cross the sea and then traverse the most desolate stretches of the Higiaz until he reached the Horse's Crypt, on the third day of the new moon in the month of Nisan.

When he left, his heart was heavy because he was leaving the oasis undefended. He knew that he would be away from Kalaat Hallaki for months and months, for the first time in his life. That was the worst sacrifice.

The men of the oasis knew that cities and villages, lakes, seas and rivers existed beyond the sands, but they considered their hidden valley the dearest place on earth, and they knew they were the only human beings in the world capable of fending off the fierce, monstrous Blemmyae. They were certain that they would succeed, one day, in invading their barren land and annihilating the ghastly creatures.

The caravan left at dawn and all the warriors, before mounting their horses, drank from the waters of the spring, still cold from the long night, so they would carry with them the taste of that life force and the memory of its coolness before facing the endless reign of thirst.

Amir carried in his soul the taste of Arad's last kiss, in his eyes the vision of her naked body reflected in the shining waters, and the ardour that consumed him in the expectation of possessing her was stronger than the burning rays of the sun.

He never looked back and, when a wind as scorching as the breath of a dragon enveloped him all at once in a cloud of dust, he knew that the golden walls of Kalaat Hallaki had disappeared behind him.

# 6

PHILIP GARRETT TURNED ON the red light in the darkroom, took out his camera and extracted the film that he had shot underground at the Franciscan monastery. He immersed it in the developing solution, anxiously watching for the chemical reaction. Just a few seconds passed and his tense features began to relax. His eyes lit up: images were beginning to appear on the strip of film. What he cared about most was the papyrus he had photographed on the table in the *tablinum*; it had been his last shot. He put on his glasses and saw the dense script that filled the sheet of papyrus emerging on the film's surface. It was cursive Greek, the same type that appeared in some of the graffiti etched on the walls of the Vesuvian city, as well as on the papyri of Herculaneum that Italian scholars had been patiently unrolling for more than a century with the aid of the machine developed by Father Piaggio.

As soon as the negative had dried, Philip moved on to the enlarger and printed a much bigger photograph. His initial joy swiftly changed to disappointment: the emotion of finding the papyrus, along with his assumption that he would have been able to take the original, had made him careless about the angle and the shot was not perpendicular enough to the table, making the last lines out of focus.

He cursed, banging his fist on the table, but there was nothing he could do; the only information he could get was there in the image. He would try to transcribe the blurred words as best he could and decipher the text down to the last readable word.

He worked for days and days, locked in his room, stopping only when Lino came in with some coffee or something to eat. When he had to go out to consult sources at the National Library or the Papyrus Institute, El Kassem would take his place in the bedroom he'd equipped as a study and stand armed guard, with orders to allow no one in. The postman, who lived in the same house, had the bad luck to enter one day. He needed to deliver a registered letter and Lino hadn't answered the unlocked door. Finding no one inside, he peered around the bedroom door and nearly coincided with El Kassem's scimitar. He was back at the front door in no time, pale as a rag, and he raced down the stairs two at a time, as if he had seen the devil in the flesh.

As the text gradually became comprehensible, Philip's mood worsened. He became tense and irritable and couldn't sleep at night, tormented by nightmares. One day, at the National Library, Philip was consulting a collection of Etruscan inscriptions, in the hopes of finding the phrase in Etruscan that appeared at the end of his papyrus, which he was guessing might be an invocation of a religious nature. He hadn't noticed that there was a young man looking over his shoulder. He was staring at the letters that Philip had transcribed on a sheet of paper and he stopped in his tracks as though he had seen a ghost.

'My God, an original, unpublished inscription!' he gasped.

Philip spun around, instinctively hiding the sheet with his hand. The young man before him was thin, not very tall, with dark eyes that glittered from behind his glasses and a tower of heavy books in his arms.

'Do you read Etruscan?' Philip asked.

'Yes, sir. It's what I study.'

'Well, you see,' said Philip, 'this is nothing but a transcription of some eighteenth-century scholar, almost certainly spurious.'

The young man gave him a penetrating look. 'Don't worry, sir, I don't want to meddle with your research. I'd just like to say,' he added with a knowing expression, 'that the inscription, in my opinion, is authentic. It's a religious invocation that perhaps accompanied the sound of an instrument . . .'

Philip started. 'A sistrum?' he blurted out.

'Could be,' said the young man. 'It's hard to say.'

'I'd like to thank you for giving me your opinion, which I will certainly take into account,' said Philip. 'You're very clever for your age. What's your name?'

'Massimo,' replied the young man. And off he went, bent under the weight of his books.

That evening, Philip closed himself in his study and started to write out the definitive translation of the document:

The Immortal One, origin of all evil and source of all human knowledge, is alive in his tomb. I, haruspex Avile Vipinas, have seen him. After he had sated himself on the blood of all the companions who had left Cydamus with me, I was able to read what was in his mind. He has witnessed all the evil of the world, and he revels in suffering and remorse. He knows the secret of immortality and of eternal youth.

For one thousand years he has lain in this tomb, which rises in the place where he first stained his hands with blood. He massacred all my companions, but allowed me to leave. The sound of my sistrum saved me, and I alone reached the shore of the sea.

I would speak to none of those who had sent us out against such a formidable enemy, but I searched among the Judaean wise men of Alexandria until I found Baruch bar Lev, a priest, son and grandson of priests. He told me of the man of the seven tombs: He who cannot be killed. Only the fire of Yahweh, God of Israel, the fire that destroyed Sodom, can destroy him.

Before I breathe my last breath, I, Avile Vipinas, hereby hand down this memory, should someone, some day, dare to set out to destroy the lair of the beast. His tomb is shaped like a cylinder and is topped by a Pegasus. It is called the Tower of Solitude and it rises on the southern edge of the sea of sand, at thirty-seven days' march from Cydamus, near the land of the . . .

Philip sat still and silent before this missive, his eyes staring into nothingness, damp with tears. He thought: 'It was you, then, Avile Vipinas, who lured me into your home, so you could impart your message. It was you, wasn't it? Or was it my father who drove me to discover your secret?'

HE PASSED DAYS and days looking through books in search of a monument that might somehow resemble the description he had read in the papyrus of Avile Vipinas, but he found nothing. A tomb shaped like a cylinder topped by a Pegasus . . . a Pegasus, the figure of a winged horse . . . What could that possibly mean?

He realized that there was no reason for him to stay in the city any longer. It was time to leave with El Kassem, in search of his father.

Before leaving, he went to say goodbye to the guardian at the Franciscan monastery.

'I didn't think you'd be back,' said the friar. 'It's been so long since we've seen you here.'

'I've been spending my time in libraries. There's something I've been working on,' replied Philip.

'Well then? Are you satisfied? Did you find what you were looking for?'

'I don't know what to say,' said Philip. 'What I've found . . . has bewildered me, put me in touch with a dimension I didn't know existed.'

The friar smiled. 'Don't tell me you discovered the secret behind the earthquake bells?'

'And if I told you that I had?'

'I wouldn't be in the least surprised. But if that's so, what could be so terrible about unravelling such a small mystery? There's one in every place in Italy: secret passageways, cursed treasures, sunken cities, ghosts, werewolves, golden goats that appear on stormy nights, witches and wizards, souls from purgatory, statues that weep tears or sweat blood ... Mystery is the rule, not the exception, my friend. That's what you scientists don't understand.'

'That may be. But then why are we even capable of rational thought? Just to make us realize that it's all no use? Are you saying that the only road is blind faith? Is that the solution?'

The monk did not respond to this provocation but fell silent for a few moments, as if devising another strategy for making himself understood. When he raised his eyes, his gaze was steady and unexpectedly serious. 'What did you find down there?'

Philip hesitated for an instant, then said, 'A terrifying message. There is a place on this earth where Evil is present with the same mystical intensity as Good is supposed to be present in the tabernacle of your church.'

'And what do you intend to do?'

'I have to find my father.'

'What then?'

'And then I'll find that place.'

'And will you destroy it?' asked the friar anxiously.

'Not before I've understood it. Have you ever thought that Evil might be the dark face of God?'

He turned and walked quickly towards the door.

The friar watched him walk off down the corridor as two tears ran down his bristly cheeks. 'May God assist you,' he murmured. 'May God assist you, son.'

When Philip's steps had faded into the shadows of the cloister, the guardian descended into the crypt, took a lantern and went underground. He proceeded at a steady step to the point where the apotropaic eye stood out on the tunnel wall. He knelt on the paving stone, the same one that Philip had put back in its place before returning to the light. He leaned his bald head against the wall and collected himself in prayer. Then he got to his feet. 'You've delivered your message,' he whispered, 'after such a long time. Your mission has finally been accomplished. Rest now, my friend. Sleep.' He lay a hand against the wall, almost a caress, then took up the lantern. His shadow disappeared, as did the sound of his shuffled footsteps, in the silent *hypogeum*.

PHILIP REACHED THE HOUSE and went into his study. He found El Kassem on guard duty, sitting on the floor with his legs crossed and his back against the wall, his scimitar poised on his knees.

'We're leaving, El Kassem. As soon as we can.'

'Finally. I can't stand it any longer inside this box. I need the desert.'

'I think I've discovered what my father was looking for in this city. Now I have to find him and tell him.'

'There is a man called Enos who was with me the last time I saw your father. He knows the road we must take and he is expecting you.'

'Where?'

'In Aleppo.'

'One of the oldest cities on earth,' said Philip. 'A fine place to start.'

He was thinking about how the difficulties he'd succeeded in overcoming had changed him profoundly. He felt ready now to solve the mysteries that his father had sown along his path, like a horseman prepared to jump the fences on a racecourse. He knew that the distance separating him from his father was growing shorter with each passing day. There was only one shadow looming on his path: Selznick.

And El Kassem feared him as well.

They left three days later on a steamer headed for Lattakia via Piraeus and Limassol. Lino bade Philip farewell, drying his eyes with a handkerchief, and sent them off with a cardboard suitcase he had filled with provisions and other things they would find useful.

'I'm afraid I'll never see you again,' he said. 'I'm old and your journey is a long one.'

'Don't say that, Lino,' protested Philip. 'People who care for each other always end up meeting again, sooner or later.'

'God willing,' said Lino.

'*Inshallah*,' said El Kassem.

Without realizing it, the old Neapolitan servant and the mighty Arab warrior had said the same thing.

THE LEGIONNAIRES ADVANCED in a single column along the gully wedged into the Amanus Mountains between Bab el Awa and the Monastery of the Ladies, so called because of the ancient Byzantine *coenobium* set between the spurs of the massif. General LaSalle, the new commander appointed by the fort of Aleppo, was keeping his eyes wide open and had sent out groups of scouts ahead of the column and on both sides, knowing that the territory had recently been subject to raids by desert marauders: Druses from Mount Amanus and from Lebanon, and bedouins from the plains.

The day was drawing to a close and the officer ordered the squad to stop at the ruins of the monastery and set up camp there. The imposing complex, reused in the Abassid era as a caravanserai for convoys from Anatolia headed east, had long been completely abandoned, but its thick walls and massive bastions made it a good refuge for the night. A flock of ravens rose croaking from the sentry tower at the entrance and LaSalle watched them with satisfaction; their hectic flight meant that no other humans had been around to disturb them.

The men dismounted, took the saddles off their horses and left the animals to graze on the tufts of yellow grass sprouting here and there among the ruins. They gathered dry tamarisk and broom branches in the middle of the vast courtyard and lit a fire to cook their evening meal.

The commander posted sentries on the bastions and thought he could allow himself a little rest until the meal was ready. He knew of the fame of that monument and he began to explore the complex structure. It had been built in the Byzantine era but its walls incorporated a quantity of material from other much more ancient buildings, so that here and there he could spot capitals from the Hellenistic and Roman periods, along with columns, statue bases and even altars, complete with dedicatory inscriptions.

He realized that one day, long ago, victims had been offered to a god on those very altar stones. The inscriptions they bore, corroded by the wind and sand, had once been carved so that the victims might rise to the heavens with the smoke of the burning incense. He wondered whether the day would come in which the God of the Christians and the God of Islam would be forgotten like Jupiter Dolichenus and Hermes Trismegistus.

Death overcame him before he could formulate an answer to his questions. Surprised by a shot to the nape of his neck, he fell, gasping, as furious rounds of musketry exploded all around him. The attackers had come from underground.

From the crypts and the galleries which were honeycombed beneath the great courtyard, hundreds of marauders sprang up and surprised the men at the very moment their dinner was being distributed. The sentries, who were looking outwards, were the first to be felled, and then it was the turn of the other soldiers, mostly gathered around the campfire. Those who chaotically tried to grab hold of their weapons were immediately mown down and the battle was over in a few minutes.

The marauders ran wild over the camp, seizing horses, arms and ammunition and stripping the corpses.

A man of impressive stature and pale skin was just coming up from underground. He wore well-buffed brown leather boots and had an automatic pistol in a holster hanging from his belt. He climbed up the ruins until he found General LaSalle where he lay dying. With the last bit of energy he had, the officer turned his head slightly towards him and recognized his icy stare, saw the yellowish stain on his shirt over his right side. 'Selznick!' he managed with his last breath. 'Your side still bleeds ... I ... I am dying, but you are cursed by God ...'

Selznick considered him for a moment or two without batting an eye, then knelt beside him and plunged a dagger deep into the general's right side. He waved to one of his men, who approached, stripped the cadaver of its uniform and handed it over to Selznick. It was just about his size, and he went inside to put it on. He removed his own jacket and shirt and glanced briefly at the bandage covering the wound on his right side, which would not heal. When he reappeared, his men saluted him by shooting into the air and he moved towards the courtyard to choose his horse. He ordered one of the marauders to put on a legionnaire's uniform and then approached the bedouin chieftain.

'You can go now,' he said. 'We'll proceed alone. I'll let you know when I need you again.'

He watched them take off at a gallop down the narrow gully, then removed a little silver box from his pocket, took a pinch of opium from it and began chewing it slowly, enjoying its bitter flavour and pungent scent.

He waited until the drug had taken effect and assuaged the pain of his wound, then mounted his horse. The two men took off at a swift pace, heading south. When they had reached the plain, they turned left, towards the east. By the first light of dawn they were within sight of the Ain Walid fort. They slowed and continued at a trot until they were in front of the entrance.

'Who goes there?' shouted out the sentry. 'Make yourselves known!'

'It's General LaSalle!' said Selznick. 'Open up, quickly! We were ambushed! We are the only survivors.'

The sentry took a closer look. The general was listing in his saddle and holding his right side. He called out to the officer on picket duty to open the gate and let him in.

The wounded man slipped off his horse. 'I'm General LaSalle,' he said in a pain-filled voice. 'The new commander of the Aleppo garrison. My men and I were attacked. We defended ourselves . . . We fought bravely, but it was no use. We were outnumbered ten to one . . .'

The officer helped him straighten up and led him towards the door. 'Don't strain yourself, General. You can tell us about it later. You're wounded. Let us take care of you.'

Two legionnaires ran up with a stretcher while the picket officer gave orders for the infirmary to be made ready. Selznick was transferred to a bed and the medical officer removed his jacket and shirt.

'A *jatagan*,' said Selznick, nodding towards the dressing on his right side. 'They gave me up for dead. I spent hours in a heap of corpses until the soldier who was with me found me.'

The medical officer removed the bandage and couldn't hide his disgust at the sight of the wound. 'My God, we'll have to cauterize it . . . It must be cauterized immediately.'

'Do what you must do, doctor,' said Selznick. 'I will leave again as soon as possible.'

'Yes, all right,' said the doctor, nodding. 'I'll put you out with some ether.'

'No,' said Selznick, 'give me a little opium, if you have any. I don't want ether. I've never lost consciousness in my life.'

He stared at the doctor with a look that did not allow objections. The medical officer gave him the opium, then scalded a blade over the flame of a Bunsen burner. When it was white hot, he placed it against the wound. The incandescent metal sizzled in contact with the flesh and a nauseating stench filled the little room. Selznick gritted his teeth but a low moan of pain slipped out nonetheless.

The medical officer disinfected the wound with alcohol and applied a fresh bandage. 'You can rest now, General. It's all over.'

Selznick dropped back onto the bed and closed his eyes.

He passed three days at the fort, nearly always sleeping, day and night, until one morning the medical officer found him on his feet, pale and silent. He left the next morning at dawn.

'You are a tough man, General,' said the fort commander at the moment of departure. 'But it's certainly not prudent for you to try to reach Aleppo on horseback. I've called in a vehicle from our logistics centre. You'll travel much more comfortably. Obviously, we immediately notified headquarters at Aleppo of the fate suffered by your unit and of your own wounds. The news was greeted with great shock. As I'm sure you know, many of your fallen officers were well known here and had old friends in the garrison. Supreme Command will certainly want a full report on the incident.'

'I myself am still in shock, Commander,' said Selznick. 'On the other hand, none of us could ever have expected an attack from under the ground, as if from Satan himself.'

'Indeed,' said the commander. 'Well, good luck, General LaSalle.'

'Good luck to you, Commander,' said Selznick, responding to his salute and shaking the man's hand as well. 'I hope we shall meet again.'

A military truck marked with Aleppo insignia was waiting for him in the courtyard. Selznick took his place alongside the driver and the vehicle disappeared in a cloud of dust.

'What a remarkable man,' observed the commander as he watched the little truck drive off down the track.

'You can say that again,' said the medical officer at his side. 'I've never seen anyone recover so quickly from a wound like that.'

'Was it serious?'

'I must say, it was the strangest thing I'd ever seen. The iron sliced through the muscles of his side without damaging any vital organs. He was lucky, but there aren't many men made of the same stuff that he is.'

'Right you are. General LaSalle was a hero of the Battle of the Somme. I'm sure we'll hear of him again. The villains who destroyed his unit have their days numbered, mark my words.'

SELZNICK REACHED ALEPPO in the late afternoon and ordered the truck to stop at the bottom of the hill on which the garrison's Ottoman fortress arose. The clay tell was scored by deep vertical furrows and the ring of walls and towers at its top shimmered in the fierce light of the afternoon sun. It was on that very hill that Abraham was said to have offered sacrifice to his God in the land of Harran.

Selznick contemplated the superb sight for a moment before he slowly began to climb the steps that led to the entrance, under the astonished gaze of the officer on duty, who'd heard that the general had been wounded in battle just four days earlier. He looked small at the bottom of that majestic access ramp, like a tin soldier, but his figure took on an imposing stature as he ascended the steep incline at a steady pace.

As soon as the officer saw him near the gate he drew up the guard and gave them the order to present arms. Without turning his head, he could see the general from the corner of his eye as he passed. The man was deathly pale, and beads of sweat studded his brow and temples under his kepi, but his bearing was erect, his gait sure.

The ranks stood proud on the parade ground for his inspection and then the general was taken to his quarters.

IT TOOK PHILIP GARRETT and El Kassem nearly two weeks to reach Limassol because of the weather, which turned bad as soon as they passed the Strait of Messina. The ship had to stop at Patras and then again at Piraeus before taking to the open sea. A storm battered the Gulf of Saronico, raging against the cliffs of Attica with incredible violence, and Philip was glad when the captain decided against moving on in those conditions. El Kassem could not have borne another moment of seasickness.

They took advantage of the delay to explore their surroundings. The two men made an excursion on horseback to the top of Mount Citerone. The landscape was incredibly beautiful and the storm clouds that raced across the Hellenic countryside, over the land green with rain and the rocks shiny as iron, made the view even more impressive. To Philip it seemed a century ago that Colonel Jobert had asked to meet him at the Café Junot on Rue Tronchet.

They sought refuge in a tavern when the wind picked up again, promising another downpour, and they sat in a corner of the little place, its only customers. Philip ordered an ouzo that tasted much like his usual Pernod and a cup of Turkish coffee for his friend. Their host never took his eyes off them as they sat waiting for the rain to stop. He had never seen such an ill-assorted pair.

'What caused their rivalry?' Philip asked El Kassem suddenly. 'What drove them to a duel?'

'I don't know if you could call it a duel exactly,' replied the Arab warrior evasively.

'Well, what happened then?' insisted Philip. He found that El Kassem had become rather reticent of late.

'Your father trusted Selznick at first,' El Kassem added after a little while. 'He had hired him himself. The man had an extensive knowledge of the terrain and *sidi* Desmond put him in charge of security for the expedition. At a certain point, your father discovered the entrance to an underground passage at the oasis of Siwa, a kind of labyrinth where it was very easy to lose one's bearings. I never understood what he was looking for down there. There was no gold, no treasure of any sort. I believe he was fascinated by the stones, old stones carved with figures of demons, etched with writing that no one could read any more. No one but him, maybe. But he was enthusiastic about his discovery. So excited that he had me travel to the coast, to send a telegram to his wife. Your mother. He wanted her to come.'

'I remember,' said Philip, 'and you can't imagine how I suffered because my father hadn't sent for me. I knew him well.

If he hadn't mentioned me by name it meant that he didn't want me. I would have given anything to be with him in the desert . . . anything.'

'Your mother was very beautiful,' continued El Kassem, and his eyes shone with a strange light in the shadows of the tavern. 'Selznick had set his eyes upon her.'

The expression sounded familiar to Philip. It was the same phrase used in the Bible when David gazed upon Bathsheba's naked body.

'That was the cause, then,' mused Philip.

El Kassem dropped his eyes.

'Tell me the truth, please, I must know!'

El Kassem turned his gaze towards the window, at the rain streaming down the glass.

'One day your father and I returned to camp,' he started again, 'unexpectedly, and he saw them together. Your mother was leaning against the trunk of a palm tree and he was very close. Your father thought he saw them exchange a glance . . . Do you understand what I mean?'

'Yes,' said Philip. 'Go on.' But his voice cracked with emotion.

'Your father was thunderstruck by that vision, by what he thought he read in their eyes.'

'He thought?'

'Yes. He suddenly realized that he had left her alone too often and for too long. I know your father. I know the nightmares that cross his mind, by day and by night. The next day he asked me to take her home. I took an escort of my men, along with a couple of women to serve her, and I accompanied her back to the coast. She did not speak my language and I did not speak hers. It was a journey of endless silence but I could see the pain in her eyes and the weight of her despair burdened my heart.

'When I returned, I tried again and again to make him understand that he was wrong, but he would not listen. He wouldn't consider sending Selznick away either. He was too proud to admit that he thought him a rival.

'But your father had changed. Something had broken in him and he lost all interest in his research. One day he closed up the site, embraced me and said goodbye. He was heading north, towards the coast, but he never said where he was going.'

Philip remembered that his father had returned, first to Rome and then to Naples, never even coming home to visit his mother. And then she had fallen ill. And her illness had taken her away. He covered his face with his hands.

El Kassem fell silent, letting Philip collect his thoughts and his memories, and then continued with his story.

'Years later, after the Great War had ended, he came back. He seemed to have regained all the energy and drive of his best days, and yet there was no joy left in him. In the evening I'd often find him alone, at the edge of the camp, watching the sun set over the dunes in silence.

'At the end of the summer, we organized a new expedition. It was then that the Legion sent one of its officers, purportedly to collaborate with us, but perhaps in reality to keep an eye on what your father was doing.

'Your father couldn't believe his eyes when that man turned out to be Selznick. He was the liaison officer between Legion command and our expedition. At first, I thought your father would abandon the expedition completely, but then he seemed to adapt to the strange situation. The relationship between them was tense but civil, and your father continued his explorations until one day the two of them – your father and Selznick – went underground. It was obvious that he'd wanted to go down alone, but Selznick's orders from the Legion permitted him to follow your father practically everywhere. I stayed outside on guard.

'Only your father came out. He was wounded, his clothing was ripped, he was dripping with sweat and his eyes were bloodshot. He was holding one of those stones, holding it against his chest like it was a precious treasure. In his other hand he held a blade of a style and a metal I'd never seen. It was bloody.

' "What happened?" I asked him. "Where's Selznick?"

' "Selznick's dead," he answered me. I imagined that there had been some accident, a cave-in, a fall.

' "I killed him," he said. He told me that Selznick had tried to rob him of the stone he still gripped so tightly and to bury him in that underground chamber. "But I found a weapon," he added, and dropped the blade he had in his hand.

'But Selznick was not dead. The wound that your father inflicted that day has never healed, and it just makes him fiercer and fiercer with every passing day. None of us will be safe until we've found him and killed him.'

FATHER HOGAN CLIMBED the stairs of the Vatican Observatory with a mixture of curiosity and deep anxiety. It was the first time that Father Boni had summoned him since he'd brought him Antonelli's translation of 'The Book of Amon'. The old priest was sitting at his desk, his back to Father Hogan as he entered.

'Sit down, Hogan,' he said without turning. 'What I have to tell you will take some time.'

Outside, the bells of Rome chimed the evening Angelus.

Father Boni got to his feet and walked, still without turning, to the window that opened onto Michelangelo's dome.

'I've finished reading "The Book of Amon",' he said, finally turning, and Father Hogan tried to hide his dismay. The old priest's eyes were sunken into dark rings, and everything about him revealed deep suffering.

Father Hogan raised his hand to switch on the light but the old man stopped him. 'No,' he said, 'not yet. It's not dark yet.

'Listen, Hogan,' he continued, 'what I've learned from reading these pages is terrifying. Truly inconceivable. I would say it was all pure invention, if it weren't for the radio signal. It's changed, did you know that? The sequence is different now and much more complex. You must be wondering why I don't just hand over the text so you can read it yourself. The fact is that it's not easy to read. It's long and complicated and Father Antonelli's handwriting is practically illegible. What's more, he's used any number of abbreviations and palaeographic symbols in his transcription. But you must prepare to leave as soon as possible, if you're ready to do what I ask, because time has run out. I will tell you tonight what is written in the text . . . if you trust me.'

'You can begin whenever you like,' said Father Hogan. 'I'm listening.'

' "The Book of Amon", ' began Father Boni, 'is a kind of sacred book – you could call it a "Black Bible" – written by different hands in different eras, in an ancient language that resembles none of the languages we know. Father Antonelli has transcribed the text phonetically and written in a translation between the lines. I'm no philologist, so any information I give you will be partial, but my predecessor has recognized here and there – especially in the more recent parts – fleeting traces of Ethiopian and of Hamite as well, which hint at a very archaic form of Egyptian. In other words, the most recent parts of this text date back to a much earlier era than the oldest documents of our most ancient cultures.

'The legendary founder of this civilization bears a name that can be identified with Tubalcain, who was descended directly from Cain himself. If this is true, if Antonelli's transcription and interpretation are correct, Tubalcain was the first man to build a city, the first man to melt and forge metal, and therefore the first human being to make weapons.'

'The evil side of human nature,' mused Father Hogan. 'So that was why Father Antonelli was in such anguish.'

'Perhaps. But that's not all. Listen. According to "The Book of Amon", the sons of Tubalcain settled in an unidentifiable place called Delfud, but never forgot the home of their fathers. They swore they would find the way to force open the gates of Eden, which were guarded by an angel with a flaming sword. They vowed to make a weapon stronger and more powerful than that sword, and to challenge the guardian angel, defeat and humiliate him, so that they could take possession of the Tree of Knowledge. They yearned to understand and control the course of the stars and the forces that move the universe. To become like God.

'The land of Delfud is described as a limitless terrain, where five great rivers with majestic currents flowed, where five great lakes, each as big as the sea, were inhabited by an infinity of scaly creatures, by crocodiles and hippopotamuses and enormous lizards. Great herds of animals came to drink at their shores: rhinoceroses and panthers, lions, elephants and giraffes, zebras and hartebeests and elands. In the sky flew enormous flocks of multicoloured birds. The hills were host to the unbridled galloping of raven horses with long rippling manes. A sea of grass rose and fell in the breeze like the surface of an emerald ocean, as far as the eye could see. In that sky the rainbow curved from south to north after a storm, when the last rays of the setting sun filtered through the last drops of summer rain. Myriad stars shone in that infinite vault on long, sweetly scented springtime nights.'

'My God!' exclaimed Father Hogan. 'You're talking about paradise!'

'I'm talking about the very origins of the earth, Hogan, when it was as yet uncontaminated . . . the power of nature still intact . . .' Father Boni sighed. Then he continued his story. 'At the centre of that boundless land stood a mountain and that's where they began to build their city. They forged an indestructible metal which they used to cut rock, raising a city of powerful walls crowned by tall, impregnable towers. They gave life to a race of invincible warriors who garrisoned the frontiers of that vast land, armed with deadly weapons. Inside the city they created gardens laden with every sort of fruit, wide fields of wheat, vineyards and olive groves. Their tables overflowed with every sort of meat, with fragrant bread, with delicious fruits. Pleasure was the recompense of every labour and every craft, and men and women became experts in the refined art of giving and receiving pleasure indifferently from both sexes.

'But there was a place, far from the city, that they kept under constant surveillance, generation after generation. A garrison manned that desolate and completely arid place, scorched by the sun in every season. It was there that – after the progenitors had been driven from Eden, naked, weeping and desperate – a barrier of basalt had burst from the ground, pushed by cyclopean forces, a mountain range that pierced the sky with the snowy peaks of its lofty volcanoes. This immense chain was eternally obscured by storm clouds shot through with lightning bolts, and the constant rumbling of thunder could be heard even at a great distance.

'And when the menacing angel that guarded this barrier chose to bare his sword, a blinding light would rend the darkness of the night, a roar would shake the earth all the way to the four corners of the horizon, a scream sounding like hundreds of thousands of warriors lined up in battle would pierce the cloud-banks all the way to the seventh heaven and fall back upon the earth like a clamouring avalanche.

'And yet the sons of Tubalcain never gave up their vigil, day and night, generation after generation. They called this desolate garrison the Fortress of Solitude. They watched and waited for the moment in which the watchfulness of the angel might abate, because they knew that only the force of God is indefatigable. And eternal.

'And then, finally, came the night of the Scorpion . . .'

Father Boni fell still for a few moments with his head low. The room was plunged into total darkness and the only sound to be heard was the incessant signal that came from the stars, amplified by the silence. On the large slate that covered the wall, one could barely make out the gleam of the chalk that the hands of Ernesto Boni and Guglielmo Marconi had used to sketch out their astral calculations on a night of toil and fatigue.

Father Hogan understood that the effort of telling the story had worn the old priest out. Like a sailor in a storm, he was trying to haul in the sails of his spirit, ripped by hurricane-force winds. The syllogisms that had always nourished his mathematical mind had collapsed around him and he was frightened to find himself feeling more and more like the delirious old man they'd seen die alone and abandoned in a hospice in the middle of an Apennine forest.

It was cold in the observatory and the room was now a little lighter, thanks to the pale glow of the moon, but Father Hogan did not have the courage to switch on the light. The words he had just heard still echoed in the darkness.

Father Boni got up and went to the window, where his shiny bald head reflected the moon's light.

'Father Hogan,' he said, 'come here to the window. Why do you think we've been talking in the dark until now?'

'I don't know. I thought that you'd strained your eyes trying to decipher the text.'

'No. You thought that what I'd discovered had so upset me that I'd turned into a creature of the darkness. Isn't that so? A kind of bat who can no longer bear the light. No, don't bother answering, I know it's true. You're an Irishman, Hogan, a dreamer, like your Yeats, like Joyce. We Latins are more rational, even . . . cynical, I'd say. Don't forget that.'

'Even the priests?'

'In a certain sense. It's the priests in Italy who've had to bear the weight of the Church's political structure. A burdensome structure, to be sure, but indispensable. They've done so with courage and with extraordinary inventiveness, but they've also had to immunize themselves with a certain dose of cynicism. Politics is no joke. But come here. Look at the sky over there. That's why we've been in the dark until now. What do you see?'

'Constellations.'

'Of course. See that one? That group of stars low on the horizon? That's Scorpio, the constellation of the scorpion. That's what "The Book of Amon" refers to. The constellation is about to enter into conjunction with the radio source that is transmitting our signal. This will conclude a cycle many thousands of years long and bring about an event of unimaginable portent.'

'But what you've told me until now is mythology. It's a powerful story, quite disturbing, but it's doubtless a myth.'

'Perhaps. But all myths conceal a historical truth, and the radio signal we're receiving is certainly the product of the civilization that wrote this book. I can assure you of it.' He walked over to the switch and turned on the light, then sat down again at his desk.

'Make us some coffee, Hogan,' he said, putting on his glasses. 'We still have a long night ahead of us.'

# 7

'THE GATE OF THE WIND,' said El Kassem, pointing at something in the distance. 'If our horses were not already so tired, we could get to Aleppo by midnight.'

Philip was soon able to make out the Roman arch of Bab el Awa and the glittering limestone slabs of the ancient Roman road that went from Antioch to Damascus. The landscape all around them was exceedingly dry and a steady wind swept the parched plains.

'It never stops. This wind blows continually, day and night, winter and summer. That's why it's called the Gate of the Wind,' said El Kassem, pointing to the monument in front of them. 'What could pass through such a gate but the wind?' he observed, as their horses went under the arch. 'A gate without jambs and without doors . . . without walls . . .' He turned back to look at it again. 'A gate which opens onto nothing . . . in the middle of nowhere.'

'It's an arch,' Philip tried to explain. 'A Roman arch. It was built to celebrate the glory of a great empire of the past.'

El Kassem did not answer or turn again to look at Bab el Awa. He continued to ride distractedly, as if he were listening to the tread of his horse on the ancient road. 'That's right,' he said, 'because the glory of men is like the wind that comes and goes.'

Philip was struck by how the rays of the setting sun, nearly parallel now to the surface of the road, flowed like liquid gold on the ancient stones, smoothed by thousands of years of passage.

After a while, they passed close to a small camel caravan escorted by a group of men on horseback, dressed in unfamiliar style. One of the camels wore on his hump a canopy with muslin curtains, which were pulled aside for a moment as Philip passed and then quickly closed.

El Kassem seemed to notice nothing and insisted that they turn off the Roman road, as its hard paving was damaging the horses' hooves. He pointed to a line of rolling hills to their left. 'It will be dark soon. We'd best go up towards higher ground. It will be easier to keep watch on the territory and find shelter for the night.'

They spurred on their horses and reached a ridge on top of the low range that stretched out as far as the eye could see. El Kassem stopped then and gathered branches to build a fire, while Philip tied his horse and unstrapped the bags containing his things.

'We still haven't had a look at what Natalino gave us as we were leaving,' he said, drawing close to the fire to see better and opening the case that was latched shut with a pair of leather straps.

There was everything in the world inside, a little bazaar: a wheel of sheep's cheese, a packet of biscuits, a needle and thread, buttons, a switchblade knife, a ball of wire, a bar of jasmine-scented soap, a slingshot with steel pellets, a bag of gunpowder, some sugar and salt, petards and fireworks. He quickly moved the bundle away from the flames.

'What's in there?' asked El Kassem.

'Stuff that can explode. Fireworks, they're called. They fly high up into the sky, leaving a long trail of light behind them, then they explode into millions of sparks of every colour. In Naples they make the best in the world.'

El Kassem seemed perplexed.

'It's a good idea, my friend. We might get separated or lose sight of each other in the desert. Using these, I can always signal to you where I am, even at a great distance.'

El Kassem shook his head. 'A strange tribe, these Napo . . .'

'Neapolitans. You're right, El Kassem, they are a singular bunch. They're like no one else in the world.'

Philip tried to imagine what thoughts had been going through Lino's head as he put together that bizarre medley, but he concluded that no reasoning had gone into it. The old man had just rummaged through the drawers where he kept his small treasures and had gathered them all up into that little case to tide his young friend over on such a long journey. It was more precious than a jewel box in Philip's eyes. He closed it and turned back towards his companion, but was surprised to see him throwing dust on the fire. El Kassem motioned for Philip to stay low and not make any noise.

Down below, just barely visible in the shadows descending on the valley, was the little caravan that they had passed before dusk on the Bab el Awa road. The silence was so deep that they could hear the grunting of the camels as they advanced with their slow gait, and the snorting of the guards' horses. But El Kassem's ears heard other sounds, his nostrils picked up other smells on the evening breeze. His eyes watched intensely in the semi-darkness that swallowed all shapes and colours in the hour preceding night.

He was stretched out beside Philip and suddenly gripped his arm. 'Down there,' he said, 'behind that outcrop.'

A group of bedouins on horseback burst into a furious gallop from that very spot, raising a white cloud of dust which snaked through the valley in the direction of the little caravan.

The escort reacted with incredible swiftness. They pushed the camels and horses down to the ground and loosed a deathly barrage of fire. There weren't many of them, but they obviously had powerful repeating rifles. The attackers scattered so as to offer less of a target and began to circle around the caravan in two separate groups. Despite their show of bravery, the defenders were not going to be able to hold out much longer.

Philip was keeping an eye on the camel with the canopy on

its back. He saw a veiled figure slip out, certainly a woman. He could see that the men were trying to protect her at any cost, shielding her with their own bodies.

'They've no hope,' observed El Kassem, but even as he spoke he had already sprung to his feet and was heading towards his horse, prepared to lend his support.

'Wait,' said Philip, seized by a sudden inspiration. 'Our help won't make any difference. Let's try Natalino's artillery.'

He grabbed one of the fireworks, plunged it into the ground, trying to roughly calculate its trajectory, and lit the fuse. A whistle and a trail of fire ripped through the darkness and the colourful explosion that resulted threw the group of attackers into a panic. Philip fired nearly his whole arsenal, one piece after another, while El Kassem took shots with his rifle. The horses were crazed and disoriented by the noise and the blinding rain of sparks. They reared and kicked, then took off in every direction, pursued by the dense rifle fire of the defenders.

El Kassem leapt onto his horse and set off after the fugitives, taking out a good number of them with his pistol first and then with his sword, a heavy scimitar in damascened steel. Philip hesitated an instant. The situation he found himself in was so different from his tranquil nights of study at the Sorbonne that it seemed like a dream to him. And as in a dream, where anything is possible and the sleeper always wakes up safe and sound, he too mounted his horse and headed off across the plains behind El Kassem.

He risked death immediately. One of the bedouins, noticing a certain lack of expertise in his riding ability, drew up alongside him and swiped at his side, slashing through his jacket and cutting his arm. Philip knew that all was lost as he felt the warm, sticky blood pouring down his side. He tried desperately to get away, shouting, 'El Kassem!'

The warrior heard him, swerved abruptly and charged Philip's pursuer. He crashed into the side of the bedouin's horse and knocked it to the ground, then swooped down upon the horseman, who was trying to get back up on his knees, decapitating him with a clean blow of his scimitar. Philip's stomach heaved as he saw the man's head rolling between the horse's legs, but he managed to control himself and took off towards the barricaded caravan, where a group of bedouins had broken through and were engaging the defenders in hand-to-hand combat. El Kassem bounded past him and threw himself into the fray, bringing down two adversaries with his scimitar and another with his dagger. Philip downed a fourth with a pistol shot and watched, stunned, as the man gasped for breath. He had killed a man, for the first time in his life.

Suddenly the assault was over. El Kassem and his wounded companion stood before the group of defenders, who finally put down their rifles. The woman who had been riding in the canopy got to her feet and walked towards Philip. Her face was covered and her right hand held a sabre but as she drew close she sheathed the weapon and removed her veil, tying it around his arm to stop the bleeding. Her unveiled face was incredibly beautiful, her skin dark and smooth as bronze.

Philip instinctively drew back, dazzled by that vision.

'Who are you?' he asked.

'It's better that you do not know my name,' replied the woman in Arabic, 'but tell me how I can reward you. Your flaming weapons and your courage have saved us.'

Philip struggled to control his emotions. The chase, the pain in his arm and the vision of her face had induced a kind of rapturous shock. Meanwhile, El Kassem had convinced the group that it was best to take shelter at the spot where he and Philip had built their fire, and he led them there. He got off his horse and blew at the nearly extinguished embers until the flame was rekindled. The woman took care of Philip: she washed out his wound with vinegar, stitched it with silk thread and bandaged it.

Philip couldn't take his eyes off her. 'The only reward I ask for,' he managed to say, 'is to be able to see you again.'

'That is not possible,' replied the woman in a calm but firm voice. His eye caught hers for an instant and he thought he saw a trace of sadness there. 'Ask me for something else.' Her manner of speaking made it clear that she was accustomed to the privilege of granting favours.

The fire was crackling now and the men were sitting in a circle all around it, putting together what food they had: bread, dates and goat's cheese. Philip remembered the cheese and biscuits in Lino's case and added those to the supper. As he stole a glance at the woman, who was sitting to the side with her back against a stone, her head still uncovered, his gaze was attracted to the pendant hanging between her breasts. It was a gold charm, a little winged horse on a kind of cylindrical pedestal. The words of Avile Vipinas immediately sprang to mind: 'His tomb is shaped like a cylinder and is topped by a Pegasus.' No, it was absolutely impossible that a chance meeting in the Middle Eastern desert could provide the key to a clue left so long ago and so far away.

'You can't continue your journey in the dark,' said Philip. 'You've seen how dangerous it is here.'

The woman spoke softly to her men and Philip was struck by the sound of their language. An intonation he'd never heard before. It sounded very vaguely like Coptic, but he couldn't be sure.

'What language were you just speaking in?' he asked her.

The woman smiled. 'I can't tell you that either!' But her gaze lingered on Philip's face and her eyes shone with amber light in the reflection of the flames.

The men found a place to stretch out, removing blankets from the horses' saddles. One of them took a place further up the hill behind a rocky outcrop to guard the others as they slept. El Kassem moved to a solitary spot and lay down, but Philip knew that his slumber was as light as the air and his senses were always alert. He would wake instantly at the slightest sound, at the merest odour carried on the wind.

Philip remained alone near the fire, poking at the embers.

The woman sat down next to him. 'Does it hurt?' she asked, brushing his arm with a light touch.

'It burns, a little.'

'You're lucky it's a flesh wound. It will be better in a few days. Keep it uncovered in the desert and bandaged in the city, then you'll heal more quickly.'

Philip turned to look at her. Her face and the curves that he sensed under her long linen tunic seemed the purest and most perfect expression of beauty that he had ever contemplated. Her straight, shining hair framed the face of an Egyptian goddess, barely touching her smooth shoulders; her long, slender fingers moved lithely to accompany her words.

'Today was the first time you ever found yourself in combat, wasn't it?' she asked after a little while.

'Yes.'

'How did it feel?'

'It's hard to say. As if I'd taken a drug. Killing is as easy as being killed. Your heart beats like mad, your thoughts come as quickly as your breath. Please, tell me that I can see you again . . . I can't imagine never seeing you again. I would have died for you today, if I had to.'

The woman's gaze changed suddenly, lighting up like the sky at sunset. She stared into his eyes with sorrowful intensity, as if a moment's look could make up for abandoning him. 'Don't torment me,' she said softly. 'I must follow my road. I have no choice. I must face my destiny, as difficult as it is.'

She fell still, lowering her head, and Philip did not have the courage to disturb her silence, or dare to touch the hands she held in her lap. She looked up again and her eyes were shining. 'But if I were one day given the gift of freedom, then, yes . . . I would like to see you again.'

'Freedom? Who is holding you prisoner? Tell me, please. I'll fight to free you!'

The woman shook her head and smiled. 'Nothing is holding me prisoner except my fate. But let us forget these sad thoughts now and drink together.' She took from her sack two cups of silver, masterpieces of ancient art, and poured some palm wine, fragrant with spices, into the cups from a flask. Philip drank with her from that marvellous cup, from her deep, dark gaze, from the starry, silent sky, and it seemed as if he had never lived before that moment. She brushed his face for an instant with a light caress and he felt heat rising to his face and tears to his eyes. He stood and watched her walk away, as lightly as if she were not touching the ground, and vanish into the darkness.

PHILIP WOKE the next day with his head confused and aching, saw that the sun was already high and that his horse was indifferently nibbling at the grass sprouting between the rocks. El Kassem was standing in front of him.

'Why didn't you wake me?' he cried. 'Why didn't you stop her from leaving?'

'If she wants you, you will find her again,' said El Kassem. 'If she doesn't want you, you could search the world over and never find her.'

'But I have to find her,' snapped Philip, and there was desperate determination in his voice. He gathered up his things quickly and packed them onto his horse under the puzzled but impassive gaze of El Kassem. As he was about to jump onto the saddle, Philip realized that his companion was watching him without moving.

'Aren't you coming with me?' he asked.

'I didn't come here to run after a woman. If you want to find your father, I've told you who you must contact. I'll see you again when you have recovered your reason.'

Philip wanted to answer but El Kassem's words rang with harsh condemnation and gave him no way out. He simply said, 'I haven't given up our search, El Kassem, make no mistake. But I have to find her.'

He spurred on his horse and flew away across the valley at a gallop. Traces of the little caravan were still visible and he thought that his speed would lead him to her, but his hopes were soon dashed. Before long, the trail he was following was lost in the close, confused web of tracks left by the caravans and herds heading into the city. When he found himself within sight of Aleppo he cursed his naïvety. He had been preceded by a tide of camels, sheep and goats, of people pushing overladen donkeys or dragging carts loaded with all sorts of merchandise.

He stopped and got off his horse, certain that El Kassem would not be long catching up, but he waited in vain. He stood for hours near the city gate, attracting the curiosity of all those who passed, until he finally gave up and entered the city alone, on foot, leading his horse by its halter. He had no idea of how to find a place to stay. He decided to follow a group of camel drivers and ended up shortly thereafter at a caravanserai where they accepted his French francs in exchange for a stall for his horse and a room for himself.

His quarters opened onto the upstairs gallery and consisted of a room with flaking plaster walls that might have once been whitewashed and a straw mattress lying on a bed of bricks. The boy who accompanied Philip left him an old lamp in exchange for a few coins and the dim light it cast revealed the bedbugs and cockroaches that would be keeping him company for the night. He shook out the mattress, beating it as best he could to get most of the parasites out, then tried to treat his wound with some methylene blue that he kept in his haversack. He reapplied the bandage, pushed a bench up against the door so he'd be sure to wake up should anyone try to get in and fell back onto the mattress as his fatigue finally got the better of him. In that filthy place, without the support of El Kassem, and with no hope of seeing the woman who had unsettled his soul and his mind, he felt terribly alone. He dozed off, drained of all energy, and soon fell into a leaden sleep.

FATHER HOGAN POURED the steaming coffee into cups and handed one to Father Boni. The priest half-closed his eyes as he sipped the boiling liquid, then set the cup down and finished his story.

'The sons of Tubalcain prospered in that boundless land, but they built no cities – other than the one on the mountain – or other stone structures, except for the Fortress of Solitude. It was from there that the attack on the Guardian Angel was unleashed on the night of the Scorpion . . .

'The text is quite difficult to interpret at this point, Hogan . . . What I could understand is that they somehow succeeded in reining in the energy generated by a conjunction of the stars and combining it with an artificial device they had created to produce an explosion of indescribable power. The result was disastrous: the basalt barrier cracked and crumbled, flames spewed forth and cut a path through the desolation as a shrill whistle tore through the air, devastating the land of Delfud. A whirlwind raised a huge cloud of dust and sand and the whole countryside became an arid wasteland. The current slowed in the rivers and the great lakes evaporated. The shores were covered with vast stretches of salt, scattered with thousands and thousands of skeletons, bones bleaching under an ever more relentless sun.

'But this disaster did not subdue the sons of Tubalcain. They did not give up. They built canals and dams to distribute the waters and cisterns to gather the rain whenever it fell. They grew plants more resistant to drought and used them to produce food. They tamed animals that could withstand hunger and thirst. But all of their efforts did nothing but prolong their agony.

'Sure now that their race was doomed to vanish for ever, those among them who knew the secrets of science concentrated all their knowledge into a single mind that shot up towards the highest heavens and disappeared into the abyss of the firmament.

'On the earth remained only the Tower of Solitude, all alone in the middle of an endless desert . . . Even the Garden of Immortality had been destroyed. The basalt barrier collapsed, and the sands covered everything. They say that a single pool of clean water survived, so cool and fresh that not even the sands could prevail over it, but that those who chanced upon it could no longer find the road of return. In other words, anyone who reached it never came back. Since there was nothing left to watch over, the Guardian Angel sheathed his sword and fell asleep.'

The priest fell still, listening to the bell of St Peter's slowly chiming the hour. Then he continued.

'Those who had survived were tormented by the scarcity of their resources and by the unbearable heat. Some of them set off in search of lands where they could give birth to a new life. They took the forefather – "He-who-must-not-die" – with them so they would never forget their origins and never lose the hope of achieving knowledge.

'Others refused to leave their lands and settled around the Tower, the only trace of their past greatness, but God punished them by taking from them their faces and their human expression. They became the "People-without-a-face" and they sought refuge under the ground.

'Those who had left in search of a new life walked for months and months under the blazing sun. They carried in their souls the memory of boundless plains, of the majestic flow of their lost rivers, of the flight of birds and the galloping of herds, of their parched lakes that had once reflected the golden clouds of the sky . . . At first, they fed upon the animals that fell to hunger and thirst, and they drank their blood, and then they fed upon each other, taking those who collapsed along the road, overwhelmed by weakness and hardship.

'Thus they pushed on until one day they found a valley confined between two arid slopes. On the bottom of the valley a great river flowed between palms and sycamores, fig and pomegranate trees. They drank that water and ate of those fruits and regained their strength, so that their race multiplied and spread throughout the valley. They hunted wild animals and built villages with reeds from the river and mud from the banks, saving the stones to build a tomb for "He-who-must-not-die".'

Father Boni dropped his head and was silent.

'It's a legend,' said Father Hogan. 'Dreadful, fascinating, but a legend nonetheless.'

'It is an epic tale,' said Father Boni. 'That's different.'

'That may be. But even so, what changes? We'll never succeed in knowing if there's a glimmer of truth in all these ravings. The book clearly has great value, but only from a literary point of view. If it's authentic, and if it's true that it's older than the pyramids, older than Sumer and Accad, that's where its value lies. We'll announce its discovery at a big conference and let the philologists and linguists have a go at it.'

'Listen to me, Hogan. I have proof, do you understand? Proof that the signal we're receiving is the last voice of the civilization that produced this text. We can't make it public until we've understood the message that's coming from space. And maybe not even then. The signals we're receiving are only the prelude. Something much, much bigger is on the way, a message the likes of which man has never received, in all of his existence.'

'Greater than the evangelical message, Father? Greater than the message of Christ?'

The old man hung his head and when he lifted it again all his anguish and bewilderment were plain on his face.

PHILIP GARRETT WAS ROAMING the bazaar of Aleppo, with its gabble of shouting and chattering voices, amid the dust lifted by the trampling of countless feet and the hooves of mules and asses laden with goods. At every corner he found another souk with dozens and dozens of stands, some of which were so small they seemed like boxes. Merchandise spilled out everywhere and the odours that wafted on the air were so strong they could knock a man out. An olfactory orgy of pungent spices, fragrant incense, cedar and Aleppo pine resins, the stink of the excrement and urine of the pack animals, the stench of the tanneries. There was a dominant smell in each souk coming from the goods on display, but the mix of odours in that enormous covered and mostly closed space was often impossible to identify.

He found himself all at once in the spice market and he wandered from one shop to the next until he found a tiny, anonymous emporium where an old man with a long white beard was crouched between the multicoloured bowls and sacks.

Philip looked at him closely, then said, 'I like the odour of sandalwood, but it's difficult to make it out in the midst of all these smells.'

'If it's sandalwood you seek, you must come to where it is kept separately from the other essences. My name is Enos.'

The old man had got to his feet and, making a little bow, turned towards the rear of the booth and disappeared behind a curtain. Philip stepped over the sacks with their rims rolled down, full of ginger and coriander, saffron and curry, and hurried after him. They went down a narrow hallway that soon opened onto a little courtyard, surrounded by tiered Moorish arches, with a gurgling fountain at its centre.

The old man turned to him. 'Are you Desmond Garrett's son?'

'Yes, I am. My name's Philip. Do you know where my father is?'

The man shook his head and frowned. 'Your father is searching for the man of the seven tombs . . . Do you know what that means?'

'No. I come from a place where we study only what we can explain and we seek only what we can touch with our hands. But I know that my father has long travelled different roads. I don't know if his search has a meaning. Who is the man of the seven tombs?'

'No one knows. It is a mystery that my people have been pursuing for millennia. Many have died terrible deaths over the centuries trying to get to the bottom of it. The man of the seven tombs has fierce, cruel servants who protect his hiding places, but when the last of his tombs is destroyed, his evil influence will cease for ever.'

The old man approached a curtain and pushed it aside, then opened a cupboard in the wall, extracted a scroll and unwound it on a rosewood book-rest. 'It is written that when the evil enclosed in that fortress of death is reawakened, it brings grief, war and famine upon mankind. It visits a violent fever upon humanity, a fever that grows for years and years until it reaches a peak . . .'

A golden light filtered in from outside through the lacy iron of the double-arched windows and shone on the old man's white hair and beard.

Philip felt a jolt of emotion. Could this Enos be speaking about the same 'Immortal One' that Vipinas the Etruscan haruspex had warned about before dying of suffocation in his home at Pompeii? A being enclosed in a tomb topped by a winged horse?

In just two days, since Philip had passed through the Gate of the Wind, he had already come into contact twice with a dimension that had never even crossed the threshold of his conscious mind before, as he had always considered superstition unworthy of his attention. So El Kassem had been wrong: Bab el Awa was not a door which opened onto nothing; it was a gateway to the infinite. The pit of his stomach churned with the sensation that all of his convictions were about to crumble.

'I know,' said the old man, 'you think it's all just ancient legends . . . You're a man of science, aren't you?'

Philip hesitated, no longer sure what to think of the science he had always trusted in. 'I want to find my father,' he said slowly, 'and save him, if I can, from the dangers that threaten him. He's exploring a world that is alien to me. I haven't even thought of such things since I was a boy. But I need to know if something still binds us together, to know if he really does need me, why he wanted me to follow his tracks after having disappeared for ten long years. Tell me, please. What do you know about the man of the seven tombs?'

The old man lowered his head. 'Since the dawn of time, his body has always been preserved in different places, each time within the domain of a powerful civilization. Whenever this power went into crisis and was no longer able to ensure the secrecy and inviolability of his tomb, he was transferred to a new mausoleum, watched over by obscure forces, guarded by a new, rising power . . .'

The rays of the setting sun that entered from the window lit up the jet from the fountain, while the rest of the square was in shadow. The gurgling of the water was the only sound to be heard as the clamour of the bazaar faded into a distant buzz, like the droning of a swarm of bees in its hive.

'But . . . who was that being? Who was the man of the seven tombs? A great king, perhaps? A cruel tyrant cursed by his people? There must be some meaning at the heart of the legend,' said Philip, as if talking to himself. He then stared straight into the eyes of the old man in front of him and said, 'Baruch bar Lev. Does this name mean anything to you?'

The old man started, as if taken by complete surprise. 'How do you know that name? Where did you find it?'

'On an old piece of paper, found by chance in a buried city.'

Enos considered him with a solemn expression. 'Nothing happens by chance. Baruch bar Lev was one of the hunters of that monster . . . a long time ago.' He began to read from the scroll that he now held open on his knees. 'The first tomb was destroyed by Simeon ben Yehoshua, a high priest at the time of King Solomon. Baruch bar Lev, rabbi of the great synagogue of Alexandria, found and destroyed the second and the third. Levi ben Aser destroyed the fourth at the time of Diogenes, Roman emperor of Byzantium. I, Enos ben Gad, am the last. I have found the fifth tomb and I have indicated it to your father, because my strength no longer sustains me. He has asked you to follow him so that, if he should fail, you can complete the task. That is why, I believe, he wants you to find the trail he has left for you.'

'The fifth tomb,' said Philip. 'Where is it?'

'Here. In Aleppo.'

'Where, exactly?'

'You will see it this very night. If you feel up to it.'

'I'm ready,' said Philip.

'Then come at midnight to the courtyard of the Great Mosque. I'll be waiting for you there.'

Philip nodded. The old man led him through the house and out through a door that gave on to the coppersmiths' market. The young man walked down a long corridor that resounded with the deafening din of dozens and dozens of hammers rhythmically beating shining sheets of copper. He disappeared into the blinding light of the western exit.

# 8

PHILIP GARRETT MADE HIS WAY through a maze of city streets lit by the full moon and cut by the long shadows of the minarets. He emerged into a vast square where the portico of the Great Mosque stood. A series of arches and columns portioned the nocturnal light and framed the inner courtyard with the font for the rite of ablution at its centre. Philip entered into the large silent space dominated by the looming dome and by the daring elegance of the minarets and a profound sensation of peace came over him. The white glow of the marble and the soft murmur of the fountains entered his soul like gentle music and the supreme harmony of the architecture engaged the moonlight like a sublime song in the darkness.

The barely perceptible sound of footsteps reminded him that he had an appointment. He turned in the direction of the scuffing noise and made out Enos.

'Shalom,' said the old man in a low voice, without stopping. 'Follow me. I'll take you to the place I told you about.'

Enos led Philip along the eastern portico to another exit and from there they went back into the labyrinth of narrow, curving streets of the old city.

'But if you've failed after trying for so many years, how can I possibly succeed?' asked Philip, as he kept up with Enos's surprisingly quick steps.

'It may not be necessary. Perhaps your father has already succeeded. But if you want to know what awaits you, you must pass where he has passed. I'm sorry, that's all I know.'

'I understand. I'm ready to do whatever I can. But tell me, if the place is here in Aleppo, why is it so hard to get to it?'

'You'll understand when you see it,' said Enos.

They silently continued along the porticoes where beggars slept curled up in their rags until finally, at the end of a winding street, they found themselves facing the dark bulk of a hillside topped by a fortress.

'Can you see now why, for years, I was unable to get to the tomb?' said Enos. 'When I began my search, the castle was guarded by the soldiers of Emir Faisal and their vigilance was strict indeed. All of the servants were close relatives or friends and so it was impossible to infiltrate the staff.' He looked at the gloomy bulwark admiringly, as if he were seeing it for the first time. 'A tomb of stone topped by a mound as tall as a hill,' he murmured. 'Do you realize that this hill may be man-made? Can you believe how powerful the protectors of the tomb are?'

Philip felt a chill run down his spine. 'My God,' he said, 'how did my father manage to get in?'

'With this,' said the old man, and opened a package that contained a perfectly pressed uniform. 'The citadel is now the general headquarters of the Foreign Legion in Syria and you speak French without an accent.' He took a sheet of paper from his robe and unfolded it. 'This is the map of the fortress and this marks the point where your father went underground. I know nothing of what happened afterwards, unfortunately. Take care. The new commander of the fort is a harsh and ruthless man. If he should discover you, you will be in deep danger. Farewell and good luck. I will wait anxiously to hear from you and I will pray that no ill befalls you.'

Philip dressed and easily passed the sentry post, saluted by the two guards on duty. He crossed the courtyard and disappeared into the shadows of the walkway that lined the interior of the fort. At that time of night the parade ground was practically empty. Almost all the sentries were posted behind the battlements on the outer wall and the watch had just left the guardhouse to make their inspection rounds up on the rampart walk. Philip slipped behind a column and took out the map to check it in the lamplight. The path he was supposed to take led to the Ayyubite mosque incorporated into the Ottoman sector of the fort. He looked around to make sure no one had noticed him, then entered. The interior was lit by a couple of oil lamps but the dim light was sufficient to find the *mihrab* marked by a cross on his map.

He felt uncomfortable treading on the carpets which covered the floor in his boots but he managed to cross in complete silence all the way to the marble pulpit, splendidly carved with geometrical motifs intertwined with flowering plants. He stopped for a moment to listen for intruders, but all he could hear were sentry calls in the distance. He carefully observed the floor behind the *mihrab* and noticed a marble square inlaid in a diamond-shaped black stone. He lit a match and lowered it to the edge of the marble slab. The flame flickered in the stream of air that filtered from an invisible crevice. There had to be a hollow below. He stuck the tip of his bayonet between the slab and the frame until he managed to lift it. An empty space yawned before him. He lit one of the candles that he'd brought and could just make out the top steps of a narrow staircase made of sandstone.

He descended with great caution, repositioning the marble hatch behind him. He found himself in what seemed to be the crypt of a Byzantine church with two side aisles separated from the nave by rows of pale marble columns topped by sculpted blocks and curved lacy capitals. The small apse at the end had an altar at its centre. The altar facing was decorated with an elaborate carving of two peacocks in the act of drinking from a fountain that poured from the foot of a cross: symbols of the soul searching for truth. The walls were adorned with frescoes which represented angels and saints whose faces had been disfigured and scraped away by iconoclasts, Philip supposed, or Muslims, both averse to the culture of the image.

The map took him directly to the altar. Could this be the fifth tomb of the man of the seven tombs? He tapped it here and there with the handle of his bayonet but the sandstone block was unmistakably solid. He examined the base all around by candle-light and noticed a slight chip at the centre of the long end. The colour of the scratched stone was lighter, a sign that it had been recently scraped away.

His father! This was the first physical trace he'd found of his father since he'd left Naples. It was evident that Desmond had used a lever of some sort to push back that mass of sandstone. Philip realized that his bayonet would break immediately; he needed something stronger. He projected the light from his candle onto the bare walls and found nothing there that could help him. He had no choice. He'd have to retrace his steps and return outside to find an object that he could use. He went back up the stairs and nudged the marble access slab with his shoulder but the sound of a voice made him freeze. A voice that sounded somehow familiar. The person who was speaking had his back turned to Philip but his uniform clearly identified him as a high officer of the Legion. Two bedouin tribal chiefs were facing him. They were armed and dressed in the same style as the bandits who had attacked the caravan between Bab el Awa and Aleppo.

The officer was speaking in Arabic. He was giving them information about a shipment of arms due to arrive from the port of Tartous. The promised weapons would give the bedouins sway over a vast region and they would be allowed to split the booty from all their sacking and robberies. The two chieftains nodded in silence and the man spoke again. What he asked for in return was that they comb the area between Wadi Qoueik and the Khabour river in search of an infidel named Desmond Garrett. When he heard his father's name, Philip recognized the voice: it was Selznick!

He held his breath and stood stock still as the two chieftains took their leave with slight nods of the head and exited through a little side door. Selznick remained alone and Philip instinctively put his hand on his bayonet. He could creep up soundlessly from behind and stab him in the back, but the thought that he might fail stopped him. If he did, he couldn't imagine what it might mean to fall into the hands of such a completely evil person, totally devoid of moral sense or restraint.

Selznick was walking back towards the main door and was still in Philip's field of vision when he suddenly slowed his pace and doubled over as if stuck by a blade. He fell to his knees and rolled onto the floor, writhing in seeming agony. Philip caught a glimpse of his face: he was as pale as a cadaver, his eyes mere slits in sunken orbs, sweat streaming down to his collarbone. He was trying to push himself off the floor, bracing himself on both arms, as if he were fighting against an immeasurable force that sought to crush him like a cockroach. He arched his back with his knees still on the ground, his forehead pressing the cold pavement. That tense bow of bone and muscle was like a steel spring tightly coiled to overcome the torment of his wounded flesh and to cram as much hate as possible into his mind. His voice came from between clenched teeth: 'Damn you, you'll pay for this wound . . . but first you'll take me to our final tryst . . . and that will be the end of it, either for me or for you . . .'

He spoke again, and it seemed to Philip that he was reciting a formula that he'd learned by heart. '"He has witnessed all the evil of the world, and revels in suffering and remorse. He knows the secret of immortality and of eternal youth."'

The words of Avile Vipinas!

Selznick continued in a low voice. 'He is just like me . . . he knows that there is nothing above human intelligence. He knows that man can fathom every mystery of this universe, that he can create anything, even God. He will heal this wound and then he will crush you, Desmond Garrett, he'll sweep you from my path for ever.'

By the dim light of the oil lamps, it looked as though Selznick was praying, kneeling on the carpet of the mosque, instead of cursing in a fit of hate. He finally forced himself to get up and made his way to the door. On the other side his footsteps, regular again, rang out on the stone pavement in the corridor.

Philip waited until the noise had completely faded away and then went to the exit himself. He considered searching the fort for an object he could use to force the altar stone, but thought it would be less dangerous to leave and then try again later. The guard had already changed and those who saw him leave had not seen him enter, but the captain's stripes on his jacket protected him from being challenged. He left by the main gate and descended the steps without haste, trying to control the tension and fear that crawled down his spine like icy water. He crossed the square and disappeared into the labyrinth of the old city.

He wandered at length without a destination for fear that someone might be following him, then sought shelter for the night at Enos's house. The old man peered through the door anxiously and after checking in every direction, let him in by a side entrance.

PHILIP APPROACHED THE FORTRESS again the next evening at dusk and waited for a group of legionnaires to enter so he could slip in with them. Under his coat he had hidden a steel crowbar that he'd had a craftsman in the market make for him.

He reached the mosque and went down the narrow steps hidden behind the *mihrab* to the crypt. Now all he had to do was push back the altar stone. He set a candle down on the floor, fixing it in place with a few drops of melted wax, and stuck the lever end of his crowbar between the stone and the step, pushing forcefully. The altar slid back with such a regular, continuous movement that Philip realized it must be on stone rollers. When it reached the end it seemed to lock into place. Philip took the candle and went into the chamber beneath.

He found himself in a room that was completely bare, plastered with some kind of old fire-hardened clay. On one side of the room was a ramp that seemed to descend to the very core of the hill. Before starting down, Philip turned back to check the altar stone and noticed that there were words scratched into its undersurface. By the time he deciphered them, he would still have had time to heed the warning they gave: 'Block the stone.' The altar had begun to slip back on its rollers to its original position! But when Philip turned to grab the crowbar, the candle fell to the ground and went out. He blindly drove the bar into place, but failed on his first try. When he tried to jam it in a second time, the stone had already rolled back completely into its housing.

'Block the stone': the words inscribed on the bottom face of the altar taunted him. He cursed under his breath, feeling like he did when his father used to correct his homework as a boy; he'd make Philip feel like an idiot every time he misinterpreted a phrase or miscalculated an equation. He took another candle from his pocket and lit it, recovered the crowbar and tried to prise it between the stone and the flooring, but the space was so narrow that he couldn't wedge the lever in. He examined the grooves and saw that for the first two-thirds of their length, they were on a barely perceptible incline, while the last third was horizontal. This last section was not quite long enough to provide a solid base for the stone, which thus remained for a short time in what seemed to be perfect equilibrium, only to roll back on the cylinders as its own weight took over.

Philip was consoled by the thought that his own father must have been fooled by the mechanism himself, otherwise he would never have left that message. He picked up the candle that had fallen to the ground and took the crowbar with him as well as he began to cautiously descend the ramp that had rough-shaped steps carved into it. He made his way down a long tunnel, at the end of which he found himself in a second chamber, this one adorned with Aramean sculptures. A cuneiform inscription was carved on the back wall and at the centre of the room a huge stone sarcophagus lay broken into pieces.

'You succeeded, then,' he murmured. 'You destroyed the fifth tomb. Only two are left. But where are you now? Where have you gone?' He walked all the way around the room, holding his candle high to examine the walls. 'You must have left me a sign . . . somewhere.' The candle had melted down to a stub and Philip lit another, which spread a slightly brighter light through the little room. He inspected the walls centimetre by centimetre and the floor as well, but found nothing. And yet his father had certainly made it this far, and he must have found his way out as well. But how? And why hadn't he left a single sign?

Discouraged, Philip sat down on the floor. An oppressive sense of despair threatened to overwhelm him in that airless chamber. He could feel the weight of the whole hill on top of him. What would happen when he ran out of candles? What chance of escape would he have in total darkness? He watched with anguish as the candle burned down to the wick. He had no choice: he would go back to the top of the ramp and yell for help until someone heard him. He'd rather be found by Selznick than die like a mouse in a trap.

He lit his fourth candle and started to walk back up the ramp, but as he lowered his head he saw what he'd been searching for. A phrase was scratched into the wall: 'Follow the air when the prayer starts.'

He realized then that his father had found himself trapped under the Byzantine crypt just as he had; then, just like Philip, he had found no exit and was forced to retrace his steps. In both situations he had anticipated that his son would be going through the same experience, to the point of knowing where his gaze would rest.

As Philip tried to puzzle out what the words meant he thought he heard a cry, distant at first and confused, but then much clearer and distinct: 'Allah-u-akbar!' It was a call to prayer! But how could he possibly be hearing it? According to his calculations, he was at least twenty metres down, in the core of the hill. Yet this must be the prayer his father had been referring to. As he was considering what to do next, he felt a strong gust of air which put out his candle, and then again heard the call of the muezzin: '*Allah-u-akbar!*'

He relit the candle and began to make his way up the ramp, shielding the flame with his hand so the draught wouldn't put it out again. When he was about halfway up, he realized that the air was being sucked towards the left wall of the tunnel, which led towards the Byzantine crypt. He turned in that direction and saw an open loophole, through which the muezzin's voice rang out loudly.

Philip felt reborn. He crawled swiftly towards the aperture that had so fortuitously appeared and found himself in another tunnel. It was very narrow and just high enough to allow him to creep through on his elbows.

He moved as quickly as he could, terrified of being caught like a rat in a trap. He was sure the claustrophobia would drive him mad.

He tried to recall the verses of the *sura* that the muezzin was reciting, in order to calculate how much time he had left before the loophole would close. His father's message made it clear that the passageway was somehow strictly connected with the length of the prayer. He finally emerged into a sort of cistern inside a thick, rounded wall. There he found another loophole, which led to a spiral staircase that rose inside a tall minaret. Philip realized that there was a counterweight system connected to the entry door which activated the shutters and exploited the flue effect of the minaret to convey the air up from the tunnels that ran through the hill, transforming the building into a gigantic organ pipe. In that way the muezzin's voice was amplified and strengthened, raining over the city with its magical vibrations. Ingenious.

Philip descended the stair in a rush, trying not to make a sound. He had decided that he would hide under the staircase until the muezzin left. As he waited he noticed the figure of a scorpion over the doorway, surrounded by some letters in what seemed to be Kufic script. He took a notebook from his pocket and began to copy them, but just then the muezzin's chanting came to an abrupt stop and Philip stared in surprise as the mechanism clicked into motion and began to close the iron door at the bottom of the stairs. The muezzin must have left by another exit.

He jumped up just in time to slip between the door and the jamb and he found himself outside without any idea of where he was exactly. He heard a voice call out in French: a Legion patrol led by a non-commissioned officer had spotted him and was challenging him to identify himself. Philip estimated the distance that separated him from the first houses of the medina and he decided to take a chance. He took off at a sprint, immediately followed by shouted warnings ordering him to stop.

Selznick was walking alongside the parapet of the entry tower and he leaned over to see where the shouts were coming from. He glimpsed a man running at the bottom of the hill and ordered the big searchlight at the guardhouse to be switched on. Philip turned just at that moment and Selznick, recognizing him, shouted, 'Capture him!'

Selznick ran down to the courtyard, jumped onto a horse and raced down the ramp, closely followed by a squad of his men. The soldiers from the patrol had set off after him as well and Philip was racing through the streets, trying desperately to find a place to hide, knowing that his strength would not hold out much longer.

He turned down a narrow alleyway in the quarter of the Great Mosque and he realized that he was not far from Enos's house. Opposite him was a slightly wider street topped by wooden balconies enclosed in grillework, in the Turkish style. He darted in that direction, but just a few steps later he found the guards running straight at him. They must have cut through the maze of streets somehow. He spun around to turn back but could hear more men arriving from behind and he heard Selznick's voice cry out, 'This way! He's got to be here!'

He pulled back and flattened himself against the wall under a dark archway, but he could see the guards coming from one direction and Selznick's squad from the other. They would spot him in a matter of seconds. He looked around for a way out but found none. He was trapped and El Kassem wasn't there to save him. There was a pomegranate tree opposite him whose branches stretched almost all the way up to a balcony. He was preparing to make the leap so he could attempt to climb up and escape over the rooftops, but at just that moment a door opened behind him and two enormous black hands grabbed him by the shoulders and dragged him inside, shutting the door after him.

Philip turned and saw a giant Nubian, who signalled for him to keep quiet. The street outside rang with Selznick's rebukes and the soldiers' voices. They couldn't understand how the prey they had thought so close at hand could have disappeared without a trace.

The Nubian gestured for Philip to follow him. They crossed a hallway dimly lit by a couple of oil lamps, went down a short corridor and entered an elegant covered patio, luxuriously furnished in the Oriental style, the floor completely covered by splendid Anatolian and Caucasian carpets. Moroccan cushions in blue velvet with gold trim skirted the side walls and an enormous tray of embossed copper at the centre of the patio was spilling over with fruit: pomegranates and figs, grapes and dates, Bursa peaches and Nusaybin apples. On the ground were an exquisitely crafted silver jug and cup with Trebisond-style engraving.

Philip was incredibly exhausted, hungry and thirsty, and he stretched out his hand to take a piece of fruit, but he saw the Nubian nod his head towards a staircase that went up to the second floor and Philip turned his head as well. It was her.

She was coming down the staircase with a light step. She wore a very simple, gauzy gown with a deep neckline that gave a glimpse of the skin between her breasts. The Pegasus pendant glittered on her brown skin, the only ornament of her beauty. Her long legs descended the stair as if dancing to unheard music.

Philip was stunned. 'You see,' he said, 'destiny has joined us again, so shortly after you abandoned me.'

The woman lowered her gaze. 'I couldn't let them capture you. You would have fallen into the hands of an evil man.'

'Is that the only reason you let me into your house?'

The woman did not answer.

'What do you know about Selznick?'

'I'm a woman of the desert and the desert knows no confines. He is a man who comes from the desert as well. What does he want from you?'

'My father disappeared ten years ago and was given up as dead, but he has recently sent me some . . . messages and I've set out to find him. Selznick thinks that by following me he will find my father. He wants to kill him.'

'What is your father searching for?'

'The truth. Like all of us.'

'What truth?'

Her voice had become inquisitive and was touched with alarm. Philip kept trying to meet her eyes. He feared that this encounter would be as fleeting as the last and he could not resign himself to it. But he saw that her mind was far away at that moment and he dropped his gaze.

'His truth is a tomb in the desert.'

The woman started slightly and appeared to reflect on his words. Then her mood changed. Her voice became gentler and more harmonious; her eyes seemed to be searching far-off horizons, endless spaces. 'Ah, it is a tomb he searches for . . . My tribe has journeyed from the peaks of the Atlas Mountains to the stony Higiaz flatlands, from Chaldea to Persia. We have seen the solitary tomb of Cyrus the Great on the high plains, and the tomb of the great pharaoh Djoser in Saqqara . . . Perhaps it is one of their tombs that your father is searching for. Or for the tomb of the Christian queen. It's as big as a fortress, standing majestic on the seashore, surrounded by a grandiose colonnade

. . . Or the tomb of the Fileni brothers who immolated themselves for their city, allowing themselves to be buried alive in the sands of Syrtis . . . The desert is full of tombs. Most of them don't even have a name.'

'No. My father is searching for the tomb of a terrible, mysterious creature, dead for millennia yet still alive. It is the dark face of human knowledge that he seeks in that nameless mausoleum . . . and perhaps he is under the illusion that he can destroy it . . .'

The woman lowered her eyes to hide a flash of recognition that Philip did not miss.

'Have you ever heard of this being? Can you help me to find my father before he loses a battle he has no hope of winning?' Philip gazed at the Pegasus that was shining upon her breast. 'I know that the tomb is shaped like a cylinder topped by a winged horse . . . like that one,' he said, pointing at the jewel she wore.

'I've studied the remains of all the ancient civilizations for years and years,' Philip continued, 'but there's nothing that I've learned that can help me now. I know of no monument that looks like that. But perhaps . . . if it stands in some remote place, in the deepest desert, perhaps no one has ever seen it except for those who live there, in that solitude.'

The woman's gaze was intense. 'There is no evil in this world that does not contain a little good, nor is there any good that cannot provoke the worst of suffering. I'm afraid I can't help you.'

'At least tell me who you are. I've never met a desert people whose women dress so proudly, without veiling the passion in their eyes, the allure of their bodies. Tell me your name, at least . . . and if I can see you again. I couldn't stand not seeing you again after finding you here. After fearing that I had lost for ever the vision of your face, the light in your eyes. I would spend the rest of my life grieving.'

His eyes were moist as he spoke and the woman was moved. She lifted her hand and lightly brushed his cheek, but the look in her eyes only reminded Philip of the impossible obstacles that loomed between them.

'Eat now, and drink,' she said, 'if you want to make me happy. You must regain your strength. You'll need it.'

She left him and returned up the stairs. Philip tried to follow her but the Nubian planted himself in front of the staircase. Philip backed off and sat at the table, hoping that she would come back down again, perhaps with an even more beautiful gown, resplendent as a Theban queen, but a maid soon came down the stairs instead with a satchel in her arms.

'My lady wants you to know that you are dear to her because of all you have done for her. You saved her from terrible danger and she wishes to show you her thanks,' she said, handing him the satchel.

'Where is she?' shouted Philip. 'I have to see her!'

His voice trembled with desperation. He lunged up the stairs but the Nubian servant rushed up behind him, grabbed him by the shoulders and stopped him with no seeming effort. Philip writhed and twisted, shouting, certain that she could hear him.

Two eyes brimming with tears watched him from behind a grating as he shouted, 'Tell me your name! Please!'

The Nubian turned Philip to face him. 'It's useless,' he said. 'She's gone.'

'Where has she gone?' shouted Philip. 'Tell me. Tell me where she is! I have to find her!'

'That is not possible,' said the Nubian. 'But if you truly care for her, respect her wishes.'

The maid handed him a bundle of Oriental-style clothing.

'You can't leave here in that uniform. Put these on,' said the Nubian. 'You'll have a better chance of slipping by unobserved.'

He walked away and the maid disappeared as well. Philip remained alone in the centre of the patio, his heart heavy and his mind confused. He had no choice but to do as they had suggested. He left the uniform behind, covered his head and face with a keffiyeh and went outside.

He found the doors of the bazaar bolted and it took him quite some time to find another way in to Enos's house from a side street. He finally recognized the double-arched windows of the patio and thought he could see a faint light within, but both the front and side doors were closed. There was no one on the streets except for a couple of beggars lying on the pavement, their skeletal bodies wrapped in filthy rags, fast asleep or perhaps already in the arms of death. But from under the portico where he stood Philip could hear a group of horses pawing the ground. Then he saw them; they were tied to iron rings that hung on the inside wall. A man in uniform was guarding them. Philip hung back so as not to be seen, then began to climb up one of the columns. He reached the gutter pipe and hoisted himself up onto the roof. He crawled across, careful not to make a sound, until he could see the double-arched windows. He peered in but immediately pulled back in shock and fright. What he saw unfortunately confirmed the premonition he'd had on spotting the horses: Selznick was inside. He was just leaving by the door that opened onto the street, followed by his men. Philip couldn't see anything else because part of the patio was outside his angle of vision. He flattened himself onto the roof as he listened to the pounding of the men's boots on the cobblestones. He waited until he heard the horses stamping, then voices, curt orders and a galloping which faded off in the direction of the citadel.

Philip moved towards the centre of the house, prised open a skylight with the tip of his dagger and dropped inside. He raced down the stair and reached the corridor that led from the bazaar to Enos's house. It was in darkness and all he could hear was the distant gurgling of the fountain in the patio.

Philip plucked up his courage and softly called out, 'Enos! Enos!' advancing towards the patio, where a flickering light seemed on the verge of going out. He thought he heard a groan and he ran inside. Enos was lying on the ground: his face was swollen, his limbs still, his eyes closed. Philip rushed over and took him in his arms, wetting his lips with a handkerchief dipped in the fountain. 'What have they done to you? It was Selznick, that bastard. It was him, wasn't it?'

Enos could barely open his eyes. 'Your father . . . find him . . .'

'Where? Where?'

'Abu el Abd . . . in Tedmor . . . he knows,' he managed to say in a whisper, before his head fell back and all life left him.

Philip shook him, gripped by uncontrollable panic. 'Enos, answer me! Answer me! Don't leave me! I need you!' Then he collapsed, weeping, the old man's body still in his arms.

Outside, the muezzin's voice flew over the rooftops of the city, chanting the pre-dawn prayer, his voice sounding like a long lament: '*Allah-u-akbar!*'

Philip roused himself. He arranged the old man's body on the floor, laying his head on a pillow and crossing his arms over his chest. He softly recited the prayer of the dead for the sons of Israel. It was the only honour that fate had allowed for a courageous man who had spent his whole life struggling against overpowering forces. That scrawny, frail body had been stronger and more unyielding than that of the most indomitable warrior. For the first time in his life, Philip hoped that God existed, so that Enos's death would not be meaningless. So that he would not have been defeated for all eternity.

Philip knew he couldn't stay in the house; it was too risky now. The city was still being scoured by Selznick's troops. Philip wandered through the shadowy streets of the district, trying to come up with the means to slip away unnoticed. He was ardently hoping that El Kassem would appear like a *deus ex machina* to lift him out of this desperate situation, but his protector seemed to have vanished. He was teaching Philip a hard lesson: that he would not tolerate him losing sight of their objective. But perhaps, mused Philip, he'd no longer be offered a second chance. The only point of reference he had was a name and a place: Abu el Abd, at Tedmor. Tedmor: the ancient desert metropolis once known as Palmyra, fabled kingdom of the great queen Zainab, whom the Romans called Zenobia. How was he to get there?

As dawn broke, Philip noticed a beggar who was just waking up and stretching his stiff limbs. He approached him, after making sure there was no one else around, and asked to buy his soiled cloak, thinking that he would use it to cover up the beautiful embroidered robes he'd been given. The old man accepted with enthusiasm and Philip bought his bowl and his cane as well, leaning on it as he hobbled away. He thus managed to pass through the Baghdad Gate without as much as a glance from the sentries. He walked off towards the east with a slow, shuffling step. The sun was just rising over the horizon and cast a long shadow behind him in the dust of the road.

When the sun had got a little higher and the city had faded into the distance, Philip tossed away the bowl and cane, stripped off the bulkiest part of his clothing and started to walk at a much quicker pace. It still took a great many hours before he came upon a rest station. He stayed clear of it for a while, as there seemed to be legionnaires in uniform inside. As soon as the soldiers had moved on he took off his tattered cloak and went in. He sat at a table and ordered a plate of rice pilaf with some boiled chicken. The waiter's confidence was easily won over with a tip, and Philip told him that his horse had been stolen and that he was afraid that his master would punish him severely unless he found another. Was there any way he could buy a horse in the vicinity? He didn't need a charger worthy of Saladin, as the waiter was quick to offer; any decent mount would do, as long as it didn't cost too much or collapse as soon as he put it into a trot.

It took two hours of exasperating haggling with a horse trader before they managed to settle on a price, so it was near dusk by the time Philip set off again. He saddled the horse and spurred it into a gallop as a huge red moon rose over the chalky rolling hills in the east.

To his right, the waters of the Nahr Qoueik flowed lazily beneath the moon, but Philip's horse flew down the road at a full gallop. Behind him, in the long train of white dust, Philip left memories and reminiscences, his childhood, his adolescence and the long peace of his studies, as he chased dreams and nightmares, shadows teasing him in the night. He urged his mount on faster and faster until the pounding of the horse's hooves matched the convulsive beating of his heart, soaring on a wave of delirium until a cloud abruptly covered the face of the moon.

The sudden darkness calmed Philip's frenzy and he pulled on the horse's reins, easing the foaming, sweat-soaked animal into a walk. He let himself slide to the ground and collapsed onto the warm sand as consciousness slipped away.

Philip awoke from that suspended state of mind with a shudder and looked around him. His horse shone damp in the shadows like a living statue of bronze and the endless plain stretched out all around him as far as the eye could see. Philip got back into the saddle and continued his journey without ever stopping again. He had no idea of how long he had been riding when, all at once, a vision loomed up in the night before him: the battered towers and crumbling walls of Dura Europos.

He dismounted and led his horse slowly by the reins towards the ancient legionary fortress. He entered through the gate, observing the innumerable graffiti that covered its jambs. He felt as though he could hear those words, carved into stone in the lost language of Rome, echoing in the vast silence like a chorus of confused cries. They seemed to flit away through the air as he passed, like startled bats. He advanced along the north–south military road amid collapsed walls and broken columns until he reached the eastern gate. The liquid majesty of the Euphrates greeted him, glittering in the dark.

He sat on the banks of the great river, surrounded by the towering ruins of the Roman fort. When he closed his eyes, he could still see Selznick writhing on the floor. But just beyond was the image of the woman he had met at Bab el Awa and glimpsed once again in that magical, fragrant place . . . Philip could not get her out of his mind, and the thought of her wounded him, filled him with an acute sense of longing and deep regret. But her image vanished as she had, like an apparition. Flocks of nocturnal birds took to the air from the towers behind him, while thousands of bats shot out of the hidden recesses of the ruins and scattered over the river and the desert.

Philip gathered some twigs and wood and lit a fire so he could have a little light and warmth in the midst of all that desolation. He toasted a bit of the dry bread that he still had in his haversack and melted a little goat's cheese on it. In that deserted, melancholy place, his scant repast gave him sustenance and the courage to go on. He added more wood and lay down alongside the bivouac in the shelter of a low wall. He rested easily, for he knew no one could see him from the desert, but someone did, from the other side of the river, and waited until morning so that he could make out the youth's features. That same day Selznick was informed about a young foreigner travelling on horseback, hiding among the ruins of Dura Europos.

FATHER HOGAN CROSSED the Vatican gardens in the dark, listening to the sound of his own footsteps on the gravelled pathways. He stared at the light in the observatory, its eye wide-open onto the night sky, scrutinizing its immensity. He knew that the old priest was waiting for him up there, waiting to relate the epilogue of a blasphemous story, the last act of a rash, arrogant challenge. He went up the stairs and, as he drew closer to the top, he could hear the signal, as persistent as a winter rain.

Father Boni was sitting at his desk. As always, with his back turned to him.

'I know what's going to happen,' he said. 'I know what that signal means.'

Father Hogan did not reply, but sat down.

'The civilization of Delfud succeeded in launching their mind into the furthest reaches of space before their elevated level of knowledge was destroyed for ever.'

'What do you mean by "launching their mind"?'

'I don't know. I'm quoting directly from Father Antonelli's translation. Maybe . . . a machine.'

'Capable of thinking?'

'What else?'

Father Hogan shook his head. 'A machine capable of thinking cannot exist.'

'The fact is that we are receiving an intelligent signal. This . . . thing was launched into outermost space for a precise purpose, for a mission that . . .' The old priest stopped, as though he couldn't find the words for what he had to say.

'Yes, Father Boni?' urged Father Hogan.

'The purpose was to probe the mind of God in the very moment of creation.' The old man fell still and lowered his eyes as if ashamed of what he had said.

'You cannot believe such a thing.'

'Oh no? Then come here, Hogan. I have something to show you. Look at this . . . The signals we are receiving give us the celestial coordinates of all twenty stars of the Scorpio constellation, plus one . . . a dark, remote star of unimaginable power, millions of times greater than our own sun . . . It is represented in the Stone of the Constellations and is described in "The Book of Amon". It is called "the black heart of the scorpion". Hogan, its position corresponds to the astral coordinates transmitted by our radio source. I believe that . . . that it is a black body. The civilization of Delfud somehow harnessed its monstrous gravity to use as an accelerator, a kind of cyclopean catapult that hurled their device at an unimaginable speed into the most remote reaches of the universe.

'Tens of thousands of years have passed and now . . . now that thing is returning. Hogan, in thirty-five days, seventeen hours and seven minutes, it will project onto the earth everything that it has learned in those lost regions of the cosmos. Do you understand how little time we have left to us? You'll have to leave as soon as possible.'

Father Hogan shook his head. 'Marconi said that the radio

source coincides with a point suspended in a geostationary orbit at 500,000 kilometres from earth.'

'That's only a relay station; the device that guides the signal to its target.'

'And where is the target?'

Father Boni opened a large map of the Sahara and pointed to a spot in the south-eastern quadrant. 'Here,' he said, 'in a place searing hot by day and bitterly cold at night, swept by torrid winds and by storms of sand and dust. A corner of hell called the Sand of Ghosts.'

# 9

DESMOND GARRETT RODE ALONE over the barren land in the midday sun. His long years in the saddle had given him a particular bearing, as if his own body were an extension of his horse's. The desert wind and sand had carved out his features and weathered his skin. He dressed like the bedouins of Sirte, with a keffiyeh around his head and in front of his mouth, but wore shiny brown leather boots over Turkish-style trousers. A repeating rifle of American make was hanging from the saddle and a damascene-hilted scimitar hung from his belt.

Desmond would stop now and then to check his compass and mark a spot on his map. The waning sun was nearing the horizon to his right when he spurred on his Arab charger. His plan was to reach the oasis just when the sky would be flaring violet over the colonnades of ancient Palmyra.

The Pearl of the Desert appeared all at once, like a vision, as he cleared a low hill. The oasis of Tedmor shone a deep, dark green in the harsh landscape that surrounded it, as thousands of palms waved their fronds in the evening breeze like a field of wheat in the month of May. The huge glittering pool at their centre flashed with the fiery evening light and the slow-moving sun loomed like a divinity over the great limestone portal, lighting up the columns of the majestic Roman portico one after another, as if they were colossal torches.

It was at that moment that the miracle took place. Just as the sun had sunk below the horizon and the ruins of Palmyra were about to be plunged into darkness, a violet flash illuminated the hills and the desert behind the city and spread nearly all the way to the centre of the heavenly vault, like an illusory dawn.

Desmond climbed off his horse and stood stock still, taking in the magic. He had seen it for the first time twenty years ago and then never again, but many a time, during long nights spent in the desert, he had dreamed of the rapturous violet sky of Palmyra as a refuge of the soul.

The purple reflection was shot through with the rosy streaks of the last tremulous light of dusk, and then began instantly to darken, invaded by the deep blue of night.

Desmond walked slowly to the edge of the pool, leading his horse by the reins. Just a short distance away, under a group of towering palms, he could see an imposing tent guarded by a pair of warriors. He tied his horse to one of the stakes and waited for someone to notice his presence. The guards did not even glance in his direction but a servant peered out from behind the flap opening and then ducked back inside. Sheikh Abu el Abd in person soon appeared at the entrance to the tent.

He strode towards Desmond and embraced him warmly, then brought him into the tent and had him sit on velvet pillows from Fez as his servants brought hot tea in little Turkish cups of silver and glass.

'Enos told me you would be coming and my heart filled with joy. I am pleased that you are my guest here, as he once was.'

'It makes me very happy to see you as well, Abu el Abd. So many years have gone by . . .'

'Why hasn't Enos come? Aleppo is not so far from Tedmor.'

'I don't know. Messages are slow to arrive in the desert. But Enos has grown very old, you know. That must be the reason. I'm sure he would have come otherwise. It was here at Tedmor that I first met him, so long ago.'

'That's true. Right here in my tent.'

'What did he ask of you then, Abu el Abd?'

'He wanted to speak with the Fateh of Kalaat al Amm. A very

difficult endeavour indeed . . . only a few people may speak with the Fateh in her whole lifetime.'

'And the Fateh agreed to see him?'

'Yes.'

'What did she tell him?'

'I don't know. But when Enos left, there was a shadow in his eyes . . . the shadow of death.'

'I am here to see the Fateh as well.'

The sheikh stared into Desmond's eyes. 'It's very difficult. Impossible, really. But if she agreed to see you, do you know what that means, Desmond *sahib*? Do you know? The Fateh can make you look your own death in the eye.'

'I am pursuing a mystery even greater than death . . . I'm looking for the man of the seven tombs.'

The tribal chief paled and his lean face turned to stone. He continued to stare into Desmond's eyes, as if he sought to explore forces in him which his words could not communicate, which his expression could not reveal. Then he said calmly, 'I have a premonition. I pray to Allah that I may be mistaken, but I fear for our friend Enos ben Gad.'

'What makes you say that?' asked Desmond. 'Have you received a message you haven't told me about?'

'No. I've received no message. I feel it. I feel that what you are seeking was the cause of it. I didn't realize what you were looking for.'

Desmond lowered his head without answering, but he was clearly distressed as an ominous certainty crept into his mind. He couldn't say another word, because he suddenly felt unbearably alone in an unequal struggle. A struggle to the death.

They walked out of the tent and looked towards Kalaat al Amm. The gloomy bulwark with its crumbling walls loomed before them, still touched with the last light of the vanished day.

'I wasn't told the true reason for your coming . . . I could not have imagined. But if what you say is true, if you are truly pursuing the man of the seven tombs, then go ahead,' said the sheikh. 'She surely knows that you are here. She is certainly speaking with your thoughts at this very moment.'

Desmond left him, mounted his horse and urged it in the direction of the mountain. He crossed the ruins at a gallop, riding swiftly along the grandiose colonnade that still shone in the darkness as if it had absorbed the last energy of the sunset and could radiate light of its own.

He rode between the tombs of the necropolis, half-sunken into the sand, and started up towards the castle. He soon had to leave his horse and continue on foot up to the ruins of the gate. He crossed the threshold and advanced among the rubble, looking around cautiously. He felt followed by a fierce, predatory gaze, intent on his every movement.

He heard the sound of gravel scattering and a bristly black dog appeared at a breach in the wall, growling and baring his teeth. He paid the dog no heed and walked right past him as the animal continued to bark furiously, barely centimetres from his knee. Could he be the Fateh?

Just beyond, Desmond heard the hissing of a horned viper but did not turn, letting the reptile slither away between the stones and undergrowth to find its prey before the chill of the night numbed its belly. Then he saw a ruddy glow behind a wall and approached. There was a old woman sitting next to a fire, her face wrinkled and her hair long and white. Her eyes were closed and ringed with dark circles. Thus he imagined the sorceress that had called Samuel's shade up from the underworld for Saul.

The woman opened cataract-misted eyes. 'I've been expecting you, Garrett. Enos told me you would come.'

'Isn't Enos dead? Isn't that true, then?'

'Not for me,' she said, impassively. 'I can still hear his voice. What do you want from me?'

Desmond felt a weight crushing his heart but he answered in the same tone, 'For you to guide me to the sixth tomb. So that I may destroy it and embark on the last leg of my journey.'

'No one has ever succeeded. Who are you to dare so much?'

'I found the key for reading "The Book of Amon" and the Stone of the Constellations. I will find the seventh tomb as well and I will destroy Him.'

'But do you know who sleeps in that tomb?' At these words, the fire flared up with a sudden roar, flames rising stronger, higher, lighter.

Desmond shook his head. 'No. Enos never told me. Perhaps he didn't know.'

'Enos didn't know. Now he does.'

'Then you tell me.'

'No. You'll have to understand for yourself, because only when you have understood can you decide. I can guide you to the sixth tomb and no further.'

'What must I do?'

'You must journey along the dead waters and descend to the valley of Sodom and Gomorrah. Leave the pillars of salt behind you, then cross the Arava Valley and the Paran Desert, until you reach Wadi Musa. Go up the wadi, following the sign of the Scorpion. It will take you to the City of Tombs. There you will do what you must do.'

'The City of Tombs? But how will I be able to recognize the tomb of "He-who-must not-die" amid all the others?'

The Fateh widened her white eyes and held out her wrinkled palms towards the crackling flames, trying to absorb its warmth into her decrepit body. 'You will be guided by the most terrible secret hidden in the bottom of your soul. The beast in you will sniff him out. Farewell. I must sleep now . . . sleep.'

She let out a deep sigh, almost a rattle, closed her eyes and pulled up the dark veil covering her shoulders so that her head was completely hidden. She looked like a grotesque idol animated only by the dancing flames. The fire seemed to die down as well, creeping low amid the glowing embers like a snake.

Desmond turned and walked off. As he descended the hillside, the whining of the dog, which had never stopped while he was consulting the Fateh, turned into a long howl that rose towards the star-filled sky that covered Palmyra like a gem-encrusted cloak gracing the shoulders of a queen.

He reached Abu el Abd's tent. The sheikh awaited him sitting cross-legged, with the palms of his hands resting on his knees. His limbs, under his light-blue linen djellaba, were as taut as a drawn bow in which all the forces of his spirit were concentrated.

'I will leave immediately,' said Desmond. 'I may be the only hunter left . . . if your presentiment is true.'

'No,' said Abu el Abd. 'Victory will not depend on a few hours more or a few hours less. The temperature is not high enough to force you to travel by night. Eat, drink and rest. I will have a bed prepared for you and a meal. You will leave tomorrow in the light of the sun. It will be a good omen for you and your spirit will be refreshed.'

Desmond thanked him. He bathed in the clear waters of the pool and then sat down to dinner, wearing a clean djellaba over his naked, purified body. Abu el Abd broke bread, dipped it into salt and handed it to his guest, then called to his servants, who entered with roasted mutton and couscous. Desmond ate and drank and in his heart continued to hope that Enos was still alive. Perhaps what the sheikh and the Fateh had perceived was some earthly suffering and not the agony of one who is leaving his life. But as they were finishing their meal the sound of galloping could be heard outside the tent, followed by a neighing and the stamping of hooves. A man was announced and soon entered. He bowed, greeting them with 'Salam alekhum', then drew close to the sheikh, whispered something in his ear and left.

Abu el Abd raised his eyes to Desmond's face and the tragic solemnity of his look foretold the sadness of his announcement. 'You are the last hunter,' he said. 'Enos ben Gad is dead. Murdered. By Selznick.'

Desmond left the tent and bellowed out all his fury and impotent rage. 'Damned wolf!' he shouted. 'Rabid dog! May you die unburied, Selznick, and be devoured by vultures. May you die screaming in pain!' He dropped to his knees, his forehead in the dust, and remained thus at length, trembling in the silence and chill of the night.

Abu el Abd's hand shook him. 'Enos ben Gad has fallen like a warrior on the battlefield, overwhelmed by enemy forces. He fought like a lion surrounded by packs of dogs, goaded on by their masters in the hunt. Let us pay our last respects to him with foreheads high. God is great!'

Desmond got to his feet and raised his eyes to the immense starry vault that seemed to be held up, from one end of the horizon to the other, by the columns of Palmyra.

'God is great,' he said, and when he turned towards Sheikh Abu el Abd, his eyes were dry and unblinking and shone with an agonized pain that had neither words, nor laments, nor tears.

DESMOND GARRETT RODE FOR days and days. He reached Bosra, and from there, Gerash and Mount Nebo. He crossed the immense valley where Moses was said to be buried and he thought of the unclaimed bones of the great leader of men buried in the sand of some unknown cave, waiting for the trumpet of God to announce the last day.

He continued from there to the valley of the Dead Sea. He looked out over that dark expanse of still water which filled the deepest wound of the planet: the wasteland where five legendary cities had once stood before they were destroyed by the hand of God and their peoples slaughtered. Which among these many pinnacles of salt – mute ghosts standing guard over nothing – imprisoned Lot's wife, with her restless spirit and her cursed nostalgia for her lost homeland?

He advanced at the foot of the mountains of salt until he reached the inlet to the Arava Valley, which stretched out before him as black as flint and completely desolate as far as the eye could see. It looked as if a hurricane of fire had ravaged it, leaving a sea of dead coals behind.

The heat was unbearable in that vast flatland, even this late in the season, so Desmond tried to save his strength and that of his horse by slowing his pace during the hours around midday. He proceeded on foot, leading the horse by its halter and wetting its nose now and then with a rag soaked in a little water from his flask. Only as dusk fell did he get back into the saddle and push on to reach a well so he could pitch camp for the night. He would stop at times, attracted by some small sign of man's presence: rock carvings or tombs marked with inscriptions corroded by wind and sand. He'd sometimes find the figure of a scorpion cut into the black surface of the flint and, in the immense silence of that valley, the image seemed animated with malevolent energy, with a wild, evil vitality.

One day, just before morning had broken, he came across a wadi which descended from an imposing calcareous massif to his left. He started to make his way up the dry river bed, which soon narrowed to become a deep gully that sliced through the mountainside from top to bottom in a nearly vertical course. Its fast-flowing waters had lain bare layer upon layer of rock which had composed it over millennia. Desmond was amazed at the infinite streaks of red, green, ochre and yellow that marked both sides of the river's passage. The wind which found its way into that narrow gully was sucked in by the play of constantly changing surfaces, and its voice altered as it moved along, like a breath whistling through the pipes of an organ one by one.

All at once, Desmond saw the City of Tombs open before him like an amphitheatre. The fabled Petra, hidden for centuries inside a hollow mountain, this narrow gully the only means of approach. It had been discovered by Johann Ludwig Burckhardt only the century before and had stirred up excitement and admiration in scholars all over the world, although very few of them had ever had the opportunity of seeing it.

Desmond unstrapped his pack and let it drop to the ground, then spurred on his horse at a gallop across the immense basin, passing in front of the monumental tombs carved into the mountainside. Their impressive façades were ornamented by sculpted columns and tympanums in the myriad colours of the rock. The soft undulations in the polychrome layers made them look as though they were immersed in ocean waves. As Desmond's horse flew over the sand which covered the enormous crater, he tried to glimpse what might be inside each one of those empty mausoleums. He listened hard for a sign of life, a breath, coming from one of those silent, yawning stone mouths, but the only sounds to reach his ears were the panting of his steed and its rolling gallop on the sand and stone, echoes bouncing from rock to rock.

He pulled on the reins and stopped, jumping from the saddle. The wind was the only voice now in that millennia-long silence, the high flight of an eagle the only hint of life in the empty, blinding sky. He climbed up onto a rock that rose from the ground like a cliff from the sea and looked slowly all around, while his horse wandered off in search of dry grass to graze on.

'It's here that you last slept, man of the seven tombs, in this secret valley. You were carried off before the valley was discovered, before human voices had the chance to echo between these cliffs. But I shall find the mark you left. I'll sniff out your trail. Enos ben Gad won't have died for nothing.'

Desmond took the saddle from his horse and settled into one of the rock tombs. He laid his blanket on the floor and found a niche for his mess tin, with the silver cutlery that he'd never done without and the silver cup which collapsed into a little round box. He placed his leather haversack with its biscuits, dried meat, dates and water flask where it would be safe from parasites and mice. He took out his pickaxe, shovel and the trowel with its beechwood handle that he'd had crafted especially for him at the hardware shop near the British Museum. He had food, he had his weapons and he was entrenched behind a stone wall: he was ready for action.

That night his campfire blazed at the centre of the wide valley under the vault of the heavens and the white strip of the Milky

Way, which crossed the mouth of the crater from side to side. The realization that the Being he was searching for had slept in that place for centuries was enough to keep his body tense and his mind vigilant, but in the end the infinite peace of that marvellous site prevailed. Desmond Garrett did not enter the mausoleum that he had chosen as a shelter, but slept wrapped in the quiet of the universe, under the mantle of the starry night.

PHILIP LEFT DURA EUROPOS the next morning at dawn after preparing his horse and filling his flask with water from the Euphrates, which he'd boiled in his field pot over the campfire. He left by the western gate, called the Palmyra Gate, heading for the oasis of Tedmor, a journey of four days, he figured. The terrain he would be crossing was completely flat and barren, a hard, yellow wasteland with a few dried shrubs scattered here and there. He decided to avoid the Deir ez Zor road, which was too heavily used. He knew he couldn't trust the bedouin tribes and he wanted his route to remain as secret as possible.

Whenever he spotted the outline of a tent in the distance, he would turn off the trail to give the camp a wide berth, circling around until it was no longer visible on the horizon behind him. He would then make his way slowly back to the trail and proceed straight ahead as long as the light of day allowed.

It was fairly late in the season and the days had become quite short, but Philip took advantage of the last glow of twilight and the first light of dawn. He even continued his journey when he could by the light of the moon, making the most of the chalky luminescence of the salty white ground.

Night was as quiet as day, and the enormous flat space that surrounded him would have seemed completely empty if it hadn't been for the howling of jackals that rose out of nowhere and faded back into nothing when the rare autumn clouds flitted past the moon. He stayed on the right track thanks to his field compass, a gift from his father many, many years before. It was a beautiful instrument of polished brass in a dark brown leather case. Every time he checked his direction he realized that his father was guiding him even then.

All that solitude brought thoughts of his father to mind. What might he be like after so many years spent so far from human society, after all this time spent in a relentless search? What would meeting him be like, if he managed to find him? What would he tell him? What would they say to each other? Would he find the words to ask him how he could have disappeared in such a way, with no warning, without even saying goodbye?

He slept whenever tiredness overwhelmed him. He avoided lighting fires even when he would have been able to gather up a sufficient quantity of twigs and sticks, so as not to attract attention, but he knew that the desert had eyes and ears everywhere, even when it seemed empty. He reached Tedmor on the evening of the fourth day, and he congratulated himself on how well he had succeeded in his solitary navigation.

He'd never seen such a marvel. He rode along the great colonnade and then turned left towards the palm grove that surrounded the spring and the pool. A little boy dressed in a long red tunic had been watching and following him since he'd entered the oasis. Philip stopped suddenly and asked him: 'What do you want?'

'What about you?' replied the boy. 'What do you want?'

'I'm looking for Sheikh Abu el Abd, may God preserve him.'

'Then follow me,' said the boy, heading towards the gigantic Temple of Baal that stood at the western border of the oasis.

The sheikh was inside the temple, sitting on the bench from which he administered justice over his tribe. Philip sat down on the capital of a toppled column and waited until the session had ended. He then approached and said, '*Salam alekhum, al sheikh*, my name is Philip Garrett. Enos ben Gad told me you would be able to give me news of my father.'

The sheikh drew closer and gave him a searching look. 'You are the son of Desmond *nabil*?' he said.

'That's right,' replied Philip

'When did you speak with Enos ben Gad?'

'Five days ago.'

'Were you present at his last hour?'

'I was. But how do you know that he's dead?'

'I know.'

'Enos said that you could tell me where to look for my father.'

'Your father did not mention you to me. Why should I tell you where he is?'

Philip lowered his head. Could his father really persist in keeping his whereabouts a secret ad infinitum? He replied nonetheless, 'Perhaps my father never mentioned me to you, but Enos ben Gad did tell me to come here, otherwise why would I have journeyed so far? It was with his last breath that he said, "Abu el Abd . . . go to Tedmor, he knows." But if you won't speak to me, I'll continue to search for my father on my own. I'll turn over every stone of this wretched desert if I must.' He fell silent, waiting for a reply.

'If you spoke with Enos ben Gad, tell me, what goods does he sell at his market stall at the grand bazaar?'

'Sandalwood. You must ask him for sandalwood.'

'And where does he keep it?'

'Not in the shop. It's in his house, in the patio, in a corner cupboard.'

'Follow me,' said the sheikh.

They went to the tent by the pool and the sheikh had him enter. 'I can trust no one,' he said, inviting his guest to join him. 'Our enemies are everywhere. Is it you who are looking for your father, or did he send for you?'

'I think he has sent for me. But I sometimes have my doubts. I haven't seen him for ten years. I'm simply following a trail he's left for me. But it hasn't helped much. The journey is difficult and the obstacles in my way seem enormous.'

'Do you know what your father is searching for?'

'I do.'

'And you're not afraid?'

'I am afraid.'

'Then why don't you turn back?'

'Because I'm not afraid enough.'

'Your father was here as Enos ben Gad was dying. We heard his soul passing in the wind.'

'But where is my father now?'

'If nothing has stopped him, he is somewhere between here and the City of Tombs.'

'Petra,' said Philip. 'I'll find him.'

COLONEL JOBERT ADVANCED with his men through the scorching desert, hoping to reach a well before nightfall. The landscape had become very different and unfamiliar. Here and there the bones of gigantic animals poked out of the sand, and the ground was covered with an endless expanse of flint, black and shiny, incandescent in the heat.

Captain Bonnier stopped in his tracks. 'Colonel.'

'What is it?'

'Look. On that stone.'

Jobert glanced at the incision. A faceless man, with a Gorgon on his chest.

'The Blemmyae again, Commander.'

Jobert did not reply and spurred his horse on to the head of the column, followed by the captain.

'How much further do you intend to proceed in this direction, Colonel? The well at Bir Akkar is the last we'll be able to draw water from. If we go on for any more than thirty kilometres beyond that point, the men's lives will be at constant risk.'

'Have you ever heard of Kalaat Hallaki, Captain Bonnier?'

Bonnier seemed disconcerted. 'Yes, I have, of course, but I've been led to believe that it is merely a legend.'

'It's no legend, Bonnier, and I will prove it. All that's needed is the courage to venture fifty kilometres beyond the well of Bir Akkar.'

'That's one hundred, of course, if we shouldn't find anything there, and if we haven't found water along the way. You risk the unit's destruction.'

'We have no choice if we want to reach the area we've been asked to explore. We must discover what has happened to the expeditions who have ventured into these lands and have vanished.'

'We'll have to see if we can find enough water at Bir Akkar. Everything depends on that,' said Bonnier.

'Yes. In that case, we will collect sufficient supplies to attempt to reach Kalaat Hallaki.'

'And if Kalaat Hallaki does not exist?'

'It does exist, Bonnier. I'm sure it exists. It's merely well hidden in one of the Wadi Addir gullies.'

It was late afternoon by the time they reached Bir Akkar and Jobert had the water level measured immediately. It was not abundant, but might suffice. He had his men light the sulphur carbide stoves and boil all the water they were able to extract. The next morning he calculated twenty litres of water for each man, a quantity that would be barely enough for four days. It would last if they found Kalaat Hallaki. If not, their fates would be in the hands of God.

They set off. Nothing particular happened for the first two days of their journey. Jobert had ordered his soldiers to economize on water as much as possible, and to save the urine of both the men and animals – they would recycle it if necessary.

On the evening of the third day they came within sight of a wadi that cut across their line of march. The vegetation on the stony bottom was sparse and stunted, but larger trees could be seen further up in the direction of the mountain.

'Do you see that, Bonnier?' said Colonel Jobert. 'Do you know what that means? We'll find water in more than sufficient quantity if we head in that direction.'

They resumed their journey, but before long the vegetation thinned out again and then disappeared completely. Jobert lowered his head; he could feel his men staring at his back, and he began to fear for their lives.

'It's useless for all of us to proceed together,' he said then. 'It would be a waste of water and energy that we can ill afford. Three of us will go on to scout out the terrain. The rest of you will remain here, doing nothing that would increase your drinking and eating needs beyond what is strictly necessary. Don't lose hope, men. I'm sure that we'll find Kalaat Hallaki before dusk. But if you don't see us return by tomorrow, turn back and may God protect you.'

He took a sergeant and a legionnaire with him, and enough water and food for twenty-four hours. They departed in a south-easterly direction, abandoning the wadi bed that seemed to be leading them astray. As he observed the surrounding terrain, Jobert realized that the arid course of the Addir meandered around a vast limestone plateau that emerged here and there from the sand; he estimated that it was many kilometres wide. From the same plateau rose an arcing range of hills that stood out against the south-western horizon. Jobert decided to cross the plateau from one side to another in the hope of finding the wadi again on the other side. The calcareous bedrock would help the groundwater to drain from the hills and to concentrate at the point in which the plateau was immersed once again in the sand. That's where Kalaat Hallaki was to be found.

Jobert and his two companions rode under the blazing sun for hours and hours, but when they were about halfway across the vast limestone plateau, a fiery western wind barred their way with a cloud of dust and sand which formed an impenetrable barrier.

Jobert turned to his men. 'This very phenomenon was described in the reports I've read. Trust me, we can't give up now. Our compass will guide us through the sandstorm. Cover your faces and eyes and we'll go on,' he said.

The men dampened their handkerchiefs and knotted them in front of their noses and mouths and followed their commander, who was urging his reluctant mount into that dense wall of dust raised by the incessant wind, which obscured the sky. They advanced slowly for nearly three hours without any change in the situation. The dust was as fine as talc. It dried their nostrils and throats and penetrated into their lungs, provoking a continuous, hacking cough.

Jobert looked back and realized that the horse of one of his men was about to collapse, overcome by strain and thirst. 'Onward!' he shouted. 'We mustn't lose heart! Onward!' But the hissing wind carried his voice off, far away. He felt doomed. He thought of his men, waiting in vain. They would surely all die in a futile attempt to get back to Bir Akkar.

He turned forwards again, to forge on in the only direction which left him any hope, and couldn't believe his eyes. As if by some miracle, the cloud of sand was dispersing. Step after step, the driving wind was becoming a gentle breeze and a vision appeared before his eyes. A green, sheltered valley, an expanse of fertile fields and lush palm groves. Pomegranates, figs, grapes. Canals intertwined around a pool as blue as the sky and as clear as crystal, and atop a granite cliff stood a colossal fortress: Kalaat Hallaki!

'My God!' he said, his voice cracking with emotion. 'We've made it.'

They descended into the valley at a slow pace as the fresh, damp air seemed to quench their thirst and to reward them for braving that hell. They crossed green fields where animals were browsing: herds of sheep and long-maned mares with their colts. They stopped at a rocky outcrop from which a jet of water spilled into a basalt basin. An old man sitting on a dry palm trunk did not even seem to notice their presence.

'We have crossed the desert and we are tormented by thirst,' said Colonel Jobert. 'We come in peace and ask if we may draw water.'

The old man replied in Arabic with a strange accent, as if he were used to speaking a completely different language.

'You may take water if you come in peace,' he said.

'We come in peace,' repeated the officer. 'Thank you, from the depths of my heart, thank you.'

The men dismounted and caught the water in their hands, bringing it avidly to their mouths. They washed the dust from their faces and hair and watered their exhausted horses. It was like living in a dream.

'I have other companions, tormented by thirst as well, and by hunger. They are beyond the barrier of wind,' he said to the old man. 'May I bring them here as well? Their lives are in danger.'

'You may bring them here,' said the old man, 'if they come in peace.'

The two legionnaires let their horses graze, watered them again and then filled their flasks with fresh water before they departed.

'We will be here tomorrow by dusk,' they promised.

'Good luck,' said Colonel Jobert. 'I'll wait for you here.'

'Who are you?' asked the old man.

'We are French soldiers,' replied Colonel Jobert.

'What are the French?' asked the old man.

Jobert lowered his head, realizing that in that place he was a human being and nothing else.

When the sun began to set, the old man said to him: 'You may eat my bread and drink my wine and sleep in my house, if you like.'

'I am grateful for your hospitality,' said Jobert. 'I am very tired and I am a stranger to this valley. I have no place to go.'

But as he was speaking, his attention was drawn by something moving up on the bastions of Kalaat Hallaki. The figure of a woman stood out against the darkening sky, the veils that covered her fluttering in the warm evening air. Jobert was fascinated and took a few steps back to be able to see her better.

The woman moved slowly along the bastions until she reached the southern edge of the crenellated battlements. There she stopped and suddenly raised her song to the heavens. Her voice rose in daring flight towards the celestial vault and then swept across the valley, as clear and sparkling as spring rain, joining with the evening breeze that wafted among the palm groves and the golden vineyards, chasing the solemn flight of the falcon which soared over the castle's towers. Then all at once the magic was shattered. Like a stone upsetting the surface of a pond, a scream tore through the last note, contorting the song into a terrifying, inhuman sound, the voice of horror greater than any imagining. Agony capable of destroying the infinite peace of that time of day and that marvellous place.

Jobert listened numbly. When he turned the old man was standing behind him.

'My God, what was that?'

The old man's head dropped but he didn't say a word.

'Please,' said the officer, 'tell me how such a melodious song can become such a frenzied scream.'

'What you hear is the song of Altair, the bride of Rasaf. One day long ago, while she was journeying through the desert to her father's oasis, she was captured by the men without a face . . .'

Jobert started and his mind was suddenly filled with nightmarish images of figures carved into stone, faceless beings with a Gorgon on their chests.

'Rasaf suffered terrible wounds and lost many men to free her, but he brought her back in this condition. She recognizes no one. She doesn't even know who she is. Every once in a while, towards evening, she goes up to the castle bastions and raises her song . . . her cry of despair. Rasaf is hopelessly in love with her and can't resign himself to her fate. He awaits the day in which the light of knowledge will shine from the desert, so he can take her there and heal her.'

'I don't understand,' said Jobert. 'What is this light?'

'Where are you going?' asked the old man.

'South.'

'Then perhaps you will see it, but you will have to venture

into the Sand of Ghosts . . . If you do, beware the people of the sands.'

'Do you mean . . . the Blemmyae?'

The old man nodded his head deeply. 'They hide in the sand like scorpions and when they catch up with you it is too late. If you should capture one of them, remember that you must never remove the black cloth that hides his face. Don't do it for any reason.' He fell still for a few moments, then raised his gaze again to the castle bastions. He waited until the screaming had softened into a heartbroken lament, then turned to Colonel Jobert.

'Turn back, if you can,' he said, 'and forget Kalaat Hallaki.'

# 10

RASAF SAT OPPOSITE HIS bride as her maidservants prepared her for the night. They undressed her, lowered her into a large tub of bronze and poured perfumed water over her dark limbs. When they had bathed and dried her, they laid her down on her bed and gave her a potion to drink, then left.

Rasaf remained there in contemplation, his fiery, tear-filled eyes caressing her face and body, but the woman was as cold and still as a statue.

'The day is drawing closer,' he whispered in her ear. 'When the moment comes I will bring you before the light that gives knowledge and you will go back to being what you once were . . . the way you were, my love.'

He sat on the bed next to her, holding her hand until he saw her close her eyes, until he heard the soft, regular sound of her breathing as she gave herself up to sleep. He left then and walked down the long corridor that ended in a staircase that led up to the bastions. The sky was full of stars and the galaxy was suspended over the oasis, as light as a sigh. The constellation of the Scorpion glittered before him like a crown of diamonds over the Sand of Ghosts.

Just then he saw a cloud of white dust approaching the oasis from the north. A man in uniform jumped on his horse and rode off at a gallop in that direction.

Rasaf turned to the commander of the guard patrolling the battlements. 'Who are they?' he asked.

'Soldiers of the desert. They've asked for food and water. They want to cross the Sand of Ghosts.'

'Do they know what awaits them?' asked Rasaf.

'They do,' replied the commander.

Rasaf scanned the shadows to estimate the strength of the squad that was just joining the man on horseback. 'Give them what they need,' he said, and walked away.

THE NEXT DAY, Colonel Jobert reviewed his column and ensured that all containers had been filled with water and that the foodstuffs had been well packed and sealed to protect them from dust, then gave the order to depart.

The old man was sitting by the spring and he watched them ride off. They hadn't listened to his advice; they were very obstinate men indeed.

The column left the oasis and Jobert saw the green fields gradually dry up as they proceeded south, until the vegetation disappeared completely and was replaced by an endless sweep of burning sand. The topographer who rode at his side took a map from his saddlebag, with the intention of marking the features of that unexplored land, in order to establish topographical points to be used as reference, but the expanse just became flatter and more empty, disturbed only by the rolling surface of the dunes.

At the end of the second day, the atmosphere became darker, and dust clouds appeared on the horizon, swirling and writhing and swelling at the top like mushrooms. There were just a few at first, but as the column advanced they seemed to multiply until they created a bizarre forest of changing, dancing shapes which gave an unsettled, eerie look to the landscape.

'The Sand of Ghosts,' murmured Captain Bonnier. His face was ashen, his jaw clenched.

'What we're seeing is a common enough natural phenomenon, Captain. And a manifest explanation for the name that the inhabitants of the oasis have given to this territory. The whirling dust looks like . . . spirits, frolicking at the horizon . . .' Jobert fell silent for a few moments as the atmosphere became even more oppressive, then he spoke again. 'I would say that it's quite an interesting effect, and that it might prove very educational to study the meteorological causes behind it.' He turned to the topographer. 'What do you say, Patin?'

His subordinate gave a faint smile, without a clue about how to answer. When he saw that the colonel was awaiting his reply, he said, 'Well, Commander, I would say that the phenomenon may be caused by an unusually large quantity of rising air currents that the particularly strong radiant energy tends to force upwards, given the total lack of natural obstacles . . .'

'What are you saying, Patin!' objected Captain Bonnier. 'We've crossed the desert thousands of times under every possible and imaginable meteorological condition and we've never seen anything like this. I think we should turn back. We have no hope of surviving in such an environment, if we insist on continuing in this direction.'

Jobert turned towards him with an irritated expression. 'I didn't ask for your opinion, Bonnier, and our mission is precisely to continue in this direction, in order to discover once and for all what is happening here . . . Those dust devils may even be part of the problem. We will proceed with all the required caution, we will not unnecessarily expose ourselves to danger, but we must seek to understand what it is we are up against.'

Captain Bonnier did not open his mouth again and thus their journey proceeded in complete silence, but he continued to glance around nervously, as though danger was threatening from every side.

The terrain they were covering was bleak and unchanging, and Jobert realized that they would soon no longer be able to continue during the day, given the intolerable heat. As soon as the sun appeared on the horizon, streams of fire poured over the dunes and stony ground and, before an hour had passed, the air caught fire as well, becoming a scorching plasma that burned their throats and nostrils and took their breath away. And the dust demons continued to twist and turn on the horizon, as if the column had not advanced by a single metre.

'Are you still convinced of your meteorological theory, Patin?' asked Captain Bonnier.

Patin did not answer, and Jobert held his tongue as well. The soldiers followed without saying a word, because their throats were parched and because their fatigue was so great that they had no energy for anything else.

The night of the third day, Jobert called his men to a halt right after dusk and personally assigned the sentries to their posts as the others arranged their beds and prepared to eat a very meagre evening meal. Captain Bonnier, who was always so attentive to every feature of the territory they were crossing, failed to see – in the darkness that descended almost immediately over their camp – the scorpion carved on a rock jutting out of the ground. Nor did he see, half-buried under the dunes, the bones and weapons of ancient soldiers corroded by the wind and sand.

It was nearly two in the morning when Captain Bonnier's sleep was disturbed by the sensation of having heard a suspicious sound. He saw a strange glow off in the distance, a reddish light like that cast by a fire, burning behind the dunes that blocked their view to the south. He realized that the sentries had seen it as well and were about to wake the colonel. He signalled for them to stay at their posts and crept close to Jobert himself.

'Commander, look. Down there.'

Jobert jumped up and went to a small rise in the ground to be able to see the strange phenomenon better. 'What could it be?' he asked.

'I don't know,' replied Captain Bonnier. 'Maybe some kind of refracted light . . . I can't think of anything else.'

'Yes, perhaps you're right, Bonnier, a phenomenon caused by refraction. Calm the sentries, will you, and let's get back to sleep. We'll sound reveille an hour before dawn. Beginning tomorrow, we'll proceed for three hours in the morning and three hours towards evening. During the day we'll build a shelter and remain at rest in the shade to save on water and energy. The daily ration of water is four litres a head. If we don't find a well in three days' time, we'll turn back.'

Bonnier spoke to the sentries and tried to reassure them with a calm, controlled explanation. He lay down again but did not close his eyes. His nerves were tense, straining to pick up any possible sign of danger from that treacherous land. The only sound he heard, some time before dawn, was the strange twittering of an unknown animal, but he could see nothing in the thick darkness that rose beyond the camp.

The odd red halo at the horizon had faded away and was just faintly visible. Bonnier managed to convince himself that it must have been, as he had hypothesized, some strange phenomenon of light refraction and, overwhelmed by fatigue, he dropped off for a few minutes into a deep sleep.

He woke with a start to the anguished screams of the sentries, who had been attacked without warning by swarms of marauders. They were shooting out of the sand all around the camp, armed with scythes fixed to their forearms, which they wielded to inflict devastating wounds. Bonnier took one look at their hooded faces, the repugnant tattoos on their chests, their bizarre weapons and had no doubts. 'The Blemmyae!' he cried out.

Jobert was already in the middle of the camp, sabre unsheathed and pistol in hand. He was yelling at the top of his lungs, 'Form up! Men! Quickly! Square off!'

But his men were unable to assemble because the enemy were everywhere, falling upon them from all directions. They faced their assailants one on one, but were often run through from behind as yet another enemy sprang from the sands.

Some of them realized that being on horseback might give them an advantage and rushed to mount their horses. Although the steeds had often been used in battle and were inured to the sound of gunfire, they reacted to those creatures as if they were surrounded by ferocious carnivores. They neighed loudly in terror, rearing and kicking, and bolted off.

Only about thirty of the men managed to draw up in a square formation around Jobert, including Captain Bonnier. Shoulder to shoulder in double file, the first kneeling and those behind them standing, they fired unceasingly at the enemy, picking them off with deadly precision, but the Blemmyae seemed to have inexhaustible energy and vitality. Shot once or even twice, they continued to advance, collapsing only when they were practically drained of blood. Some of them had circled around the other legionnaires who had been cut off from the formation and they lunged at them in packs, like beasts falling upon their prey. The screams of the victims were so bloodcurdling that Jobert, imagining that the monsters were tearing them to pieces alive, gave his men orders to shoot any comrade who was under attack or who had been snatched away from the formation.

The fight was unequal now and, although the ground around him was scattered with the bodies of the Blemmyae, Jobert realized he had only a few moments of life left to him. He reloaded his pistol constantly, fiercely determined not to be taken alive. The enemy were so close that he was using his sabre now. He had to run them through, repeatedly, from side to side, even after they'd been shot, before one of them would fall.

They did not cry out, not even when they were fatally wounded. A squeaking sound was all they ever made, more terrifying than the most excruciating scream.

Bonnier fell, his arms lopped off and his belly ripped open, and then Patin, decapitated by a single swipe of one of those lethal scythes. Jobert's soul was filled with horror, his head was bursting and his heart pounding so hard he thought he would suffocate. He had never felt this way before, not even in the midst of the most furious battle.

One after another of his last soldiers fell, and he thought his time had come, but just then a burst of rifle fire tore through the air, and then another, and another. The desert resounded with a powerful cry and with the galloping of hundreds of horses. He turned slowly as if in a dream and saw a squad of horsemen wearing light blue *barrakans* with a purple standard at their head: the warriors of Kalaat Hallaki!

They attacked the Blemmyae frontally in such a close formation that there was no space between one horse and another, unleashing a barrage of firepower so intense that no corner of the desert that lay before them was sheltered from their shots. Jobert was miraculously unharmed while the troops passed to his left and right, driving back the enemy. When they were out of bullets they took their halberds in hand and strung the scorpionmen up like fish. They dragged them over the sand for metres and metres, waiting until they went into spasm to extract their blades. They killed every last one of them: no one escaped, no one surrendered or laid down his arms. The warriors then grouped around their leader, shouting and cheering. At a sign from him, they jumped onto their mounts and again rode back to where they had come from.

Colonel Jobert knew he had to return and decided to leave immediately. He gave a last glance at the battlefield but did not notice that one of the thousands of dunes stretching out to the horizon had a shape that was too perfect. By the time he had disappeared over the northern horizon, the wind had bared the hemispherical mound and the sun sculpted its smooth basalt surface.

It took him nearly four days to reach Kalaat Hallaki. When he saw the oasis sparkling like a jewel with its glittering canals and springs, the fruit-laden palm trees waving their leaves towards the sky, the children frolicking in the pools, he could not hold back his tears.

'What will you do now?' asked the old man when he saw him, tattered and bleeding, his face burnt and his lips cracked. 'How can you go back alone? How will you explain the loss of all your men?'

'I have fulfilled my mission, at this terrible price,' replied Jobert. 'Now I know what is hidden in that stretch of the desert . . . and to think that I refused to believe . . .'

'To believe in what?'

'In a legend. The legend of the Blemmyae. But, my God, how is such a thing possible?'

'You know nothing,' said the old man, 'and your mission has failed. You have lost all your men but you have nothing to report.'

'Nothing?' Jobert said, turning towards him with wild eyes. 'I saw faceless monsters who lurk in the sand like scorpions, capable of striking out with deadly strength even after they'd been hit by two, three bullets . . . and you say that I didn't complete my mission?'

'No,' said the old man. 'You don't truly know what those beings are, and how they can live on such barren land, without water, plants or animals. You don't know who they are, or what they think, or if they have feelings. If they feel pain or despair.'

'They're monsters. They're nothing but monsters.'

'We're all monsters. We who live at Kalaat Hallaki can afford to have noble sentiments because we have everything we need. The blazing sun is tempered by the shade of the trees and the cool waters, we harvest our fields three times a year, we have a choice of fresh, abundant foods, the sky is clear, our women and children are beautiful . . . You stayed a mere week in that hell and there is more hate and savagery in your eyes than you have ever felt in your whole life. The Blemmyae have been confined to that furnace since the beginning of time . . .'

'I'm familiar with this sort of philosophical digression, my friend. I chose to leave the empty quarrels and gossiping of the city to live in the austere immensity of the desert. I'm a man worthy of your respect.'

'You are,' agreed the old man. 'That's why I'm telling you that you are still far from the truth. Have you ever heard of the Tower of Solitude?'

Jobert shook his head.

'That's where you'll find the answer, if you ever get there. The tower is beyond the Sand of Ghosts, at the very end of the sea of sand, but if you want my advice, forget everything, even Kalaat Hallaki. This war is too tough for even the most inveterate soldier.'

Jobert did not reply, overcome by emotions too diverse and too strong.

'Sleep now,' said the old man. 'Rest. Tomorrow I'll give you abundant food and water so that you can cross the wall of dust and the arid lands that separate you from your territory. Forget what you have seen. Tell your commanders that your men died of hunger and thirst. Fight your battles against men who look like you do and have the same weapons. Forget Kalaat Hallaki and the Sand of Ghosts for ever.'

DESMOND GARRETT WAS SLEEPING soundly under a starry sky in the middle of the wide valley. The dying embers of his campfire cast a faint glow on his face and on the sparse bushes around the clearing. His horse was grazing nearby, abruptly raising his head and cocking his ears now and then when there was a rustling in the undergrowth or the hoot of some nocturnal bird.

He suddenly snorted and kicked at a rock, letting out a low whinny of alarm.

Desmond threw back his blanket and jerked into a sitting position, looking all around. Silence and tranquillity reigned. Even the birds were sleeping in the niches they'd found between the rocks or inside the tombs dotting the mountainside. His attention was attracted to one tomb in particular, a monumental mausoleum with an impressive decorated pediment resting on a row of Corinthian columns in ochre-streaked brown stone. With every passing moment, a reddish glimmer became more apparent in the inner chamber, as if someone had lit a fire there.

Perhaps a shepherd had entered the valley to find shelter for the night, thought Desmond, but the hour was late and he could not understand why he would have waited so long to start a fire. The light was becoming stronger now, setting the inside of the tomb aglow, flames flickering outward as if licking at the columns. The tomb opening looked like the mouth of a furnace. Or the gate to hell.

Desmond had already got to his feet and drawn closer, to try to understand what was causing that strange phenomenon, when he saw a black figure wrapped in a cloak standing out against the red glare. The cloak fell to the ground and a sabre flashed in the hand of the mysterious man.

Desmond bent to unsheathe his own scimitar and continued to advance slowly towards the tomb entrance. The other man turned his head to face him and Desmond recognized him: it was Selznick!

'It's you, you dog!' he shouted, and lunged forward with a downward slash of his weapon.

The other side-stepped the blade and responded with a sudden thrust; Desmond just barely managed to avoid a direct blow to his chest by twisting to the side. The sabre grazed his flesh under the armpit and blood began to pour down his side. He could feel its heat on his skin and smell its cloying odour in his nostrils. The wound intensified his energy because he had no idea how badly he was hurt and did not know how much longer he had to live. He had to strike back and kill his detested enemy.

Desmond launched an all-out attack, lashing out again and again until his adversary began to draw back. But as Desmond was seeking a way to stab him in the exact spot where his blade had already penetrated once, he felt his strength leaving him. He focused all of his hate into a single thrust and drove the blade into his enemy's side. Selznick's face twisted into a mask of pain as Desmond struck out again and again.

The clanging of the blades as they collided with such violence echoed between the walls of the valley and roared inside the tomb itself. But every swing, every jab, was slower, more sluggish. The two bodies clutching at each other in the ultimate struggle seemed to be floating in the air now, weightless, even as their movements became more and more arduous.

Selznick's voice seemed louder than ever, nonetheless, as he shouted, 'We'll see each other in hell, Desmond! We'll finish this fight in hell!'

Desmond felt Selznick slipping away from him; his foe was losing a great deal of blood from the reopened wound and was retreating towards the mausoleum's back wall. Desmond couldn't follow, couldn't finish him off with the one last blow that was needed. His limbs were stiff, wooden, no longer responding to his will. Not even the hate he felt was sufficient to instil strength into them. With a last, impossible spurt of energy he forced himself to get up and make his way down the long corridor at the end of the funeral chamber.

He found himself inside a vault carved into the solid rock. Drops of water seeped from the many cracks in the walls. It felt refreshing at first, but then he understood with horror that the drops were blood, not water. The entire mountain was bleeding on him.

The insistent neighing of his horse woke him and Desmond scrambled up from his bed, somewhere between waking and sleeping, and brought his hands to his face. It was wet, from the rain! Clouds had gathered over the valley, driven by a strong western wind, and the sheer walls of the immense basin were lit up now by flashes of lightning. He ducked into one of the tombs to seek cover from the storm. The same one he had seen in his dream.

It was dark and silent, now.

Desmond lit his lantern, took a look around and was gripped by a strong, precise sensation. The Fateh's words came back to him: 'The beast in you will sniff him out.'

He said, out loud, 'This is where he is, then. This is where he slept in his sixth tomb.'

He took the lantern and went in, past the great stone façade. At the back, in what had once been the funeral chamber, there were signs that the room had been reused as a chapel in the Christian era. The same circumstance as he'd found in Aleppo. Perhaps these ancient believers had sensed the traces of an enemy presence and felt they had to neutralize it?

On the back wall, amid a number of pagan motifs, he saw a painted crucifix. The wound on Christ's side was in relief, looking like living flesh.

'The beast in you will sniff him out,' he repeated to himself. His hand mechanically reached for his belt and he took out a long dagger. What he was about to do revolted him and his forehead beaded up with sweat in that airless atmosphere. He drew close to the painting. Although his posture had been stiffened by death, this Christ had the serene expression of one who has found peace after a long martyrdom. Desmond could hear the sound of thunder in the distance. It was raining upon Petra, a winter rain, a useless rain that would not help anything to grow.

His features hardened at the moment in which he drove the blade into the wound in Christ's side, and he felt something snap inside of him. He knew that he had cast off another of the moorings that had once kept him anchored to the rest of humanity.

A sharp click shook him from that painful tension. He thought with relief that his intuition had been correct, but nothing happened. He tapped the wall to check for hollows, using the round pommel at the end of his dagger, but his raps sounded as dry as if he were hitting solid rock. Perhaps he'd been fooled; he'd let a dream get the better of him and now he had no idea of the direction in which to go.

Desmond turned back towards the monumental gate of the tomb and leaned against its gigantic columns to contemplate the rain falling on the valley. He listened to it pelting against the rocks and the ruins of the vanished city.

In that atmosphere outside of time and place, he imagined that he could see his wife rising up at the centre of the valley under the silvery rain. He imagined her walking towards him without even touching the ground, a light gown clinging to her body as if she were a deity sculpted by Phidias.

For years now, ever since he had chosen to leave civilization, he had grown accustomed to seeing her in his dreams, to calling up her ghost and seeing her appear like a desert flower after a rainstorm, but his absorbed contemplation was abruptly broken by a noise like that of two boulders grinding one upon the other. It was coming from behind him.

Desmond turned around and saw, to his great amazement, a crack snaking through the plaster on which the crucifix was painted. It split open above the cross and at its sides, and then the entire portion of the wall began to tilt inwards like a drawbridge, revealing a dark opening that descended into the centre of the mountain.

He held out his lantern to light up the tunnel that branched off from the wall. He looked down and saw that beneath his feet a deep trench had opened. The painted plaster slab stretched over the void like a bridge. To cross it he would have to tread on the crucifix. 'This certainly won't stop me,' he thought, reasoning that the mechanism must have been devised in ancient times for those who lived their religion as superstition. Yet he couldn't help but recall how he had become imprisoned in the crypt under the mosque in Aleppo and so, before he proceeded, he stuck two large wedges of stone between the base of the painted slab and the sides of the opening so that no one could close it behind him. He tied a rope around his waist and got out his pickaxe. Then he went forward, holding his lantern high to illuminate the passage in front of him.

Desmond considered trying to balance his weight on either side of the slab, but he saw that he would only risk falling into the abyss yawning at his feet. He had no choice but to walk over the body and the face of the sacred image. The tunnel continued with a slightly downward slope, and he began to make his way along the passage at a slow pace, taking care to light up every centimetre of the ceiling, walls and floor. At a certain point he saw several asymmetrical niches off to his left containing images of Romanized Nabataean divinities carved into the limestone.

The smell of burning petroleum that came from his lantern stagnated in the heavy, still air, creating a suffocating atmosphere. Rounding a bend in the tunnel, he found himself in front of a massive structure unlike anything he had ever seen in his life.

In the middle of a vast chamber was a cubical structure, completely carved in stone, as tall as the ceiling. A round opening in its front wall was closed by a millstone. There were no other chambers or niches, nor were there any other passages leading out of the main room. The walls were bare and rough, cut from solid rock. He examined the system of closure attentively; the millstone had simply been rolled along and inserted into the wall opening. The words of the Gospel came to his mind: 'They rolled a stone in front of the entrance and left.' This is how he imagined the tomb of Jesus.

He approached and saw that the track that had been used to slide the stone forward was nearly flat and that the stone itself was not very large. He slowly nudged it sideways using the lever on his crowbar, and once the entrance was free he placed a quantity of debris from the floor into the track to block the stone in place, making sure that there was no way its weight could make it slip forwards.

He entered and found himself inside a chamber measuring four metres by four, at the centre of which there was a Nabataean sarcophagus of painted wood in the Egyptian style. The paintings depicted peasants working in the fields, sowing or pushing ploughs. Others held sickles and were harvesting wheat or tying it into bundles. There were pastoral scenes on the other side: flocks at pasture, sheep being shorn, women weaving cloth and carpets on their looms.

He forced the lid with the tip of his dagger and lifted his lantern to look inside. The coffin was empty, but the bottom was crawling with scorpions.

They were mostly females, with clusters of young, their bodies still transparent, clinging to their backs. They'd found an undisturbed, well-sheltered place for reproducing. But how had they got in?

Desmond spilled a little of the petroleum from his lamp onto the bottom of the sarcophagus, then lit a match and dropped it in. The decaying wood caught fire all at once, in a huge blaze that lit up the funeral chamber as bright as day. Amid the hiss of the flames, he could hear the crackling of the scorpions' bodies as they burst, and he recalled being told that a scorpion hemmed in by a ring of fire will kill itself by injecting its body with its own poison.

He watched the fire as if hypnotized by that explosion of light. He had destroyed the sixth tomb! Only the seventh was left: the last, the most remote, the most hidden, the most difficult. An impregnable fortress, watched over and defended by formidable forces.

The Fortress of Solitude!

Desmond turned to retrace his steps and what he saw changed his elation into the deepest despair.

Sand.

The access tunnel was full of sand, which was pouring slowly into the underground chamber, spreading out in the shape of a fan across the floor. He rushed forward to search for a way to get out, but he sank in all the way up to his waist. He floundered through the river of sand, trying desperately to make his way back up the ramp, but the sand was sucking him down, making every movement incredibly difficult. This time he really was in a trap.

He looked at the rope, the pickaxe, the steel crowbar – objects that his experience in the Aleppo tomb had suggested. All completely useless. What an idiot! He'd been tricked into thinking that what had got him out of trouble the first time would work a second. The components of this new trap were totally incongruous: solid rock and sand. Two elements which were the exact opposite of each other, yet equally unyielding. Whoever had designed the sixth tomb had factored in the presumptions of the hunter who would succeed in destroying the fifth. But . . . where had the sand come from, if the ceiling and the walls of the tunnel were carved into solid rock?

The slab with the crucifix! Moving the slab must have activated some sort of delayed mechanism that poured sand into the tunnel from a reservoir up above. And he, Desmond Garrett, the last hunter, was a prisoner in the bottom of an hourglass. When the lower compartment was filled with sand, the monstrous machine would mark the hour of his death.

He looked at the tunnel. The top of it was still open and a fair amount of air was flowing through it, but there was nothing along the passage that he could grasp on to, nothing that would help him get out. He tried tapping the walls again with his pickaxe, to see if he could find some hidden compartment or crumbling stone, but all his efforts were in vain.

He would stop every now and then, sitting in the corner furthest from the opening to regain his strength and catch his breath, hoping for some last-minute solution: a stone, a chunk of clay, anything that he might use to block the passage and stop the flow of sand. Might it even stop on its own? How could any rock basin designed to hold and feed in the sand still be as smooth and clean as a glass jar after all these centuries? Might there not have been some landslide, or an infiltration of some sort? After all, Petra was built of carboniferous rock, which dissolved in water. And plenty of water had fallen over twenty centuries in a land so vulnerable to erosion. It was raining at that very moment . . .

He thought of Philip.

HE SAW A FLICKERING LIGHT for a moment in that total darkness, like a fire blazing at the end of the valley. But how could a fire be burning there after an hour of rain? He urged his horse in that direction at a trot, careful not to let him stumble on the jutting rocks, and watched as the light flared up again, coming from some kind of hollow in the ground, and then died out.

The storm had subsided a little but was not over, and Philip took shelter under a rocky outcrop near to where he had seen the flashing light. He began to dry off his horse with the sponge that he always kept in the saddlebag.

He suddenly heard a muffled but distinct sound, a kind of dull pounding that seemed to be coming from the hollow. He lit his lantern to inspect the bottom. There was a hole there all right and that's where the pounding was coming from. He took a rope from his saddle, tied one end to a dry acacia trunk standing at the edge of the hollow and cautiously lowered himself down towards the hole. The sound was even louder now, but Philip could still not tell what it was. It would sometimes stop for a few minutes and then start up again.

He felt that he needed to know who or what was making that noise. He leaned over the edge of the hole and shouted in Arabic, 'Who's down there?' He waited, then shouted again even louder, 'Is someone down there?'

Desmond stopped the pickaxe in mid-stroke and strained to hear. The voice repeated, 'Is anyone down there?'

'Philip!' he said, thinking he'd gone mad. Then, as loudly as he could, he shouted back, 'Philip! Philip!'

'Father!' replied his son's voice. It was muffled and distorted, but he was sure it was Philip's voice.

Desmond started shouting again, pronouncing one word at a time so he was sure he'd be understood. 'Philip, it's your father! I'm trapped in an underground room that's filling up with sand. From where you are, can you see what's beneath you?'

'Wait!' replied Philip.

He dropped slowly down into the hole. When his foothold felt secure, he let go with his hands and lit the lantern. Below him was a big funnel-shaped bowl, a seemingly natural structure that had been artificially modified in order to create a smooth surface down which a large quantity of sand was pouring. The hole at its bottom was partially clear, for a space of about fifty centimetres. So that was where the reflection of the fire that had caught his attention had been coming from, and from where he could hear his father's voice.

He shouted, 'The sand is coming from here! There's a big reservoir but I can't tell how deep it is. The sand is pouring down towards an opening. I could try to descend with a rope.'

'How long is the rope?' asked his father.

'About fifteen metres.'

'That's not enough. You wouldn't even get within sight of me. The corridor leading to the room I'm in is at least eight metres long on its own.'

'I'm going to try to get down to you anyway,' said Philip.

'No! Don't do it, for the love of God! You would only sink into the sand.'

'How did you get down there?'

'From the valley of Petra. From the big stone tomb with the Corinthian portico.'

'Can I try to get in that way?'

'No, it wouldn't work. You'd have to get past the sand and that's impossible from there. The tunnel is two-thirds full!'

'Damn!' cursed Philip. 'There's got to be a way. Don't you have anything with you?'

'A pickaxe, a steel crowbar and a rope. All useless in this situation.'

'No, wait,' said Philip. 'I've just had an idea. How long is your rope?'

'About ten metres.'

'Tie it to something heavy. The crowbar. Maybe I've found the way to get down.'

'Be careful!' shouted his father. 'If you fall into the sand we're both lost!'

'Don't worry,' said Philip. 'We'll make it.'

The idea of rescuing his father from a trap like this made

Philip euphoric. He would show him now! After all those years of trying to solve impossible conundrums, all those years of trying to earn his father's esteem.

He climbed up out of the hole and went to examine the acacia tree at the rim, where he had tied his rope. As he had thought, the trunk was much longer than the opening at the bottom of the hole was wide. He took an axe from the gear he'd packed onto his horse and began to hack at the tree's roots. He had heard that acacia wood was hard, but he would never have imagined how hard. It was like trying to cut stone.

He put everything he had into the task, realizing that his father's life might be hanging by a thread; even a few minutes could make all the difference. Finally, the last root was cut and the trunk, about twenty centimetres in diameter, fell to the ground. Philip tied one end of the rope to the centre of the trunk with a double slipknot and secured the other end to his waist. He dragged the trunk down and fitted it across the hole at the bottom. He tied a handkerchief over his mouth and stopped up his ears and then began to lower himself down. When he touched sand, he let his arms and legs slide over it so he wouldn't sink in. He slipped through the bottom opening and into the access tunnel, closing his eyes and holding his breath as though he were diving.

He was buried under cascading sand, and an atrocious sensation of suffocation and panic threatened to overwhelm him, but he didn't lose hold of the rope and managed to pull himself back up to the surface with immense effort. His eyelids and ears were full of sand and his heart felt as if it would burst, but as soon as he had his head out and drew a breath, he knew he would make it. He let himself slip forward, holding the rope tightly. After the first stretch he found he could control his movements much better because the speed of the sand had greatly diminished. He was almost at the point where the tunnel opened onto the underground chamber when he felt a sharp tug:

the rope was stretched taut and he could go no further. He tried to wipe his eyelids as best he could before opening his eyes and he finally saw his father. He was just four or five metres in front of him. The sand had already flooded the entire room and was at his waist.

'Throw me your rope!' Philip shouted.

Desmond tossed the crowbar from which his own rope dangled. After missing it a couple of times, Philip managed to grab it and tie it onto his.

'We'll go up now!' he said. 'Cover your mouth with a handkerchief and try to protect your eyes and ears. This is the hard part. We have to make our way up the stream of falling sand. There's no alternative!'

'I'll follow you,' replied Desmond. 'Go on.'

Philip began to haul himself back up on the rope. It wasn't too difficult, until he reached the cascade. He took a deep breath and let himself go into the onrushing sand. He thought his chest would explode. It was impossible to breathe and the exertion required to go on was tremendous. He forced himself to think of all the obstacles he'd overcome to get where he was, and to think of the man dragging himself so laboriously behind him. He tightened his grip, knowing that his father's life was in his hands. The sand grated his bare hands and got under his clothes, weighing him down and creating an incredible amount of friction. But he had calculated the height of the sandfall on his way down and he knew that each time he managed to put one hand over another he was twenty centimetres closer to the top.

When his head finally burst from the sand inside the reservoir he was close to passing out. He ripped the handkerchief from his mouth and took two or three rapid, deep breaths. The oxygen restored life and lucidity. He turned around, as he continued to hoist himself upwards, and shouted, 'Stop before the sandfall, father! Did you hear me? Don't try to get through the sandfall!'

'I heard you,' answered his father.

'Good! Wait there until I'm out completely. Don't start to pull yourself up until you feel me tugging the rope. That way I can help you from here.'

'All right, I'll wait.'

As Philip made his way up, he saw that the top part of the reservoir was already free of sand. He pushed off the nearly clear surface and hoisted himself up to the acacia trunk, which had performed its task as an anchor perfectly. He was outside, finally, and the last drops of rain from the storm were an immense relief. The sight of the stars glittering here and there among the clouds reminded him of the sublime verses with which Dante concluded his *Inferno*: 'Thence we came forth to see again the stars.' He turned back towards the hole, pulled the rope taut and gave a sharp tug.

'I'm coming up!' shouted his father.

Philip began to pull with all his might, bracing his legs against the acacia trunk. He could soon feel that his father had come past the critical point, but he continued to pull nonetheless to help him up. When he saw his head emerging from the hole, he couldn't believe it was true. He stretched out his hand and helped him up and into the night air. They were on their feet, facing each other.

'Hello, father,' said Philip with a calm voice.

Desmond wiped the sand from his eyes and face, then said, 'I'm happy to see you, Philip.'

Philip had tried so many times to imagine this meeting with his father and what he would say to him. He had thought of reproaching him for all his absurd behaviour, or of calling him a bastard for forcing Philip to follow him in a stupid game of hide-and-seek. Or else, he had thought, he would punch him first and then hold him in a long embrace, like Ulysses and Telemachus.

Instead, all he had managed to say was, 'Hello, father.'

'Let's go down to the valley,' said Desmond. 'I've got bread in my bag, some salt and olive oil. And maybe even a drop of whisky.'

'But, father,' said Philip, 'it's three in the morning, not time for dinner.'

'Yes, it is,' said Desmond. 'I've destroyed the sixth tomb and you're here with me. You do know what I'm talking about, don't you?'

'I do,' said Philip.

The rain had stopped. The smell of fragrant herbs and wet dust rose from the ground, and the stars twinkled even more brightly among the scattering clouds.

'Find some wood,' said Desmond, when they got to the bottom of the valley. 'It won't have rained hard enough to soak it through. Light a fire if you can and we'll toast a little bread.'

'I have some things too,' said Philip.

He went to get the bag that the woman in Aleppo had given him and then lit a fire under a rocky outcrop. The damp wood smoked at first but then burst into flame, crackling and giving off a slightly bitter aroma. Philip opened the satchel and placed his remaining delicacies on a little cloth: honey, dates, sweets, fruit jellies and walnuts. But as he was rummaging through the satchel his fingers stopped as he touched an object that he would never have expected to find there.

He took it out, amazed, and admired it against the fire which was blazing now. His father was no less surprised.

'My God, that's beautiful. What is it?'

'A Pegasus on top of a tower.'

Desmond examined the magnificent jewel: crafted in the late Hellenistic age, he thought, or perhaps even Roman. The winged horse was rearing up on its hind legs and its eyes glowed with sapphires, while the little tower below was realistic-looking, with fluted columns and stone blocks.

'What does this represent?' he asked his son.

Philip set the jewel on a stone in front of the fire and sat watching it in silence, as if fascinated by the play of reflections on the sparkling surface, by the perfect anatomy of the miniature steed.

'What is it?' his father asked again.

'It's the seventh tomb, father. The last.'

# 11

THE LITTLE LIGHT BULB pulsed rhythmically at the top of the glass pyramid in Father Boni's secret study. The old priest had Father Antonelli's breviary open in front of him, while on the wall behind him was a huge celestial map of the northern hemisphere. Every centimetre of his large working table was covered by sheets of paper containing scribbled mathematical equations. The strain of the enormous job he'd taken on was plain in his face; it was ashen and furrowed by deep wrinkles. He lifted his head from the page he was reading when he heard a light knock at the door.

'Is that you, Hogan? Come in and sit down.'

'You're not well, Father Boni,' said Father Hogan. 'You must rest. Stay away from that damned text for a couple of weeks or you'll end up like Antonelli.'

'You are strange, Hogan,' said the scientist with a tired smile. 'We are about to bear witness to an unrepeatable event, unique in the history of the universe, and you tell me I should take a couple of weeks' holiday.'

'I'm not strange. I'm a priest and a believer. I am therefore convinced that my soul will survive my biological death and that I will see the face of God and contemplate His mind, with all the secrets and mysteries it contains. I am convinced that the time that separates me from this event, be it dozens of years or a single day, is nothing compared to eternity, and very little compared to the history of our planet or the history of humanity.'

'Absolutely. So why the hurry, right? Next you'll be saying that Bellarmino had a point in gagging Galileo.'

'I said I'm a believer, not that I'm stupid,' retorted Father Hogan. 'And you know me well. I'm as anxious as you are to find out how this adventure will end, but I feel that it was a very serious mistake to keep the whole thing secret. We need help. Other experts could be involved. The Church has an enormous wealth of experience and knowledge at its disposal. Our own wretched forces are simply not enough. If you want to know the truth, I still can't get the thought of Father Antonelli out of my mind: his bewildered expression, the anguish in his eyes, the tremor in his hands.'

'It's not true that we didn't ask for help. Do you call Guglielmo Marconi no one?'

'A single man is not enough. Think about it. What we've chanced upon is the story of a civilization that violated every law of nature in their supreme arrogance, in their belief that they were capable of achieving ultimate knowledge, ignoring the path that God himself had carved out for mankind.'

'Yes. The folly of taking on God himself. It is this titanic challenge that fascinates me. You know "The Canto of Ulysses" in Dante's *Divine Comedy*, don't you?'

'Of course. One of the most sublime expressions of universal literature. Ulysses dares to go beyond the Pillars of Hercules to look upon the holy mountain of purgatory, which is forbidden to mortals, relying stubbornly on his own strength and defying the decreed limits of what mankind can do. This is precisely what I fear: that you have fallen under the spell of this temptation, of this civilization that imagined it could subjugate nature and challenge God. Ulysses, remember, ended up entombed in the abyss.'

Father Boni's forehead and temples were damp with heavy perspiration, his eyelids were constantly twitching.

Hogan insisted, 'Tell me, what is it that you expect to come out of this revelation? Tell me. I need to know.'

Father Boni wiped his brow with a swift gesture, as if he didn't want to let any weakness show. 'Hogan,' he said, 'this is the point. Think about it. Man is continuously challenging God: when he kills, when he rapes, when he curses. But God does not respond to these provocations. He merely marks everything down in the eternal book of His everlasting memory until the day when each man is judged for the good and the evil he has done. God gave man his freedom; that explains it all. In other terms, man is free to offend God, and thus damn himself for all eternity.'

'True,' said Father Hogan.

'This is why God never responds to any of our challenges.'

'That's right.'

'But this is different. Here we have a civilization that has challenged God in a direct, inescapable way. They've challenged Him head on. More than that, even. They've gone off to search for Him in deepest space. They've gone back in time to spy on what He was doing at the exact moment of creation. Don't you get it, Hogan? Don't you understand what's been attempted here?' The old scientist seemed transfigured. A visionary light sparkled in his eyes. 'Hogan, do you remember when I read you the translation of "The Book of Amon"? You said it sounded like a myth, didn't you? Do you remember?'

'Of course. And I say so again.'

'And I told you that wasn't quite right. That it wasn't a myth, but an epic tale – that is, the transfiguration of events that actually occurred . . .'

'But the origins of such an ancient epic are completely beyond our reach . . .'

'No. You're wrong. I can tell you exactly what was meant. Do you remember the part that says that the inhabitants of Delfud manned a garrison, that they stood watch day and night for generations and generations, waiting for the Guardian Angel to doze off so they could force the gates of the Garden of Immortality and reach the Tree of Knowledge? That story symbolizes the most extraordinary endeavour that has ever been undertaken in the history of mankind. These ancestors of ours actually attempted a journey to the origins of the universe. And their purpose was even more extraordinary: to understand God's plan at the moment of creation, or even to force His hand, to modify His plan ... to originate a new creation on earth. And we know where, Hogan. At the point where the message is to be delivered, in the heart of a sun-scorched desert. Where the Tower of Solitude stands.'

Colour had returned to the old man's cheeks and his eyes shone with hallucinatory excitement. Father Hogan looked at him in dismay, but did not dare to contradict him.

'Go on,' he said.

'Hogan, none of us is free of doubt. Not even the Pope himself.'

'So?'

'I don't want to wait until I die. I want to know now. You see, I believe that, if God exists, He could not refrain from responding to such a tremendous provocation. And so, Hogan, when the transmitter is in conjunction with the black body at the centre of the constellation of the Scorpion – that is, in exactly twenty-nine days, seventeen hours and thirteen minutes – we will have the answer to all the questions that man has ever asked, ever since the moment at which he became conscious of his existence. Or we'll have God's response to the insult of Delfud. In any case, we will hear His voice and His message – even if that means a howl of anger – in a direct way ... No longer through books that we can't interpret, or through signs and symbols, no longer hidden behind an elusive pattern of chance happenings. We will hear and we will forever remember the sound of His living voice ...'

'Father Boni, what if there is no message? No answer? You must take this possibility into account.'

Father Boni fell silent and the flickering light on top of the pyramid was reflected in his dilated pupils. He turned then towards the little bulb. 'Look,' he said. 'The intervals between one sequence of symbols and the next have become, just over the last few days, much shorter. They've been reduced by nearly one per cent. Do you know what that means?' He pointed at the heaps of papers covered with figures. 'If you take a look at my calculations you'll understand what I've managed to demonstrate: the transmitter is approaching along a parabola at a speed that we cannot even imagine. Faster than the speed of light! It is advancing through the cosmos, distorting space and time as it proceeds, bouncing from one peak of distortion to the next, like a stone skips along the surface of a lake. A stone tossed by an immeasurable force . . .'

Father Hogan stared at the endless sequences of calculus, then looked back into the eyes of his superior and mechanically repeated the same question: 'And if there is no message? No answer?'

'Then that would mean that . . .'

'That God does not exist?'

The old man lowered his head. 'Worse,' he said. 'Much worse.'

Father Hogan covered his face with his hands to hide the tears rising to his eyes. 'Oh, my Lord,' was all he could manage.

Father Boni regained his composure instantly with a total change of expression. He seemed to be in a completely normal frame of mind when he spoke again. 'Let's drop this discussion for now. I didn't call you here to talk about philosophy, but to give you some news. I've managed to calculate the exact location where and the exact time when the event will take place. Marconi is still working with us and, as you know, he has come up with an extraordinary invention: an ultra-short-wave radio combined with another instrument which has revolutionary capabilities.

'You will be waiting there at the precise place and time of signal impact, Hogan, and you will capture the message coming from the most remote regions of the universe with this radio of ours. The message will be imprinted using a system that will conserve it for years and allow us to decode it. Although there may well be no need to decipher it. In any case, Hogan, I've prepared everything, down to the very last detail. I've already been in touch with the . . . powers that be, to obtain authorization and assistance for your journey. You will be travelling to a practically inaccessible desert area at a great distance from the last outposts of civilization. Of course, our . . . collaborators will be demanding something in exchange. But there's no other solution.'

'What?'

'They've asked to be told of the results of our experiment.'

'And how will you . . .'

Father Boni made an eloquent gesture with his hand. 'Not really a precise request, wouldn't you say? I don't see why our response needs to be any more so.'

'Is that all?'

'There's something else they're very interested in.'

'That is . . . ?'

'They're searching for an individual who seems to be very important to them. It just so happens that we have a great deal of information about this person. I'll be telling you about that shortly. And then you'll leave. As soon as possible.'

'What do you mean by "as soon as possible"?'

'The day after tomorrow at the very latest.'

'I can't. There's no possible way I could be ready by then.'

'There's nothing to prepare. It's all ready, even your bags. The trip has been booked. Your secretary will bring you your ticket and the money you will need tonight.'

Father Hogan seemed lost in thought for a few moments. 'All right, I'll go,' he said finally. 'What time am I scheduled to leave?'

'Ten in the evening. Now, Hogan, listen to me. The person I mentioned a short time ago is an officer who deserted the Foreign Legion. He calls himself Selznick. Some years ago, the Legion assigned him to collaborate with Desmond Garrett in research he was doing in the south-eastern quadrant of the Sahara desert.

After an initial phase in which there were apparently no problems, the two of them became sworn enemies. Their animosity culminated in a sword duel in which Selznick was wounded in his right side. They say that he still suffers the consequences of that day; that the wound has never healed and has fuelled a deep, deep hatred.

'In truth, no one knows Selznick's true identity. Except us. This sealed envelope I'm giving you contains everything we know about him. You'll give out this information a little at a time and only when you are certain you'll be getting the support they've promised.

'This evening, the Pope's physician will be vaccinating you against the main tropical diseases, but I'm trusting that you won't be exposed to anything dangerous. The desert is one of the cleanest places on earth. I'll come to say goodbye before you leave.'

Father Hogan left and returned to his own study. He picked up the telephone and began to dial a reserved number.

'This is Father Hogan. I'm calling from the Vatican. I would like to speak with the marquis.'

'I'm sorry, Father,' replied a man's voice, 'but the marquis is occupied at the moment.'

'Please tell him that I've called and that I absolutely must see him tomorrow on a strictly confidential matter. I will wait for his answer.'

A few minutes later the same voice said, 'The marquis will see you tomorrow at five o'clock in the evening.'

THE NEXT EVENING at dusk, Father Hogan left, in a rented car and civilian dress, for an elegant quarter of the city. He stopped in front of a seventeenth-century gate guarded by a uniformed porter. He went up to the second floor and stood in front of a dark walnut door with no name plate. He rang the doorbell and waited until he heard the sound of approaching footsteps. The butler who answered wore a black dress coat and white gloves. He greeted the guest: 'The marquis is expecting you, Father. This way, please.'

Father Hogan followed him to a large study with parquet flooring and ceiling-high walnut bookcases, filled with both ancient and modern books. On a large solid-walnut desk which stood to one side, near the window, was an Art Nouveau lamp in the form of a semi-nude nymph bearing the green opal-glass lampshade. There was no trace, in the large beeswax-scented room, of any of the complex technical devices which had made the master of the house famous throughout the world. Near the desk was an antique globe, and Fra Mauro's famous planisphere adorned the wall behind an armchair.

Guglielmo Marconi entered a few minutes later through a side door. 'I'm pleased to see you,' he said. 'I was sure you would have called. If you hadn't, I would have called you myself.'

'Mr Marconi,' said Father Hogan, 'I'm about to leave for the Sahara. I'll be taking the apparatus you've built with me.'

'I know,' said Marconi. 'When are you leaving?'

'Tomorrow. But before I go, I have to find answers to several questions that are troubling me. Some of them concern you directly.'

Marconi nodded. No emotion was evident on his face. 'I'm listening,' he said.

'Father Boni summoned me about a year ago to assist him in research which, according to his own words, was of enormous interest and great importance. I accepted with enthusiasm and left my teaching position at the University of Cork. Now I find myself imprisoned in a nightmare, involved in an experience the conclusion or consequences of which I can't even predict.'

'I think I understand how you feel,' said Marconi.

'When we last saw each other that night in the Vatican Observatory, you told me to be careful, remember?'

'Yes, I remember very well.'

'Why?'

'Because Father Boni never told me how he knew about that signal, or what he would do . . . later.'

'And yet you worked for him in absolute secrecy, developing a futuristic apparatus. What do you expect in return for your silence?'

'Nothing. Sometimes there's no recompense needed for a scientist beyond the results of his work.'

'But do you know what Father Boni is expecting from this endeavour? Do you know what use he means to put your devices to?'

'That was never an issue for me. Father Boni is a man of God, as you are.'

'You have not answered my question.'

'What I know is that we are picking up a signal from space and that this signal is transmitting an intelligent message from a rapidly advancing source. Father Boni and I made a pact.'

'Can you tell me about it?'

'There's no reason why I shouldn't. Father Boni promised to share the contents of that message with me when he has deciphered it.'

'Technology in exchange for knowledge.'

'Yes, in essence that's it.'

'So, I'm leaving now, and I must find myself in twenty-eight days' time in a precise place . . . the point at which the orbiting receiver will concentrate the final flow of information.'

'I imagined that this task would fall to you. That's another reason I told you to be careful.'

'What could happen?'

'No one can say . . .'

'Father Boni told me that the apparatus I'll be taking with me there, into the desert, is capable of fixing the message onto some sort of medium which will preserve it. It that true?'

The scientist nodded but said nothing. He lasped into silence for a few minutes and Father Hogan noticed small drops of perspiration beading at his temple, as on the night they had spent in the observatory, listening to the signal that came from space.

'You can count on me, Hogan,' he said, finally. 'Do what you've been asked to do and then bring everything back to me. Do you understand? Back here to me. Before you return to the Vatican.'

'I will.'

They walked towards the door and Marconi reached out his hand before opening it. 'Good luck,' he said, and stood there watching Father Hogan as the priest descended the stairs and until he had disappeared into the dark hallway.

PHILIP FELT DEADLY TIRED but he continued his story, reconstructing every phase of his journey through Rome and Naples, up to the discovery of Avile Vipinas's house. He told his father about the woman he'd met after passing through the Bab el Awa Gate, and what happened in Aleppo and Palmyra.

'This is it, father. It's the seventh tomb. This monument described in the papyrus I found in Pompeii, a cylinder topped by a Pegasus. When I saw that woman and the charm she was wearing at her neck, I realized that it had to be the image of the seventh tomb. It's an unbelievable coincidence, I know. But how else can you interpret it? Look. There's no doubt. It's a cylindrical tower, topped by a winged horse.'

'But we have no idea where it is.'

Philip turned the jewel over in his hands and showed his father the words in ancient Arabic carved into the base. 'You're wrong. This charm comes from Jebel Gafar.'

'Jebel Gafar,' mused Desmond. 'That's over the border, in Saudi Arabia. I'm almost certain of it. It's a desolate, unapproachable place. It seems strange that a similar monument could exist there. But Baruch bar Lev's map is no help either. The seventh tomb is not included, but, if I remember rightly, he says to seek it in the southern desert. There's something unconvincing about all this. The text that you found in Pompeii said that the Roman expedition had departed from Cydamus, right? And Cydamus is Gadames, in Libya.'

'There's a Cydama in Syria as well. That would fit with Jebel Gafar.'

'But why did that woman give you such a gift?'

'I'm not sure, but . . . it makes me hopeful,' said Philip.

'Are you in love with her?'

'I've thought of nothing but her since the moment I met her. I can't get her out of my mind. That's why El Kassem left me. I knew I had to follow her, at any cost, but he had prepared an entirely different route, and he went his own way. There was no convincing him. That's why I've been acting on my own, without any help. I've risked failure again and again. My only real regret is Enos ben Gad's death. If El Kassem had been at my side, we might have been able to save him. But I think I did the best I could. I did what I thought you would have done if you had been in my place.'

'You did well,' said Desmond. 'The proof is that you're here with me and that you saved my life.'

Philip raised his eyes towards the horizon, where the pale light of dawn was beginning to show in the east. 'But why did you put so many obstacles in my path? Why did you treat me like a child?'

'Don't you understand? The desert may have kept my body lean and made me tough and resistant, but I'm getting on in years, Philip. What if I fell along the way? I had to be sure that someone else could pick up where I left off and bring my mission to its conclusion, destroying the seventh tomb. You, Philip!

'I wanted you to be the last hunter, but you were so far away. Far away in time, in space, in feeling. How could I hope to initiate you? How could I steel your mind and your body? How could I devise a tough enough test? I decided to set up an assault course for you, ready for the day when you decided to follow my trail. If you succeeded, it would mean that everything I had worked towards for my whole life would not have been in vain.'

'Yes, but I might have failed. Didn't you ever consider that?'

'Yes,' said Desmond, 'and that possibility troubled me greatly. But I've always thought that most human beings die as though they had never lived. I was certain that when you found the road I had mapped out for you, no matter how steep or how difficult, you would risk your life to succeed. That you would have been won over by the challenge. I did it because I think highly of you, son, because I knew I could trust you, more than any other person on this earth.' He put his hand on Philip's shoulder and Philip covered it with his own and squeezed it, for the first time in his life.

'You were saying that finding that jewel made you hopeful,' continued his father. 'You're hoping that the woman you met intentionally left it in your bag as a message, so you could meet up with her again at Jebel Gafar.'

Philip nodded.

'That's possible, but all this reminds me of something else. Don't you remember the story of Joseph the Israelite? He hid a gold cup in the sacks of wheat that his brothers had bought in Egypt, so he could accuse them of stealing it and thus hold his brother Benjamin hostage. There may be another reason for her wanting to lure you to that hell on earth. Stay on guard.'

'You're so mistrustful,' said Philip, with a trace of resentment. He was thinking of his mother. Desmond too was struck by the memory of the woman he'd lost, and silence fell between father and son.

'What else do you know about the man in the house in Pompeii?' asked Desmond after a while.

'Avile Vipinas was an Etruscan haruspex. He was the only survivor of that unfortunate mission, and he says he witnessed an event so horrifying that he was never able to speak of it again.'

'As if he'd experienced some sort of supernatural phenomenon.'

'Yes, you're right. And do you know what saved him? The sound of his sistrum. The instrument was still there, in that buried house, hanging at the entrance to the *tablinum*.'

'My God!' said Desmond. 'But then . . .'

'Exactly. The "earthquake bells" were actually the tinkling sound of the sistrum. The sound that you tried to have reproduced in a music box. Do you remember? Why?'

'I don't know. I heard that sound one night in the Franciscan monastery and I couldn't get it out of my head. I knew that I absolutely had to find the source of those notes. I even went down once, during an earthquake, and I followed the sound from one tunnel to another until I got to that wall, and realized that the other side was hollow. But I didn't have the proper tools with me. When I went back up to look for something I could use, I was informed that your mother had fallen ill . . . Where is the sistrum now?'

'Here,' said Philip, reaching into the inside pocket of his jacket. A flash of deep disappointment immediately crossed his eyes. 'Oh my God,' he said. 'The uniform jacket!'

'Don't tell me that . . .' began his father in consternation. But he never finished the phrase.

'Desmond Garrett!' The voice echoed harsh and strident among the rocks of Petra, thundering down from above.

'Selznick!' cried Philip, shuddering. 'How did he get here?'

'Damn him. He must have followed you. Quick, take cover.'

Philip grabbed his bag and ran off behind his father, who had already jumped into a deep hollow in the ground.

'Desmond Garrett!' shouted the voice again, and this time it came from another direction.

Desmond fired three fast pistol shots and the walls of the crater multiplied the sound infinitely. The shots echoed in the hollow rooms of the rock tombs like roars of thunder. Desmond took off again at a sprint, followed by Philip. There was a ruin about fifteen metres in front of them that would offer better protection.

The sky was just starting to lighten and against the pale horizon they could make out a group of bedouins on horseback who were scattering in various directions as if obeying precise orders.

'My God, look!' said Philip. 'They're trying to block every way out of here.'

'Right. And then they'll come for us. Are you armed?'

'I've still got my pistol, but I don't have much ammunition.'

'Let's see what we can do here.' Desmond turned back towards his horse and whistled sharply.

The horse whinnied and ran towards him, and they managed to pull him behind a wall before the bedouins' shots could hit him.

Desmond took a rifle and some ammunition from the saddle and began to shoot at their attackers, who were drawing closer as Philip buried his bag under the sand.

'You get behind me and fire in that direction,' said Desmond. 'Don't shoot unless you're certain of hitting your target. We can't waste a single bullet.'

The bedouins continued to advance, covering each other, as Selznick shouted, 'I want them alive!'

Desmond and Philip kept up their defensive fire until they were down to their last bullet and then pulled out their blades. Selznick ordered the bedouins to surround them, then he advanced until he was close enough to speak to them.

'Those whom death does not part are destined to meet again,' he said from the shadows.

Desmond did not see the grimace of pain that distorted Selznick's features or the hand pressing against his aching side. 'I don't know what demon has saved your life, Selznick,' he said, 'but don't be fooled. Death is an old acquaintance who never forgets. It's just a matter of time, you can bet on it.'

'You'll go before me,' said Selznick. 'I'll live, and heal ...

when I've entered the sanctuary of the being who knows the secret of immortality and eternal youth. And now your son will tell me what was written on the other half of the papyrus!'

'What's he saying?' Desmond asked Philip in an undertone.

'There was an argument that night between Selznick and the men who had brought him down to the underground room. The papyrus was damaged in the tussle. The photograph that I took a few minutes earlier contains the only integral copy of the text. It's in there,' he said, pointing towards the spot where he had just buried his bag.

Selznick had drawn closer, flanked by two bedouin warriors who had their guns levelled.

'I didn't have time to read it, Selznick. I'd just found it when you walked in. It takes time to interpret such ancient script. Not just a few minutes. Days.'

The sky in the east was light now and the valley was emerging from the shadows. Selznick drew his sabre and pressed its blade against his old enemy's throat.

'Don't try to trick me, young man,' he said, still facing Philip. 'I know you have a copy of that text. Those long hours – days! – you spent in libraries did not go unnoticed. Search him!' he ordered the bedouins.

They found nothing on his person or in the pack he had left next to the campfire.

'I told you,' said Philip. 'I don't have it with me. It's still in Aleppo. In the pocket of my uniform jacket.'

Selznick cursed. 'You don't want me to cut your father's throat after all the trouble you went to to find him, do you?'

'Don't tell him anything, Philip,' said Desmond. 'He's a man without honour. He'll kill us anyway.'

'But not because of me,' said Philip. 'You'll never get me to come down to your level, Selznick. I've no need for any photograph. I know that text by heart. What you're looking for is a cylindrical structure topped by a winged horse. You'll find it at Jebel Gafar, over the Saudi border.'

Selznick sheathed his sword. 'I was sure of the noble sentiments that bind you to your father. Now the two of you will
stay here in this fine company, while I go to check whether
you've told me the truth.'

But at the very moment Selznick turned towards his men to
give them their orders about the prisoners, a couple of gunshots
downed the two bedouins at his sides and a third burned a hole
through the cloth of his jacket as he rolled to the ground to take
cover behind a low wall. A black shape plunged to the ground
from above, firing a barrage of bullets from two revolvers.

'El Kassem!' shouted Philip.

'You rogue! I knew you'd show up sooner or later!' exclaimed
Desmond.

El Kassem tossed him a cartridge belt and shouted at Philip,
'Run! Get out of here! There's a horse in the gully of the wadi
and I've taken care of the guards. The road is clear now, but it
won't be for long. You've only got a few seconds.'

'Go!' shouted his father. 'Go now or everything we've done
will be worthless. We can cover you from here.'

Philip scrambled to unearth his bag and was about to set off
at a run when he stopped a moment and took out the photograph
of Vipinas's text. He handed it to his father. 'I've got it all in
here,' he said, pointing at his head. 'This will be more useful to
you. Good luck, father!'

He sprinted off towards the mouth of Wadi Musa, as his
father and El Kassem kept the bedouin sharpshooters at bay. He
spotted a horse whose reins were looped around a stone; he was
pawing at the ground and trying to get free, frightened by the
bursts of gunfire. Philip leapt into the saddle and the last thing he
saw in the light of dawn, before he galloped away, was his father
and El Kassem being overpowered by a swarm of enemies.

SELZNICK DREW CLOSE, livid with anger. 'I greatly appreciate
your loyalty to your master, El Kassem. A fine quality in a dog
like you.'

El Kassem spat into his face.

'Have no fear, you'll pay for this as well,' said Selznick without losing his composure. 'After all, it's easy to let go of one's life in a gunfight or when crossing swords. We'll see if you're capable of hanging on now.'

He had his men drag them inside one of the tombs, where an intact stone sarcophagus still stood.

He ordered the bedouins to remove the lid and had them put in one of the corpses that was still lying on the ground, then turned to the men holding El Kassem. 'Put him in there as well and close it up.'

The Arab warrior struggled, trying desperately to get free and win himself a quicker death. But Selznick ordered two more men to help the others in forcing him into the sarcophagus.

Some time later, from the darkness of his horrifying abode, already saturated by the stench of the corpse it contained, El Kassem heard Selznick's voice. 'You can breathe. The lid is not sealed tight, but if you try to lift it you'll pull the trigger of a rifle aimed at your master's chest. If you're not both dead when I come back, I'll set you free. It's a promise that I'll keep. There are certain limits I respect. I am human, after all.'

El Kassem could hear him walking off and then heard his voice again, a little further away, ordering two of his men to remain at the entrance to the chamber, where no one could take them by surprise.

In the meantime, in the near-total blackness of his tomb, El Kassem had not lost his lucidity. His finger examined every millimetre of the large sarcophagus and then began to search the cadaver. He knew the customs of the Middle Eastern bedouins well and in the end he found what he was looking for: a small, very sharp blade concealed in a fold of the man's belt. He breathed a sigh of relief. If the worst came to the worst, at least he could cut his wrists.

Desmond's voice, speaking in French, was the only thing that kept him connected to outside reality.

'You've got no choice, El Kassem. We'll wait until it's dark, then, when I say the word, you'll push open that lid and make a run for it. It will be over in a minute. I won't suffer and the darkness will make it easier for you to get away. If they kill you, at least it will be with a rifle shot. If you do manage to escape, you can find Philip and help him to carry out our mission. Do as I say. You can't last in there without going mad.'

El Kassem's voice was low, barely perceptible. 'Don't worry, *el sidi*, I can hold out. I found a dagger on the corpse and this sarcophagus is made of sandstone. In a couple of days we'll be out of here, if you can bear the hunger and the thirst. Groan if you hear someone coming and I'll stop.'

Desmond soon heard the blade scraping against the sandstone sarcophagus.

'It's crazy,' he objected. 'You'll never make it. You'll soon run out of strength. Wait and try to stay calm until tonight, then, when I give the signal, lift the lid and it will all be over.'

'No,' replied El Kassem stubbornly. 'I can do this. And if my strength gives out . . . I've got meat here.'

Desmond fell silent. He knew him well enough to realize that he was serious. He listened to the sound of the knife chipping at the stone for a while, then began speaking again. 'If that's what you've decided, follow my instructions. That way you'll bore through where the string is rigged up. Try to get to the front right corner. Are you there? All right. Now move a hand's span up and then go back by the same distance towards the right side. That's where you want to dig. The string goes through a fork stuck into the ground at exactly that point. You'll be able to reach out and cut it.'

'I understand, *el sidi*. You try to hold out. I'm sure I'll succeed.'

Desmond immediately heard the scraping of metal against stone again. The sound was slow but continuous, unflagging. El Kassem would stop to rest for about ten minutes every hour, then continue.

The first day passed, and the first night. Desmond was bound by his wrists and ankles to a rock wall. He felt extremely weak and was tormented by thirst. But the sound of the knife against the sarcophagus wall never stopped and prevented him from losing heart.

He couldn't understand how that man, shut in for the last twenty-four hours with a cadaver in such a confined space, was not already dead of claustrophobia or sheer horror. How could he still have enough energy to continue the job? As the hours passed, his spurts of activity lessened and the intervals of silence increased. Desmond could barely control his anguish when the noise stopped, but he did not dare speak. Could El Kassem be sleeping in those interminable hours of silence? What nightmares preyed on his mind? How much torture could he withstand?

The chamber echoed with the loud laughter of their guards, who were whiling away the time playing *tawlet zaher*.

Desmond swore that if he found Selznick again he would make him suffer the same monstrous punishment.

At sunrise on the third day, after a long silence, Desmond – who was fighting off the hallucinations caused by thirst, hunger and exhaustion – heard a noise. The barely perceptible noise of a stone falling to the ground from a few centimetres' height. In the deep hush of dawn that small, sharp sound exploded in his mind like thunder. His gaze shot instinctively to the point the sound was coming from and his heart leapt. The wall of the sarcophagus was crumbling under his eyes, at the exact point where he had told El Kassem to dig.

'You've done it!' he said. 'Can you hear me, El Kassem? You made it!'

'I know,' hissed a voice from the little hole. 'I can see the light. What time is it?'

'Dawn of the third day.'

'The third? Damnation! I'd calculated nightfall of the second.'

'Don't stop now! Widen the hole. You have to make it big enough for your fist to fit through.'

It took four more hours of patient work before El Kassem's

fist pushed through the hole he'd managed to make in the sarcophagus wall. Desmond guided his fingers towards the string. The knife's edge had been considerably blunted by long hours of scraping at the sandstone and the blade was little more than a stump. It wouldn't cut unless he could put enough pressure on it, but too much pressure would set off the trigger and fire the gun.

El Kassem worked at sharpening what was left of the blade, honing it against the sarcophagus wall for over half an hour. He stretched his hand out of the hole once again and began patiently sawing at the string, stopping whenever Desmond warned him that the trigger was about to trip.

Each time that he had to stop he was obliged to start all over again, since he couldn't see what he was doing. But his phenomenal patience finally paid off and the string snapped in two, dismantling Selznick's trap.

El Kassem lay still and silent for a little while to recover his strength and concentration. Then he said, 'Be ready, el sidi. I'm coming out.'

He turned onto his knees and braced his back against the lid, pushing with all his might until the slab rose and shifted to one side. El Kassem gave a last desperate shove and the slab slipped to the ground.

Startled by the noise, one of the two bedouins on guard ran inside but El Kassem was ready with his knife. It flew into the base of the bedouin's neck. The man collapsed, holding both hands over the stream of blood that gushed from his severed carotid artery. El Kassem was quick to pick up the rifle that had been rigged to kill Desmond and shot the guard's companion as he was running up. He took the men's weapons and handed them to Desmond after he had freed him from the ropes that bound him to the wall.

They advanced, sliding against the walls, to the entrance of the tomb. There were four more armed men outside who had all taken cover when they heard the gunshots and seen that their comrades had not come back out. El Kassem retreated to where he couldn't be seen and fired two more shots into the air.

'Why?' mouthed Desmond.

El Kassem motioned with his head towards the two fallen men. They swiftly stripped off their keffiyehs and black *barrakans* and put them on, then walked back towards the entrance.

'Everything's all right. We've taken care of them,' El Kassem called loudly, and gestured for the men to come out of hiding. The four of them got to their feet, ready to follow those they thought to be their comrades back into the rock chamber, but as soon as they were close enough, Desmond and El Kassem spun around and shot them down with a volley of pistol and rifle shots. The field was clear.

They went to the bedouins' campfire and drank thirstily from their water skins. Desmond found some food in a sack and offered it to his companion.

'No, thank you, *el sidi*,' said El Kassem, 'I'm not hungry.'

Desmond never found out whether his companion was telling the truth or just saying that to make him believe he was able to bear anything. He was even capable of that, El Kassem.

Both men were exhausted. They found a hiding place and fell into a deep sleep for several hours.

When Desmond awoke, there was a fire blazing and El Kassem was skinning a snake so he could roast it. 'They come out looking for sand mice at this time of day, but there's no hunter that can't be hunted. It's good and it's . . . fresh meat.'

'I know, El Kassem,' said Desmond. 'It won't be the first time I've eaten snake.'

The warrior crouched near the fire, cut the reptile into chunks and skewered them onto his scimitar, which he held over the embers. Meanwhile, Desmond had gathered his bags and taken out the text by Avile Vipinas that Philip had given him before escaping.

'Jebel Gafar,' he mused, repeating the word several times. 'I'm not convinced . . . I'm just not convinced . . .' He got to the line where the ancient haruspex described the mysterious monument. 'There's a magnifying glass in my saddlebag,' he said to El Kassem. 'Could you get it for me?'

El Kassem laid his improvised spit on a couple of stones so that the snake would keep roasting, and went over to Desmond's horse. Inside the saddlebag was a large entomologist's lens, something Desmond always carried with him to use to inspect inscriptions, graffiti or stone carvings. He handed it to Desmond, who took it without removing his eyes from the document he was examining. The magnified script revealed every last detail of the writing and Desmond stopped at the words which described the monument from which the devastating fury had exploded. 'A cylinder topped by a Pegasus . . . no, a Petasus. Oh, my God!'

'What is it?' asked El Kassem. 'What have you seen?'

'There's a letter that's slightly irregular . . . See? I'm sure – look – that this stroke shouldn't continue downwards, towards the left. It's mould, not ink that's making the mark. Incredible! The *gamma* then becomes a *tau*. The word is no longer "Pegasus" but *"petasus"*!'

'Oh, merciful Allah, my snake!' exclaimed El Kassem, detecting a burning smell. He took the meat from the flames and drew up alongside Desmond again. 'So, what does that mean?' he asked, perplexed.

'It's simple,' replied Desmond. 'In ancient Greek, the letter *tau* was written like this,' he said, tracing a letter in the dry soil with the tip of his knife, 'and it was pronounced "t". But if a spot of mould alters this part of the letter,' he continued, using his index finger to amend the letter he'd drawn, 'then the *tau* becomes a *gamma*, which is pronounced like a hard "g", understand? So, what we thought was "Pegasus" is, in reality, a *"petasus"*.'

'What changes?' asked El Kassem.

'Everything, my friend. In ancient Greek, a Pegasus is a winged horse, the creature of fables. A *petasus* is a type of flat hat with a broad brim that the ancients wore. So, our monument is a cylinder topped by a hemispherical cap . . . like this.' And he etched out another small drawing with the tip of his knife.

Desmond could not help but notice El Kassem's involuntary start.

'Does it remind you of something?' he asked.

The warrior scowled. 'Yes. Something I heard about a long time ago . . . when I was very young. A man coming from the southern desert told a terrifying tale, but we all thought he was mad . . . Have you ever heard of the Blemmyae, *el sidi*?'

Desmond looked into his eyes and for the first time ever saw a shiver of fear there.

'Give me some of that snake,' he said to change the subject. 'I'm hungry.'

They ate sitting by the fire in silence. The Arab warrior was thinking of the nightmares that had tormented him as a boy, after he'd listened to the stranger's stories, while Desmond tried to imagine the dreaded monument, solitary as a lighthouse in a sea of sand.

It was El Kassem who broke the silence. 'What have you decided?'

Desmond raised his eyes to the sky, where the constellation Scorpio was glittering over the valley of Petra. His gaze was drawn to the pulsing red star of Antares and to the black space above it.

'Philip is in great danger, alone as he is against Selznick,' he said, 'but I cannot go to Jebel Gafar. There's no time. I'll leave here tomorrow morning at first light. You go, El Kassem, and make sure that nothing happens to him. I'll be grateful to you for as long as I live. He's my only son, El Kassem. Don't let me lose him.'

'Nothing will happen to him as long as I am with him. But what about you? Where are you going?'

Desmond spread a map on the ground. 'I'm going to try to work out the itinerary described by the man who wrote this letter two thousand years ago. I believe that he and his comrades were searching for Kalaat Hallaki and that they ended up in the Sand of Ghosts. The Tower of Solitude is there, I can feel it.'

When they had finished eating, they buried the dead so that their corpses would not attract animals during the night, then Desmond spent the rest of the evening poring over his maps, reading and rereading the words of Avile Vipinas and weighing them against all the secrets that he had wrung from the desert in his years of seeking and wandering. Among his papers was a drawing that he had made some ten years earlier that represented the Stone of the Constellations, the relic that Father Antonelli had shown him in the hidden recesses of the Vatican Library. He examined it at length, by lamplight, and then took a sextant from his bag. He raised it to the heavens and pointed it at Acrab in the Scorpio constellation. The star shone with icy light in the clear sky. El Kassem heard him murmur, 'There's no time left . . . There's no time.'

FATHER HOGAN DISEMBARKED in Tunis, where the papal nuncio was waiting for him with a car. Before getting in, he had watched as his luggage was unloaded and made sure it was carefully secured onto the roof rack.

'It would have been a pleasure for us to have you as our guest here,' said the nuncio, 'but we've been told to accompany you to El Kef, to the Oasis Hotel. Actually, we've been given no explanation or further instructions. Quite an unusual procedure, if I may say so. The position I so unworthily hold would suggest that I be informed of every detail of any operation that the Holy See wishes to carry out in this territory, yet I have been told nothing. Perhaps you have been instructed to communicate with me directly regarding such a delicate mission. In that case, I would certainly understand . . .'

'I'm sorry, Monsignor,' said Father Hogan, 'but I can tell you nothing. I myself have no idea of what awaits me at El Kef.'

The prelate fell silent as the car drove off towards La Marsa, heading for the interior. When the last houses on the outskirts of town were behind them, his taciturn companion had another try. 'I see that you've brought quite a lot of luggage with you. Perhaps some equipment for a mission of ours here? Times are changing and technology has made such extraordinary progress that even we of the Church have to keep up with the latest developments, for the glory of God, of course . . .'

Father Hogan, who had opened his breviary, closed it again and turned towards the nuncio. 'Monsignor,' he said, 'your curiosity – that is to say, your interest in this matter – is certainly legitimate and I understand it completely. But I have received explicit instructions from my superiors and yours not to say a word regarding the reason for this mission or the contents of my luggage.' Then, noting the nuncio's peeved expression, he continued. 'You see, Your Excellency, if you want my point of view, just between the two of us, this obsession with secrecy has taken over all the chancelleries lately, and I fear it has caught on in the Secretary of State's office as well, with due respect. All this secrecy may merely be motivated by banal customs requirements or something like that. I'm sure you've grasped my meaning. Sometimes, for the greater glory of God, as you have so rightly mentioned, it becomes necessary to get round petty bureaucratic or administrative obstacles by using methods and means that are not entirely orthodox . . . All to a good end, of course.'

The nuncio seemed content with this interpretation and said nothing more. He was comforted by the fact that the young Irishman spoke using the familiar, tortuous language of the curia, even though it certainly wasn't, all told, much better than total silence. The car proceeded quite quickly along a tarmac road at first and then, as they went further into the interior, on a dirt track.

Every so often they would have to stop to allow a herd of sheep or a caravan of camels to pass, resuming their journey in a cloud of dust.

They arrived at El Kef towards evening and Father Hogan

made sure that the porters carried his luggage to the room with the greatest care. He thanked the nuncio, who left to return to Tunis. Father Hogan had some dinner brought to his room, then retired almost immediately. The journey had been fatiguing and the African sun had already reddened his freckled Irish skin.

The next day he was woken at dawn by a knock on the door. He put on a robe and opened it to find an officer of the Foreign Legion standing there.

'I am Lieutenant Ducrot. You are Father Hogan, correct? I'll wait for you in the lobby. We'll leave in a quarter of an hour. I'll send two men to load up your luggage. You should get something to eat downstairs in the meantime. They make delicious crêpes here. If I were you, I wouldn't pass up the opportunity.'

Father Hogan washed and went downstairs, where Ducrot was waiting for him. The lieutenant's men loaded his luggage onto a little truck and sealed it into a crate, after which they departed. The vehicle soon turned off the road onto a track that proceeded in a south-eastern direction to the Algerian border. After a little while, the officer pointed to something on their left and Father Hogan saw a military aeroplane waiting with its engines running on a beaten-earth strip bounded by empty petroleum drums painted red and white. They boarded the craft and journeyed for nearly seven more hours, flying over thousands of kilometres of desert in a south-easterly direction until the plane began its descent to another strip similar to the one they'd departed from, near a small clump of dusty palm trees surrounding a well.

Another Legion officer was awaiting them. He introduced himself as Major Leroy. 'Welcome to Bir Akkar, Father Hogan. Please come this way. I'll introduce you to the person who will be taking you to the zone you are interested in. He's one of our best men, but he has recently suffered the loss of his entire unit in an exceptionally difficult operation, conducted in totally unexplored territory.' He continued in a more confidential tone, 'This will explain why some of his behaviour may seem unusual or even alarming at times.'

They entered a low, mud-plastered building that had been whitewashed. Major Leroy led him to a room where another officer was standing waiting, his back turned to the door. The room was simple and bare. It contained nothing but a desk with two chairs and a large map of the Sahara on the wall. On the opposite wall was an old print with scenes of Kabila folklore. The man turned as soon as he heard them enter. He was tall and thin, with short hair and a well-trimmed moustache, but his eyes glinted with signs of insomnia and his expression seemed to be that of a man used to living with nightmares.

'My name is Jobert,' he said. 'Colonel Charles Jobert.'

# 12

'SIT DOWN, FATHER. You've had an exhausting trip and must be tired. Would you like a glass of Arabic tea?'

'Yes, I would, thank you,' replied Father Hogan.

Jobert opened the window and called out to a boy running down the road, then came to sit opposite his guest.

'We've received instructions from our military authorities and our intelligence services to collaborate with you on an important joint mission. I must confess, Father, this is the first time that, as a military man, I've been asked to work with the Holy See. Consider me at your disposal immediately if you wish, although I expect that you would like to rest after such a long journey.'

There was a knock at the door and the boy entered with tea. Jobert poured the steaming amber-coloured brew into a couple of glasses and passed one to Father Hogan, who sipped it slowly and with great pleasure, although it was quite different from the blend he was used to drinking at the Vatican, which he had sent from London.

'I'm really not all that tired,' said Father Hogan, 'and we don't have much time. If you don't have anything to suggest to the contrary, I'd prefer it if we begin to lay down the terms of our collaboration.'

'That's fine with me,' said Colonel Jobert. 'Well, then, if I've understood correctly, you want to enter one of the most impenetrable zones of the south-eastern quadrant. Is that so?'

'Yes. And you're the only man in the world who can take me there. Is that right?'

'No, not exactly. There is someone else who has managed to reach the heart of hell and make his way back. His name is Desmond Garrett. We have not yet succeeded in contacting him, although we still have some hope.'

'Would you go back out there if I weren't asking you to?'

'At the first chance I had. My soldiers were slaughtered out there, down to the very last man. I want to go back, suitably prepared this time, and settle the score.'

'Who killed them? Marauders?'

'You wouldn't believe me if I told you.'

'Try me. I'm a priest, so I'm used to dealing with the incredible.'

Jobert's eyes twitched with a rapid, repeated beat. 'Have you ever heard of the Blemmyae?'

'The Blemmyae? But ... they're the stuff of myths! If I remember correctly, it was Pliny, in his *Natural History* . . .'

'They really exist, Father. I met them. I saw them hack my men to pieces. I saw them charging and wielding their weapons even after they had one, two, three bullets in them. I heard the monstrous squeaking noises they make, more terrifying than the roar of a wild beast. Whether you believe me or not, they exist, and it is into their territory that we must go. It's an inferno. There's a temperature difference of fifty degrees centigrade between the daytime and the night. Not a blade of grass grows there. There is not a dry twig to be found. The wind whips up dozens of dust demons that writhe at the horizon like ghosts. Thirst is a fiery claw that rips at your throat. That's where we'll be going, if you truly desire it.

'I'll have fifty light cavalrymen with me, armed with repeating rifles and heavy machine guns, along with ten camels laden with water, food and ammunition. There's a place where we can stop on the way, an incredibly beautiful oasis with plentiful water, fruits, every sort of crop. It's called Kalaat Hallaki. People have always thought it was a mere legend, but it's a real place, the most enchanting thing you've ever seen.'

'I'm ready to leave, Colonel. I'm ready to follow you anywhere. We can leave tomorrow.'

Jobert noticed that Father Hogan was continually swatting at the flies hovering around his tea glass. 'Flies. That's all there is at Bir Akkar. Nothing but flies. They came in with the first caravan that ever stopped at this dusty hole and they took it over. They thrive here. We're just like the flies. We've conquered Bir Akkar and we maintain control over this outpost. But we cannot grow, or multiply.'

Father Hogan noted the lost expression in his eyes in contrast to his sardonic smile. Sometimes it seemed as if he wasn't even there; as if his eyes were chasing figments of a dream, or a nightmare.

'All right,' Jobert began again abruptly, returning to Father Hogan's offer to depart immediately. 'But there's a pact between us. We provide complete logistic support and protection, and you agree to let us in on the results of your . . . experiment.'

Father Hogan nodded. 'If there is a result.'

'Naturally. Ah, yes, there's one more thing . . .'

'Selznick,' said Father Hogan.

'Correct.'

'Do you know where he is now?'

'Perhaps,' Jobert sighed. 'We have learned that one of our officers, General LaSalle, the commander of the fortress of Aleppo, recently disappeared, quite suddenly, without leaving any trace. Strange . . . strange indeed.

'What's more, LaSalle was injured when he reached Aleppo. He had a deep knife wound to his right side, resulting from an ambush in which he lost his entire unit, except for one or two men. And this is very strange as well.'

'The same thing happened to you, from what I've heard. Why do you find it so strange?'

Jobert started imperceptibly and his eyes narrowed into slits, as though they had been wounded by the blinding sun of the desert. 'Because I know LaSalle. He would never have left his command post like that, for any reason whatsoever. And he would never have willingly survived the murder of his men.'

'But you did,' said Father Hogan.

'Against my will and by pure chance. What's more, I had a duty to save myself. I had been entrusted with a mission and I had to return to report the outcome. And there's that wound to his right side that could only have been inflicted by a left-handed man. Like Desmond Garrett. A strange coincidence, wouldn't you say?'

'Yes. But pure conjecture.'

'That's right. But let's get back to us, Father Hogan. We have been informed that you possess intelligence regarding Selznick that could be of vital importance to us.'

'That's right,' said Father Hogan. 'We'll have plenty of time to talk during our long journey, but I can tell you now that Selznick is not his name. He doesn't have a name, actually, or rather he has many. He was the child of rape. His father was a Hungarian renegade who became an officer during the reign of Sultan Hamid. But the identity of his father, although we have that information, is not very important. What is truly surprising is his mother's identity.'

Colonel Jobert shifted on his chair, crossed his legs and lit a cigar. 'I'm listening,' he said.

From outside came the cries of camel drivers from a caravan that had got as far as that lonely outpost and were drawing water for themselves and their exhausted animals. The aeroplane that had brought Father Hogan to Bir Akkar was lifting off at that very moment against the setting sun. It made a wide turn and headed north. The young priest followed it for a while with his eyes and, when he saw it disappear into the twilight, he felt his heart sink.

'I'd prefer to talk about it another time,' he said.

SELZNICK'S COLUMN advanced through the blinding light of the Arabian desert, over a flat, uniform expanse in an absolutely motionless atmosphere. There was not a single well on the entire route to Jebel Gafar, and both the men and the animals were still drinking sparingly the water drawn from the well at Petra.

One of his bedouins belonged to a tribe from the south and had fought against the Turks in the last war. He knew the way to Jebel Gafar although he had never been that far. No caravan routes passed through the place, and there was said to be no water on the way in or on any of the ways out.

When they came within view of the first heights, Selznick assembled the men and had them split into a number of small groups, both so that they'd be less noticeable to anyone who might be in the area and so that they could take off in different directions to search for an object that he described to them carefully: a tower topped by a winged horse.

Selznick waited in a gorge between two hills where the erosion had created deep furrows that provided a little shade in the oblique rays of the setting sun. One by one, the squads returned to report that they had seen nothing corresponding to his description. These men were trained to discern every last detail of the desert terrain, and there was no reason to doubt their judgement. If Desmond Garrett was still alive upon their return, he would pay for this idiotic prank.

Selznick decided nonetheless to spend the night there and make another attempt the following morning. The night sky was extraordinarily clear and a full moon was rising on the western horizon, flooding the plain with a crystalline glow that high-lighted every stone and rock on the uniform backdrop of the vast dusty wasteland. He distanced himself from the men, who were gathered around the campfire, well aware that the sight of his solitary figure would inspire fear in them, and rode up towards the hills of Jebel Gafar to observe the lunar landscape.

It was then that he noticed something strange at a distance of about a kilometre, where the hillside had eroded into a shape that looked rather like an amphitheatre. The ochre-coloured surface layers had crumbled, revealing a chalky layer underneath which, in the light of day, reflected an indistinct, glaring whiteness. But the low, oblique rays of the moon brought out a series of pinnacles sculpted by the wind and the rare winter rains. One of them, in particular, seemed to have too regular a shape to have been created by nature.

He made his way closer, sheltered by a rocky ridge that separated him from the object of his curiosity. When he was near enough he left his horse and approached on foot, moving in such a way as not to be seen and confident that the tan colour of his uniform would blend in well with the sand.

He climbed over the one last hillock that had been blocking his view and found himself in front of a cylindrical construction built of dry blocks of stone taken from the mountain behind it and thus of the same white colour, making it undistinguishable under the direct light of the sun. The top of the tower had partially collapsed, making its shape even less apparent, but at its centre was a figure that had been corroded over time by the elements but was still recognizable: a winged horse on its hind legs, supported by a brace that the ancient artist had crafted to look like a rock on which its front legs rested.

Selznick wanted to shout out in that empty immensity, to cry out in victory and triumph. He had finally found what he had been seeking for so many years. And he had made it there first, suffering more than anyone else, fighting longer, overcoming hunger and thirst and the proximity of the coarse and stupidly ferocious beings he'd had to surround himself with. He dropped down to the ground and took out his binoculars to examine the top of the tower, but what he saw left him astonished and furious. There were armed men on the bastions and for a moment he thought he could make out a woman as well.

He shook his head in dismay and mentally counted his men: not enough for a frontal assault. Just then, more men on horseback appeared at the base of the tower on one side, raising a white cloud of dust under the moon. There were at least thirty of them, well armed and in a compact formation. They were patrolling the surrounding territory.

Selznick returned to his camp and ordered his men to extinguish the fire they had built with a little wood they'd found on the bottom of a wadi and to seek shelter wherever they could. He found a point from which he could observe the tower and again he thought he saw a woman walking on the bastions and then disappearing.

SHE WENT DOWN THE STAIRS to a walkway that encircled the tower's inner courtyard and provided access to the rooms all around it. She went into her room, a plain bare space with solid stone walls. One corner of the room was covered with carpets and blankets, while another had a number of cushions arranged around a copper plate holding bedouin bread and a clay water jug. Next to the door was a rack with rifles, sabres and pikes and a round shield of damascened steel. The room was lit only by the reflected moonlight on the white limestone walls.

Her attention was suddenly attracted by a clear but very soft noise, barely perceptible, coming from outside. She leaned out of the narrow window and started. A man had tossed a rope onto the bastions and was climbing up the shadowed part of the outer wall. She instinctively ran to the weapons rack and seized a rifle. She aimed at the man, who was close now to the parapet, but something stopped her finger from pulling the trigger, a presentiment. The intruder swung out of the shadowy area and turned to face her. It was Philip!

The woman dropped the gun and ran out of the door to the stairs and the upper walkway just in time to call the guard. 'I heard a suspicious noise coming from over there,' she said. 'Go and check.'

The sentry rushed off in the opposite direction and she reached the spot on the bastions where the rope was hanging from a hook jammed into a crack between two stone blocks, just as Philip grasped the parapet to hoist himself over the side. He was rooted to the spot at the shock of seeing her in front of him.

'Oh, my God! Is that you?'

She pulled him away from the guard's range of vision. 'You're mad!' she said. 'Why did you do it? You might have died . . . You may die still.' Philip could hear a deep note of anguish in her words. 'Follow me, quickly,' she said, and led him down the stairs to the lower walkway and to her room. Panting, she closed the heavy door behind her.

Philip held her close in a feverish embrace, as though he feared she might once again vanish without warning. 'What are you doing here?' he asked. 'What is this place?'

The woman shook her head.

'This is the place I was searching for, that my father is searching for, isn't it? Tell me, you must tell me. You can't deny me an answer. It was you who had me come all this way.'

'No,' she said, 'that's not true. I didn't want to see you again.'

But Philip felt her trembling in his arms. He pulled the winged-horse pendant out of his bag. 'You're lying,' he said. 'This is yours and you put it in here that night in Aleppo. The name of this place is carved right here. You wanted me to come here.'

'No, this is not what I wanted to happen,' said the woman. 'I thought I would be long gone from here by the time you arrived. But unfortunately, that's not the way it went. I was forced to stop here, to wait . . . That's the only reason you found me here.'

She spoke resolutely, staring right into his eyes with such a steady look that Philip felt lost once again.

'But then . . . why? Why did you want me to risk my life to find this desolate place . . . Just so that I would find what I was looking for?'

The woman nodded.

'That's not possible. I don't believe you. You would have left this place without waiting for me, knowing you'd never see me again?'

She raised her eyes to his and they were moist and so dark that Philip felt seized by sudden dizziness. 'My life . . . it's not up to me, Philip,' she said again.

'But right now it is up to you. Your beauty is a treasure and you can do as you like. But don't reject me, I beg of you. If you do, I'll go right out onto those bastions. I won't hide and I won't defend myself. I heard you call my name for the first time,' he said. 'Let me say yours, please, now.'

'Arad.'

'Arad,' he repeated, as if he were saying a magical word capable of opening a door that had always been closed to him.

The palms of her hands had been on his chest, but now she let them slip up to his shoulders and around his neck. Philip felt a rush of blood shooting through his veins like a river of fire. He kissed her lips, warm and sweet as fruit in the sun. She responded to his kiss and pressed against him, and Philip trembled with indescribable emotion. He caressed her thighs and her stomach and her magnificent breasts. He undressed her and contemplated her body in the moonlight as she opened her arms to him. He embraced her, awed by the paleness of his skin against her dark beauty.

She climbed on top of his body and towered over him for an instant like a black idol, like a goddess sculpted in basalt. Then she took his hands and placed them on her hips so he could guide their surging dance, long and lingering in the lunar silence. He followed her every move, sought her in every sigh, every shiver. He touched every centimetre of her splendid skin until the slow, majestic roll of her hips turned into a paroxysmal tremor. He responded hard and violent then, inebriated by the odour of that primordial woman, that black Eve born of mystery. He drew her in beneath him and clasped her in a frenetic embrace, sinking into her torrid flesh and escaping the world and the desert and the whitewashed walls of that lonely tower. He fled far, far away, soaring into the light of the moon like a wayfaring spirit, a quivering Pegasus, flying over the dunes and mountains, over the empty silent plains, all the way to the white foam of a remote sea . . . Then he fell, collapsing into her warm dampness and her still-panting breath. He was exhausted, his mind lost in the abyss of her black shining eyes. They slept.

THE DISTANT SOUND of a gallop shook her from a deep sleep and Arad leapt to her knees, limbs taut, like a lioness ready to strike. She ran to the window and saw a long wake of dust with the tips of spears glittering here and there in the moonlight, gun barrels as well. A large purple standard was fluttering in the wind against the light blue of long cloaks. She ran back to the bed, where Philip was still lost in sleep. She shook him hard to wake him. 'Hurry, you must leave immediately. If they find you here, they'll kill you.'

'Who? Who wants me dead? Selznick? He's been searching for this place just as I have. You know who I'm talking about, don't you? The man who was after me in Aleppo. I'm not afraid of him. I won't go.'

Arad dragged him to the window. 'Do you see them? They are the ones who will kill you if you don't go. I can't explain it all now, but I swear to you, they'll kill you without a moment's hesitation.'

'I don't want to lose you again. I'm staying.'

'They'll kill me as well. Is that what you want? You must go, Philip! Listen to me. If my destiny allows it, I will search for you and I will find you, wherever you are, because it's true, I lied to you. I left that jewel so that you would join me here, but I thought I would be alone. Destiny has decided otherwise. Come with me, come right now, I beg of you.'

'There's one thing,' said Philip. 'I left something in Aleppo, a little silver musical instrument, in my uniform. I have to have it.'

'Your uniform,' murmured the woman. 'I kept it to remember you by, to remember the way you smell . . .' She rummaged through a sack and Philip heard a silvery ringing. The sistrum shone a moment later between her long fingers.

'Thank you,' he said. 'Thank you for saving it for me.'

The galloping was closer now. They could hear pounding hooves, neighing, men shouting.

'Follow me,' said Arad.

She led him down a small spiral staircase on the inside wall that ended in a hidden cell closed by a hatch. As Philip was making his way further down, she let the hatch fall behind him and bolted it shut.

'Forgive me,' she said, 'but this is the only way to save your life. Someone will come to open the hatch in two days and you'll be free. Farewell.'

Philip pounded his fists furiously against the hatch, but no one was there to hear. Arad was already on the upper walkway, leaning over the courtyard, when the gate burst open and a large group of warriors surged in. At their head was Amir.

'I've been deprived of your beauty for too long, Arad,' he called up in greeting. 'I couldn't wait to see you. I hope you are well.'

'I am well, Amir. And I too am happy to see you.' She went down to the courtyard as the men drew water for themselves and their horses from the well at its centre.

Amir drew closer. 'The moment is near, my lady. Five weeks from today the cycle of the constellations will be complete and the light of knowledge will shine resplendent on the Sand of Ghosts and on the Tower of Solitude. The queen will be healed.

'The time to take the treasure has come. I have already procured an enormous quantity of naphtha from the Caldaean merchants and it is on its way to the sea. A consignment of weapons – the most modern and deadly that money can buy – are arriving from Tartous, and invincible blades are being forged in Damascus as I speak. Now we must take the gold we need to pay for these things. But there is something else you must take from the treasure chamber: the standard of the black queens. We have practised for the trial that awaits us thousands of times. We cannot fail. If you succeed, if your key strikes at the same moment that mine does, the door will open and the standard will be yours. You will perpetuate your dynasty, and I will kneel at your feet, should you wish to cast your eyes upon me.'

'I thank you, Amir. I've awaited your arrival with great longing as well. I will go to my room now and wait for dawn, when you will call me for the trial. Refresh yourself and rest. Allow your men to rest as well. I shall keep vigil alone, and gather all the strength of my mind and of my body. I've waited all my life for this moment.'

Amir bowed and returned to his men to give orders for the first light, which would not be long in coming. He retired, then, to a room near Arad's, to wait for dawn.

INSIDE HIS ROOM, Amir shut the door behind him and then lay a small carpet on the floor. He sat on his heels and opened the little leather satchel hanging from his belt. He took out his key: an arrowhead made of burnished steel, shaped like a star. He had chosen the most difficult for himself because he was certain that he would succeed, so great was his desire to be chosen as the companion of the future queen of Kalaat Hallaki.

Arad and Amir, closed in their separate rooms, never took their eyes off the arrowhead each had laid on a carpet, waiting until the light of the new day would make it shimmer like a diamond, providing the signal that the moment for their test had come.

The rays of the new sun struck the head of the winged horse on top of the tower first, then descended along his chest and his broken wings and moved down the stone walls, slowly, steeping them in pure light. They entered Amir's room, which faced east, first, and then Arad's.

Amir and Arad each rose to their feet and took a bow from the wall, fitted the gleaming head onto the shaft of an arrow and hefted it carefully, passing it from hand to hand.

They left their rooms and met at the centre of the deserted courtyard, which was still in shadow, and stood facing each other in silence. Amir saw something different in Arad's gaze, a wavering light, as if her soul, flitting behind her eyes, were troubled. He looked up at the bastions where the sentries were mounting guard at every point along the horizon. He waited until one of his men stepped forward and brought his rifle to his shoulder. He nodded, then turned to the woman and said: 'Let us go now, Arad. It is time.'

They descended a stairway that led underground. It opened onto a corridor which went towards the centre of the compound. They walked alongside each other in silence, gripping their bows and looking straight ahead, but Arad could still hear Philip's words in her ears, still feel the shiver of his hands on her skin.

They reached a vast circular room, also built of big blocks of white limestone. Light spilled in from an opening in the ceiling. At the centre of the room was a round stone whose grey colour stood out from the rest of the yellow sandstone floor. Neither raised their eyes so that the glare of the sky would not trouble them. The natural lighting coated the walls with a diffuse liquid glow that was just below the threshold of distinctness, so the only objects that were completely clear were two silver stars set into the wall, level with their eyes, one exactly opposite the other. Arad and Amir exchanged glances and then slowly walked backwards, step by step, until the stars lined up precisely with their right ears.

'The signal will reach us in a few moments,' said Amir. 'Nock your arrow and draw the bowstring.'

He did the same. They were exactly opposite each other, and each could see the tip of the arrow that the other was aiming, as if each were ready to kill the other, aiming directly at the face. Not a bead of sweat touched the brows of the two young people, not a tremor ran through their arms. They were as still as statues, at the supreme height of tension. But Amir, gazing at the woman he loved, felt that she was as distant as a star in the firmament, and Arad felt his torment and her soul was greatly disturbed. They were staring into each other's eyes, just as they stared at the stars, and somehow, strangely, each could feel, with pain, the emotion crossing the mind and the eyes of the other.

A rifle shot sounded above, shattering the harsh truths of dawn. The two arrows shot out like lightning, each driving deep into the hollow of the star it had been aimed at.

A dull roar exploded as the big circular stone dropped below floor level and moved aside, revealing the sparkling of an immense treasure beneath. Amir descended into the underground chamber and returned with a bronze rod and a standard bearing the emblem of a rampant gazelle. He knelt before Arad, offering the standard up into her hands. 'You are the last queen of Hallaki, the last of the blood of Meroe. You are the thirtieth black pearl of Kush.'

The rays of the rising sun licked the gold and silver, the bronze and glass, the ivory, the ebony, the gems, the marble, the coins, the jewels. There were statues and idols from ancient Egypt, necklaces that had encircled the necks of the queens of the Nile, breastplates of warriors and conquerors of the Land of the Two Rivers, bracelets and amulets of priests and wizards from Anatolia and Persia, braziers and thuribles that had burned Arabian incense to all the divinities that man had created to his own image and likeness between the Indus and the Pillars of Hercules. There were coins with the symbols of the cities of Hellas, with the effigies of the kings of Macedonia and Syria, of Lydia and Bactriana, with the profiles of the emperors of Rome and Byzantium, with the monograms of Abbasid, Ayyubite and Almoravide caliphs and of the sultans of the Sublime Gate.

The crypt contained the symbols of power and prestige of every civilization, all of which had paid tribute to the standard of the black queens. To do so their leaders had breached familiar boundaries, had left the known world to challenge the unknown. The little kingdom of Kalaat Hallaki had outlived them all.

'We have succeeded,' said Arad. 'Let us take what we need, Amir, and depart as soon as we can. We have a long road ahead of us.'

'We have succeeded,' said Amir, 'and this means that we are made for one another.' He looked over at her as she stood cloaked in the light of day that poured down from above. He would have given all the treasures of the crypt just to hold her in his arms for a single kiss, but he felt deep down that she was more distant now than on the day he had seen her dive naked into the spring of Hallaki.

ARAD TRIED ALL THAT DAY to find a moment when she could go down to Philip's cell, to talk to him, to give him hope. It was just not possible. All her time was taken up by the preparations for their journey and, when night fell, the guards swarming over every part of the tower made it impossible to do anything that might seem suspicious.

They left the next morning, before daybreak.

Amir's warriors were in formation in the courtyard, ready to depart. They had prepared the pack animals, loading them with bags of wheat and barley within which the precious objects from the crypt had been hidden. They had drawn water from the well and filled wineskins and flasks and big clay jugs, which they tied onto the camels' packsaddles.

Arad appeared dressed as a warrior herself, with a light blue *barrakan*, a damascened shield, scimitar and dagger. Her left hand held the standard with the gazelle. An old servant approached her, leading her horse – an Arab thoroughbred with big liquid eyes – by the halter. As she took the reins she slipped something into the old man's hand: the key that opened the underground hatch. She whispered an order: 'Open the hatch tomorrow at dawn, Alì, and set the prisoner free. Give him a horse and enough water and food for five days.'

Amir had had the gate opened and awaited Arad at the head of the column. She spurred on her mount and flanked him, then slowed her horse to a walk. The warriors separated into two columns on either side of the supply train. Another couple of squads acted as the forward and rear guards. The old man made his way slowly up to the bastions to watch the spectacle of that small sky-blue army moving west towards a battle that had never been fought.

The column was already just a streak of dust in the distance and yet the pounding of hooves seemed stronger, the horses' neighing closer. The old man could not explain what could be causing such a strange phenomenon and went down to the courtyard to see what was happening.

As he was opening the north gate he was suddenly confronted by a stone-faced horseman surrounded by a group of bedouins who burst in at a gallop, jumped off their mounts and thronged around the well to drink.

Selznick did not even get off his horse. He rode slowly around the entire courtyard, looking up and all about. He seemed disappointed, as though he had expected something very different. He observed the statue of the winged horse that was illuminated now by the first rays of the sun. The closer he got, the more it seemed a shapeless torso, mutilated and corroded by time and by countless sandstorms.

He stopped in front of the old man, who beheld him with astonishment and fear. 'Who are you?' he asked.

'I'm the custodian of this place,' he answered.

'You expect me to believe that you live here alone?'

'It's true. The caravans headed to the Mecca stop here and leave me food in exchange for water and shelter.'

'What is this place?' Selznick pressed.

'It is the tomb of a holy man venerated and respected by all. You must respect him as well.'

'Liar!' shouted Selznick. 'How can a holy man be buried under a pagan image?' he said, pointing at the marble statue at the tower's summit. 'The column of warriors that I watched leave here before dawn was certainly no caravan of pilgrims headed for the Mecca!'

He turned to his men. 'Search this place from top to bottom!' He got off his horse and went up to the inner walkway, entering the rooms facing it, which still showed signs of having been occupied a short time before. He went down to the underground chambers and his attention was immediately drawn by the sounds of a quarrel. He ran along a corridor and down a flight of stairs and found three of his bedouins heatedly arguing about something they'd found on the floor.

'Stop!' he shouted.

At the sound of his voice, they got to their feet, panting. A silver coin glittered on the ground and Selznick bent to pick it up. On one side was the effigy of a man with a strong, square jaw and drooping eyebrows, a diadem crowning his head, on the other an eagle holding a serpent in its claws.

'Have you found others?' he asked. 'Where?'

One of the bedouins gestured with his eyes towards a comrade standing to his left and Selznick forced him to open his fist. He was holding two gold coins.

'They were scattered on the steps here,' he admitted.

'Then there must be more,' said Selznick. 'Bring me the old man!'

PHILIP, LOCKED UP in his prison, was aware of shouts and cries, horses whinnying and galloping. At first he tried to make himself heard by shouting out himself, but he soon fell silent, realizing that no one was listening, or that even if his yelling was heard, it would be confused with the din outside. After a while, he began to hear a man's cries of pain, becoming more and more agonizing. He realized then that Selznick must have taken control of the place.

The man's cries grew weaker as time passed and finally died away completely. Philip became convinced that no one would arrive to free him and that he would die of hunger and thirst in that rat hole. The only alternative was to shout loud enough to be heard by Selznick's men once night had fallen – an option he didn't want to think about.

He had already explored his prison thoroughly without finding any way out. There was an air flue on one side that rose from his cell to the top of the tower, but climbing out was impossible because the opening in the ceiling was covered by a heavy iron grille, through which he could see a bit of the darkening sky.

He had assuaged his hunger pangs slightly by eating a few crumbled biscuits from the bottom of his haversack, but his thirst was becoming unbearable. He looked through his bag to see if there was anything that could help him out of his plight. He noticed that he still had some of the fireworks that Lino Santini had given him as he was leaving Naples. He thought of using the powder to blow up the hatch, but it was made of solid iron and looked too heavy and out of reach. But he reasoned that Arad's column could not have covered more than fifteen or twenty kilometres in a day's journey and that they would surely see the light of a rocket if he could manage to shoot it directly up the flue through the grating. Arad had already seen that kind of explosion on the Bab el Awa road and would immediately connect it with him. It was his only option besides revealing his presence to whoever had occupied the tower. He tried to build a support for the gunpowder-filled cardboard cylinder that would keep it in a perfectly vertical position, attempting to aim it at one of the central openings of the grille. If it exploded against one of the bars, the din of the explosion would attract someone to the chimney. Even that would probably mean a way out, although he'd have to deal with the consequences.

He waited until the sky was completely dark, then lit a match and held it to the touchpaper. The rocket flared and took off with a sharp whistle. It shot through the grille and soared into the sky, exploding into a cascade of light and colour. The bedouins on guard, startled by the piercing whistle, watched the fabulous spill of lights in wonder and fear. They ran to knock at the door of the room that Selznick had occupied, but their description was so excited and confused that Selznick, who had heard the sound of the explosion himself, could not figure out what they had actually seen. He ordered another inspection of the monument, inside and out. He was worried about a superstitious reaction on the part of his men and didn't want them running off on him.

He walked around the structure with a torch in hand, examining every recess of the ancient building. The phenomenon that his men had described as a supernatural event had left him sceptical. He passed alongside the tortured body of the old custodian, who had died without revealing a thing: neither whether there were treasures hidden underground, nor who the warriors he had seen leaving were.

The old man lay on the pavement with his arms splayed and eyes wide open. Nothing would wake him again. Of all the dead men that Selznick had seen in his life, what struck him most was the fixity of their stares. He had always tried to search for an epiphany, a preview of infinity, in their petrified expressions, and sometimes he had even succeeded. Their cold pupils had allowed him, he felt, to face the abyss. Strangely, he had experienced no terror. He realized that it was no deeper, blacker or icier than what he had inside him.

The turmoil of shouts and agitated footsteps in the underground chambers and along the stairs in the tower reached Philip and he decided that he would wait until the next morning before making himself heard.

ARAD'S COLUMN HAD long passed the Jebel Gafar ridge and neither she nor anyone accompanying her could see the small luminous trail streaking through the sky, but someone else did. A horseman who was following Philip's tracks through the desert: El Kassem. He had ventured this far alone, leading another horse laden with water and food. He had taken the road to Jebel Gafar in the hopes of getting there before Selznick, but the signs left on the ground by the passage of numerous horsemen left him with little hope.

The fireworks at Bab el Awa instantly came to mind and El Kassem spurred his horse in the direction of the fountain of coloured lights which had blossomed in the middle of the sky. He almost drew up short against the white stone tower before he had realized it was there. He tethered the horses in a sheltered position and approached the imposing bastions, creeping through the darkness. It didn't take him long to sense the presence of guards on the upper walkways. He recognized them immediately, from their style of dress and the weapons they carried, as Selznick's men.

El Kassem continued to make his way all around the tower with his back up against the wall, looking for an access other than the gate guarded by more sentries. He eventually found a rope hanging from the rim of the walls and he thought that Philip must have got in that way. He began to pull himself up with his feet propped against the wall, hidden from sight by the shadows covering that side of the structure. As he climbed up, his gaze spread over an ever vaster territory and his head spun wildly, making him feel completely disoriented. El Kassem had grown up with the endless horizontal dimension of the desert, but rising in the direction of the sky while hovering over the void gave him a nauseous, suffocating feeling that he hadn't experienced even when locked in with the cadaver in the tomb in Petra.

He drew a sigh of relief as he gripped the rim of the parapet. He found himself just a few steps away from a sentry who was rounding the corner. El Kassem's knife flew through the air and put a sudden end to the warning cry that was about to rise from the guard's throat. He donned the fallen man's black cloak, picked up his rifle and continued on the inspection round so he could get a feel of the situation. He saw more of Selznick's men in the courtyard and another guard on the bastions opposite him. He realized that in completing his own round, the other man would soon stumble upon his comrade's dead body, so he deliberately rushed up to him as if he had something to say. When the other realized who was facing him, it was too late. He fell without a whimper, his throat slashed from side to side.

El Kassem was alone now and could calmly continue to inspect the entire upper terrace. He noticed the iron grate that closed the chimney flue. It seemed to be the only way to get into the building, which, as he had seen, was completely surrounded by Selznick's men.

He hauled in the rope from the parapet, but before dropping down the chimney, he decided to check the bottom of the flue to make sure that there were no traps or other dangers lurking there. He tore off a strip of his cloak, set it on fire with a lighter and let it fall to the bottom. He watched the flickering flame until it settled on a stone floor where no danger was apparent. As he began to tie the rope onto the grille so he could lower himself down, he saw a man appear below, looking up with a bewildered gaze. Philip!

'Who's up there?' asked the young man.

'Philip, it's me, El Kassem. I'm going to throw down a rope. Climb it as fast as you can, before they find out that I've killed the guards up here.'

Philip seized the rope dangling before him and started to pull himself up with enormous effort, exhausted by over two days of complete fasting. When he was about halfway up, he realized that he wouldn't be able to make it. He was about to fall; his hands were aching and racked with cramps every time he tried to raise one above the other.

'I can't do it, El Kassem!' he said in a faint voice. 'I'm not strong enough. I can't make it up.'

El Kassem could not see him but heard the immense strain in his voice.

'No!' he shouted loudly. 'Don't let go! I'll pull you up. Tie the rope around your body so you won't fall. Are you there? Are you there? I can't see a cursed thing in this darkness!'

'I'm here,' said Philip. 'I've tied myself to the rope.'

El Kassem looped the rope up over his shoulder and stood firm on the grille. He started to pull with all his might, stepping down on the rope with every yank so that it couldn't slip back. He took a deep breath and readied himself for the next heave. Philip remembered the lighter he had in his pocket and he flicked it once, then twice, and a little flame lit up. 'Can you see me?' he asked.

'I can see you,' said El Kassem. 'You're nearly up.'

At that moment, a voice rang out in the courtyard. 'Ahmed!' Again, a little louder and with a note of alarm: 'Ahmed!' El Kassem realized that someone was calling one of the guards who had been out of sight for some time now.

'Fast!' he urged Philip. 'Pull yourself up or we'll both be dead in a matter of minutes.'

Philip started to hoist himself up again, as his friend continued to pull on the rope. As soon as Philip grabbed the grille, El Kassem tied one end of the rope to the parapet and then turned back to help him out. Just then, the man who had been calling his comrade appeared on the upper walkway and saw the two intruders and the corpses of the guards. His surprise caused him to hesitate a moment, long enough for El Kassem to pull out his revolver and fire.

'Come on! Fast!' he exhorted. 'They'll all be up here in a minute.' He tossed the rope over the other side of the parapet, but when he turned to lower himself down he saw Philip still standing at the base of the winged horse. 'Are you mad?' he shouted. 'Can't you hear them?'

Philip shook himself and both of them began to slip down the rope as Selznick's men burst onto the bastions. They soon spotted the rope and leaned over the parapet. The two men were running towards their horses. They aimed their rifles and were about to fire when Selznick stopped them.

'Let them go,' he said. 'They know where the treasure we're looking for is. There's nothing here.'

EL KASSEM AND PHILIP rode long hours in the light of the moon along the Jebel Gafar ridge until they found a cave where they could pass the rest of the night.

Philip was completely worn out by his exertions, the excitement and lack of food, and he fell rather than descended from his horse. El Kassem handed him his water skin and Philip drank slowly, in little sips, as he had learned to do in the desert, then collapsed to the ground, drained of all strength.

'In a few moments we would have both been dead,' said El Kassem. 'Why did you stop on the walkway instead of coming down the rope with me?'

'There's an inscription under the statue of the horse. The entire construction is the trophy of an ancient Roman emperor called Trajan. He had it built to celebrate his victory over the Nabataeans, an Arab tribe from this region. It can't be what we're looking for.'

'If we'd had time, I could have told you that myself. You're father has discovered where the seventh tomb is and what it looks like. It's a cylinder topped by a cap – that is, like a hat, not like a horse . . . That's what he said . . . He said that you had read the word wrong, that mould had altered part of a letter . . . He drew something that looked like this,' and he used the tip of his dagger to sketch out the drawing that Desmond had made at Petra.

'A hat . . . my God, you mean a *petasus*. Is that what he said? A *petasus*?'

'Yes, I think that was the word. But if an hour of rest is enough for you and we can set off again, perhaps he can tell you himself. There will be a felucca waiting for him in four days' time at Al Muwailih on the Red Sea to ferry him to the Egyptian shore. If Allah assists us, we can be there as well.'

The next day Philip and El Kassem found traces of Arad's horsemen, but soon realized that their path had turned south, while the two men had to go west. Philip looked over at El Kassem but he had such a determined glint in his eye that he didn't even dare mention what was passing through his mind. Philip followed him without saying a word under the flaming sun, along the trail that led to the sea.

'Did you find her?' asked El Kassem after a while.

'Yes,' replied Philip. 'And I've lost her again. For ever this time.'

# 13

COLONEL JOBERT WOKE before dawn to make sure that everything was ready for the departure of their expedition. He wanted
to see to his own horse personally, checking trappings and gear.
In reality, ever since he had joined the Legion, he'd always been
on his feet to watch the sun rise, the light sweeping from the
horizon and whitening the black desert sky, the shadows dissolv-
ing – evaporating, really – under its dazzling rays. The dunes
coming to life like the waves of a fossil sea shaken from a long
slumber, as the nightmares of the darkness dissipated.

For a few minutes, the temperature was marvellous, neither
cold nor hot, and the light was perfect. The deafening drone of
the flies had not started up yet and all the animals rested
peacefully. The entire world silently witnessed the miracle of the
daylight which returned to visit the earth.

That morning he was not the only one up, nor the first.
Father Hogan was a couple of dozen metres away, standing on
a dune, seemingly absorbed in prayer. Jobert watched him for a
while, then approached.

'Say one for me as well,' he said. 'I haven't been able to pray
for many years.'

'What are you truly looking for down there, Colonel Jobert?'
he asked without turning.

'A passage.'

'To where?'

'I don't know. The desert is a prelude to infinity: a territory
without borders and without limits that lies between the civilized

world and the chaos of primordial nature. What am I seeking in that desolate place, guarded by creatures which are no longer human? Perhaps ... I'm thinking I may find the Pillars of Hercules of this sluggish ocean, this expanse that changes as you're watching it, conjuring up spectres and mirages. Reality is always elusive here, fleeting ... What about you, Father Hogan? What do you ask for when you pray?'

'Nothing. I raise my voice, calling Abba, Father!'

'What answer do you get?'

Father Hogan hesitated a moment, then turned and said: 'The voice of God is like ...' but Jobert had already walked off, as silently as he had come.

JOBERT ENTERED HIS QUARTERS and gathered his personal things, but as he was about to mount his horse, a staff officer ran up to him with a dispatch. 'This just arrived, Colonel. It was sent from an Egyptian port on the Red Sea.'

Jobert nodded and took the paper. It was signed Philip Garrett, and read: 'I've found my father. We are travelling towards Kalaat Hallaki. Selznick is free and probably on our tail.'

Finally! Everything would be concluded where it had begun. The old hunter had emerged out of nowhere again and was on his way to Wadi Addir and the Sand of Ghosts. And where Garrett was, Selznick was sure to follow.

They left soon after sunrise, heading south-east. Jobert rode at the front of the column and Father Hogan was at his side. He had never ridden a horse before and the commander had chosen a placid animal for him, a mare who'd always served as a packhorse. Behind them were two camels, one behind the other, carrying between them a sort of litter on which Father Hogan's gear was being transported, carefully sealed inside a double layer of oilcloth.

Jobert turned to make sure that everything was in order. 'You say that there's a radio in there?'

'That's right.'

'How will you power its batteries?'

'Using a charging system connected to the blades of a small rotor that can be turned by the wind or by manpower. Energy won't be a problem.'

Jobert rode in silence for a while, then said, 'It may be that a fierce battle awaits us when we reach our destination. Will you fight if necessary or will you simply let the rest of us kill for you?'

'I haven't come to kill, Jobert, but to listen to a message. I'm aware that this may involve considerable risks, and I'm neither a coward nor a hypocrite, if that's what you're wondering. Look, I realize that a man who has made a choice like yours must have had a tough, tormented past, but remember that a man who makes a choice like mine must follow a road that is not easy or without obstacles either. Don't put me to the test, Colonel. You might be surprised.'

They journeyed all that day and all the next along the same route that Jobert had taken on his return. The temperature was barely tolerable, although the winter season had begun. On the evening of the third day, as the men set up camp, Jobert approached Father Hogan holding a topographic map.

'Your radio might be able to help us if you are willing to lend us a hand. Before leaving I sent dispatches to our informers and our outposts along the different routes travellers would be bound to take. Philip and Desmond Garrett are heading towards Kalaat Hallaki and Selznick is surely after them. If we can manage to learn which of the three routes that depart from the Red Sea they have taken, we might be able to lay a trap.'

'The radio is at your disposal,' said Father Hogan. 'Just give me time to open the case. I packed it personally and must open it with my own hands.'

In a short time, the radio had been freed of its wrappings and was ready to use once a long antenna had been attached. Colonel Jobert couldn't help but notice that Hogan hadn't touched the much larger package that sat alongside it. It was sealed with great care and protected by steel padlocks.

'And what's in there, Reverend?' he asked with a hint of sarcasm. 'A secret weapon of the Holy Roman Church?'

'There's a powerful magnetic recording system in there, Colonel. I wouldn't hesitate to define it as a sort of mass memory.'

'I'm afraid I don't understand.'

'Now that we've set off on our mission I can tell you. At the Vatican, we've been picking up a signal from a mysterious transmitter that, in exactly twenty-five days, seventeen hours and seven minutes, will concentrate a gigantic flow of data at a precise point of the south-eastern desert. Since we haven't been able to calculate its speed or the rate of flow, we've prepared an instrument that will, in theory, store this information and allow us to decipher it at a later date.'

'In theory?'

'That's right. It's an experiment that's never been attempted before.'

'But how do you know that the capacity of this . . . box will be sufficient? If you're trying to collect all the water in a waterfall, what difference does it make if you're using a glass or a cistern? Most of the flow will be lost anyway.'

Father Hogan could feel the evening breeze stirring as he attached the rotor and turned on the radio. 'Give me the frequency of your station,' he said. When he had tuned the instrument in, he continued, 'Do you imagine that we hadn't considered that possibility? Let me tell you about something that once happened to me. I was at a mission in central Africa, in a village that had been isolated for days and days by civil war. The old people and children had already started to succumb to starvation. Finally, one day we got news that a lorry full of flour had managed to make its way through and would be arriving the next morning. Before dawn, anyone who was still capable of standing was waiting at the side of the road with every imaginable sort of container. As soon as the lorry came into sight, they all started running towards it, but before they got close the vehicle hit a landmine. There was a terrifying explosion and a white cloud rose to the sky. After a moment of shock, the people kept running, holding out the containers they'd brought, their skirts, their scarves, their aprons. That flour seemed so precious that saving any amount, no matter how small, was better than seeing it go completely to waste.'

Jobert did not answer and went off to complete his inspection rounds.

Father Hogan sat next to the radio all evening, having his rations of food and water brought to him, but the instrument remained mute. Just as he was about to give up and get some rest, a voice came in, calling from a locality on the coast. They had received a dispatch via telegraph reporting the sighting of an officer of the Legion with a group of bedouin horsemen journeying towards the south-eastern quadrant on the Al Shabqa trail. From the description of the officer, it was Selznick.

Father Hogan sent a man to call Colonel Jobert, who arrived immediately.

'Well,' Jobert said, laying a map out on the field table, 'he's attempting the route from the north, through Egypt and Fezzan. He'll be certain that he's chosen the safest option, where no one can intercept him. Except us.'

'What do you intend to do?' asked Father Hogan.

Jobert ran his finger down the map, along the itinerary that was taking form in his mind. 'If Selznick, as I believe, is coming from here, he has no choice. There's only one well on the road before reaching the valley of Wadi Addir, where he's planning to meet up with his old enemy. And that's where we'll wait for him,' he said, pointing his index finger at the Bir el Walid well on his map.

Father Hogan shook his head. 'How can you possibly find one man in a sea of sand? In an area millions of square kilometres wide?'

'The desert does not forgive mistakes,' said Jobert. 'It's not as if you can go whichever way you like. You only go the way you can – that's where there's a well. We can easily calculate his rate of advance by the route and the time of year. Selznick will be at Bir el Walid in two weeks' time, at the very latest, and we will be there waiting for him. If my hunch is correct, it was Selznick who ambushed the unit of my fellow officer LaSalle in Syria. He wiped out every last one of them, including the commander, and took his place. He must be captured and brought before a firing squad.'

'Two weeks!' said Father Hogan. 'At that point, we'll have less than two more to reach the Sand of Ghosts. I'm sorry, but that's too high a risk.'

'Selznick free and on our trail would be much worse.'

Father Hogan rose to his feet. 'This trip is already risky enough on its own, Colonel, and full of unknowns. The detour you're proposing is not justified. Selznick cannot be so dangerous as to pose a threat to a Legion unit in full battle order, equipped with heavy arms. Or is there something else I'm not aware of?'

'There's nothing else,' said Jobert. 'The slaughter of an entire garrison seems sufficient to me, without counting desertion and other crimes.'

'I can't agree with you,' repeated Father Hogan. 'Our expedition is based on a specific agreement, and this deviation could seriously jeopardize its outcome. If the mission fails, you will be held responsible.'

Jobert smirked. 'You wouldn't want to provoke a diplomatic incident between our countries, would you? Between the Holy Mother Church and her beloved firstborn daughter?'

'Worse,' said Father Hogan, who was becoming suspicious of the officer's obstinate attitude.

Jobert turned serious, which convinced Father Hogan that he'd hit a nerve. 'Why should I listen to you?' he asked.

'Because, as you know, we can provide you with information regarding Selznick's identity.'

'Not much. At least up to now.'

'I'll tell you what we know, as I promised. But I can also tell you that our investigation is still under way.'

Jobert seemed noticeably disconcerted by his words and Hogan, who had actually been bluffing, realized that there must be some shameful, highly embarrassing secret that the Legion was eager to bury as soon as possible by executing Selznick.

'Tell me what you know,' Jobert demanded. 'That was part of the agreement as well.'

'As I had begun to tell you, it's not Selznick's father that interests us, but his mother: Evelyn Brown Garrett. The mother of Desmond Garrett.'

'Are you sure of what you're saying?' asked Jobert, frowning.

'Absolutely. It all goes back about fifty years. Jason Garrett was an American engineer working in eastern Anatolia, on a project building a road that would cross the Pontian mountains, connecting Erzurum and Trebizond. Rioting broke out in the area and there was armed conflict with the local Kurdish tribes. The sultan sent troops in to quash the uprising. Garrett was worried about the safety of his wife and son, and decided to send them back to Europe, but as they were travelling through the village of Bayburt, their carriage was stopped by a patrol for what seemed to be a routine check. However, the patrol commander was so struck by the woman's beauty that he did away with her escort and had her brought to his quarters. He tried first to seduce her and then to threaten her, but she would not be swayed, so he resorted to violence. He raped her and forced her to stay with him for the entire operation. Then he brought her back to Istanbul and had her accompanied to the border.

'Evelyn Garrett was so shaken and distressed that she did not dare let her husband know what had happened. She sent word that she had taken ill on the journey and had sought shelter at a monastery in Smyrna. But her troubles were far from over. When she reached Salonika, she realized that she was pregnant. She continued on to Belgrade and then to Vienna, where she put her son Desmond in a boarding school. He was young enough not to have realized what had happened and he believed her series of merciful lies.

'She told him that she would have to be away for some time to regain her health and she went to a clinic, where she gave birth to a boy, whom she turned over to a Passionist orphanage.

'Her husband never learned what had happened. She hid her rage and humiliation, along with her remorse for abandoning a blameless child to his destiny. Evelyn Garrett was a cultured, sensitive woman from a prominent New England family. She paid dearly for her decision to follow her husband into such difficult and dangerous territory, in defiance of her family's wishes. You see, they were completely against her marriage in the first place, because the young man she had chosen, though certainly intelligent and willing, was from a lower social background. And they were even more against her taking a small child so far away, to live among people they considered little more than barbarians.'

Colonel Jobert took a puff on his cigar and shook his head. 'The power of the Church!' He sighed. 'You have eyes and ears everywhere. You hear people's most shameful secrets in your confessionals. You have no arms, yet you can move the armies of kings and nations. You have no territory, yet you are everywhere. Any other state must struggle to recover after a war, but you fight your battles everywhere without ever stopping, with no restrictions.'

'We can't stop,' said Father Hogan. 'We have to bring the Word to all people before the end of time.'

'How do you know that Selznick was that child abandoned in an orphanage in Vienna?'

'As far as possible our organizations follow the affairs of those who were left in their custody as children. Especially when these affairs turn out to be particularly conspicuous one way or other. In the sphere of good or of evil.'

'I see,' said Colonel Jobert. 'Especially when they stand out. Is that all you have to tell me about Selznick?'

'For the moment,' said Father Hogan. 'The rest depends on the outcome of my mission.'

'Then don't worry about it. I will assume all responsibility. First I will capture Selznick and then I will take you to Kalaat Hallaki and the Sand of Ghosts. I wouldn't want to miss the show myself. If a priest threatens me with political blackmail at the prospect of turning up late, he must be anticipating something quite special . . . Isn't that so, Reverend?'

Father Hogan did not answer. Jobert got to his feet and ground his cigar butt under his heel. 'Tomorrow we have a tough journey ahead of us. Thank you for your help, Reverend. Without that radio of yours we would never have been able to get the information we needed to help us capture such a dangerous criminal. Who would have thought, just a few short years ago, that a voice could cross the limitless expanse of the desert in a heartbeat and reach a lonely squad of soldiers hidden in the dark of night? We would have imagined that only the voice of God was capable of so much!'

Father Hogan raised his eyes to the constellation of Scorpio, to the cold light of Acrab. 'The voice of God . . .' he mused, as if talking to himself. 'As a child I would hear His voice in the wind and thunder, in the billows crashing against the cliffs . . .'

'There's nothing but silence here,' said Jobert. 'The silence that reigned before man existed and that will continue to reign unopposed on our planet after we are gone, until the end of time. The desert is a petrified prophecy. Goodnight, Father Hogan.'

He walked off into the darkness.

THEY SET OFF the next morning before dawn. The land they rode across was rough and even rocky at times, covered by dust as fine as talcum powder. They continued in the same direction for the whole day. The next morning they saw a caravan in the distance proceeding in the opposite direction; Jobert observed it at length through binoculars before it disappeared among the dunes. They never saw another living soul on the entire journey. Their direction had to be worked out with a compass, since long stretches of the route had been completely erased or were just barely visible.

Father Hogan had initially felt acutely uncomfortable in the suffocating conditions, so completely devoid were they of any nuances, but slowly, day after day, he had become fascinated by the violent light and the vivid colours of the desert, by the extreme purity of the air and land, by the sky where the alternation of day and night was the ultimate expression of light and darkness.

That landscape, which in the beginning had seemed a skeleton of nature condemned to hell, revealed a hidden, secret life with every step: tenuous scents carried on swift, uncontaminated winds to distant lands and seas, fleeting shadows and sudden flashes of light, concealed presences which gave the only hint of their being in the unreal silence of dawn or the flames of sunset.

He realized that they were walking along the beds of evaporated rivers and lakes; they were crossing the ancient plains of Delfud, where endless meadows had once been teeming with vast herds of wild animals. This very land – in a remote time, in a mysterious way – had bordered upon the Garden of Immortality.

When they neared Bir el Walid, Jobert took half a dozen men and reconnoitred the entire area. Only when he was sure that there was no one for a radius of several kilometres around the well did he allow the men and animals to drink and to replenish their water supplies.

That night he let them pitch camp near the well, but then he had them carefully remove any traces they had left and retreat to lower terrain a few kilometres away. He sent scouts out along the trail that came from the east so they could warn him of anyone approaching. The weather had been good up to that point and they had not encountered any insuperable difficulties on their journey. Everything seemed to be going well and Jobert calculated that Selznick would show up in three or four days, but the time passed without anything happening and Father Hogan grew more anxious with every passing hour. There was so little time left! He imagined the voice plunging through infinite space and couldn't help but compare the immeasurable speed of that message, devouring the distance between the stars, with the slow plodding of the mules and camels all around him. A sense of impotence consumed him. He would turn on the radio whenever he had the chance and seek out an ultra-short-wave frequency, pointing the antenna towards the constellation of Scorpio. He would then sit for hours and listen to the insistent signal as it became more and more frequent.

On the evening of the fifth day, Colonel Jobert, who had been observing him for some time, approached, silent as always. 'Is that it?'

'Yes.'

'Where does it come from?'

Father Hogan looked up towards the constellation, low on the tropical horizon.

'From there,' he said. 'From a dark spot in the constellation of Scorpio, a little above Antares.'

'Are you mocking me?'

'No. We are certain of it.'

'So that's what you're waiting for ... My God, a message from another world!'

'Do you understand now? At least allow me to leave. I can go alone. All I need is a small escort and enough supplies to make my way there. I can't wait any longer.'

'I do understand, but you mustn't let yourself panic. It would be a terrible mistake to attempt the journey alone. The risk of never arriving would be much greater than any delay involved in waiting here an extra day or two. It won't take them much longer, I'm sure of it. If in two days' time we still haven't sighted them, I'll concede that something has happened and give the order to move on myself. I've already instructed the men to prepare for departure.'

Father Hogan nodded resignedly and started to walk off, but Jobert called him back. 'Wait, there's something there.'

The priest spun round and saw that Jobert was staring at a little hill about a kilometre to the east of their camp.

'I don't see anything at all,' said Father Hogan in disappointment.

'The scouts are signalling something. Look.'

Hogan could indeed see a flashing light on the hill now.

'There's no doubt about it,' said Jobert. 'Someone is approaching. It may very well be him. Stay here and don't move. This is a matter I want to see to personally.'

He called the men and divided them into groups, then summoned his officers. 'Gentlemen,' he said, 'it seems likely that the individual who has just been sighted is Selznick. He is a deserter and a murderer and he absolutely must be court-martialled. Each of you will now take your positions, giving the area of the well a wide berth, so that he'll have no escape route. We'll wait until they set up camp and then, at my signal, you'll come out of hiding but remain outside shooting range if possible. Selznick is not alone. If there is a reaction of any sort from his men, don't hesitate to fire, but leave Selznick out of it. He has to be taken alive.'

The officers gathered their units and mounted their horses, proceeding swiftly and silently towards the post to which each had been assigned.

Father Hogan approached Colonel Jobert. 'Do you mind if I come with you?' he asked.

'No, as long as you give me your word that you will keep your distance and not interfere in any way.'

Father Hogan nodded and, as soon as Jobert had jumped onto his horse at the head of his group, he mounted the mare he'd been given and followed a short way behind. When they were near the well, Jobert ordered his men to dismount and to remain hidden. He himself crawled even closer on his hands and knees, creeping along until he was about thirty metres from the well, then lay on his belly and took out his binoculars. A group of men on horseback was coming from the east, followed by a small caravan of camels. They were preceded by two bedouins armed with rifles, who were approaching the well at a trot. They made a brief tour of inspection before rushing in to draw water. The others followed their lead, spurring their horses to the well, and lined up next to their comrades. They filled their flasks, passing them down the line, then began to gather wood for a fire. The last to get off his horse seemed to be their leader. He was wearing the uniform of a Legion colonel with leather boots, but his head was covered and his features were hidden by a keffiyeh. When one of the men brought him a flask he bared his face and dismounted from his horse, nearing the fire. It was Selznick.

Although he had been practically certain it would be him, Jobert still stared at the sight of the man he had been hunting for so long and who would at last have no escape. He checked his watch and calculated that the others would be securely in position by now. He waited a few more minutes, then fired a shot into the air. The sound of galloping briefly filled the air as three squads of legionnaires drew up in a wide semicircle around the well.

There was no resistance. Seeing that they were completely surrounded and outnumbered, with no way to break through, Selznick's men tossed their weapons to the ground and surrendered. Not even Selznick himself put up any opposition, handing his arms over to the officer who arrested him. The bedouins who were escorting him, about ten of them in all, were disarmed, allowed to stock up on water and then sent back in the direction they had come from; any of them who dared show his face again would be shot without hesitation.

Selznick was handcuffed and brought before Jobert. The two men stared at each other for some time in silence. The air of tension that enveloped them was so palpable that, one by one, the other soldiers disappeared. Even Father Hogan left them alone.

'Quite a stroke of luck, Colonel. Nothing short of incredible, actually,' said Selznick after a while. 'Two grains of sand on opposite sides of the desert had about as much chance of meeting up as we did.'

'No, that's not true, Selznick. I was here waiting for you. You'd been spotted on the Shabka trail. I was informed of your movements thanks to a high-powered radio we have with us.'

'A radio?' said Selznick. He sneered. 'Well, then, it wasn't a fair fight, Jobert. You've contaminated the last place on earth where a man could still be free, like a fish in the sea or a bird in the air.'

'Free to kill, to steal, to betray . . .'

'Just free,' said Selznick.


THEY STARTED THEIR journey again without delay that very day and Colonel Jobert resumed his place at the head of the column.

Father Hogan approached him. 'What do you intend to do with Selznick?' he asked.

'What did you expect, a summary execution without a trial? I'm an officer, not a hangman. There's a redoubt five days from here. We'll be able to reach it with a slight detour. It's used to store supplies and water for our troops who are crossing through this area, and it is usually garrisoned by a small unit. I'll turn Selznick over to them and we can proceed without worrying about him. We'll be at the Sand of Ghosts in a week or so and he'll be facing a court-martial . . . Who can say which is the better fate?'

They continued south, crossing first a rocky ridge that jutted out of the sand here and there, and then a flat, barren stretch of hammada that was strewn with dried thornbushes. On the fourth day they arrived at a wadi and Jobert ordered his men to follow its course from then on.

During the journey, Jobert allowed his men to remove Selznick's bonds so he could defend himself against the flies and gnats that accompanied them, incessantly tormenting the men, horses and camels.

On the evening of the fifth day, they came within sight of the redoubt. Nothing but a low drystone wall and a flag that hung from an acacia-wood flagpole. The place appeared to be deserted. It was very small and only one of the three companies could camp inside. The others set up outside.

A strange crepuscular light hung over the desolate site. Selznick was tied to a pole and given a blanket to protect him from the chill of the coming night. Colonel Jobert entered what must have been the commander's quarters: a hovel with no doors or windows, covered everywhere with dust. A couple of sheets of yellowed paper lay on the table and several heat-curled books sat on a shelf. Insects, big ground beetles with long legs, scrambled off to find somewhere to hide, surprised by the intruder. Jobert left that ominous place and went towards the desert to walk off his tension and anxiety. When he returned, the men had eaten and were already resting, worn out by their exertions, but Selznick was still awake.

'Can't sleep, my friend?' he asked Jobert with a mocking smile.

'Don't call me that, Selznick. You are a murderer and a deserter. You and I have nothing in common but the uniform that you have dishonoured and I would strip that from you with my bare hands if I could.'

Selznick smirked. 'Not what you were expecting, is it? There's not a living soul here. What are you going to do with me? Is that what's keeping you from sleeping, Jobert? There's a remedy to every problem: a nice, quick summary trial and off to the firing squad. Then you can continue untroubled on your way.'

'Shut up, Selznick. Who do you think you're talking to? I'm not like you. I have principles. I believe in a code of ethics.'

'Do you think that makes you better than me? Tell me, then,

what are you willing to shoot and kill for? What are you fighting for here, Jobert? Why are you wearing that uniform?'

'I . . . I'm fighting for the values of the civilization that I believe in.'

Selznick shook his head. 'Western Christianity . . . would not exist without Judas. Tell me, Jobert, have you ever known what it feels like to be detested, to bear the weight of the contempt and hate of your fellow men? To be the wolf driven from the pack? True heroism is . . . the courage of people like me. We are the only ones who dare to face the final challenge . . .'

Jobert considered him with an expression of dismay. 'That won't save you from the firing squad, Selznick. I swear it.'

'No one can foresee when or whom death will strike, Jobert. You who are a soldier should know that.' He fell silent for a while, then looked at the rudimentary flagpole standing at the corner of the enclosure wall. 'Have you noticed that flag? If the men here were forced to leave, why did no one lower it? How is that possible?' A breath of wind set off a mild flutter in the torn flag that hung from the pole. 'Haven't you asked yourself why that flag was never lowered, Colonel Jobert?'

The officer shuddered at the thought of what Selznick was implying. He went back, nearly fleeing, to the miserable hovel at the end of the camp. He lit a candle stub and put it inside a lantern, then left the compound to reconnoitre the desert to the east and the south, where the scouts had not yet been. He finally found a little group of mounds, nearly flattened by the wind. On one side were the unburied remains of an officer. A Legion captain's uniform still dressed the mummified body.

Jobert felt a wave of panic rising. What could have exterminated that garrison if not an epidemic? There were no signs of fighting either inside or outside the camp. Just the traces of abandonment; of a slow, inexorable agony.

He went back to the redoubt and walked slowly among the slumbering men, holding the lantern high to illuminate their faces. Perhaps they'd already been contaminated; perhaps some incurable disease was already worming its way through their bodies. Perhaps he himself was doomed.

Jobert walked towards the pole that Selznick was tied to. He seemed to be drowsing, but as soon as Jobert passed, he opened his eyes and stared at him with a contemptuous expression. 'An epidemic,' he said, shrugging. 'You've no hope.'

Jobert regained his composure. 'That may be,' he admitted. 'But you'll have no chance to celebrate, Selznick. You're going back with them and if for any reason the unit does not reach Bir Akkar, I'll order the commander to kill you.'

'You'll have to kill me now,' said Selznick. 'Because I shall accuse you of having abandoned them to their destiny, fully realizing that they would all die on the way back of the same disease that wiped out this garrison. I'll say that you did not eat and drink with them because you didn't want to risk contagion. You'll be lynched, Jobert. Don't forget what sort of men these soldiers were before they joined the Legion. Under the present circumstances, they have nothing to lose. Unless . . .'

'Unless what?'

'Unless you agree to take me with you.'

'Where?'

'To Kalaat Hallaki and the Sand of Ghosts.'

'You're mad, Selznick! I am not . . .'

'Spare me your lies, Colonel. On such a long, boring journey, men talk, and I'm neither stupid nor deaf. There are only two roads leading away from here. One that goes back to Bir Akkar and another that leads into the heart of the south-eastern quadrant, towards Wadi Addir and Kalaat Hallaki. If you're sending your men back to Bir Akkar without you, that means you intend to proceed south.'

'Kalaat Hallaki does not exist. It's a legend, like so many others that the peoples of the desert tell tales of.'

'You forget that I worked with Desmond Garrett. Kalaat Hallaki exists and that's where you're going. Why? And why this deployment of forces?'

Jobert realized that he had no choice. He either gave in to blackmail and took an extremely dangerous man with him on a mission that was already high-risk to start with, or he finished him off then and there. After all, if he chose to do so he would just be carrying out an act of justice which would not be long in coming in any case. He could free Selznick of his chains and kill him, and tell his men that he had managed to get loose and was trying to escape. He slipped behind the pole, released the man's bonds and put his hand on his holster.

Selznick understood his intent immediately. 'Yes,' he said, 'this is surely the wisest decision. But are you sure that you're not murdering me in cold blood? Are you sure you want to commit the most shocking injustice of all?'

'I would have preferred to hand you over to the law, Selznick, but you've left me no choice,' said Jobert, pointing his revolver at him.

Selznick stared straight into his eyes without a tremor, without the slightest hesitation. 'Death cannot be worse than life,' he said, 'but before you pull that trigger, answer me one last question, Colonel. You know the true reason my superiors have hunted me down so tenaciously, don't you? That's why you want to kill me.'

'Desertion. The massacre of General LaSalle and his men.'

'Don't be naïve, Jobert. If you allow me five more minutes of life I'll tell you the real reason. A reason that will set your heart at ease if you're cynical enough, or that will torment you with remorse and shame for all the rest of your days if inside you there is the merest hint of that decency that you like to flaunt so much.'

Jobert's finger was already curled around the trigger, but something stopped him. He knew that Selznick had been used during the war by his own motherland, sent out on secret missions. He had neither known nor cared to know any more, assuming that Selznick's fierce, ruthless character made him suitable for such work.

Selznick realized what was going through his mind and kept talking. 'I was assigned by your government, during the war, to command the units in charge of executing individuals who had been accused of cowardice before the enemy. Thousands of young men, Jobert, whose only fault was refusing to submit to butchery without a reason, unlike the hundreds of thousands of their companions mown down by machine guns, forced to advance in suicidal attacks by obtuse, incompetent generals. This is the true reason why they've been searching for me since I fled the Legion. They want to find me and execute me, and bury this whole story. This is the true reason why you, now, will pull that trigger.'

Jobert lowered his weapon and returned Selznick's wild stare. 'You'll come with me,' he said, replacing the other man's handcuffs. 'Killing you now would only serve to lock the past up for all time.'

He returned to the little cemetery that he had discovered behind the redoubt and dug a grave for the unburied body, then covered the remaining mounds with sand so that his men would not see them at daybreak. When he had finished, he leaned against the wall to reflect on what he would do when the sun came up, evaluating all his possible options. He could not send his men back to Bir Akkar because he wouldn't be able to justify such a decision, but nor could he take them with him. If they'd become infected, the disease could spread to the entire contingent. He would order those camped inside to remain at the fortress to repair it and act as a garrison there while he proceeded with his mission. If the source of infection was no longer active and they survived, he would join up with them again on his return journey. If they were condemned to death, at least they would have a shelter in which to await their end.

He dozed off shortly before dawn, seeking a little respite for his tormented mind and spirit.

# 14

THE FLAMES OF THE little campfire cast the only light in the immense, empty expanse; the voice of the jackal the only sound in the vast silence.

Philip got up and joined his father, who was adjusting his sextant to a precise point in the clear winter sky. 'What are you looking for in that constellation?' he asked.

'How much time we have left.'

'Can you predict how long we have to live?'

'No. I'm trying to calculate how much longer our journey will last. I have seen the Stone of the Constellations in the most secret archives of Rome and I've read the testament of Baruch bar Lev. I am the last hunter of the man of the seven tombs. The last tomb can be destroyed when the star of Antares mirrors its vermilion light in the spring of Hallaki, when Acrab in Scorpio enters the centre of the firmament over the Tower of Solitude.'

A neighing rang out in the dark and Philip turned to see El Kassem, who had just mounted his horse and was riding towards a little rise north of them in order to scan the horizon. He was waiting for Selznick to reappear, so that the final duel could be fought. His silhouette was clear and still against the basalt hill, and his Arab charger seemed an enchanted Pegasus poised to take flight.

Philip turned towards his father again. 'You know where the spring of Hallaki is, don't you? It's there that we're going, isn't it?'

Desmond laid the sextant on the ground. 'Finding Hallaki was my dream as a young man, my secret Utopia. I pictured it in my mind's eye for years, as I spent days and nights in my study, and I always refused to consider it a legend. I saw it as the last remnant of a natural world which had ceased to exist, the last memento of an ancient state of bliss. During my expeditions, I would wander for months through the desert at the edge of the southeastern quadrant, searching for it, but more than once I was prevented from going on by a sandstorm . . .'

'How did you finally manage to find it?'

'It was when I understood that the sandstorm was a sort of permanent barrier, a shield that the desert had raised in protection of that last paradise. El Kassem had prepared my way by leaving water supplies along the entire route, the same that we've been using on this journey, and I decided I would attempt a crossing. I risked death that day. I forged ahead through that burning wall in a kind of delirium, and even after I had lost my horse I continued to advance for hours and hours with the sand scratching at my face and hands until they were bleeding. The wind was so strong it was stripping off my clothes. All at once, my strength abandoned me and I collapsed to the ground. I covered my head with the edge of my cape and, before I slipped into unconsciousness, I sought the face of your mother, the only woman I ever loved, and I thought of you, Philip. I thought I would never see you again.'

He fell silent for a while, straining to hear in the darkness, lifting his head as if he could pick up his enemy's scent on the night breeze. El Kassem had vanished, but he soon appeared again, at a different spot, for a moment, in the shadow of a dune.

'When I opened my eyes again, I found myself in the greenest, most lovely meadow that you can imagine. I was stretched out on the grass, bathed in the light of a golden sunset. The bleating of sheep and the songs of birds filled my ears. Brightly coloured creatures soared over my head in a violet sky.

'When I saw that place, I swore I would never leave. Your mother was already gone and you were practically a man. I thought I had found the mythical land of the Lotus Eaters, where Ulysses' companions sought rest after their endless journey and found oblivion instead. I would live in that inaccessible refuge and serenely await my last hour. I deluded myself into thinking that a man can flee from his past, from the people he has loved and those he has hated. I wanted to believe that there was a place in the world where a man could utterly forget himself.

'Until I discovered that that gorgeous hideaway was a citadel at war. I realized that a terrible threat loomed over those gardens and orchards, that that enchanted oasis was the last outpost, beyond which the undisputed reign of a mystery darker than any nightmare was to be found – a mystery that I myself had tried in vain to flee many a time. Hallaki is the metaphor of our human destiny, my son. We'll never stop searching on this earth for the paradise that we have lost, but each time we think we've found it we discover ourselves before an ocean of darkness. There is no day without night, no heat without cold. There is no reign of love that does not share a border with the empire of hatred.'

'But then why struggle at all?' asked Philip. 'Why face risk and hardship and pain to take on an impossible challenge? When you've destroyed the last tomb, if you ever manage to do so, will you have tricked destiny? Will you have halted the fist of God that looms over us? You're chasing after some magic ritual that will satisfy your thirst for adventure, your curiosity about the unknown.'

'Perhaps. But it's a war we can't avoid, a fight without quarter. The battlefield is everywhere. There's nowhere for deserters to seek shelter. The only possible course of action is choosing sides. And since you're here with me, it means that you have decided what side you're on. That's the answer to your question.'

Philip looked up towards the starry vault and the movement of his eyes gave him the sensation for a moment that the stars were falling down, were being sucked into a vortex.

'But . . . mightn't the power of suggestion have something to do with it? This wouldn't have happened back in Paris . . .'

'No. There are things that happen only in those places where the work of creation has not been interfered with. Have you ever crossed a forest on your own at night? You can call upon all your rationality but you'll always be spooked, you'll always feel that something is after you. The ancients believed that the boundless solitude of the desert, the forests and swamps, the never-melting ice fields, were the exclusive domain of the gods. They were right. Avile Vipinas truly saw what he described; he could not have lied on the brink of death. He took up his pen with his heart pounding and his breath being sucked from his throat . . .'

'Tell me what your ultimate objective is. Where will we have to fight this battle?'

'Reading the words of the Etruscan haruspex convinced me. What the inhabitants of Kalaat Hallaki call the Tower of Solitude must be the last resting place of the man of the seven tombs. If I'm right, we have to look for an object that resembles a cylinder topped by a hemispherical cap, the *petasus* that Avile Vipinas speaks of.'

Philip sat on the still-tepid sand, watching the flames of the campfire as they blazed, creating a small island of light in the dominion of night. He searched for El Kassem among the uncertain shapes of the landscape.

'What do those words you told me mean?' he asked his father all at once. 'What did you mean when you said, "When the star of Antares mirrors its vermilion light in the spring of Hallaki, when Acrab in Scorpio enters the centre of the firmament over the Tower of Solitude"?'

'I think that those words allude to a particular astral configuration. The tower can be destroyed when Antares is at its zenith directly above Kalaat Hallaki—'

'But don't you see? The second part of the phrase doesn't make sense. If Antares is at its zenith directly above Kalaat Hallaki, how can Acrab, which is very close to Antares in the Scorpio constellation, be at the centre of the firmament?'

Desmond shook his head. 'I've thought it over at length,' he said, 'and I've never managed to find a plausible explanation. It may be an error of some sort, or a mistaken interpretation. You're right, the phrase just doesn't make sense as it is. All we can do is reach Kalaat Hallaki and then look for an answer in the sky.'

The luminous halo at the centre of the little valley shrank little by little until it was no more than a glimmer and the sky, glowing with millions of stars, appeared even vaster and deeper. Man's solitude seemed limitless, making Philip feel giddy, as if he were poised to topple into a chasm.

Sleep seemed the only refuge.

Philip lay down near the campfire, but before he closed his eyes he heard the distant, muffled pounding of a horse's hooves. El Kassem was passing like a ghost in the darkness, mounting guard on the borders of infinity.

THE LONG CARAVAN descended from the hillside and wound its way over the plain like a snake, delineating the features of the terrain with sinuous grace. The warriors on horseback led the column behind Amir, who was preceded by the purple standard. Arad rode at his side, carrying a staff topped by the rearing gazelle of Meroe. Behind them was a long line of camels, laden with wineskins and big clay jars tied to their saddles with strong rope. More warriors on horseback brought up the rear of the column. Others were scattered at a distance on both sides of the column as guards.

'No one has ever crossed the wall of sand with such a large caravan,' said Arad. 'If we lose the animals, all our efforts will have been in vain.'

'I've been thinking about it since we left,' replied Amir. 'There's a point in the wall of sand where the wind abates at night. We'll proceed until we come within sight of the barrier, then stop and allow the men and the animals to rest for a while. From there we'll find the crossing point, which is slightly to the east of the direction we are travelling in. We will wait for night to fall and for the wind to drop, and then we will descend into the wadi, which will provide us with shelter. Before day breaks we'll see the stars twinkling over the bastions of Kalaat Hallaki. You will enter under the banner of the gazelle of Kush, and embrace your father and your mother once again.' Amir's eyes shone as he spoke. He never took his eyes off her unless it was to scan the horizon before him.

They crossed another chain of low, wind-worn hills and then descended into the valley below. Suddenly a strip of what looked like fog came into view at about one hour's march from where they were – a barrier that extended across the plain as far as the eye could see.

'The wall of sand,' said Amir. 'Beyond it we'll find grass and water, fruit on the trees and birds singing in the sky.'

'Beyond it there's the madness of my mother . . .' said Arad. Her eyes were fixed on the swirling dust.

'Not for long,' insisted Amir. 'Before the full moon rises again, your mother will have regained her sanity. I swear it.'

They stopped when the sun began to sink, its light drowning in the thick dust carried by the wind. Amir gave orders for the animals to be allowed what was left of the water and for the men to descend from their horses and rest as they could. Upon his word, they would blindfold the horses and camels and tie them one to the other so that they could not stray from the caravan. Then they would begin the crossing. They waited for the sky to darken completely and for the evening star to appear, shining in the deep blue like a diamond on Damascus velvet. It was time. The wind was dropping.

He turned towards Arad, who was waiting on her own, at some distance from the others. 'I feel ice in my bones when I gaze into your eyes, Arad. Why won't you look at me?'

Arad did not answer.

'Not very long ago, you promised that you would welcome me into your bed if I succeeded in leading our warriors through the Sand of Ghosts.'

'I will,' said Arad. 'Wipe out the Blemmyae, spill their infected blood onto the earth, and I will hold true to my word.'

Amir's eyes were full of sadness. 'I don't want your word, Arad. I want your love,' he said. He jumped onto his horse and galloped away.

He rode up to a slightly elevated ridge, covered his face with his *barrakan* and raised his arm as a signal. The warriors mounted their horses and the caravan drivers goaded on the camels, who set off with their slow, swaying gait and filled the air with mournful grunts. The column plunged into the fog that swallowed up shapes and sounds, the voices of the men and the animals. They all vanished into the milky mist.

But the long column that snaked through the desert, raising a white cloud in their wake, had not passed unnoticed. Perched on the saddle of his horse, Colonel Jobert was watching as the long line of horsemen and camels was slowly engulfed in the curtain of dust. 'Those people know of a passage through the sandstorm,' he said. 'All we have to do is follow them. They'll take us to Kalaat Hallaki.' He turned towards Father Hogan. 'I promised you that we'd get there in time and now this unexpected stroke of luck will certainly shorten our journey. Be prepared. We'll attempt the crossing immediately, as soon as the last of those horsemen has disappeared into the cloud.'

In the meantime, Amir was keeping his head down and urging his horse on with his heels, although he would stroke the animal's neck now and then to reassure him. In his other hand he held high a flaming pitch-soaked torch so the men behind him could see. He was searching the terrain for traces of a stony path, the bottom of the wadi. He could feel the wind abating slightly, and then he realized that his horse was trying to step around the big stones that were jutting out of the ground. He'd found the path.

After a brief stretch where it was practically level, the wadi sank between two banks tall enough to provide shelter from the wind, which was hitting them obliquely now instead of head on, and the long caravan was able to proceed without the risk of straying off in the darkness. Amir felt immense relief and new hope. He knew that he would succeed in an endeavour that no one would have thought possible. He advanced for hours in the dark without seeing the face of Arad, although she was right beside him. He held the torch high the entire time with an aching arm until he could feel the wind dropping and then dying away completely. The suddenly still air was fragrant with grass and flowers and bore from faraway the cries of the sentries standing guard on the bastions of the castle and the song of the night birds. Amir contemplated the quiet valley. Hallaki slept stretched out in the shadows like a beautiful woman in her sweetly scented bed. He looked back and saw Arad emerge from the fog cloaked in moonlight, like an apparition.

'We're home, Arad, my lady, my beloved. We're home.'

The caravan reached the edge of the oasis when the stars were beginning to pale and the sky to whiten behind the bulwarks of the fortress. At that moment a trumpet blared, then a second and a third, and the whole valley echoed with the sound. The great gate was opened and a squad of horsemen rushed out to welcome Amir and Princess Arad.

The squad escorted them to the castle as dozens of torches were lit on the bastions. Others lit the walls of the inner courtyard and bathed the carvings on the great portal in their reddish glow. The bridge shook under the pounding hooves of Amir and Arad's horses and the warriors poured in, continuing their gallop around the big courtyard and finally drawing up in single file all around the vast square.

Rasaf el Kebir appeared bareheaded, with a long blue cape thrown over his shoulders. His scimitar hung from his side in its silver sheath. He threw his arms open wide and welcomed both of them, his daughter and the young leader of his warriors, clutching them to his chest as if both were his children.

'You are home!' he said. 'Kalaat Hallaki wasn't the same place without you, and I was beginning to despair.'

'Our mission was a complete success,' said Amir. 'We passed

every test. Outside is a caravan of seventy camels laden with the jugs that hold the naphtha which flows from the well at Hit. I will lead the charge of your warriors between two walls of flames, all the way to the Tower of Solitude. Your bride, Altair, will regain the light of her mind on the day upon which knowledge shines forth from the tower. Allow me to return the key of the Horse's Crypt, the steel star that brushed your daughter's cheek like a caress without doing her any harm.'

'I too give you the key,' said Arad, 'that brushed Amir's cheek like a caress, without doing him any harm.'

Amir watched her as she said 'without doing him any harm' and felt his heart filling with anguish and grief instead. He felt that she was more distant than the stars he contemplated in the desert sky every night before succumbing to sleep.

'That day is coming,' said Rasaf. 'If we win, and my wife is healed, I think that the greatest happiness that could befall me would be to see the two of you united, and the race of the queens of Meroe perpetuated.'

He looked his daughter straight in the eyes but she lowered hers, as if she wanted to hide from her father the thoughts that were passing through her mind at that moment.

'Rest now,' he said, 'from the hardships of your journey. The women have prepared a scented bath for you, and a soft bed. This evening you will both dine with me in the great hall of the castle, along with all of those who are most dear to me. We will enjoy happy hours in the expectation and hope that our vows will be fulfilled.'

As evening fell, both Amir and Arad left their separate apartments and went to the great hall, where dinner had been prepared for them.

Rasaf met them at the door and embraced them. 'Come,' he said, 'take your places next to me so we can celebrate your return. We will eat and drink and prepare our spirits for the last battle.'

'My mother,' said Arad, 'where is she? Is she well?'

'Your mother is resting,' replied Rasaf. 'She has drunk a potion that will help her sleep until the moment of our departure. But don't let yourself feel troubled for her now. You've done everything possible: you've suffered trials and tribulations, you've crossed the desert twice. Allow your heart to feel a little joy, and share it with the man before you, the strongest and most generous of the sons of this land.'

'Yes, father,' said Arad with a faint smile. And she turned and graced Amir with the same smile. But her mind had never left the bare room where she had given herself to a stranger, a pale young man with blue eyes. In that place she had believed for a few moments that she could live like any woman who is born and dies beneath the heavens, bearing children so she can watch them grow and work in the fields and tend to the flocks. She had given in to an emotion that she had never felt before, to a force that was stronger than the wind, hotter than the rays of the sun, softer than the evening breeze.

She had believed for a moment that she could run off with him and live for ever in a distant secret place where destiny would never find her. She had deceived herself, and now she knew that she could no longer flee. She would fight. She would face the horror of the Blemmyae, the immensity of the mystery that sometimes flashed on the horizon at night in a bloody halo. She smiled again when Amir handed her a cup of palm wine and she drank from it, hoping that one day she would forget.

When the evening was drawing to a close, one of the guards entered and approached Rasaf. 'My lord,' he said, 'the soldiers of the desert have crossed the wall of sand and their chief has come to us unarmed, requesting to meet with you. He is the same man whom we once saved from the Sand of Ghosts. He says that he comes in peace and offers you his allegiance. He puts the powerful weapons he has with him at your disposal and your command.'

'Wait until everyone has left the hall and then bring him here to me. Draw up the guard at the entrance to the oasis and put sentries on every bastion. Their every movement must be under our surveillance.'

The man responded with a nod of his head and left.

Rasaf turned to Amir and Arad. 'I would like you to stay. A stranger, a soldier of the desert, asks to speak with us. He is the same man you once saved from certain death, Amir. I want to listen to what he has to say.'

Eventually, the guests took their leave, one after another, and the great hall was soon empty. When they had all left, the door opened and Colonel Jobert appeared. He was covered in dust and his eyes were bloodshot and weary.

'I have been told that I am in the presence of Rasaf el Kebir, the lord of this place.'

'The lady of this place is not with us because her mind has long been steeped in darkness. I am her husband.'

'I know,' said Jobert. 'I heard her song of enchantment from the bastions, and her cry of terror. I have come to offer my allegiance against a common enemy. Against those monstrous creatures who have ravaged the mind of your bride and massacred my men under my very eyes.'

'You insisted on venturing into the Sand of Ghosts without knowing what awaited you and you paid dearly for your presumption.'

'I know,' replied Jobert, 'but we soldiers of the desert are accustomed to obeying the orders we receive from our superiors. I had been ordered to explore the territory that you call the Sand of Ghosts and I had no choice. I owe my life to you and I have returned to offer my allegiance. I want to avenge my fallen comrades and give them an honourable burial. I have powerful weapons capable of killing hundreds of men in a mere instant, and a group of loyal and valiant soldiers. We shall march forward together and annihilate the Blemmyae. I promise and I give you my word of honour that afterwards I will leave this place for ever and never again will any of the soldiers of the desert cross the wall of sand. Kalaat Hallaki will go back to being a legend.'

Rasaf considered him in silence. The man was exhausted and could barely stand, but his eyes glittered with desperate determination and steadfast will. Rasaf understood that honour was not merely a word for this man, but he also realized that such sacrifice and risk could not be explained away simply by a desire for revenge, by his resolve to bury bones bleached by the sun. He turned to Amir and saw that he was thinking the same thing.

'It is not only vengeance that you seek. You haven't returned simply to lay your dead to rest. What else are you looking for? I will not allow you to pass unless you tell me honestly.'

Jobert lowered his head. 'The wise men of my people say that a message will arrive from the stars in five days, seventeen hours and seven minutes, and they have sent one of them with me to listen to this message. But the place where it will arrive is in the Sand of Ghosts, in the territory of the Blemmyae.'

Arad started and even Rasaf could not contain his surprise. 'The wise men of your people have told the truth,' he said. 'And we mean to listen to that voice as well.'

Amir interrupted. 'What do we need this foreigner for?' he said. 'We have powerful arms of our own that I have brought with me from across the desert. We have already saved him once and thus we are stronger than he is. After all, we cannot be sure of his true intentions.'

But Arad drew closer and rested her hand on his shoulder. 'We face a bitter battle, Amir, perhaps the last we shall ever fight. Allow these allies to do combat at our side. It will not diminish your valour and I will keep the promise I have made to you, because you will be in command. You will draw up the forces and move them on the battlefield.' She kissed his head and left the room.

She went down the stairs, crossed the courtyard that was still illuminated by the torches and walked out into the silent valley, wandering through the orchards and shadowy palm groves, breathing in the scent of the fields. Clouds covered the vault of the sky except for a brief gap towards the west, where a slim crescent moon hovered over the tree tops. The murmur of the spring was close now; a sound that she'd always listened for since she was a little girl, delighting in its gentle song. She approached the water's edge and tossed a stone in, as children are wont to do, watching the little concentric waves ripple outwards. The clouds parted then and a strip of sky was reflected in the water. Arad saw the red light of Antares sparkling like a ruby in the shiny black pool.

THE THREE HORSEMEN were transfixed, watching the dense cloud of dust that covered the southern horizon. They were waiting for the light of the sun to disappear so they could read the destiny that awaited them in the stars. But when the last gleam of daylight had been extinguished, a new glow rose above the cloud against the dark sky. A thick, bloody halo which expanded and contracted like a beating heart.

'My God, what is it?' said Philip.

'It's Him,' said Desmond. 'It's Him. He's waking up. The star of Antares is mirrored in the spring of Hallaki. We must go, now.'

He urged on his mount. But the horses were nervously pawing the ground, bucking, reluctant to proceed towards the grim light that stained the sky like an infected sore.

'The horses are afraid,' said El Kassem. 'We won't be able to cross the cloud.'

'We'll go on foot, if necessary,' said Desmond. 'We'll follow the red halo. It will guide us even from inside the cloud.' He dug in his spurs and rode on, followed by Philip and El Kassem, but they soon stopped dead in their tracks. 'Look,' said Desmond, 'the cloud has dissipated.' And indeed, directly in front of them, precisely where the vast halo throbbed with the most intense light, the cloud was disappearing like morning mist in the heat of the sun. The wind dropped and the crescent moon was soon visible in the west.

'We can go now,' he said. 'The road is open.' He turned

towards Philip with an ironic look. 'This would never have happened in Paris, would it?'

Philip did not smile back, but he was the first to spur on his horse. The three men galloped along the arid banks of Wadi Addir.

They didn't stop until they had reached the hidden valley and the wonder of Hallaki loomed before them. The castle, a solitary giant, kept vigil in the darkness. Lights pulsed behind its windows, while others vanished only to reappear elsewhere; calls echoed from the bastions, muffled at this distance. The valley itself seemed deserted and nothing could be heard save the calls of nocturnal birds. Here and there, amid the deep green of the trees, water glittered, reflecting the silvery glow of the moon.

'Can you understand what I felt when I first found this place?' asked Desmond.

Philip nodded his head in silence, not finding words to express the emotion that had gripped him. He turned towards a line of low hills stretching out to their right. The reddish halo had shrunk considerably and seemed to be vanishing.

'It's still there,' said his father. 'It's that we have shifted towards the south-east to follow Wadi Addir.'

They descended into the valley to draw water from a spring that flowed at the entrance to the oasis. 'This is where I awoke that first time,' said Desmond, indicating the meadows on which their horses were grazing. 'I was surrounded by children who were watching me in silence. They must be warriors by now . . . and perhaps some of them are riding over the Sand of Ghosts at this very moment by the light of the moon. We must go on,' he said. 'Look, Antares is shining directly over our heads.'

Philip approached him as El Kassem saw to watering the horses. 'Father,' he said, 'we don't know what awaits us tomorrow in the desert, nor whether we'll still be alive when the sun sets again. There's something I've wanted to ask you, for a long time now.'

Desmond looked at him. 'It's about your mother, I know . . .

but it's the same question I've asked myself all these years without ever finding an answer. I loved both of you, Philip, in the only way I could love you, but this didn't stop you or your mother from suffering . . . It's like when you're sitting in front of a campfire in the winter: your chest is warm in the reflection of the flames, but your back is stung by the chill of the night.'

'And you believe that this battle will absolve you of blame and do away with my regrets?'

'No. But it will be the most challenging moment of our lives. If we survive the fire and the sword, whatever part of us remains will be closer to our true nature than anything we've ever known. If we fall, at least we shall cross the bounds of night at a gallop.'

They jumped into their saddles and rode across the oasis, advancing into the open desert. Three kilometres on, the track split in two different directions: one led due south, while the other took off in a south-westerly direction, where the strange bloody aurora had nearly vanished. Without getting off his horse, Desmond unfolded a sheet reproducing an ancient map of Ptolemy's. He used the flame of his lighter to illuminate the area crossed by the trail on their right. A word was splayed across the empty space in cursive characters: Blemmyae.

'Let's go,' he said, spurring on his mount.

COLONEL JOBERT STOPPED on the top of a dune that was flushed with the last light of sunset, then got off his horse, took the compass from his saddle and marked a spot on his military map. 'We're here, Hogan,' he said. 'That's where we were attacked, in that valley down there. The topographical site you are seeking is a few kilometres beyond the valley, more or less where we saw that red halo shining last night.

'Amir and Princess Arad will be approaching from that direction any minute now. If the Blemmyae appear, our friends will attack from that side. We'll hem them in on this side and tear them to shreds. How are you feeling?'

Father Hogan had his binoculars out and was scanning the

sinuous line of the dunes, where the wind was whipping up tall swirls of dust. He suddenly stopped. 'My God!' he said. 'What is that?'

'What?'

'There's something down there, in that saddle between the dunes, a construction of some kind. Look. That's where the halo of light was coming from . . . and we haven't heard the signal since the light went out.'

Jobert grabbed his binoculars and looked in the direction Father Hogan had indicated. He saw a cylindrical construction that looked as if it might be made of stone, although no joints were apparent; it seemed to be a gigantic monolith. It was topped by a hemispherical dome made of the same material, with a seam running all the way around its edge.

'How is that possible?' he mused. 'Who could have cut such a colossal structure out of stone, transported it here and erected it in the middle of all this desolation?'

'That's it,' said Father Hogan. 'It's the receiver. I have no doubt.'

'The Tower of Solitude,' said a voice behind them. 'Finally . . .'

They turned to see Selznick staring at the huge monolith with a strange smile on his lips and a hallucinatory ecstasy in his bloodshot eyes. He had lost weight, and his face was tired and gaunt. The yellowish stain seeping out onto his uniform jacket was the revolting reminder of his curse.

'Take off my shackles,' he said. 'Where could I run to? And give me back my sabre, at least. Those monsters could attack us at any time. Let me have a blade so I can take my own life if they capture me.'

Jobert hesitated.

'Come now, Colonel, where is your spirit of humanity? Your values?'

'Give it to him, Colonel,' said Father Hogan.

'All right,' said Jobert.

He loosed Selznick's bonds, then slipped the sabre from his saddle and handed it to him.

Jobert turned to his men. 'We'll advance now,' he said, 'in a double file. Keep your weapons ready. Two men on foot for each machine gun, at the head of the column. At the slightest sign of danger, drop to the ground and open fire at will. Remember that this sand covers the bones of your fallen comrades.'

He turned to Father Hogan, who was putting on a sort of backpack with the radio inside. 'What do you intend to do?'

'I've connected the radio via a cable to the magnetic recorder that the camels are transporting. I'm going to try to get as close as possible to the receiver. The cable is quite long. You see? It's wound up here in this coil. I'll have sufficient freedom of movement,' replied the priest.

'Stay between the two lines for protection. Do you want a weapon?'

'No, I don't need one.'

'Take something,' insisted the officer. 'You haven't seen what I saw. They're absolutely atrocious, beyond any imagining.'

Hogan shook his head. 'I'll be too busy with this,' he said, nodding towards the radio. 'I wouldn't be able to use a weapon.' He hadn't finished speaking when the signal echoed clear and strong from the radio, while a blaze of bright light flared from the monolith. The dome seemed to become luminescent, casting a vermilion halo into the dark sky.

'It's the signal,' shouted Father Hogan. 'Forward, we must go forward!' But his voice was drowned out by a bloodcurdling sound, like a deep, hollow death rattle. The soldiers blanched and remained rooted to the spot, paralysed by fear.

'Forward!' shouting Jobert, unsheathing his sword and urging on his steed.

But at that very instant he heard another sound behind him and it filled him with dread: the bestial screeching that marked the presence of the enemy, the scorpion men who populated the sands. He turned around and terror twisted his features into a grimace. 'The Blemmyae!' he cried out at the top of his voice. 'The Blemmyae! They're behind us! Fire, men! Fire! Where is Amir? Damn it! Damn them all!'

Father Hogan turned round and saw the advance of the nightmarish creatures that Jobert had described so often around their desert campfires. He felt his blood freeze in his veins, but he forced himself to turn back towards the tower, dragging the camels behind him. The soldiers manning the machine guns turned as well, but they could not shoot, for fear of mowing down their own comrades, who were already engaged in hand-to-hand combat.

'Look! Amir's warriors!' shouted one of the officers.

'Square off, men!' shouted Jobert. 'The machine guns! Let the machine guns through!'

He had the guns moved to the flanks, one on the right side to cut down the advancing Blemmyae and the other on the left, turned in the opposite direction, to cover Father Hogan, who was making his way undaunted to the tower.

On their left, about a kilometre away, the column of Hallaki warriors suddenly appeared. A shrill cry echoed and two squads rushed headlong down the dune in two parallel columns, urging their horses into an unrestrained gallop. The monolith's dome was throbbing more intensely, its bloody light flashing even brighter, and Father Hogan realized that the bursts coincided with the signal, which was becoming increasingly loud and clear and more frequent. His face was dripping with sweat and his eyes felt wounded by the continuous flashing, so strong now that it was lightening the darkness that had fallen upon the desert.

He suddenly saw the sand stirring up under the feet of the blue warriors' steeds, as though it were teeming with thousands of monstrous insects. The Blemmyae burst out in every direction and flung themselves upon their adversaries, waving their shiny black metal scythes in the air. Amir's warriors forged onward, dropping the jars that were hanging from their saddles onto the ground, while fending off the attack of the scorpion-creatures that rose from the sands. The horsemen who fell were replaced by a continuous stream of fresh warriors who pressed on towards the tower, from which the beastly growl was unleashed once again, only louder and more cavernous.

Another couple of squads rode in to attack the Blemmyae, shooting at them with repeating rifles, spraying their bullets over the entire surface of the desert sands. Some of the soldiers leapt from their horses and took the enemy on in close combat.

Amir appeared then at the top of the dune, with Arad at his side. Both held lit torches in their raised hands. They exchanged a glance and then hurtled down the hillside until they had reached the tower, where they threw their torches to the ground. Two high walls of fire shot up and everything in their way burst into flame, including the Blemmyae and warriors locked in mortal combat.

The flames opened a corridor from the top of the hill all the way to the tower. Between them descended Rasaf at a mad gallop, holding a terrified woman in front of him on the saddle: his bride, Altair!

Father Hogan continued to advance through that incredible bloodbath, not really understanding how he could still be alive. He was astonished to see Selznick running towards the empty black portal at the base of the monolith, ripping off his clothes as he ran, stripping them from his bleeding wound. He was shouting, 'Heal me, Lord of Solitude!' He watched as Selznick crossed the threshold of the wide red halo that issued from the tower and then fell to his knees, screaming and pressing his hand against the wound that was sizzling as if it was being cauterized by a red-hot iron.

Father Hogan felt a sharp yank. He turned and saw that the camels behind him were terrified and trying wildly to escape, and he felt an ever deeper anguish wash over him. All would be lost if the cable broke! He grabbed a rifle that was lying on the ground and aimed it at the two animals, discharging all the rounds in the chamber in quick succession. When he saw that he had brought them down, he turned and continued to make his way towards the black doorway leading into the tower.

But a cry echoed to his right, over the din of the battle: 'Selznick!' Three horsemen were rushing down the hillside at a gallop, brandishing their sabres.

Selznick turned. 'Garrett!' he shouted. 'This time will be the last!' And he drew his own sabre.

The growl that was emanating from the tower was transformed into a thunderous roar which seemed to instil new courage into the Blemmyae as their comrades continued to rise from the sand. At that moment, Desmond raced past Father Hogan and then jumped to the ground with his sabre in his hand, engaging Selznick in a furious duel. The man was back on his feet and was returning every blow with wild, unsuspected energy.

The battlefield all around the tower was an inferno of fire and smoke, human screams mixing with the eerie sounds made by the Blemmyae. Philip found himself surrounded by four of the creatures, who had suddenly burst up around him, and he fought them off desperately. El Kassem flew to his side, cutting down one and then another. He shouted, 'The fire! Race to where the fire is. They won't dare to get close to it.' Philip dug his heels into his horse's flanks. The animal seemed ready to drop, attacked on every side, but with a powerful effort he righted himself, reared up and galloped off as El Kassem, like a lion surrounded by a pack of hyenas, spun his scimitar, spraying sparks off the black scythes of the Blemmyae. With every blow, he cried, '*Allah-u-akbar!* God is great!'

Philip tried to drive his horse towards the wall of fire but the animal was terrified by the blaze and bucked at the last moment, throwing his rider to the ground. Philip rolled through the flames and found himself inside the corridor. He got to his feet and found Arad in front of him, supporting her mother with Rasaf's help. The woman was unconscious, but they were still trying to lead her towards the luminous halo that surrounded the tower, so that the supernatural light could clear the darkness from her mind.

'Arad!' Philip shouted. 'Arad!' She looked at him in astonishment, but did not stop. The roar that was erupting from the tower ripped through the air, even louder, like a howl of infinite pain, and a strong wind gathered out of nowhere, raising a dense cloud of dust. The fire was abruptly extinguished and the Blemmyae resumed their advance. Philip caught a glance of a brave young warrior who was completely encircled, fighting on with unflagging fury. He heard the crackling shots of the machine guns coming from another direction. He desperately sought Arad in that swirling soot. 'Arad!' he shouted out in anguish. 'Arad!'

He saw her all of a sudden, distinguishing her by the light blue cloak that fluttered in the fog. There was something in front of her, a shadow in the wind, a dark shapeless mass that advanced slowly, letting out a long, low growl. He tried desperately to reach her, struggling against the strong wind. He found her and shielded her body with his own against the beastly sound that was drawing closer and closer. The dark mass was looming before him. He fired one, two, three shots with his pistol. They had no effect and he tossed it to the ground.

Philip retreated slowly, seized by terror, his foremost thought that of protecting Arad. He could already feel the beast's hot breath upon him. Backing up one step at a time, he tripped on a discarded weapon and the metallic clang reminded him of what he had in his pocket. The sistrum. He searched frantically through his jacket until he found it. He clasped it tightly in his fist at first, then held it out and waved it in front of him until the argentine sound flew over the scorched field and pierced the dust. The wind and the roaring stopped all at once. The beast's voice became a hoarse, panting breath, a pain-filled wheeze, and then vanished completely. Isolated shots could still be heard, suffocating cries, the distant whinnying of horses running wild, and then nothing.

The only sound still to be heard was the furious clash of swords inside the tower. The duel was not over. Selznick was still striking back hard, raining down close, incessant blows on his enemy. They flew at each other, soaked with sweat, animated by raging hate. Selznick fought as if he were possessed and Desmond felt his strength waning; he realized that he would soon no longer be able to resist the furious onslaught of his enemy.

The red glow descending from the vault dimly lit up the vast interior cavity as well, allowing Desmond to make out a large black stone sarcophagus that stood alone at the centre of the chamber. He sought shelter behind it, hoping to gather his strength. Then, sensing a moment in which his enemy was off guard, he lunged forward with a sudden thrust, holding his sword out in the same way as he had when he wounded Selznick that first time. But Selznick eluded his blade with a swift sidestep, sending Desmond rolling in the dust. His adversary was immediately upon him, ready with a cleaving blow, but Desmond managed to dodge it with a wrench of his shoulders. Selznick's blade plunged deep into the ground and Desmond violently smashed it with his own as he twisted away, breaking it in two. He sprang to his feet, pointing his weapon at Selznick's throat, forcing him to retreat until he was backed up against the sarcophagus. Fine, thought Desmond, this would be his sacrificial stone. He'd nail his enemy's evil spirit right to that tomb. He had raised his sabre when Father Hogan's voice sounded loudly behind him.

'No! Do not bring this crime upon yourself! He is your . . .'

But the whirling wind had now invaded the tower, blinding the two contenders. Desmond stumbled backwards, trying to shield his eyes from the burning dust while holding the sabre out before him. He fell back against the wall and, when he was able to see again, Selznick was gone. Only the bare sarcophagus remained before him. The wind had swept away the thick layer of dust that had covered its surface, uncovering seven inscriptions. He scanned them feverishly, one after another. All said the same thing in ancient lost languages, all screamed the same tremendous words:

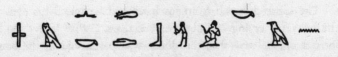

אף אחד לא יהרוג את קין

ΜΗΔΕΙΣ ΚΑΙΝ ΦΟΝΕΥΣΗ

NEMO CAIN OCCIDAT

THOU SHALT NOT KILL CAIN!

The sabre dropped from his hand and he raised his eyes to the heavens, crying out between his tears, 'Why? Why?' As he looked up, he saw that the dome was perforated in the same pattern as the constellation of Scorpio and he saw the gelid light of Acrab piercing the middle hole. He remembered the words of Baruch bar Lev: 'when Acrab in Scorpio enters the centre of the firmament over the Tower of Solitude'. The 'firmament'. In Hebrew 'firmament' could also mean 'dome'!

'Run!' he shouted. 'Flee this place, everyone!'

Outside, Father Hogan was on his knees in front of the door in the raging wind when he heard the signal increasing beyond measure in both intensity and frequency, until it became a paroxysmal fibrillation that shattered his eardrums and made his whole body clench in stabbing pain.

'Get out!' yelled Desmond, running out of the entrance. 'Out of here!'

But Father Hogan was not moving. His brow was beaded with sweat, his jaw tightly clenched. 'I must stay,' he said. 'I must receive the message.'

Desmond saw a figure arriving against the wind at a gallop: El Kassem.

'Get him out of here!' he shouted. 'Take him away with you! Now!'

El Kassem ripped the backpack from Father Hogan's shoulders, knocking him to the ground. He grabbed him by an arm and dragged him off in the dust, as Desmond tried laboriously to run after them, fighting against the wind. The signal, still growing, had became an acute, lacerating whistle. The dome of the monolith was now red hot and was flashing with a blinding light. It exploded, suddenly, with a fearful roar, raising a globe of fire that scorched the sky all the way to the horizon.

Desmond turned. 'The fire of Yahweh . . .' he murmured, as if speaking to himself.

The signal was extinguished into a deep, dull tone. Darkness and silence descended over the deserted expanse.

COLONEL JOBERT APPEARED before their eyes just then. His figure emerged slowly, like a ghost, as the wind cleared away the smoke and soot. He had his back turned to them and was kneeling over the body of a dead Blemmyae, which had been mangled by machine-gun fire. When he stood up and came towards the hill, his eyes were as empty and dull as though he had left his soul on that battlefield. He looked back. Nothing remained of the tower except for the great black stone sarcophagus, which the desert wind was already slowly covering with sand.

He turned to the others. 'I've seen nothing,' he said. 'Those of my men who have survived will be split up and sent to distant outposts. The desert swallows up everything, even memory. Farewell.'

He observed the march of the Hallaki warriors with shining eyes: they bore the dead bodies of Amir, Rasaf, Altair. He touched his spurs then to his horse's flanks and rode off to reach those of his unit who remained.

Father Hogan packed his equipment onto a couple of mules and took them by their halters. 'I'm going with Colonel Jobert,' he said. 'May God bless you all.'

Philip turned to Desmond. 'Farewell, father,' he said. 'I'm going to remain at Kalaat Hallaki. Maybe I'll succeed in doing what you never could. I have someone to love, someone who needs me to share the burden of pain and grief . . .'

They embraced. Then Desmond leapt onto his horse.

'Will I see you again?' shouted Philip with moist eyes as his father rode off.

El Kassem turned back. '*Inshallah!*' he shouted. 'Farewell, *el sidi!*' He spurred on his thoroughbred and disappeared with his companion in a cloud of dust.

# 15

Selznick was captured the next day as he was dragging himself through the desert. He was on his last legs and put up no resistance. Colonel Jobert took him into custody and continued down Wadi Addir until they reached the redoubt where he had left his garrison.

Jobert entered, accompanied only by Father Hogan, as his men watched silently without dismounting from their horses. He found no one waiting for him because they were all dead. The corpses lay where each man had breathed his last and the Legion standard still hung limply from its pole, even more faded than it had been. No one had lowered it.

He did not dare to bury them, afraid of risking contagion, but above all so as not to further unsettle his surviving men, who were still reeling from what they had been through. Father Hogan recited the De Profundis and made the sign of the cross over each dead body.

'I'll leave him here,' said Jobert suddenly.

'That would be condemning him to death,' said Father Hogan. 'You may as well have him court-martialled.'

'No,' said Jobert. 'The reason for which my superiors would like to see him executed is even more despicable than his misdeeds. I won't absolve them of their nightmares. I'll set him free tonight and I'll say that he escaped. At least he'll have a chance. No one should be denied a chance, not even the worst of murderers.'

THEY REACHED BIR AKKAR on the day of the winter solstice and Father Hogan waited there two more days for the plane to come and fetch him. When he was told that the pilot had arrived, he went to say goodbye to Colonel Jobert. The officer was standing in front of the window looking out, just like the first time they had met.

'Mission accomplished, Father Hogan,' Jobert said as soon as he heard him enter. 'You've imprisoned the message in that machine of yours and now you're taking it home. I'd be willing to wager that no one will ever hear another word about it. Although, in theory, we should be kept informed . . . Wasn't that the deal?'

'Yes, you're right,' said Father Hogan. 'That was the deal. But even I don't know what's been recorded on that memory. It will take time – a long, long time, I suppose. But would you really like to know?'

Jobert shook his head. 'I want to know nothing. I want only to forget.'

Father Hogan approached him with his hand extended, but when Jobert turned towards him, he let it fall and said, 'You didn't tell me everything either, Colonel. I saw you lift the veil that covered the head of one of the fallen . . . one of the Blemmyae. But nothing has happened to you. Nothing that I can see.'

Jobert's face tensed, his eyes clouded over.

'What did you see, Colonel?' insisted Father Hogan.

'Do you really want to know?'

'Yes.'

'Myself,' he said with a disturbing light in his eyes. 'A shapeless, repugnant mass, which transformed under my eyes into my face but it was . . . different. I saw an atrocious mask and yet it was my own. The dark side that we hold prisoner in the bottom of our souls so that no one will ever glimpse it. The wickedness, corruption, unconfessed foulness that we've removed from our conscious minds. Shameful desires, bestial violence, infamy. I saw all of it in that horrendous mask. They are us, those monsters . . .' he said. 'They are us . . . So now you can imagine what you would have seen had you been in my place, Hogan. Force yourself, strain your imagination . . .'

His voice trailed off and Father Hogan looked at him in silence. That hollow tone, that bleak gaze, left no doubt that he was telling the truth.

'Evil always seems invincible to us,' replied the priest. 'Especially the evil within us, but that's not true. When you wake up tomorrow, before dawn, watch as the light advances over the world, stare at the rising sun. You will find your face there as well, Jobert, the part of you destined to live. For ever.'

He went to the airstrip, where the plane was waiting to take him to El Kef. Jobert did not accompany him, but Father Hogan caught a glimpse of his dark, still shape, arms folded, behind his office window, through the swirling dust raised by the plane's propellers.

FATHER HOGAN REACHED ROME one stormy night a few days before Christmas. The rain pounding on the shiny tarmac, the dark, swollen clouds in the sky and the air laden with humidity made him feel as if he were on another planet.

He waited on the airfield as the big black oilcloth-wrapped crate was unloaded. A cart was ready to transport it to a warehouse. He followed it on foot, as one does a coffin. Two security men who were there to ensure its safety brought up the rear of the little procession.

When he walked out onto the street, he saw a man dressed in a raincoat, with a hat low over his eyes, waiting. Father Hogan approached him. 'You're already here,' he said. 'I would have kept my promise to come to see you.'

'I know,' said Marconi. 'But I couldn't sit there waiting. Come with me. I have a car.'

Father Hogan returned to make sure that the warehouse was locked and guarded, then got into the car that was waiting for him, shiny under the rain, door open.

The two of them dined alone in Marconi's house, in the big library, and Father Hogan told the scientist everything that had happened from the moment he had landed at Bir Akkar. Marconi listened intently, never missing a word, never interrupting.

'What became of your friends?' he asked at the end.

'Desmond Garrett disappeared into the desert with El Kassem and I don't think we'll hear from him, or of him, again. He lives in a place now where time and space fade into infinity.'

'And Philip?'

'His life is in Kalaat Hallaki now. He was the one who saved us, you know, with the silvery sound of his sistrum . . . My God, it was incredible . . . As we were leaving that awful place I asked him how he could explain such a miracle. He told me that he had no idea of how it had happened.

' "The sistrum saved us like it did an Etruscan haruspex two thousand years ago," he said. "He was the only survivor of a Roman army unit that had ventured into the desert and been attacked by . . . that very same creature, I suppose . . . I was in an absolute panic until I thought of the sistrum, and when I held it out and shook it, the fury stopped all at once. And then something extraordinary happened. For just a moment all of that horror surrounding me disappeared, the screaming and shouting were hushed and that field of blood and fire was transformed into the most peaceful setting you can imagine. I was in a field of grass, flocks of sheep all around. I heard the voice of a little child crying, crying in despair, and I saw a woman, a beautiful woman with black hair, bending over a rough cradle and singing. Singing and shaking a rattle made of little bits of bone and wood. And the baby stopped crying, all at once. The sound, that sound, was the same as that of the sistrum."

'That's what Philip told me before he joined the woman he loves and has bound his life to . . . before he disappeared into the shadows of that marvellous, forgotten place. Perhaps the vision that he had – of such a remote event – gives us the key to understanding not only what happened out there in the desert, but perhaps even, who can say, the mystery of our life on earth and of our death.

'As for me, I managed to save the machine from destruction, at the risk of my own life. The recorder received the flow of that signal which originated from the furthest reaches of space. You deserve credit for the success of this operation as well, Mr Marconi, and I intend to respect the pact that you made with Father Boni. The recorded memory is not in the crate that I left under lock and key in the warehouse. It is in a crate that is being unloaded at this very moment probably, along with a consignment of Oriental carpets. That's what you wanted, isn't it? Isn't that why you wanted me to come to see you first?'

The scientist stared deeply into his eyes in silence for a moment. Then he said, 'No, that's not the reason. I wanted to prevent Father Boni from having access to that memory. There's only one man on this earth who can decide the fate of that message and he's waiting to see you. Go now, Hogan, go to him and tell him how you saw the fist of God strike down the Tower of Solitude in a lonely spot in the middle of the desert.'

'But what about Father Boni?'

'I don't know. I've heard that he has fallen gravely ill and that he's been taken to a quiet, secluded place where he may be able to recover his health and, above all, the serenity of his mind and spirit. If that's possible.'

From the street Father Hogan could hear the muted, singsong notes of a shepherd playing on an Italian bagpipe. He felt a lump in his throat and thought of a bare room and an old priest who died trembling with fear and pain. He took his leave and went down to the street, where a car was waiting to take him to the Vatican.

He asked to get out at the entrance to the square so he could cross the immense colonnaded area on foot. He looked at the nativity scene on display in a corner, with its Christ child, shepherds and shooting star, and he stopped for a while to listen to the murmuring fountains. He closed his eyes and saw, for the last time, the clear waters of Hallaki. He raised his head before setting off again and at that moment a light appeared in a window on the top floor of the Apostolic Palace, like an eye opening wide onto the darkness of a sleepless night.

Visit **www.panmacmillan.com** to read more about all our books and to buy them. You will also find features, author interviews and news of any author events, and you can sign up for e-newsletters so that you're always first to hear about our new releases.